9/6/09

3/30/14

Sophie's Dilemma

Books by Lauraine Snelling

A SECRET REFUGE

Daughter of Twin Oaks   Sisters of the Confederacy
The Long Way Home

DAKOTAH TREASURES

Ruby   Opal
Pearl   Amethyst

DAUGHTERS OF BLESSING

A Promise for Ellie
Sophie's Dilemma

RED RIVER OF THE NORTH

An Untamed Land   The Reapers' Song
A New Day Rising   Tender Mercies
A Land to Call Home   Blessing in Disguise

RETURN TO RED RIVER

A Dream to Follow   Believing the Dream
More Than a Dream

LAURAINE SNELLING

Sophie's Dilemma

BETHANYHOUSE
PUBLISHERS
MINNEAPOLIS, MINNESOTA

Sophie's Dilemma
Copyright © 2007
Lauraine Snelling

Cover design by Koechel Peterson & Associates

Published by Bethany House Publishers
11400 Hampshire Avenue South
Bloomington, Minnesota 55438

Bethany House Publishers is a division of
Baker Publishing Group, Grand Rapids, Michigan.

Printed in the United States of America

ISBN-13: 978-0-7394-8712-9

꧁ **DEDICATION** ꧂

To the members of the Ox Cart Trails Historical Society in Drayton, North Dakota, who are spearheading the drive to bring Blessing and Drayton together—my thanks and excitement. Who knows where this wagon is going, but we're all along for the ride.

LAURAINE SNELLING is the award-winning author of over fifty books, fiction and nonfiction, for adults and young adults. Besides writing books and articles, she teaches at writers' conferences across the country. She and her husband, Wayne, have two grown sons, a basset named Chewy, and a cockatiel watch bird named Bidley. They make their home in California.

Bjorklund Family Tree

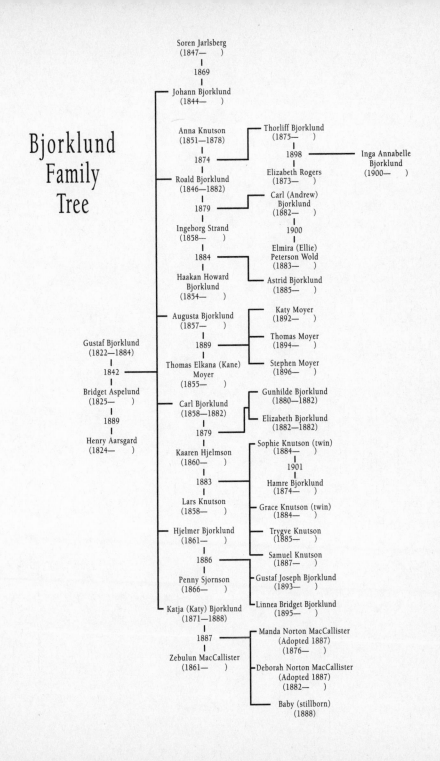

Soren Jarlsberg
(1847—   )
|
1869
|
Johann Bjorklund
(1844—   )

Anna Knutson
(1851—1878)
|
1874
|
Roald Bjorklund
(1846—1882)
|
1879
|
Ingeborg Strand
(1858—   )
|
1884
|
Haakan Howard
Bjorklund
(1854—   )

Thorliff Bjorklund
(1875—   )
|
1898
|
Elizabeth Rogers
(1873—   )

Inga Annabelle
Bjorklund
(1900—   )

Carl (Andrew)
Bjorklund
(1882—   )
|
1900
|
Elmira (Ellie)
Peterson Wold
(1883—   )

Astrid Bjorklund
(1885—   )

Augusta Bjorklund
(1857—   )
|
1889
|
Thomas Elkana (Kane)
Moyer
(1855—   )

Katy Moyer
(1892—   )

Thomas Moyer
(1894—   )

Stephen Moyer
(1896—   )

Gustaf Bjorklund
(1822—1884)
|
1842
|
Bridget Aspelund
(1825—   )
|
1889
|
Henry Aarsgard
(1824—   )

Carl Bjorklund
(1858—1882)
|
1879
|
Kaaren Hjelmson
(1860—   )
|
1883
|
Lars Knutson
(1858—   )

Gunhilde Bjorklund
(1880—1882)

Elizabeth Bjorklund
(1882—1882)

Sophie Knutson (twin)
(1884—   )
|
1901
|
Hamre Bjorklund
(1874—   )

Grace Knutson (twin)
(1884—   )

Trygve Knutson
(1885—   )

Samuel Knutson
(1887—   )

Hjelmer Bjorklund
(1861—   )
|
1886
|
Penny Sjornson
(1866—   )

Gustaf Joseph Bjorklund
(1893—   )

Linnea Bridget Bjorklund
(1895—   )

Katja (Katy) Bjorklund
(1871—1888)
|
1887
|
Zebulun MacCallister
(1861—   )

Manda Norton MacCallister
(Adopted 1887)
(1876—   )

Deborah Norton MacCallister
(Adopted 1887)
(1882—   )

Baby (stillborn)
(1888)

1

Early September 1901

THE SAME. Everything was always the same.

Sophie Knutson glared at the face in the mirror. Her face, her hair, her home, Blessing, and now that school had started, it was one more same old thing. The final same old? She'd not heard from Hamre in over a month. Not that it mattered, of course. She pinned her hair in a swirl on top of her head, but when she moved, it slipped and fell about her shoulders. Slamming her comb down on the dressing table, she leaped up and returned to her pacing.

"I hate school!"

Grace looked up at her sister stomping from one side to the other of the bedroom they'd shared all their lives, just as they'd shared their mother's womb seventeen years ago. Grace spoke slowly, as if choosing her thoughts with great care. She kept her fingers in her lap, fingers that spoke far more swiftly than the tongue she'd trained with great difficulty to form the words she could not hear. "Sophie, look at me. What did you say?"

"I said I hate school."

"I know. But this will be our last year, and you promised to finish." Grace picked up the hairbrush lying in her lap.

Sophie clamped her fists on hips clothed by a white lawn chemise, trimmed in lace, all sewn with love by Grace, who was now sitting cross-legged on the bed. As usual, Sophie had started something and never gotten around to finishing it. Months ago she'd cut out the lawn pieces, and when Grace tired of looking at them, she finished the garment for her sister.

"I wish . . . I wish I . . ." Sophie's eyes grew dreamy, looking into some faraway place. "School is so boring." She plopped down on the bed, facing Grace so they wouldn't have to sign. Grace had been born deaf but was liberated from her silent world when Kaaren, their mother, learned sign language and taught the skill to all of them, which led to starting the school she now ran for the training of deaf people.

"What do you wish?" Grace asked.

Sophie knew her sister already knew the answer, since it had been the same since their childhood. Nevertheless, Grace indulged her.

"I want to go places, see new things, meet new people." Sophie flung her arms dramatically wide. "There's a whole world out there, and we are stuck here in Blessing."

"Not forever."

"I know, but the *ever* seems so far away!" She flopped back on the pillows. *I don't want to go to school. That's all there is to it.*

"What would you do if you didn't go to school?" Ever practical, Grace unplaited her daytime braids with graceful fingers.

"I could help Bestemor at the boardinghouse or work for Penny in the store, since Rebecca will be back in school. I could even help Dr. Elizabeth in the surgery." *Maybe I could find work in Grand Forks or Grafton. Grafton—Ellie's family lives there. Surely Goodie could find me something to do.*

"But you don't like blood."

"Better than school." Sophie ran her fingers into her dark hair and pulled it straight up. "Maybe I should cut my hair into a fringe."

"Now that would be an adventure."

"I saw it in a magazine. It's the latest rage. If I get the scissors, will you help me?"

"But your hair waves back so beautifully. Not like mine." Grace pulled a hank of what she called mouse brown hair over her shoulder and waved it at her sister. She'd gone back to braiding it to keep it out of her way.

"Be right back." Sophie signed with flying fingers as she leaped off the bed. Racing down the stairs, she snatched the scissors out of the sewing room and raced back up. Sophie never walked if she could dance or run. She paused in the doorway. Grace lived up to her name. Right now she sat on the bed with her arms raised, braiding her thick hair for the night. The light from the kerosene lamp outlined her in gilt.

If I leave, or rather, when *I leave, what about Grace? How will I live without her? Yet I know she won't want to go along.* Grace loved school, loved being at home, loved helping their mother with the deaf school. Her patience with the new students was never ending, forming their fingers into the signs that would free them from their silent prison. After all, she had once been where they were. She understood.

Sophie crossed to stand in front of the mirror. Did she dare cut her hair? Just a few strands right in front. She tried folding her hair to hang short in front on her forehead to give her an idea what it would look like. She turned without thinking so that Grace could read her lips.

"Would you help me please?"

"Hadn't you better think on it more?"

"No. At least I will look a little different. Hold the hair in back so I can drop just the ends over my forehead."

Grace did as she asked and looked over her sister's shoulder to stare into the mirror. Their eyes met, Sophie's dancing with the thought of such daring, Grace's caught in a question mark.

"I'm going to do it." Sophie handed Grace the scissors. "I'll hold the comb; you cut."

"No. If you want them short, you cut."

"I know. You cut mine, and I'll cut yours." Sophie whirled and, with the comb, tugged a few strands of Grace's hair loose from the night braid. While the two girls looked much alike in stature, Sophie had a wider forehead, an upturned nose, and darker eyes to match her hair. Grace's face was more oval, with a straight nose and dreamy gray eyes with thick lashes. While Grace called her hair mousy, Sophie referred to it as tawny, shot with gold. Together they decided to call Sophie's hair nutmeg with cinnamon trails. They'd been on a spice-searching mission that day, with Sophie dreaming of the lands that grew the spices they used to flavor food. Pepper had been too dark, cinnamon too red, allspice too strong, and nutmeg just right.

Grace hefted the scissors, opened the blades wide, slid one edge along her sister's forehead, and pulled away. "I can't do this."

"Of course you can. Just cut right above my eyebrows. I read that was best."

"But what if I slip and cut you?"

"You won't." Sophie combed the long strands all the way out and started again at her scalp, stopping at eye level. "There, now cut." She adopted a frown of command on her face, knowing her sister well enough to understand she would dither and back out unless she took a firm stand.

"Sophie Knutson, if Mor scolds you, don't you dare blame me." Grace slid the scissors back in place and snipped. The newly released long tresses slid through the comb and drifted to the floor. Both girls studied the results in the mirror, mouths matching in perfect Os.

"Do you like it?" Sophie asked, breaking the silence.

"Not much. Do you?"

"I think it will take some getting used to."

"What will Mor say?"

"What will Mor say to what?"

The voice from the doorway spun Sophie around with a shriek. "Ah, I . . . ah . . ."

Grace followed, her eyes as round as her sister's.

"Sophie, what did you do?" Kaaren stood stock-still.

"Ah, Grace . . ."

Grace gave her a shove and stepped backward, her fingers flying so fast even Kaaren couldn't keep track.

"Sophie made you?"

Grace nodded vigorously.

Sophie felt like she was three years old again and caught with her finger in the cookie dough. She straightened her shoulders and huffed,

"I've wanted a fringe for a long time."

"I see." Kaaren crossed the room to peer more closely at the damage. "Is it supposed to look ragged like this?"

"No-o." Sophie turned and stared in the mirror again. "The pictures in the magazine showed them even and puffy. Maybe we should cut it all off, right at the roots."

Kaaren shook her head, the lamplight catching highlights in her golden coronet that had always reminded the girls of either crowns or halos, depending on what they were reading at the time.

"Mother, don't laugh," Sophie wailed.

"I'm trying not to." Kaaren took the scissors in one hand and the comb in the other.

Sophie backed away, her hands splayed in defense in front of her. "What are you going to do?"

"I'm going to fix the mess you made. Now hold still. Unless you'd rather leave it the way it is." She turned to hand the scissors to Grace, who backed away, her hands locked behind her back. When she offered the tools to Sophie, she got the same reaction. "All right, then, go the way you are or let me fix it."

Sophie gulped and nodded. Surely her mother could redeem the efforts. She'd always been able to do so with everything else. She scrunched her eyes closed and offered her face as if going to the guillotine.

"Just look at me like you usually would, or I will not be responsible for the way it looks."

Sophie opened her eyes wide, then blinked and focused on her mother, her shoulders tense, arms rigid at her sides. Kaaren snipped a bit here and trimmed a bit there. The hair fell, and Sophie sneezed.

"Sorry."

"Good thing I wasn't cutting right then." Kaaren trimmed up the sides, dipped the comb in water from the pitcher, and combed the hair up and over her finger. "There, I think that will do." She stepped back. "Not bad if I do say so myself." She turned to Grace. "What do you think?"

"Better, much better, but I'm still not sure I like it."

"I'm afraid it will take some getting used to." Kaaren studied her daughter. "But I think it looks good on you."

"Now it's Grace's turn." Sophie gave herself a doubtful look in the mirror one more time.

Grace shook her head. "I am not cutting my hair into a fringe." She signed at the same time, her fingers slashing the air.

"But you said . . ."

"No. You said I would." Grace knelt down and swept the fallen hair into one hand with the other.

"I'll bet you a penny that the other girls will have theirs cut like mine within a week."

"There will be no betting in this house." Kaaren brushed short bits of dark hair off her daughter's chemise. "Now, it is bedtime, and you should be grateful your pa is off with the threshing crew. The shock of this might be too much for him."

"Ma, you really—" Sophie caught the glint of teasing in her mother's eyes and tone. She shook her head and turned back to the mirror. "I think it does indeed grow on one." She fluffed the fringe with her fingers.

Kaaren kissed each of her daughters good-night. "You get to sleep now. Morning will come far too soon, and the cows need to be milked before you leave for school."

"I know." Sophie left off studying her new hairstyle and pulled her cambric nightdress over her head, then shimmied out of her chemise and camisole underneath it. She tied the blue ribbon at the neckline and folded back the blue-and-white nine-patch quilt they'd helped their mother make years before. "Come on, Grace. 'Night, Mor." She slid under the sheet and puffed her pillow behind her.

After Kaaren left the room, Sophie turned on her side to watch her twin finish getting ready for bed and waved to catch Grace's attention. "I haven't heard from Hamre for more than a month now."

"I know." Grace tied her pink neck bow. Their light nightdresses matched, including the deep ruffle edged with lace at the bottom and the bodice trimmed with a dainty row of tatting, but for the colored ribbons. "He is either fishing or forgetting."

"Hmm." Sophie pursed her lips and slitted her eyes. "We've been corresponding regularly. Why would he forget?"

"Maybe he found a girlfriend. Can I blow out the lamp now?"

Sophie nodded and sighed. "I guess." She stared at the ceiling in the darkness. Hamre wouldn't forget her, would he? Unless he had indeed met someone else. The thought made her roll over to her other side and clutch her pillow. Seattle was so far away. He'd said there were lots of Norwegians there; there must be plenty of attractive Norwegian girls. And he always signed his letters, "Your friend." Did he care for her or not? She tossed to the other side, and Grace reached over to pat her shoulder. Sophie rolled on her back and held her sister's hand until they both fell asleep.

2

"YOU WON'T BELIEVE what Sophie did!"

Ingeborg, her golden hair now shot with silver, turned as her daughter barreled through the doorway the next afternoon. "She cut her hair in a fringe."

"Tante Kaaren told you." Astrid, her Bjorklund blue eyes flashing, set her lunch bucket and two books on the counter. "Now the girls are all talking about cutting their hair in fringes too." She shook her head, setting the single wheaten braid she wore to swinging. While the other girls her age were putting their hair up to look older, Astrid, like her cousin Grace, chose convenience, both in fixing it and keeping it out of the way.

"You aren't wanting to do that too?" Ingeborg knew she wasn't ready for fringes or short hair like some of the women she'd seen, and she hoped her daughter wasn't either.

"No." Astrid's tone dismissed Sophie and the fringe as she galloped off to a new topic. "Just because this is our last year, Pastor Solberg is going to work us to death. You should see all the assignments he wrote on the blackboard."

Grateful for the change of subject, Ingeborg returned to rolling her molasses cookie dough. Jars of pickled beets lined the counter, ready to be carried down to the root cellar. She had relish, using up the last of the cucumbers, simmering on the back of the stove, ready to pour into jars shortly.

"As soon as you change your clothes, please bring in the rest of the wash, unless you'd rather fill the jars."

"The wash. I've been inside all day, and I need the sun."

Astrid leaned around her mother and sneaked a piece of rolled dough. Laughing at her mother's halfhearted grumble, she mounted the stairs to her bedroom to change into work clothes. She hung her new red-and-white gingham dress on the hook on the wall rather than in the clothespress because she would wear it again tomorrow. The blue calico dress she'd started sewing the week before had yet to be hemmed and so still hung down in the sewing room. While she'd not had to cut her dresses longer for the last couple of years, she'd had to add more fullness in the bosom area. There hadn't been a lot of time for sewing with the rest of the garden ready for canning and drying. The race to finish before the first frost arrived happened every year. Sometimes they won, like this year, and sometimes the frost caught them unprepared.

Back downstairs, clad in a faded shift that often needed the ministrations of needle and thread and a full apron with deep pockets on the front, she poured herself a glass of buttermilk, grabbed a handful of cookies, and headed for the clothesline. The world outside seemed strangely silent with all the men and machinery gone threshing. The dried sheets and towels barely flapped in the lazy breeze. Though halfway to the horizon, the sun streamed warmth onto her head and shoulders. Instead of lying flat out on the grass like she might have a few years earlier, she sat down and leaned against the post that held up the clotheslines while finishing her drink and cookies. A robin fluttered down and, keeping a beady eye on her, watched for worms with the other one. She tossed him a bit of cookie, and he snatched it up, watching to make sure she didn't make any rash moves.

Astrid stretched her arms over her head, pulling out the tightness that came with starting school again and sitting for so long on the wooden benches. There had been some new students this year, including a boy named Heinz Geddick from the German family that had recently moved to the area. He was a senior but spoke very little English. While Pastor Solberg spoke Norwegian for him at times, he had asked Astrid to help also. Though they communicated well enough because of the similarities in Norwegian and German, she could see he was frustrated. There were several German pupils in the lower grades too, so she would most likely be tutoring them all in English. It was a shame her older brother, Thorliff, didn't have time. He spoke all three languages fluently.

She folded the towels and sheets as she took them down, inhaling the clean fragrance that came from the sun and the wind, and laid them in the oval willow basket. One of those Metiz, a French Canadian Sioux woman who became their friend and mentor, had woven for them before she died several years earlier. With her hands busy, Astrid's mind roamed across the small pasture to think of Sophie. Why Sophie wasn't happy here she just didn't understand. And dreaming about Hamre Bjorklund. Astrid shook her head. While she was sure Hamre, a distant cousin, had grown up since he left Blessing years ago and went to Seattle to go fishing, all she could remember was his silence. Getting him to talk more than a sentence or two was harder than splitting kindling with a dull ax.

Off in the distance she could see Andrew, the brother closest to her in age, striding across the fields. He'd stayed home from the threshing crew to keep the home chores done. Milking forty cows and hauling the milk to the cheese house took full-time male help, not that the girls couldn't have handled it, but not along with school starting. Besides, his wife, Ellie, was very large with their first child, and Astrid knew her sister-in-law had some deep fears about having a baby. She waited for Andrew to join her before taking the wash inside.

"How was school?" he asked, pushing his straw hat back on his head.

"Sophie cut her hair in a fringe."

"A what?" Andrew made a noise of disgust, matching the look on his face.

She motioned across her forehead. "Short here above her eyebrows."

"Why would she do that?"

"You know Sophie. She wants the latest thing. Before you know it, she'll be wanting a horseless carriage." Astrid raised her eyebrows. "Anything to be different and in the fashion."

Andrew snorted and shook his head. "Leave it to Sophie."

"You should see our reading list for this year."

"Most likely the same as ever. I didn't think I'd get through it all." Andrew whistled for his dog, Barnabus, who came running from inspecting a gopher hole. "Go get the cows, Barney." He waved toward the pasture, and the dog charged off.

"I'll be out pretty quick, soon as I gather the eggs and feed the chickens. How's Ellie?"

"Looks like she swallowed two watermelons." Andrew held his hands in a circle, way out in front of him.

"I know that. I meant any changes?"

"Nope, but she sees Dr. Elizabeth tomorrow." Andrew headed for the barn, and Astrid took the wash inside.

"Mange takk," her mother called. "There's a bucket of scraps on the back porch for the chickens."

"I'll get it. Do we need to take eggs to Garrisons'?"

"Andrew can take them in tomorrow along with the cheese. I have a big shipment going out." Ingeborg's cheese house had grown through the years and now shipped wheels of cheese to many of the major cities of the United States. The Norwegians, especially, enjoyed being able to get their favorite cheeses made here just like in their homeland.

Ingeborg threatened Haakan often that they should invest in goats so she could make gjetost, but her teasing only got teasing back. They fattened many hogs for the market on the whey and had expanded the cheese house itself twice. Garrisons' Groceries, the new store in town, bought eggs, cheese, and smoked hams from the Bjorklunds. Penny had turned her mercantile into a dry goods store and no longer carried the foods needed in the community.

"We've got a hen that's eating eggs," Astrid announced when she brought the eggs to the well house, where her mother was cleaning eggs and packing them into crates to ship. "Thanks to her, some of these are pretty dirty."

"If we can find who it is, she'll go in the stewpot." Using a damp cloth Ingeborg wiped a spot of manure off an egg and set it tip down in the slatted wood crate that held twelve layers of twenty-four eggs. "We need more straw in the nest boxes." The chickens too ate the whey from the cheese house, and as soon as the garden was finished for the season, they would be loosed into the fenced plot to clean up the garden residue.

While some people burned back the tip of their hens' upper beaks to prevent them from cracking eggs or pecking at each other, Astrid refused to do that to hers, choosing instead to keep an eye on them and discover the culprits. The chickens were her responsibility, and she and her mother split the money from the eggs, which gave Astrid some school money. She was still intent on going to Chicago to train as a nurse with Dr. Morganstein, the same doctor her sister-in-law, Elizabeth, had trained with for her physician's license. Astrid had spent much of the summer helping at Dr. Elizabeth's surgery.

"Is George milking tonight?" Astrid asked.

"Far as I know. Why?" Ingeborg paused in her egg cleaning.

"He hurt his back falling off the ladder yesterday while fixing something at Tante Kaaren's."

"She never mentioned it." Kaaren and Ingeborg had taken time out for coffee that morning, the last opportunity for Kaaren before the students started arriving for their sessions at the school for the deaf. Some of the older boys and girls would help with chores on the farm; others would learn woodworking from George McBride, a former student who also worked on the farm and was married to Ilse. Lars taught machinery repair, and Ilse taught weaving. The deaf students attended Blessing School too, once they learned signing well enough to be able to participate in class.

"Maybe no one told Tante. Grace told me at school. And I thought I would laugh myself silly when she and Sophie talked about cutting *the fringe...*." She emphasized the words and rolled her eyes at the same time. "Now Sophie is ready to cut hair for everyone." Astrid and

Ingeborg shook their heads at the same time. Sophie's antics had caused plenty of laughter through the years as well as a few tears.

"She was flirting with Heinz today. The poor boy wore a red face much of the day, even though he didn't know what she said." Astrid shook her head again. "And she thinks she's in love with Hamre, so how can she be making eyes at Heinz?"

"I'm sure she said nothing improper."

Astrid laughed again. "It isn't what she said, but how. You know Sophie." Astrid picked up four milk buckets, slipping the handles over her arm, and out the door she went.

Still smiling at her daughter's comments, Ingeborg set the dirty eggs to soak in water while she buffed and dried the remainder. While her hands did the mundane chore, her mind roved off to pray for Haakan and Lars with the threshing crew, asking guidance from her Father for the cheese business as to adding more varieties, asking blessing on the new year of school and all the students, and praying for strength for herself.

The bleeding had started again this afternoon. If it got bad again, her daughter-in-law, Dr. Elizabeth Bjorklund, Thorliff's wife, had threatened her with surgery to remove her female parts inside. Hysterectomy, she called it. Such a strange name. *Lord, I thought we were through with all this foolishness. I felt better again. Uff da, can't you please take care of it so that we don't have to resort to cutting everything out? You said to ask in faith, that I can say to that mountain, "Be cast into the sea," and it would move. Well, I've never tried to move real mountains, that's for sure, but this seems like a mountain to me. Just as that woman in the Bible touched your garment, Jesus, I ask for you to stop the flow of blood. It's not been going on for twelve years—I don't know how she stood it—but it has come back. So I ask for this healing, knowing that you are our great healer and you can do this. If only you will.*

3

Mid-September

Two whole weeks and he had yet to smile at her.

Sophie listened to Grace slightly puffing out her sleep breaths. While Heinz seemed like a boy compared to her, his was the only new male face that appeared even slightly interesting—in school that is. His older brother, Abram, was another story. But he saw her as still a schoolgirl, even with her fringe. This Sunday for church she decided she'd put her hair up. Surely that would help her appear older. But then again, if the threshing crew had returned, perhaps some of the other young men would be in church.

"Sophie, time to wake Grace," their mother called from the bottom of the stairs. "Please call the boys too." Trygve and Samuel slept in the room next to the twins, and no one could sleep harder than those two. They'd probably sleep through until dinner if no one woke them.

At least when the threshing crew got back, the girls wouldn't have to milk the cows before school. She tapped her sister on the shoulder and threw back the covers to go shake the boys. None of the new students for the deaf school were ready for milking cows yet, most of them being younger this year, but two boys Samuel's age from last year would be waiting at the barn to help.

After rousing her brothers, Sophie returned to her bedroom to dress. She and Grace slid into their chores clothes and then made their way downstairs. Trygve sat on a chair tying his boots. A big yawn traveled the air and made her yawn too.

"Looks like it froze last night." Samuel, the youngest of the family, turned from looking out the window.

Sophie handed Grace a shawl and threw another one over her own shoulders. "Let's go. Andrew will have all the cows in and fed. You know how snappy he gets if we are late."

"Bring a couple pails of milk back. If there is extra cream in the springhouse, we need to churn today." Kaaren leaned over to check the oven. Whatever she had baking smelled heavenly as they all trudged out the door. "Breakfast will be ready when you return."

"You're late," Andrew announced as soon as they came through the barn door.

Sophie poked Grace and mouthed, "I told you so."

Since Andrew was in charge of the home farms while the crew was off threshing, he took his responsibilities very seriously, no longer the easygoing youth he had once been. They all took a bucket and a three-legged stool and started down the aisles, each of them having favorite cows to milk. A newly freshened first-time cow still needed the kickers, so Grace, who was more sensitive to the cows, chose her. Murmuring her own off-key tune to the cow, she stroked its neck before sitting down to wash the udder and set the bucket between her legs. The song of the pails commenced as the milkers all fell into the rhythm of squeeze and pull, releasing the milk to froth in the buckets. As one finished, they poured the milk into a can with a metal strainer set on top and moved on to the next cow.

"You kids go on and get ready for school," Andrew said when they were down to the last couple of cows. "George and I will finish."

"You'll feed the calves too?" Samuel asked. Feeding the calves had become his job when Trygve took over the market hogs. The sows now lived in Andrew's newly built barn, and the dry cows and heifers grazed the pasture around there.

"For today. Saturday you can work with the deaf boy from Fargo. He seemed to really like the young animals and has lived some on a farm."

"Good. You want me to bring another team out to plow?" Trygve had tried to talk his parents into letting him drop out of school to work on the farm, but they were adamant that he finish, just as Andrew had.

"Ja, you can get in a couple of hours. The girls will take your place milking."

Sophie gave him a half glare. "Thank you, Sir Andrew." Milking was one of those chores she would never miss when she went on her travels. Nor working in the cheese house, where the odor of sour milk bonded to one's hair and hands no matter how clean they kept the floors and equipment. She picked up the last bucket of milk, and she and Grace stopped by the springhouse to get a can of cream to take home with them. They walked across the field carrying the can between them. *Should have brought the wagon*, she thought as their burden grew heavier with each stride.

Halfway home Samuel and Trygve took the can and the buckets.

"Thank you, kind sirs."

Her brothers looked at her as though she were daft.

"Tell Mor I'm going to hitch the wagon before I come in," Trygve said when they reached the house.

Samuel took the can they'd set on the porch and carried it into the kitchen, which was abuzz with activity as the deaf students made their way to the long table that sat eighteen in the dining room.

"You'd better hurry," Kaaren urged when they'd washed and sat down with the students. "Let's pray. I Jesu navn . . ."

The Norwegian table blessing flowed from the lips of the family as easily as one in English would have. Grace signed the words in English for the students who shared the dormitory-style rooms on the second floor of the school section of the house. Expecting them to learn Norwegian was beyond the possibilities.

Kaaren had baked cinnamon rolls for breakfast to accompany the oatmeal that had been cooking all night on the back of the stove. They poured cream and molasses over the cereal, a much more simple meal than they would have when feeding the men too.

As usual, Sophie was the last one out the door, kissing her mother's cheek as she picked up her lunch pail. "I didn't get that wool carded yet, but I will tonight."

"Yes, you will. I need it to teach my first class on spinning. I'll have two of the students help you after supper."

Sophie sighed and flew out the door, knowing if she didn't get to the wagon when Trygve was ready to leave, she would walk the mile to school. It had happened before.

Once Sophie was in the wagon, Grace, with a patient look, handed her sister the book she needed to take back to the library. Her smile acknowledged her twin's shrug of apology.

"You are so good to me. Pastor Solberg said if I forgot it today, I would have to walk home to get it."

"I know."

How Grace knew and did so many things when she couldn't hear, Sophie now took for granted. Some of the time she forgot to turn so Grace could read her lips and would get a tap on the shoulder in reproof. Like the chemise, Grace would often pick up something Sophie had left unfinished for a long time and quilt, knit, or sew it herself and then leave it on their bed for Sophie to find. Guilt used to assail her, but now it barely nibbled, or she could ignore it more easily. She was never sure which, nor did she spend much time dwelling on it. Instead, she gave Grace's hand a squeeze while bestowing her best smile of gratitude.

The day dragged by like all school days. Sophie received a reprimanding look from Pastor Solberg for doodling flowers and trees on her tablet rather than writing the essay he'd assigned. She sighed and flipped the page, but words failed to come to mind. What did she care about the forming of unions to supposedly help the workers? Now, if he'd let her write about Teddy Roosevelt and his adventures in the West, that would have been another matter. He was hero material for sure, even if he did wear those funny glasses. Clara Barton and the American Red Cross or Susan B. Anthony and the suffragettes—now those were things that truly interested her.

Or Hamre. Why had she not heard from him for so long? Two letters she'd sent with no reply. Perhaps he had found someone to love out there on the West Coast. But his earlier letters had sounded like more than something just written from distant cousin to distant cousin. Had she been reading more into them than what he'd really meant? There were lots of Norwegians out there; he'd told her that, but surely he wouldn't settle for a dull Norwegian girl. Hamre needed someone with fire in her soul, and Sophie knew just the Norwegian girl with that.

"Miss Knutson, would you please stand and read your essay?" Pastor Solberg stared right at her.

Her forehead, under her fashionable fringe, blazed hot like it might sizzle the hair. "I-I'm sorry, sir, but I have no essay. I couldn't think of a thing to say." If only the earth would open up and swallow her. She might not like school, but she liked being embarrassed even less.

"I see." He stared at her over the top of his glasses. "Is there something you'd rather write about?"

She shook her head. "No, sir." She heard a titter from behind her. The heat bathed her cheeks also. Better not say what she was thinking or she'd be in deeper trouble.

"You have until the end of class today or as late as you would like to stay to get something down on that paper." While the tone was mild, she knew he meant every word.

"Yes, sir."

He moved on to one of the others. Rebecca stood and read her essay supporting the unions. Then Trygve read his, opposing them.

Sophie listened carefully and then began writing, using some of their ideas but wisely putting them in her own words. She felt a slight nudge on her shoulder and slid her hand back along the seat. Grace placed a bit of paper in her hand. While Pastor Solberg was questioning one of the others, she read four words, *Remember Thorliff's newspaper article* to give her more clues.

I hate school. I hate politics, I hate essays. She remembered her mother's admonitions against hating anything and revised her thoughts. *I intensely dislike school, politics, and essays.* If only she could have written about that. But she wrote away while the others read theirs and Pastor Solberg moved on to one of the other grades. With Miss Isabelle

Rumly, a new teacher who had come from Grand Forks to teach in Blessing, instructing the lower grades in the new addition to the schoolhouse, Pastor Solberg could concentrate on those from the seventh grade up through the twelfth.

She reread her piece and nodded her satisfaction. As her mother said so often, *"All you have to do, Sophie, is concentrate."* She'd not have to stay after school after all.

Pastor Solberg nodded when she showed it to him. "You can read it tomorrow, then."

A half an hour later she was grinding her teeth at Latin translation. As if she would ever need to understand Latin. If she could learn French, the language of culture and love, she would excel in that, she was sure. And she would actually use it when she went to France. France . . . Paris . . . her mind floated off on another daydream.

Pastor Solberg's voice made her jump. "You're finished with your translation?" he asked, standing right over her. France disappeared in a puff.

"Yes, sir." She handed him her paper.

He read it standing right beside her. Watching his face, she was sure he was going to give her a failing grade and then her mother would have plenty to say. But he marked a few things, nodded, and handed it back. "You see, you can do even Latin when you buckle down and work at it."

I know that. It's just that Latin is so boring. "Thank you, sir." *And you let your mind wander off to Seattle and Hamre and France.* Her inside voice scolded better than her mother did.

The creak of the door opening at the back of the room made her look over her shoulder. A tall, broad-shouldered man who looked vaguely familiar stepped inside holding a seaman's cap in his hands. Was it—could it be—Hamre?

Pastor Solberg blinked, and a smile broke across his face. "Hamre Bjorklund, it is you." The pastor strode down the aisle, hand outstretched.

"God dag. Ja, it is me."

Sophie swallowed and swallowed again. This was the person who'd been writing to her? She'd still thought of him as the gangly young man who left, who rarely looked anyone in the eye, and only dreamed of going fishing. She put her hand to her chest; her heart had picked up speed like a sled going down hill. This was Hamre!

"Come in, come in. Let me introduce you." Pastor Solberg led him forward to the front of the classroom. "Everyone, this is Hamre Bjorklund, who emigrated from Norway to here and then headed west when he was twenty-one to go fishing in Seattle. Is that what you do now?"

"Ja, on a cod boat."

Even his voice had changed, deepened. Sophie wished she had a fan for her hot cheeks. Maybe someone would open a door.

"Could you please tell our class what life is like out there?"

"Ah, well . . ."

His voice used to be raspy, but now . . . She turned and caught Rebecca's eye. The two swapped wide-eyed secret smiles that said the same thing. This Hamre was indeed easy on the eyes and his voice deep music to the ears. She felt Grace's foot nudge the back of her leg. She didn't dare turn fully around. But oh, how she wanted to. Do you need me to sign? Her fingers flew. Grace shook her head.

"We fish in dories off the main boat, pulling in cod mostly. We row the dories and catch the fish in nets. The fish is then salted down in the hold. Sometimes we fish in the Puget Sound, which is a huge bay, and in the winter go out to sea and north to Alaska."

Seattle, Alaska, faraway places, and Hamre was having adventures. She heard herself sigh again.

"Where do you live?"

"Just north of Seattle, near the docks in Ballard. There are many fishermen there."

"Do you mind if the class asks you some questions?" Pastor Solberg asked.

"Not at all." He pointed to the first hand to go up.

"Do you sail the boats? I mean, do you use sails or engines?" Trygve asked.

"Some boats use one, some the other. I've shipped on both. But sails are used mostly." He pointed to another hand.

"Do you own the boat?"

"That is what I want." His answer brought a couple of chuckles.

He caught Sophie's gaze and looked away. She now knew what was meant by *swooning*, as she'd read in some books. Her head felt as if it might float right off her shoulders.

"How many fish do you catch at a time?"

"Sometimes the net brings in so many that the water slops over the gunwales."

Hamre stared right into her eyes, setting her fingers to tingling and making it difficult to swallow. "Fishing is big business in Seattle."

"Do you want to buy your own boat?"

"Ja, I do. Someday."

Did you come back for me? Questions chased one another through her mind like kids out at recess. *Where are you staying? Will you come for supper? When will you kiss me?* The racing questions skidded to a stop. She ducked her head so he couldn't see the heat creeping up her neck. She remembered his letters. He'd written that he wanted to own a fishing boat or perhaps a whole fleet of them someday. And he was saving all he could to do that. He'd written of riding out a storm with waves crashing over the bow and the sail being ripped off. One letter told of meeting some other distant Bjorklund relatives. Adventure, travel, excitement. Hamre was a "same soul" with her.

She brought herself back to the classroom as Pastor Solberg was thanking him for speaking to the students. "Where will you be staying?"

"At the boardinghouse." He was looking directly at Sophie again; she could feel it clear to her toes. "I heard my soddy washed away in the flood."

"Welcome home, son. We'll enjoy visiting with you." Pastor Bjorklund glanced at his pocket watch and spoke to the students. "You all know your assignments for tomorrow. I'll excuse you a few minutes early today."

Sophie forced herself to leave the building with Grace and Rebecca, even though every ounce of her soul wanted to run to the front of the room. Heinz smiled at her as he passed, but her earlier scheme to flirt with him meant nothing. Was Hamre behind her? Would he catch up?

A warm hand touched her elbow, sending tingles like apple cider bubbles up her arm and across her entire body. Hamre's voice, deep and husky, said, "We will talk, ja?"

"Ja." She caught herself. "Yes. Would you like to ride home with us in the wagon?"

"I thought perhaps we could walk."

"Oh. Oh, of course." She was sure her heart just flew out of her chest and went dancing in the sunlight.

4

HAMRE IS HOME.

Ingeborg rejoiced at the news. "He can stay in Andrew's room."

"He said he was staying at the boardinghouse." Astrid looked up from setting the table. "He certainly looks different from how I remember. You should have seen him up there in front of the room, talking and answering questions. He didn't used to say ten words—in a day."

Ingeborg chuckled. "I know. I was never sure if he was so terribly shy or just never had anything to say. But he was a hard worker."

"He always wanted to go back to the sea. He didn't like it here very much." Astrid glanced up at the whistle from outside. "Trygve's on the way to the barn. I sure will be glad when the men come back and we don't have to milk all the time."

"In Norway the women do all the milking."

"I know. You've said that, and they go up with the cattle to the mountain camps in the summer and make cheese. Did you do that?"

"A couple of times, but then I worked for a family in town until I married Roald and came to this country. At least I had learned to make good cheese."

Astrid took a piece of cheese from the cutting board. "Very good cheese." Out the door she went, heading for the barn. She'd already gathered the eggs and fed her chickens. Since she'd caught the renegade hen there had been no more eaten eggs with sticky yolks all over, and the hen had sure tasted good with her mother's dumplings.

She had just picked up the pails from the springhouse and started toward the barn when Barney charged from behind it and ran down the lane, barking as if his life depended on chasing away whatever he heard. Shading her eyes, Astrid shrieked, "The men are coming! The men are coming!" She dropped her buckets and ran back to the house. "Mor, they're home. Pa's home."

Ingeborg flew out the door and picked up the iron bar to clang the triangle. She beat it from side to side, laughing all the time, tears streaming down her face. Haakan was home! She and Astrid grabbed hands and trotted down the lane to meet them. How could six weeks seem more like six months, or years even? *He's home again. Thank you, Lord, he's home again. You know how I've missed him. Thank you for keeping them safe. Thank you, thank you, thank you.* Letters just weren't the same as seeing his dear face and finding refuge in the strength of his circling arms. She waved the dish towel she'd forgotten to put down.

Either Haakan or Lars pulled the whistle on the steam engine, the blast scaring up a flock of blackbirds feeding on the dried seed heads along the lane. The caravan drew closer, the steam engine leading and pulling the thresher, followed by the small house on wheels for the cook and her crew, and finally three wagons pulled by four-up teams.

Haakan waved his hat from up in the engine cab as the mighty behemoth clanked along at one speed. While Lars constantly modified the machinery, this one still had three settings—start, go, and stop.

"Uff da. Will we have enough for supper?"

"Most of the others will go on home without waiting to be fed. You know that," Astrid said.

Together they watched as the remainder of the crew drew near, Toby Valders driving one wagon and his brother, Gerald, driving one of the others. The two older Geddick sons, Joseph and Elmer, brought the third, and Mrs. Geddick and her daughter drove the cook shack. Haakan's letters said she served plenty of good food, keeping up the Bjorklund good name of caring well for their crew.

The steel monster complained to a stop, and Haakan reached down to help his wife up the ladder. Astrid scrambled up behind. Five people crowded the cab, but with Ingeborg tucked under one of Haakan's arms and Astrid the other, they all fit. Lars put the machine in gear and steered it forward.

"So all is well?" Haakan shouted above the roar and clank.

"Hamre is home to visit," Astrid shouted back.

"Really?"

"Sophie walked home from school with him. She's all moony, and so are the other girls. He looks lots different than he used to." She glanced up to her pa. "He's almost as handsome as you."

Haakan tugged on her braid. "Flattery will get you everywhere." He leaned his cheek on her head and didn't let go of either her or his wife.

"She's right, you know." Ingeborg stood on tiptoe to speak right into his ear. "I was beginning to think you were never coming home."

"Missed me?"

"More than you know."

"Ah, I know." He pulled her closer to his side, if that was possible.

"You want off here?" Lars indicated the end of the Bjorklund lane.

"You need me for anything tonight?" Haakan asked.

"No. I'm just going to park, shut her down, and send everyone on home. The Geddicks can take one of the wagons and drop the Valderses off."

"Sounds good." When the machine stopped, Haakan swung down first so he could help his wife and daughter. "See you in the morning." He waved to those following to bring the wagons and cook shack into the yard.

"You want a ride?" Toby asked when he pulled even with them in his wagon.

"Nope. We'll walk. Leave the wagons by the machine shed and unharness the horses. Then you two ride home with the Geddicks."

"I need to hurry for the milking," Astrid said and swung herself up on the tailgate of Toby's wagon since he was in the lead. She waved at her ma and pa and swung her legs in the dust kicked up by the trotting horses.

"What's for supper?" Haakan asked.

"Baked rabbit, potatoes, creamed carrots with turnips, fresh bread, and I baked an apple pie. Shall we invite the Geddicks? I can stretch it some." Ingeborg leaned into the shoulder of the man walking beside her. How she had missed his shoulder to press against.

"No. The missus has supper ready in the wagon for the crew. They can eat before they head on home. I hate to be selfish, but eating in the peace of my family sounds mighty close to heaven for me. It seems I've been gone months rather than weeks."

"Ja, it does."

"Any applications for running the flour mill?"

"Several. Hjelmer has them all. He and Penny came to dinner after church last Sunday, along with Thorliff and Elizabeth. That little Inga, wait until you see her. She's running now, up on her tippy-toes. She's quicksilver. If you want to hug her, you have to snatch her up and do it quick."

"And Ellie?"

"Growing rounder all the time."

"I'll go tie things up and then wash for supper." Haakan left her with a hand squeeze, heading for the barn with his fedora pushed toward the back of his head. His whistle floated back over his shoulder.

His hair is getting darker so the silver shows more. Ingeborg watched him walk. Was he limping slightly? For sure the lines in his face had deepened over the weeks, or had that been going on and she'd just not noticed? He worked so hard taking care of everything and everyone else. He was surely ready for some wifely care. "Thank you, Father," she whispered to the freshening breeze, "for bringing him home safely and with good success." She knew from his infrequent letters that the harvest had been good, both for the farmers and for the threshers.

An hour later Haakan and Astrid came through the door, laughing at something. Ingeborg watched them through a sheen of happy tears. She knew he would tease her for being weepy, but the joy that welled up insisted on overflowing as liquid happiness. *Thank you, Father*, ran through her mind again, weaving in and among all the other thoughts of gratitude residing there.

"Mor, Hamre came and helped with the milking. I told him he probably forgot how, but he just shook his head and took a bucket and a stool and sat down like he'd been milking just this morning."

"I've never heard as much laughter in that barn unless we were having a party. Well, it was a party welcoming us all home." Haakan surveyed the cheery kitchen. "You made new curtains."

Ingeborg nodded as she glanced at the red-and-white gingham fabric that now covered the windowpanes. "The kitchen needed cheering up, and Penny ran a sale on her cottons." She pulled the roasting pan from the oven, inhaling the rich aromas that announced the meal, and enjoyed the laughter as Astrid teased her father about something.

Haakan hung his hat on the peg by the door and rubbed his hands together, callouses scratching against each other, then smoothed his hair back with both palms. "Coming home is always the best part of any trip, or any day, for that matter."

His words couldn't have pleased her more. Ingeborg set a dish of pickles on the table. Only three places. How their family had shrunk. Or rather, how it had grown. Ellie and Andrew were living at their own house, Thorliff and Elizabeth with little Inga at theirs. And Hamre had come back. She wondered if he would stay.

"Let's have grace," Haakan said as they settled into their places.

Ingeborg waited for him to start with *I Jesu navn*, but instead he spoke in English. "Father God, I come with a heart full of thanks for bringing us home safely without any accidents, for providing for us beyond our needs, for my home where live those I love most dearly. Thank you for taking care of things here, for the privilege of being able to trust you with all the bounty you have poured upon us. Bless this food and the dear hands that prepared it. In Jesus' precious name, amen."

Covering her surprise, Ingeborg sniffed as she rose to bring the platter and bowls off the warming shelf. As she set them on the table, she rested her hand on Haakan's shoulder just for the joy of having him there. So many things she missed when he was gone.

Haakan took a piece of bread from the plate and brought it to his nose. "No one makes such good bread as you do." Slathering it with butter, he took a huge bite and closed his eyes as he chewed. "And fresh butter. We couldn't always buy good milk and butter. Sometimes even the water was bad."

As they passed the bowls, he heaped his plate. "Mrs. Geddick did well, but no one compares with you."

"I am going to get a swelled head with all your compliments." But she enjoyed every one of them. She glanced up to see Astrid giggling into her milk. "What?"

"Nothing."

"Then why are you laughing?" Haakan stopped with a fork of food halfway to his mouth.

"Because I'm happy too. If Andrew and Thorliff and their families were here, it would be perfect."

"We'll do that tomorrow night," Ingeborg said with a nod.

"So how is school going?"

"Good, although the reading list is enough to choke a cow."

"Don't feed it to one, then." He studied his bread. "Although cows eat most anything. Not like us."

Ingeborg nibbled on her bottom lip to keep from laughing out loud. Haakan had such a droll sense of humor. She caught his glance and let her smile widen.

Astrid rolled her eyes, the dimples in her cheeks deepening. "P-a-a. I wasn't planning on it." She took another bite, started to prop her elbows on the table, but caught the look from her mother and sat up straight again.

The conversation continued, catching one another up on all the news. Ingeborg made sure the bowls kept passing until Haakan waved her off and patted his stomach. "Got to save room for that pie."

Astrid mopped up the last of her gravy with a bit of bread. "Sophie cut her hair in a fringe. I think I will too."

While Haakan shrugged, Ingeborg's eyes headed for her hairline.

"Well, it is the fashion."

"Since when did you care about fashion?" Haakan dug his pipe out of his overall bib pocket.

"I am growing up, you know."

"No. You are still my little Astrid."

"Pa."

He held the match up like he used to for her to blow out, but when she shook her head, he blew it himself. A deep smile of satisfaction softened his face at the first draw on the pipe.

At her mother's nod, Astrid stood to clear the table, scraping the plates into the bucket kept for the chickens. She kept the bones out for Barney, for when he came in the morning with Andrew. When Andrew and Ellie moved into their house, Barney went to live with them, leaving a hole in the life at the homeplace. Setting the dishes in the pan of soapy water heating on the stove, she put the food away and then washed the dishes.

Ingeborg poured her husband another cup of coffee to go along with his pie and picked up her knitting to sit beside him while they talked.

"Any idea why Hamre came back?" Haakan asked.

"Sophie's been writing to him," Astrid told him, "but he didn't tell her he was coming. She was as surprised as the rest of us." Astrid kept up with the conversation in spite of the slosh and clink of the dishes in the pan.

"She's been writing him?" Haakan looked from Astrid to Ingeborg.

Ingeborg shrugged. "I didn't know it. Kaaren has never mentioned it."

"What's wrong with her writing to him?"

"Nothing. Not one thing. It just doesn't seem like Sophie. Now Grace, yes, but Sophie?" Haakan stared back at his daughter. "You're not corresponding with any young men, are you? Or is anyone calling that I don't know about?"

"Pa . . ."

"All right." He raised his pipe. "Just asking. After all, I've been gone, and who knows what all could have transpired."

"I'm going to nursing school. Remember?"

"As I said, just checking."

Some time later when Ingeborg had brushed her hair the requisite one hundred strokes, loving the feel of Haakan watching her, and had blown out the kerosene lamp, she lay back on her pillow with a contented sigh. Her husband had come home, and she had ceased bleeding, a very good combination. When he put his arm around her, she went to him with joy.

The next evening with the whole Bjorklund family home—as well as Hamre, who provided them with sea tales during the meal—and supper finished, the women cleaned up the kitchen and rejoined the men still gathered around the kitchen table. The talk turned to the flour mill that the town co-op had been building and when it would be ready for business.

"We're getting the machinery installed now," Thorliff, the elder of the Bjorklund boys and owner and editor of the now-weekly paper, the *Blessing Gazette*, leaned forward and wrote himself a note in the small notebook he always carried with him. "Hjelmer has the applications from those who answered our ads for the position of manager, and we will be interviewing next week. I am partial at this point to a man named Garth Wiste from Minneapolis. Hjelmer is leaning toward another. We have written to three men to come for the interviews."

"One is from Chicago," Elizabeth added.

"Wiste is younger than the others but has plenty of experience in the flour mills of Minneapolis."

"Is he married?" Ingeborg asked, dividing her attention between the conversation and watching Ellie, who couldn't seem to get comfortable on the kitchen chair. "Andrew, why don't you bring the rocking chair closer for Ellie?"

With a concerned look at his wife, Andrew brought the chair closer, and Ellie, sitting down, sighed in relief. "Thank you." She picked up the baby sweater she'd been knitting and set the rocker in motion with the toe of one foot.

Thorliff turned to his mother with a frown. "Now that is one question we didn't ask. What difference does it make?"

"If he is married, he will need a house built for his family and will be more likely to stay here."

"True, and there are none available for sale in Blessing right now." Thorliff got a faraway look on his face.

"All right. What scheme are you coming up with now?" Elizabeth poked her husband with her elbow.

"Well, I was just thinking maybe we should build a house or two, you know, and have them ready to sell when someone new moves here." He made another note. "Think I'll mention that to Hjelmer."

"I'd think with finishing the mill, you'd have about all the construction you can handle." Haakan blew a smoke ring from his newly lit pipe.

"Never hurts to think ahead. When that mill gets going, everyone in Blessing who has shares in the co-op will benefit. We've kept the construction costs down real well, coming in under estimates." He tapped his notebook with the pencil. "Who'd have thought we'd be looking for more people to work here?" He glanced up at Hamre. "Sure you wouldn't rather stay home? We could use another pair of good hands."

Hamre shook his head. "Sorry."

"You wouldn't have to milk cows." They all chuckled as Hamre flexed his fingers and shook his head again.

"You're gaining a good reputation with the building," Ingeborg added.

"Just taking after the rest of the family." Thorliff smiled at his mother and father.

Ingeborg returned the smile. Her cheese house did have a good reputation, as did the men and their farming methods. The Bjorklunds and Knutsons were known to be progressive farmers, willing to try new machinery and new crops. While she knew pride was one of the seven deadly sins, she believed it referred to pride in oneself. Hers was more for her family and this small town that had built up around their farm, starting with the school and the church.

"I'm thinking of adding on to the surgery." Elizabeth shifted her daughter's sleeping form to her other arm.

"You want me to put her on my bed?" Ingeborg asked.

"I can."

"Let me." Ingeborg stood and picked up her precious granddaughter, swaying gently from side to side until little Inga sighed into deeper sleep.

Astrid looked up from the book she was reading and smiled at her mother. "What a lovely sight."

"What?"

"You holding Inga. Love shines golden all around you."

"Ah, just the lamplight." But the words warmed her heart as she laid the little girl on the bed and covered her with the shawl she kept on the bedpost. Finally, after all these years, there was a baby in the house, even if only once in a while. It helped make up for the lack she'd always pleaded for God to change. She, who'd wanted a house full of children, had only three. Now that the canning and gardening was finished for the year, she would have to bring Inga out more, or go to her house. She leaned over and kissed the child on her forehead, tenderly stroking back the wisps of sunlight hair. "God bless you, little one," she whispered. "Oh, Lord, keep her and the other babies safe."

Soon there would be another one to chase after—Andrew and Ellie's coming baby. She had yet to finish the quilt for their little one. *Tomorrow*, she promised herself. *Tomorrow I will work on it. Perhaps now that she no longer needs to milk, Astrid can help me with it.*

"Mor, you want me to cut the cake?" Astrid asked from the doorway.

"Yes, please." Ingeborg stopped in the doorway and turned to look again at her granddaughter.

"I think we better be heading home," Andrew said when she returned to the table. "Ellie is feeling a mite poorly."

Ingeborg stopped with her hand on Ellie's shoulder. Was this her time already?

5

"COULD I BE IN REAL LOVE?" Sophie asked the face in the mirror.

Grace stopped in the doorway, reading her sister's lips in the mirror and shaking her head. "He just came here. Do you think he came for you?"

Turning from the glass, Sophie squared her shoulders. "Maybe. I've been writing to him for almost two years."

"What? Ten letters, perhaps twelve? That is not a basis for love."

Sophie could tell how upset her twin sister was by the stumbling of her speech and her flying fingers.

"What do you know? You've never been in love." When she saw Grace's jaw tighten, she knew her words hurt even worse.

"I should hope not. We are too young for that." Grace didn't try to speak, and her fingers slashed the air.

Maybe you are but not me. His touching my elbow . . . just being near him makes me shiver. "Many women marry at fourteen, some even younger."

"They are not women; they are girls. Oh, Sophie, please . . ." Grace dropped her hands to her sides and, slowly shaking her head, sat down on their bed.

There was no point in continuing this with Grace. "Well . . ." Sophie turned and tipped Grace's face up by placing her finger under her chin. "There's nothing to worry about. He'll go back to fishing and nothing will have changed." The thought made her want to throw herself across the bed and wail. He was so handsome, so manly, not a boy like those her age.

A picture of Toby Valders flitted across her mind. He was not a boy either, and his kisses had felt more than sweet, but Hamre looked like she'd pictured the old Norse gods. Strong enough to pick her up and carry her off to his Viking ship, his eyes burning blue sparks, his lips carved like stone, only warm stone and . . . She jerked herself upright, wanting to fan her face. My, how her imagination could carry her away.

She thought back to their walk home from school. He'd told her about some of his adventures—fishing for cod, rowing a dory, and pulling in fifty, a hundred, a boatload of twenty-pound cod. Someday he planned to have a schooner of his own, his dream a three-masted ship to sail to the Bering Sea, where the fish were so thick that all the dories came back full twice a day and the men cleaned the cod and salted them down in the hold, silver in his pocket.

Surely he could afford a home and a wife if fishing was so profitable. . . .

"So how long are you gone?" she'd asked him.

"There are two seasons, winter and summer. I came off the summer run and caught the train for here. I need to be back and ready to go in November."

He would not be staying in Blessing? Her heart took a dive. *Then why did you come back?* But she was afraid to ask that question and instead asked what Seattle was like.

"It rains all winter there but not much snow. There are mountains to the west and the east, and Mount Rainier sits like a king on a throne to the south. Sometimes you go for days without a sighting, but when the sky clears, there it is in all its snowy majesty."

"I'm jealous. I've only seen pictures of mountains." *Ah, to see mountains, huge trees, the Pacific Ocean. Maybe I could even go to Alaska with him.* She brought herself out of her daydreams. "How come there is so much water there?" She knew Seattle wasn't on the coast because they had looked it up on a map once to see where he had gone to.

Hamre took a stick and bent down to draw in the dirt. "Here's the coastline, and here the ocean comes in the Strait of Juan de Fuca and flows south into an inland waterway like none other. Up here is Canada, Vancouver Island." He drew more shoreline. "So many islands, I could have one of my own if I wanted. But Seattle is a growing city. Many of the provisions for the Yukon gold strike flowed through Seattle. There are forests with trees thick as the fur on Barney's back. Like the north woods where Haakan was a lumberjack, the trees in Washington are being cut and shipped up and down the coast for lumber."

Never would she have believed Hamre would say so many words, and without digging them out of him. Sophie watched his hand on the stick, leaning close enough to almost touch him. Rich blond hair curled slightly from behind his ear, circling the lobe. He was clean-shaven and his square jaw moved beneath his skin. If she leaned just a mite closer . . . She inhaled his scent of soap and . . . and . . . She sniffed again. Man. That's what it was. Hamre's own manly scent. Her knees threatened to quit on her.

Surely he could hear her heart, it thundered so hard . . . as if it wanted to leap out of her chest and dance with his. If his wanted to dance, of course.

He turned to look at her. His eyes, those Bjorklund eyes, blue as the deepest sky, eyes one could get lost in. She swallowed and tried to break away, but her eyelids refused to flutter in the way that enticed the boys she'd known. He held her gaze and straightened, rising so she had to tip her head back. Her legs turned to mush, and she feared she might fall against him. Even her fingertips tingled.

He stepped back, breaking the mood and causing her to sniff.

"Ah, Sophie, I . . ."

She had waited for him to continue, her breath catching. . . .

Even the memory caused a like reaction. She cleared her throat, hoping Grace, already in bed, hadn't seen her flush, and ordered her heart to get back to normal.

Once in bed Sophie watched Grace's face, outlined by the moonlight streaming in the window. She knew Grace was either praying or thinking hard, because her breathing had not slipped into the evenness of sleep. But talking in the dark was not easy, and she knew Grace didn't want to hear what she wanted to talk about.

Why couldn't she tease Hamre like she did the others? Why did she not feel that power over him that she knew over the other boys? Down bone deep, she knew males of the species found her attractive, and what she could get away with, she did, always a breath from the edge that would incur a scolding from Mor, a look from Pa, and a lecture about nice Norwegian girls. Then, what her parents didn't know wouldn't hurt them. Or so the old saw went.

Grace did not see things the same way she did.

Sophie studied her sister's profile. Of the two of them, Grace was growing into a real beauty, while she . . . There was a wide river of difference between the two sisters. Grace lived up to her name, beautiful deep down like their mother. Once Sophie had looked up the meaning of her own name, and when she discovered it meant wisdom she'd laughed for weeks.

If Hamre came and tossed rocks at her window, would she go down and walk with him in the moonlight? She made herself roll over and close her eyes. She knew both Grace and her mother would say she needed to pray about her feelings for Hamre. She thought about what to say. *Dear God, make him love me?* That wasn't it. *Dear God, keep him from going back to Seattle until I can go with him?* No. *Dear God, help.* At the thought of real help, she matched the rhythm of Grace's breathing that led her into sleep of her own. Better not to ask if one didn't want to hear the answer.

The next day at school she took the teasing of her friends with a flip of her hair and a saucy look. Let them think what they wanted. But she could tell Grace was still upset with her, and that let in a niggle of fear that tormented her far more than she'd ever thought it would. What if she really was on the wrong track? So she plied her books with more concentration than usual and even raised her hand to answer a question, bringing an astonished look from both her sister and Pastor Solberg. Astrid gave her a secret smile of congratulations. Little did they know that her mind answered every question with Hamre.

On the wagon ride home she wrapped her new navy serge skirt around her bent knees and laid her cheek on her knees. *Let Hamre be at our house. Let me see him today.* Was it a prayer if she didn't say "Please God" first or "Our Father"?

No Hamre. No, he hadn't been there. No, no one had heard from him. He was probably visiting the rest of his relatives, Ilse suggested. Sophie thought up reasons to go visit Tante Ingeborg.

When she cleaned the schoolrooms, she checked the windows to see if Hamre was coming. Sitting out on the porch peeling potatoes, she had a clear view of the road and lane. No Hamre, and she hated peeling potatoes anyway, along with most other homemaking things like cooking, sewing, knitting, cleaning. Although she did them at her mother's insistence, she always dreamed of adventures far away from Blessing.

By bedtime she'd still not seen Hamre.

The next afternoon when the wagon stopped at their house, she saw a familiar figure talking with her pa at the machine shed. Her heart picked up a beat and her feet a skip. "He's here," she signed to Grace, nodding toward the men.

"I can see even if I can't hear." Grace didn't bother to speak, just signed back, her fingers flashing.

Sophie stomped up the porch steps and into the house. Why couldn't Grace be happy for her?

"Hamre will be staying for supper, so set an extra place," Kaaren said. She glanced over to see Sophie staring out the window toward the barn. "Perhaps you should milk all the cows. All by yourself tonight. In an hour."

Grace rolled her lips together to keep from laughing.

The banter between Grace and Mor laid a background as Sophie's thoughts ranged far afield. *Mrs. Hamre Bjorklund. Sophie Marie Bjorklund. We will own ships instead of farmland. Hamre will be a fine father, teaching his sons about the sea.* She leaned against the window frame. *Hurry up, Hamre.*

"Sophie!"

Returning from her dreaming, Sophie turned at the insistent tone of her mother's voice. "What?" She knew her voice was not the most pleasant, and the raising of her mother's eyebrows said she recognized that too. "Sorry."

"You have your good dress on?"

"I . . . ah . . . well, we're having company." Sophie refused to look at Grace. She could feel her twin's secret laughter. She sucked in a breath and slapped a smile on her face. "What was it you wanted?" Sweetness worked better than snapping, in her mother's outlook.

"We need some help here. Would you go out to the well house and bring in the jug of cream? Also I have a new mold of butter we'll use."

"Yes, of course." She flew out the door. The springhouse was closer to where the men were leaning into part of the steam engine. Perhaps she could go ask if they wanted anything. She thought of taking cookies down to them, but that might be a bit obvious. *Please be thinking of me, Hamre.*

As she opened the door set in the stone wall that helped keep the well house cool, Sophie eyed the two men still talking. They were spending too much time talking about farming, she was sure. Why didn't they come up to the house? Didn't Hamre want to see her? If he knew she was waiting and he was tormenting her . . .

Water ran from the windmill into a pipe that poured into a concrete trough and ran out the other end via a pipe into the watering tank for the cattle. Crocks and jars set in the cold tank stayed fresh. Eggs filled a basket with straw in the bottom. Smoked meat hung from hooks in the rafters, as did spekekjøtt, haunches of mutton dried in the top of the barn in the hot summertime. It would be sliced paper thin and served on bread or with cream. Like the cellar under the house, the springhouse spoke well of the larder and the hard work of the family. When the weather cooled enough for butchering, crocks of sausage patties and headcheese would line the floor against one wall. Ropes of sausages would hang in loops from the rafters. On a hot day the well house was a great place to work.

Sophie took the wooden butter mold and the jug of cream her mother needed and closed the door carefully behind her, dropping the bent nail into the hasp to lock it. She glanced around, only to see the men were no longer by the machinery. Had they gone to the house? Surely Hamre would visit with her before he returned to the boarding-house. What had they been talking about all that time? If only she could read lips long distance.

Supper at the Knutsons', when the deaf school was in session was always an adventure, especially at the beginning of the year while every-one was still in training. The older students took turns helping with the meals and serving; the younger ones set the table and helped with the cleanup afterward.

With Lars at the head of the table and Kaaren at the foot, closest to the kitchen, Sophie, Grace, Trygve, and Samuel, along with Ilse and George, spaced themselves along the long table to help the students, who were required to use the proper signs to ask for what they wanted.

Sophie paid more attention to Hamre sitting next to her pa than to the children around her until the milk from an upended glass flowed into her lap. She pushed back her chair and leaped to her feet, ready to scream at the offender, but her mother's clearing her throat stopped her. *Here I have my good dress on for company, and this happens.* She'd taken off her apron, which added to the mess. But since looking at her mother would yield nothing but a note of censure, she fetched a couple of towels, one to hand to the child to wipe up the mess on the table and another to clean her dress. Now she'd have to rinse out the skirt tonight because she'd hoped to wear this to school the next day.

Smiling sweetly on the outside, she took her place again and passed the bowl of potatoes to the person on her right.

When supper was finished, the adults moved into the parlor while Ilse oversaw the cleanup and homework time.

Hamre, look at me. Sophie tried to catch his attention, but he fol-lowed her family as if he had all the time in the world. Surely this wouldn't be an ordinary evening with homework and casual conversation.

She felt as trapped as a mouse caught by the tail.

Kaaren picked up her mending and Grace the sweater Sophie had started knitting but quit weeks earlier after dropping some stitches. Lars indicated a chair near him for Hamre, leaving Sophie to finally flounce into a chair by her mother. If Hamre had just paid attention to her, they might have gone out on the porch to talk or walk, and perhaps she would take his arm and he would cover her hand with his and hold her snug against his side. Instead she had to endure another look of reprimand from her mother. What a wasted evening, and she had yet to rinse the milk out of her dress.

"So how long do you plan to stay in Blessing?" Kaaren asked.

"The schooner will leave for the Bering Sea about November first, and we have some work to do to get it ready. So another week at the most."

Sophie felt her jaw drop and snapped it shut before her gaffe should become obvious. Only another week. She tried to smile, but her chin quivered in spite of her attempt.

Lars cleared his throat and looked at his wife. "Hamre has asked me if he can court our Sophie."

Her heart stopped, fluttered, and raced off. Had she heard right? Court our Sophie? *Oh Hamre* . . . She looked up and into his eyes. Finally. Could he read her soul? The happiness in her gaze? Sitting still took all her will when she only wanted to fling herself across the room and into his arms. Hamre!

Lars shifted his attention to his restless daughter. "But I told him you are too young and have promised to finish school. You may write to each other with our blessing, and we'll see what all comes by next summer."

Sophie stared at her father. No! He couldn't do that to her.

6

"BUT I WANT TO GO with you!"

"Sophie, you know what your pa said. I was hoping we could be married now, but we can wait. It won't be long."

"It will be forever." Sophie spun away and went to stand at the porch railing, staring out over the moon-washed fields. Frost was in the air, causing her to pull her shawl more closely around her shoulders. She felt his hands cup her upper arms, and heat poured through her body. What if she turned into his arms? Would he kiss her? What would his lips feel like?

"Sophie, I dreamed you would feel this way, but we must abide by your pa's wishes. I will go to sea for these months, and if all is well, I will come to visit again between the seasons. Do I dare to believe that you love me?"

"Oh, Hamre, I do." She turned and stared up into his eyes, darkened now in the night. She paused. "Do you really love me?"

"Would I have asked to court you did I not?"

"But I need to hear you say the words." Her voice softened, and she put all her heart in her eyes.

"Ah, Sophie, I think . . ." He sucked in a long breath, and his voice deepened even more. "When I was a boy, I believed I loved Ilse, but I went away and couldn't even remember her face. I wrote to you because your face, your laughter, never left me. I believe I have always loved you. But I was waiting for you to grow up." He stroked the line of her jaw. "And now you have."

"You never said. All those years."

"I could not say anything. Words never came easily for me. And you were a little girl."

"But now they do?" *And I have grown up. So romantic, waiting for me to grow up. Writing to me as a friend. Ah, this is what stories are made of.*

"I think I grew up. Maybe talking to the cod fish helped."

Chuckling at his response, she felt his hands wrap hers in a warmth that penetrated clear to her backbone and down to her toes. Leaning closer, she turned her head and rested her cheek on his chest. His breath feathered her bangs. If she looked up, leaned closer, could she kiss his chin? Surely his heart beat in time with hers, not a steady beat but more a race. He released one hand, keeping it caught between them and used his calloused fingers to trace a line along her jaw. Ah, the bliss of his touch. So rough like sand but so gentle, as if afraid she might break. The trail of his touch burned like the sear of a flatiron.

"Ahem." Her mother's voice came from the parlor behind them.

They drew apart to the decorous distance of society's strictures. Her whole front felt chilled, missing his touch. She sighed, a sigh that came from deep inside. A year seemed an interminable time. Why was there always something or someone to keep her from her dreams?

"I better go."

"I know. Ma is giving the signal." *But I don't want you to go.* "Will I see you tomorrow?"

"Ja, I will meet you after school for a buggy ride. Haakan said he would loan me theirs." He brushed his fingertips over her cheek again. "Good night."

He left her standing there, still dreaming of a kiss.

Back in the kitchen, Grace took one look at her sister's face and shook her head. Returning to the book she was reading for school, she ignored Sophie's pleading look. Fine. If Grace didn't want to talk about the love of her life, she would not tease her to do so. Sophie flounced up to their bedroom to dream of Hamre.

Sophie woke in the predawn hours, her dream still a living part of her mind—she and Hamre married and riding the train to Seattle. What could she do to change her father's mind? And her mother's? The two were always in solid agreement. If she could get Grace to help her, perhaps she would have a better chance. She turned on her side and watched Grace sleep, her twin's face only a pale form in the dimness. She choked on the pain of the next thought: *I'll have to leave Grace behind.*

They'd never been apart—not even visiting overnight at Astrid's or Rebecca's. Always where one went, so did the other. Would marriage to Hamre be like her and Grace, so close they knew what the other was thinking, and if one hurt the other felt it? She thought of the time Grace had had such a terrible cough. Her own throat had hurt, and she'd not coughed once.

But Hamre. Warmth puddled in her middle at just the thought of him. So tall and strong, so gentle, the sparkle in his eyes, the set of his chin. The thrill when they touched. *Go back to sleep*, she ordered herself. But when she did, she could feel the rock and sway of the train, feel the warmth of his arm next to hers in the seat. She slept again, feeling his shoulder beneath her cheek.

She woke with a plan.

"Sophie, time to get up," Kaaren called in her normal greeting.

Sophie lay still a moment longer to savor her plan before waking her sister. Surely she could accomplish this. After all, Hamre was male, and according to whispered conversations she'd overheard, all men had the same kinds of urges. She'd even read of them in the Bible, not that she was supposed to understand it. But she hadn't grown up on a farm for nothing.

She touched Grace's shoulder and watched her come awake. Her eyes fluttered open, and as always, she turned to smile at Sophie.

"Good morning."

"Ja, it is a good morning."

Grace narrowed her eyes. "What?"

"Nothing. I am just grateful I don't have to go milk cows every morning. Come on."

By the time they were dressed and had brushed their hair, Sophie could hear Ilse and their mother talking in the kitchen but was not able to make out the words. Was it Norwegian? This was a morning like all school mornings, yet it wasn't. Five days left until Hamre would get back on the westbound train. Five days to convince him to take her along.

She forced herself to pay attention to her schoolwork rather than keep checking the back door to see if he'd arrived yet. When Pastor Solberg dismissed school and she walked out the door, sure enough, there he was sitting in Haakan's buggy waiting. Her heart leaped, and a smile split her face. "Tell Ma I'll be a bit late," she told Grace and headed for the buggy before Grace could reply.

Hamre stepped down to help her in, his hand burning hers. She settled her skirt and smiled at him as he climbed back in the buggy. "Where are we going?"

"Where would you like to go?" His voice ran deep like the river. Again the puddle in her middle.

"Anywhere, but I have to be home in time to help with supper. You will come for supper again, won't you?"

"I'm sorry. I promised to go to Thorliff's for supper tonight."

"Oh." She let her lower lip pout just enough to attract his attention. He turned to look at her, his blue eyes growing sad. "I'm sorry. I . . ."

"That's all right. I just want to spend every minute I can with you." She let her eyelashes feather across her cheeks, raising her chin slightly to see if her action had the desired effect.

It did. He looked at her with a smile that encouraged her to tuck her hand through his arm and lean against his strong shoulder. The horse trotted onward, head up, ears flicking, and the buggy's swaying gave her a good reason to lean against him more firmly.

"Tell me about your fishing trips."

"What do you want to know?"

"What have you seen?"

"Whales longer than this horse and buggy rise out of the water like gray monsters. You see a puff of mist where they release their air, then their backs arch, and finally the tail fins flip as they let out sounds." He drew the arch with the sweep of one arm.

"Sounds?" *Oh, I want to see whales, the ocean.*

"Then they go down under water again. We've seen gray whales, humpbacks, and killer whales. They're a striking black and white with a big dorsal fin." He turned to look into her eyes. "Did you know that whales sing?"

"Hamre, you're teasing me." She looked at him from under her lashes and swallowed at the glint in his eyes. Surely her ploy was working.

"No, they really do. Underwater sound travels for great distances, and that is how they communicate."

"Well, I never . . ." She shook her head. "Whales . . . what else?"

"Seals, sea lions, dolphins, grizzly bears along the shores of Alaska, moose, elk, deer, sea otters. You cannot believe all the wildlife up there, not that there is not a lot in Washington too. You will love it there."

"I know already." She sighed. "Such a long time away. What if you find someone else to love?"

"Do not fear for that." He covered her hand with his other. "I have waited these years already for you to grow up."

"If we could go together now . . ." She let the sentence slide ever so gently into silence. She felt his body stiffen next to her. So he thought the same, did he?

"I know . . ." He tipped his head to the side to touch hers.

"I think my heart might break right in two if you leave me."

"It won't be that long. You'll see."

She left it at that, only sitting closer so she could feel his leg through her skirt.

"I better get you home, eh?"

"I guess." She laid her head against his shoulder. "I miss you when you are not with me." She looked up at him. Her breath caught in her throat when he stopped the buggy. He stroked her jaw with the tips of his fingers, leaning closer. She raised her mouth, and slowly he leaned down. With a sigh, he covered her lips with his, turning at the same time so his other arm circled her waist.

This was not the light peck of the other boys. She'd always drawn away after a brief contact, but this time she melted into his arms and let the kiss linger. As if she had any choice. When he raised his head, he whispered against her lips.

"You are so beautiful."

She'd read of a heroine melting into the hero's arms. Now she knew what that meant. With great effort she straightened and stared into his eyes. "Oh, Hamre. I never knew a kiss could be like that." Her whisper made him smile.

He nodded and clucked the horse into a homeward-bound trot.

Say something. Her mouth dried with the wanting. *Take me with you. Say something.*

He pulled the horse to a stop in front of the Knutson home and stepped down, then handed her down. "That was nice." He touched the brim of his hat, climbed back in the buggy, and turned to drive back out the lane.

Nice? That was all he could say? Nice? With all her wiles and a kiss that sent her spiraling into space, he left her with a tip of the hat and "nice"?

She stamped her foot and stormed into the house, ignoring Grace's questioning look and stomping up the stairs to throw herself across the bed and let the tears flow. He didn't really love her after all. The kiss that had sent her into the clouds meant nothing to him or he wouldn't have left her with "That was nice." To top it all off, she was no closer to leaving with him.

She fell asleep that night dreaming of a kiss that went on and on.

"Sophie, whatever is wrong?" Kaaren laid the back of her hand against her daughter's forehead. "No fever, but are you sick?"

Sick with longing. "I didn't sleep well, that's all." She knew she had black smudges under her eyes. The mirror had told her so. Oh, to crawl back in bed and pull the covers up to hide her misery.

That evening she watched him come striding across the pasture, and when they met, he kissed her in spite of her pale cheeks and dark shadows. While she fought to keep to her resolve to be cool and proper with him, all she wanted to do was burrow into his chest and rest in the strength of his arms. A teasing smile was beyond her. This wasn't the way she'd planned any of it.

She poured his coffee and helped her mother serve the dessert as Lars and Hamre talked about the changes the mill would make in town and which was better, gasoline engines or old-fashioned steam. But when she walked with him out to the porch as he was leaving, he kissed her again. She knew then he no more wanted to leave her than she him, and he pulled away with great reluctance.

"Oh, Sophie, how will I leave you?"

"Don't. Take me with you."

He laid a finger on her lips. "Hush, don't talk like that." Then he kissed her on the forehead and strode back toward town.

Sophie watched him go, her hands clenched at her sides. "You cannot leave me, please don't leave me." When she went into the house, she walked past the others and climbed the stairs, her feet weighing more with each riser. Three more days before her life ended.

She woke in the night, her pillow damp from her tears. "God, if you hear me at all, could you please let me go with Hamre?" She whispered the prayer, grateful for the first time that her sister could not hear her. But when Grace's hand covered hers lying between them, she knew Grace understood. No longer a game, Sophie sighed and turned over to lay her hand on Grace's shoulder. Three taps, their signal of thank-you, but this time with a far deeper meaning. No words but a heart-to-heart message between two who had shared one womb.

One more night before he left. Sophie could no longer summon a smile. "I cannot bear for you to leave." She blinked to keep the tears from falling and failed utterly.

"Ah, my Sophie." Hamre wiped her tears away with his thumbs, cupping her jaw between his hands. When he pulled her into his arms, she burrowed in like a lost child, wrapping her arms around his waist. This time when he kissed her, he lingered on her lips, whispering words of love, holding her close against him. When he broke away, she swayed until he caught her close.

"I'll ask your father again."

"No. he won't relent. Just come for me, and I will go with you. I don't care about anything but going with you. Once we are married, they will forgive and forget. All will be well." *And if not, we will be too far away for it to make a difference. Except for Grace. Can I not at least tell Grace? No. She will tell Mor. She cannot help that.* What she thought would be a thrill had now become desperation. She clung to Hamre. Why did love have to hurt like this?

"I will have a bag packed and hidden in the haymow."

"Sophie, let me ask your parents again."

"No. Then they will not allow me to see you. I know my pa. He seems gentle, but when he makes up his mind, he does not change it. This is the best way. Trust me."

Hamre turned away. "I should say no to this scheme, but so help me, I cannot leave you behind." He wrapped her in his arms and buried his face in her hair. "This is not right."

"Perhaps not right, but necessary." Why did she feel years older than she had a week ago? Was it only a week, or had she loved him already for a lifetime?

When she said good-night to her mother, she hugged her close and breathed deep of the fragrance that was her mother. *Forgive me, Mor. I don't know what else to do.* She kissed her father's cheek. *Good-bye, please forgive me, but I have to leave.*

"Something is happening," Grace said as they crawled into bed.

"I had to say good-bye to the man I love, so yes, something is happening. My heart is breaking." Sophie hugged Grace and whispered against her ear. Knowing her sister couldn't hear her made it worse. "Forgive me. I'll write to you."

You can still back out, a small voice whispered inside her mind.

No I can't. I have to live up to my word. But which word? The one to Hamre or the one to her father? Hamre would come back for her in a year. But what if he didn't? She was certain she could feel her heart ripping in half. *What if they never speak to me again?*

Later, when the whole house had quieted, she slipped out of bed and tugged her resolve into place while she dressed in her warmest wool skirt and a long-sleeved waist with a cameo at the neckline. After tucking her nightdress into a small bag she'd stowed in her chifforobe, along with her brush and comb, a washcloth, towel, and soap, she snapped it shut. Surely they would send more of her things when she wrote and asked for them. A tiny shiver of dread spilled on the excitement. Wouldn't they? The note she had written she propped on the chest of drawers, where Grace would see it. Tiptoeing down the stairs, she let herself out the back door just as Hamre approached the steps. She stepped into the comfort of his arms.

"I have your bag in the buggy. We will go to Pastor Solberg to ask him to marry us."

Where had all her excitement gone? Married? Wasn't that what she wanted? Sophie shook her head. "He won't."

"We will ask."

She let him take her small bag, and together they stole away. When she was sitting in the buggy, she looked back at the house, where those she loved most lay sleeping. *Good-bye, I love you. Don't forget me.* She half rose, the urge to return home so strong she felt sure someone was tugging on her shoulder, drawing her back. Then Hamre settled into the buggy and took her hand in his.

"Your hand is like ice."

Sophie swallowed, a sigh of pain nearly choking her. *And so is my heart. I never thought leaving would hurt like this. Grace . . . oh, Grace, don't hate me.*

As they pulled up to the ranch house where Pastor Solberg lived, she could only think, *He'll never do this and then he'll ride over and tell*

Ma and Pa, and they'll drag me home again.

"I'll go talk with him and be right back." Hamre gave her a hug that should have been comforting but wasn't. She couldn't stop shivering.

When he returned, it wasn't with a smile but with a shake of the head. He climbed into the buggy and drove in a circle to head back to town. "We will drive to Grafton and find a minister or a justice of the peace to marry us there."

"Will Pastor Solberg tell?"

"He does not know you are with me."

As the miles passed beneath the buggy wheels, Sophie slumped against Hamre until he put his arm around her and let her sleep against his chest.

She woke to find herself sheltered in his arm. How many miles had they come? Was he having second thoughts like she was? "Hamre?"

"Ja."

She reached up and smoothed her hand over his cheek. "I love you."

He turned his face into her hand and kissed the palm that smelled faintly of soap. "Ja, that is good."

❧

They were married just before breakfast by a black-robed judge who invited them to join him after they'd said their brief vows.

"Thank you, but . . ."

"No buts. Mrs. Johansen, put two more plates on. These young people need a good meal to start their new life."

Once on the train Sophie stared out the window. She had her wish and her prayer. She was now Mrs. Hamre Bjorklund. What would the future hold?

7

"INGEBORG, SOPHIE IS GONE." Kaaren nearly fell in the door as it crashed against the wall.

"Gone?" Ingeborg reached to catch her sister of the heart. They couldn't have been closer were they truly sisters, they'd been through so much together. Oh, how could Sophie do this to her mother? "What happened?"

"She ran off with Hamre last night." Kaaren wiped her eyes with the corner of her apron. "Lars is searching for her, but I know they are gone." She handed Ingeborg the note Grace had found on the chest of drawers.

Ingeborg guided Kaaren to a chair and sat her down. "Have you eaten?"

"I cannot eat." She tipped her head back, tears leaking from under closed eyelids as though getting those three words out were all she could manage. "How could she do such a thing? Lars asked them to wait only for a year, until she graduated. We didn't tell her she could never see him or anything so dramatic."

Ingeborg sat Kaaren down on a chair and poured a cup of coffee for each of them before sitting down herself to open the envelope and take out the sheet of paper.

Dear Grace, Ma, and Pa,

Hamre and I left during the night. We will be married.
Once we are in Seattle I will write to you. Please forgive me,
but I cannot live without him.

Sophie. She cannot live without him when ten days ago she was
flirting with Heinz. Ingeborg reached for Kaaren's hand. Like a trapped
bird, it trembled beneath her own. "Oh, my poor dear. All I can say is
that God will keep her in the palm of His hand. And He will give you
strength." Ingeborg continued reading.

You know Hamre is a good man and will provide for me.
I love you all.
Sophie
P.S. Please don't hate me.

Seeing Kaaren's ravaged face, Ingeborg wished the girl were right
there to be shaken soundly. How could she do such a thing to parents
who loved her so dearly? And not just to them, but to Grace.

"How's Grace?"

"She went to school. She hasn't cried."

"She's angry?"

"Oh ja, she is that. So are Lars and the boys. I keep telling myself
God is taking care of her, but right now . . . I just want . . . her home."
She took a handkerchief from her apron pocket and blew her reddening
nose. "Trygve was all for getting on the train and going after her."

"How did they—? Hamre must have rented a horse and buggy
from the livery and driven them to Grafton." Ingeborg thought a
moment. If someone caught the train this morning, it would be the
same one Hamre and Sophie would take west. But would it make any
sense to try to stop them?

"Hamre gave Lars his word. Doesn't that mean anything anymore?"
Kaaren's tears flowed in spite of her mopping efforts.

Ingeborg read the note again. *Please don't hate me.* Uff da. What
was the child thinking? She put the note into the envelope, handed it

back to Kaaren, and rose to cut some cheese. "Here, eat this and a piece of toast. That will taste good. Ilse is taking care of the school?"

"Ja." Kaaren took a sip of her coffee, clenching the cup between her cold shaking hands. "To think Hamre would . . ." Her sentence trailed off as she shook her head slowly, as if even that little motion took what energy she had left.

Of all the children, Sophie was the most headstrong—had been from the time she was tiny. But she had always watched out for Grace. Or was it during these later years that Grace had watched out for her sister? The twin bond between them was far stronger than between other brothers and sisters. Ingeborg thought back to when the girls were babies and were most content sleeping cuddled together, how Kaaren and Lars had learned Grace could not hear and their resolve to help their baby daughter live in the hearing world around her. As close as their families were, Ingeborg loved the twins like she loved her own children.

Uff da, Lord. You know all, and you knew Sophie would leave. Nothing surprises you. Comfort Kaaren and Lars—and Grace. She's been put out with her sister the last week or so—Sophie's cutting her hair, fussing about school. Ingeborg shook her head and got up to refill their coffee cups. *How would I feel if Astrid did something like this?*

"Mange takk," Kaaren whispered. "One minute I am so angry, and the next, all I can do is cry and pray." She chewed on her lower lip. "And Lars. He is so angry."

❧

That afternoon after school was out, Pastor Solberg came to the Bjorklunds' door.

"Come in, come in," Ingeborg said.

"No, I've come to ask a favor."

"Of course. How can I help?"

"Would you go with me to talk to Kaaren and Lars?"

"Of course. Let me change my apron and get my shawl. It's brisk out here; fall has come." *Oh, Lord, now what?*

He helped her up into his buggy and climbed in himself. "This is a sad day."

"Ja, that it is. A shock. Kaaren came to us this morning with the news." She watched her pastor and longtime friend as he stared straight ahead. Something was bothering him. *Lord God, you know what is wrong. John has been with us for all these years and seen it all. Life, death, sickness, health, joy, and sorrow. Help him now with whatever is bothering him. Give him an extra measure of grace to sustain him.*

He stopped the buggy in front of the picket fence that fronted the Knutson house. Hog wire continued on the other three sides, enclosing the yard and garden for protection in case the cows got out, which had happened more than once. He got down and came around to help her out, his shoulders rolled in as if he carried a burden far heavier than he could manage.

Together they mounted the front stairs to the porch instead of going to the back. This was indeed a formal call.

"Oh, I didn't see you come up," Kaaren said after opening the door to their knock. "Come in. I'm afraid you won't find us very happy here today."

"We need to talk about that." He indicated the parlor. "Can we sit down? Is Lars near?"

"I'm right here." Lars came in from the kitchen.

"Good. I'd just as soon talk to you both at the same time."

When they'd all taken a seat, Solberg sighed and began. "I have a confession to make."

Kaaren looked to Ingeborg, who shrugged and looked to their pastor to continue.

"We were all in bed when someone knocked on the door last night. I got up to answer, and it was Hamre. He asked me if I would marry him and Sophie right then."

"Was Sophie with him?" Lars asked.

"She didn't come to the door with him, but I assume she was. I invited him to come in, but he just stood there. I-I didn't know what to say. I prayed for God to give me wisdom. I thought that if I said yes, it might delay them, but then I wondered if I said no what would happen. So I said I would be delighted to marry them, but that Sophie needed to have your permission, and then we could have the wedding in a day or two, when their families could rejoice with them." He stared at Kaaren and Lars sitting side by side on the horsehair sofa. "I was hoping to buy time, to keep them from making a big mistake."

"It wasn't your fault. It was theirs." Lars's voice wore a hardness not heard before.

"Then today when Grace said Sophie was gone, I was heartbroken, as I know you are. I . . . I'm sorry. I should have gotten on the horse and come to tell you then, but I thought they were going to wait. Hamre thanked me and said something about changing plans. Please . . . will you forgive me?"

"There is nothing to forgive." Kaaren took Lars's hand and, glancing at his face, turned back to Pastor Solberg. She shook her head, carefully, as if she had a headache. "We can all say 'if I had done this' or 'if we had done that,' but that does no good." She studied their clasped hands. "My mind says I will trust God, but my heart screams I want my daughter back."

"To hurt her mother like this . . ." Jawline tight, Lars narrowed his eyes. "That is unforgivable."

"No. Please don't say that." Kaaren squeezed his hand.

"I asked at the livery. Sam said Hamre rented a horse and buggy, and it hadn't come back yet." Lars covered his wife's hand with his other.

"You think they drove it to Grafton?" Ingeborg asked.

"Possibly. Take most of the night."

Ingeborg knew Kaaren was thinking the same thing she was: Surely they wouldn't live in sin. Surely Sophie wouldn't be that wild. Would a pastor or a judge marry them there? How were they going to live? Hamre said he lived in a boardinghouse. Uff da! No answers. The note said Sophie would write when they got to Seattle. But that was three days on the train. It would be at least a week before a letter could get back to Blessing, perhaps two.

"How is Grace?" Solberg asked.

"Angry. Disappointed. The same as the rest of us."

"So all we can do is pray for her—for them—and wait," Kaaren said with a catch in her voice.

"Unless we send out a posse." Lars leaned back, arms clamped across his chest.

"Like her brothers?" Kaaren raised an eyebrow.

"Good thing they aren't older or I'm sure they would go." Ingeborg felt a knot loosen inside. Kaaren had smiled on that last comment.

"Well, we have God's promise to care for His wayward children." Pastor Solberg shook his head again. "If He can take care of sparrows, He will watch over them."

Ingeborg stood. "I need to be getting on home. You'll let me know as soon as you hear anything?"

"Ja, we will do that."

"Could we pray, please?" Without taking time for answers, Pastor Solberg bowed his head. "Lord, we come to you with pain that hurts even more when it involves our children. Thank you that our children are your children, as are we. We know you will watch over Sophie and that you will heal our hurts, for so you have promised. Let us cling to you, and I pray for extra grace and wisdom in the months ahead. In your son's precious name, amen." He stood. "I'll be praying extra hard for all of you."

"Thank you, Pastor." Kaaren sniffed and forced a partial smile.

Lars thanked the pastor and shook his hand, but the tightness had not left his face or his voice.

After Pastor Solberg dropped Ingeborg off at her house, a thought stopped her on the back steps. Wait until Hildegunn Valders got a hold of this. All in the name of Christian caring, of course, but gossip was gossip, and this was going to cause a storm of it. How could she protect Kaaren from the worst of it?

8

September 9, 1901

"I'M SORRY . . . she's gone."

Garth Wiste stared at the midwife as if looking at her the wrong way through a telescope. "And the baby?" He forced the words past the block in his throat.

"Still alive but weak."

My Maddie . . . how will I live? "I will see her now."

"If you would wait until I clean things up a bit—"

"Now." He pushed past the woman blocking the bedroom door and crossed to the bed to kneel by his wife's side. Taking her hand in his, he kissed the skin so transparent he might look right through. The blood. All over like there had been a battle fought here. All her life drained out. "Oh, Maddie, I . . ." He fought the tears, but like stopping the ocean, it was impossible. He stroked her cheek, tucked her hair behind one ear with a tender finger. Never again would she tease him, make him laugh, hold him, play with her children, love him.

He gathered her close as if willing life back into her cooling body. "God, how could you? She had so much to live for, and you took her away. How could you?" Anger flared, a rage so hot that surely the tips of his fingers burned her skin. He kissed her forehead and laid her back down, arranging her hair, tucking the sheet around her arms. "Oh,

God!" His groan rent the stillness. "I cannot do this. You ask too much of me."

A whimper came from the basket in the corner. Who would feed this baby? Surely the midwife would know someone to wet-nurse it. It? One did not refer to one's infant as *it*. Was it a boy or a girl? He'd not bothered to ask, so concerned he was for his wife.

"Mr. Wiste, please let me clean things up in here," the midwife said from slightly behind him.

He'd not even heard her come in. "About the babe?"

"Your daughter, sir."

"Ah, yes. Do you know someone who could take her, a wet nurse?"

"I have a friend who would help out, yes."

"Fine." He got to his feet and stared down. Were it not for the drying blood and the blue of her skin, he might think Maddie only slept.

"It's God's will, Mr. Wiste."

He turned on her, impaling her with his eyes. "No! I cannot believe this is God's will! If He is a God of love, this . . . this horror cannot be His will!" *And if it is, I want nothing to do with Him!*

He strode toward the door without a backward look. He'd said his good-bye.

"Don't you want to see the baby?"

He jerked the bedroom door open and slammed it behind him.

A thin wail heaped flaming coals on his agony. Treating the stairs and the front door with the same force, he thundered down the side-walk and onto the street. He recognized no one, heard nothing. Had he been at the mill, the heat of him might have caused an explosion—when heat and flour dust combusted it could bring down a mighty building.

He pounded the earth for miles until pain radiated from his feet, up his legs, and finally registered on his brain. He sank against a fence post, dazedly looking around, with no idea where he was. Other than in the country. Cows grazed in the field, unaware of his pain, as if nothing mattered but the next mouthful of grass. How could the birds fly about so unconcerned? The sun shone when surely it should be shrouded. He propped his elbows on his bent knees and buried his face in his hands. The tears drizzled on his chin, ran through his fingers, and soaked his sleeves.

When the deluge had put out the fire, he tipped his head back against the wood and permitted the setting sun to dry his face. Finally staggering to his feet, he found the cows in a semicircle behind him, watching him and chewing their cuds.

"So do you know the way home—to my home in Minneapolis, that is?" He must be deranged, talking to cows like this.

One swished her tail and belched up another chaw.

"No, I guess you don't." He looked around. A farmhouse lay up the road to the west. But which side of the city had he come through? He set off to ask his way.

❧

The burial took place on Wednesday. Garth felt as though he were hovering up in the tree limbs, watching the action and not a part of it. Maddie was laid into the ground, and the mourners returned to the church for a noonday meal. He knew he'd accepted condolences and made the appropriate responses because later one of his brothers told him he had done well. What he didn't know was how he would keep going day after day without her.

"Grant is crying for you," his sister Helga Larson announced while she and their two sisters cleaned up the kitchen at his house after the funeral. "He doesn't understand why he can't come home. He stands at the window watching every time you leave your house."

"And what? Bring him here?" Even though Garth lived next door to Helga, he couldn't bear the thought of having his son around. He knew how terrible he looked when he'd shaved that morning. Mirrors never lie. The thick mink-colored hair that Maddie loved to stroke looked like rats were nesting in it. His hazel eyes peered coldly out of black circles. A cut on his square chin told of his carelessness with the razor. "Can't he stay with you?"

"He can, and after this babe is born I can take your daughter too." She rested her hand on the mound that looked large enough for two in spite of the full dress designed to disguise her pregnancy. "She won't need to stay with the wet nurse much longer." Helga sank into a chair with a sigh. "But Grant needs his father."

"He needs his mother, but we know how impossible that is." Garth hated the words that were spewing forth, revealing his barely banked rage. He couldn't look at her, despising the pity he knew to be in her eyes. "I-I'm sorry. I can't."

☙

"You have to name the baby," Garth's mother said several days later when she came to make sure he ate something.

"You name her."

"Didn't you and Maddie discuss baby names?"

He shook his head. Perhaps, but not that he remembered.

"Grant is asking for you. I'm taking him home with me when I leave here. Helga thinks her baby will come tonight." She poured him a second cup of coffee, patting his shoulder at the same time.

"Good. Mange takk." He didn't realize he'd slipped back into the language of his grandfather and father—the language he'd spoken until he had turned three and his father remarried.

On Monday he returned to work, for only there did he not see his Maddie's beloved face or something that reminded him of her.

The flour mill became his refuge.

"Hey, Wiste, you heard about that new mill they're opening in a place called Blessing, North Dakota?" one of the millmen asked.

"No. What about it?"

"They're looking for a manager."

That night after gathering all the needed information, Garth sat down and wrote a letter to Hjelmer Bjorklund of Blessing, North Dakota, and posted it the next day.

☙

One week later, after receiving a telegram from Hjelmer saying to come right away, Garth arrived in Blessing and asked the stationmaster for information.

"The mill's right down the street. You can't miss it. Shoulda seen it coming in on the train like you did."

"Thanks. Is there a place where I can get a room for a night or two?"

"Blessing Boarding House—good beds, good food. You can't beat it. It's right next door." He indicated to the south.

Since Garth had been sitting on the other side of the train, he hadn't seen much but farmland and farm buildings, but he nodded and walked toward the door.

He stepped out of the station house, looked to the south first, and saw a warehouse, a grain elevator, and the flour mill dwarfing all the other buildings. On the same side of the street as the station stood a three-story building with several additions, painted gray with white trim and a long porch facing the street. Although right next to the train tracks, the building had been recently repainted, and tieback curtains made it look right friendly.

Up the other way he saw several stores and a fairly new building that flew a United States flag in front. That must be the post office. A sign said *Bank of Blessing* on another corner of the building. A church steeple pointed above the stores a block or two away. While Blessing wasn't a big town, it looked prosperous. He took the steps to the boardinghouse with a lighter stride than he'd used of late. A cheery woman of indeterminate years, but for sure plenty, greeted him from behind a low counter.

"How can I help you?" Her Norwegian accent could not be missed.

"I'd like a room for one night, maybe more." He returned her smile. She reminded him so much of his grandmother, he almost greeted her as Bestemor.

"Ja, I have a room. Meals are included, and that will be one dollar—pay in advance." She pushed a ledger toward him. "Please sign here. Where you from?"

"Minneapolis. I've come to interview for the manager of the flour mill."

"Ah, my son and grandson built that. We"—her *w* as *v* made him smile again—"in Blessing have a co-op that owns the mill."

"What a good idea. More communities should do that." He signed his name and address as he chatted. "It looks like Blessing is growing."

"Ja, that we are. You will meet my son Hjelmer Bjorklund and my grandson Thorliff Bjorklund. I am Bridget Aarsgard." Her smile showed her pride, as well as several missing teeth. She wore her snow white hair in a braid that circled her head. Pleasantly rounded with her apron as white as her hair, she came around the desk. "Come, Mr. Wiste, I will show you your room." She led the way upstairs and opened the third door on the right. "This be good?"

"Ja, it will. Mange takk."

She beamed at his response. "Supper at six."

He set his bag on the floor, sat on the bed, and stared out across the fields framed by white curtains that looked like they'd been washed and starched just the day before. The patchwork quilt on the bed reminded him of his mother's house. Maddie would have loved it here. The thought stabbed like a well-aimed spear.

He fled the house, heading for the mill and, he hoped, a new life.

9

"ARE YOU ANGRY AT ME?" Sophie asked, turning from the train window.

Hamre shook his head, but he didn't turn to look at her.

It feels like it. What's wrong? Why are you sitting there like a wooden statue? He'd been like this ever since they found their seats on the westbound train at Grafton. It felt like hours ago, but in reality was probably less than an hour. Sophie caught herself rubbing her hands together as if she were cold. She turned to stare out the window again. Houses, barns, cattle in the fields, all passing at an alarming rate. Here she thought she would love riding the train, but with Hamre so silent, her joy had seeped down through the floor and was flattened by the clacking wheels.

What would Mor do in a situation like this? The thought caught her by surprise. First of all, her mor would never get herself into a situation like this. Secondly, she would say pray. *I did pray, and I sort of thought that God thought it's all right.* Then she remembered some things Pastor Solberg had said about God's will and . . . She had the tiniest but very certain feeling he'd said something about never crossing God's Word. The words in her mind keeping in clack with the wheels on the rails repeated the fourth commandment: *Honor thy father and thy mother; honor thy father and thy mother.*

"Hamre?"

When there was no answer, she glanced up at him. His eyes were closed and his mouth slightly open. He was asleep! Here she was worrying over what she'd done, and he was sound asleep. A slight snore confirmed it. Her fingers clenched each other, as if seeking comfort from the familiar. But there was nothing about sitting on a train heading west that was even vaguely familiar. *I am married. I am now Mrs. Hamre Bjorklund. Sophie Knutson is gone forever.* She had gotten her dream. She was on an adventure. She'd left Blessing. And if her brand-new husband was sound asleep . . . Well, he'd driven the buggy all night while she slept. He was exhausted.

Taking that into consideration, why, then, did she just want to hide her head in her mother's lap and cry until the tears that threatened to drown her were no more?

If I had paper and a pencil, I could at least write a letter home. But she'd not thought to put such mundane things into her bag. *You didn't think about a lot of things*, a little voice whispered. *But now you have to make the best of it.* What did one do on a long train ride? Look out the window to see plains, farms, a small town once in a while. Just like home only not as flat. Haystacks, grain elevators, stops for water and coal, people getting on, others getting off. A woman across the aisle was knitting. Another was reading a story to two small children. A man puffed a cigar, the stink of it making her wrinkle her nose. Could she ask him to put it out?

Hamre woke with a start. He yawned and turned to smile into her eyes. "Sorry. I didn't have much sleep last night."

"I know." Not that she did either. Sleeping in a swaying buggy was nothing like her bed at home, curled next to Grace. *Grace—does she hate me?* She forced a smile to answer his.

"Are you hungry?"

She nodded.

"We can eat in the dining car, you know."

"Really?"

"Yes. Come on." He took her hand, and all of a sudden her world felt better and her smile came back.

She touched the sides of her hair, smoothing loose strands back into the upsweep. She fluffed her fringe and turned her face up for him to inspect. "Do I look all right?" When he didn't respond right away, she peered at him from under her eyelashes, only to find him staring at her. "What?"

He cleared his throat. "You are so beautiful."

Her heart skipped a beat, and her lips trembled on the way to a smile. "Thank you." Sliding her arm through his, she leaned her cheek against his shoulder. She could do that now. They were married.

He patted her hand. "Let's go eat, Mrs. Bjorklund."

In his voice the name gave her an even greater thrill. "Yes, let's."

He motioned her to go ahead of him. She kept reaching for a seat back to keep from being swayed right off her feet and landing ignominiously in someone's lap.

Hamre pushed open the door at the end of the car, and she stopped stiff at the sight of the roadbed flashing beneath their feet, the grate looking far too flimsy to be trod upon.

"Keep going."

"I can't."

"Of course you can. It's perfectly safe."

"But it's moving. Look."

"The plates overlap so they cover the couplings between the cars." He nudged her with a hand to her back.

"You go first."

"All right." With both hands on her waist, he squeezed around her and, taking one of her hands, led her over the moving floorboards. "See, I told you." His smile once they were in the next car allayed her fears that he thought her young and silly.

Tables dressed in white linen cloths with fancy silverware and stemmed glasses that caught beams of sunlight from the windows and sparkled at her made her catch her breath. A flower in a bud vase centered every table, and white folded napkins lay under polished silverware. Here was the life she'd dreamed about, with Hamre by her side. Thoughts of Blessing faded away to the accompaniment of clacking wheels.

"Are you sure we should eat here?" She tugged on his hand and kept her voice low.

"Yes. It comes with the ticket." He pulled out a chair for her and motioned her to sit down. A black man in a white buttoned-up coat smiled at her.

"I be your server," he said.

"I see." She looked to Hamre as he sat down across the table from her. They had never talked about what money he had, only about the fish he caught. She'd seen pictures of fancy table settings, and Bestemor had white tablecloths at the boardinghouse. But here there were two forks, lying on top of a starched stiff napkin, on one side of her plate and a knife and spoon on the other. A small knife lay at the top of the plate. Whatever was that for? The small plate to the left was maybe for desserts?

Their server set a leather-bound book upright in front of each of them. "Your menu." He picked up her napkin and, giving it a shake, laid it across her lap. "Would you care for coffee, tea, ice water to start with?"

Sophie stared at the man across the table from her. Wasn't her husband supposed to be the one to guide her? Right now she needed real guiding. Hamre glanced up over the top of the menu he was reading and winked at her. *I can do this*, she decided and smiled at their server. "I'd like a cup of coffee, please."

"Cream and sugar?"

"No thanks." So many choices. He appeared again at their table, a silver coffee server in hand. Tipping her fine china coffee cup upright, he poured a stream of rich brown liquid without spilling a drop on the tablecloth. Wondering how he did that, she shook her head slightly and trapped a chuckle inside. She smiled and stumbled over thank-you, nearly saying mange takk, which he probably would not have understood at all.

"And you, sir?" he asked Hamre.

"Yes, please." Hamre leaned forward a bit to read the copper nameplate on the white uniform jacket. "Jason?"

"Yes, sir." A different accent softened the r to sound more like *ah*.

"I think we'll have the roast beef with mashed potatoes and gravy, and we'll decide on dessert later." He smiled at Sophie. "Is that all right?"

When the man left, Sophie leaned forward. "How did you learn all this? You grew up the same as me, and we don't eat fancy like this."

"No, but we sure ate good food. I missed that on some of the boats I've been on. Especially when the seas are rough and they don't allow the stoves to be lit."

"But this . . ." She indicated the table setting with a sweep of her hand.

"I worked in a hotel for a month or two between fishing seasons. Had to set the table like this and clear away. You learn a lot by watching."

"You did?"

"Ja. I don't like to go hungry."

Sophie picked up her coffee cup to have something to do with her hands. This man was one surprise after another. And she was married to him. A frisson of delight climbed her spine. She sipped the coffee, watching him over the brim. "What else have you done in the years since you left Blessing?"

He thought a moment. "I've scrubbed boats to rid the hulls of barnacles."

"Barnacles?"

"Kind of cone-shaped little armor-plated creatures that grow on rocks and anything under water. They slow the speed of the ship if not removed. So once a year we scrape them off."

"I see. What else?"

"I can mend nets or sails."

"You know how to sew?"

"Different from any sewing you've done, but I got good at it. You need to know how to do it if you are going to own a fishing boat of your own."

"You said you wanted a three-masted schooner."

"You remembered." His smile warmed her clear to her toes.

"You drew me a picture of one once." She thought back to the letter. "You drew it very well. How come when you were in school in Blessing, you never said anything, and now you can talk about so many things?" *Except when you go silent on me? Why is that?*

"I was a boy who didn't want to be there on the farm. I guess that's my only excuse. When I left Blessing, I learned that if I didn't ask and answer, life got really lonely, and I missed out on too much. Out on the boat, though, when you're the only one in the dory, the fish don't answer back."

"Excuse me." Jason had returned with small plates of pickled green beans, carrots, and beets to set before them, along with a basket of rolls that made her mouth water. The delicious bread smell sent her mind skipping back to her mother's kitchen.

Pushing away the memory, she waited to whisper until Jason had bowed and left. "I thought we were having roast beef."

"We will. This comes first."

She tasted the beans and grinned in delight. "This is delicious."

"I know."

Two plates later, brown gravy filled a hole in the mashed potatoes and swirled over onto the slice of meat. Green beans with bits of red sat off to the side of the plate, and a bright green piece of something decorated another.

"What is this?" she asked, pointing to the green sprig.

"Parsley. Taste it."

She did as he said and nibbled the curly leaves. "It's good."

"It's an herb."

"Oh." She took a fork of potatoes and gravy. It was good, but to be honest, her mother's was better. The intrusive thought made her throat clog. What were they doing at home? Were they furious with her? How was Grace?

"What is it?"

She glanced up to see Hamre studying her. She shook herself. Looking back did not help, but this would be even more delightful if Grace were here to share it with her. She straightened her shoulders and sniffed. "I'm fine, just . . . just thinking of home. For a moment." She cut another piece of meat and ate. *Do not think of home. Blessing is no longer home. My home is now with Hamre. And I am on an adventure, the biggest adventure of my life.* She sent Hamre a wide smile along with a look from under her eyelashes, the kind of look that always brought a smile from the man across from her. Her husband. How she loved that word.

By the time they finished, she wished she could loosen the button on her skirt. How could she describe it all in a letter? They wouldn't believe her. Well, Hjelmer would. He rode the train all the time to Bismarck for the legislature, to Grand Forks, even to Minneapolis and Chicago. How she wished she could talk to Dr. Elizabeth. Hadn't she known wealthy people in Chicago when she was going to medical school? But then, perhaps her family had been served like this. Amazing how the questions rose now, but when she could have asked them, she hadn't.

Later in the afternoon, she dozed against her husband's shoulder. He said they'd see mountains too, like those he remembered from Norway. So many new things as they traveled farther and farther from the flat river valley where she'd grown up.

That night after eating supper again in the dining car, Hamre went silent on her once more. He'd been telling her about fishing and his life on fishing boats. He'd described pewing the fish from the dory to the schooner, which sounded like forking hay, since he described the tool he used much like a three-pronged hay fork, and then he had mentioned the name of a man he knew. He quit smiling, and it was like he pulled a curtain over a window and went behind it.

And she was alone again.

10

"I BELIEVE WE HAVE FOUND the man," Haakan said that evening.

"To run the mill?" Ingeborg smiled at her husband. "But isn't this the first man you've talked with?"

"True, but Thorliff and Hjelmer feel the same way I do. He can start work in a week or two. He has plenty of experience and really wants to move out of Minneapolis." Haakan washed his hands and took his place at the table.

"Is he married?"

"Widowed."

"Ah, the poor man. Has he children?"

"Ja, but he will leave them with relatives for the time being. We all walked through the mill, and he approved of the way things are set up."

"Of course he did. You always do things the best way."

"Hjelmer was right. Hiring a manager with plenty of experience to make sure all the machinery is installed right is a good investment."

Astrid came down the stairs, a frown wrinkling her forehead. "Mor, how could Sophie go off like that without even telling Grace good-bye? I don't understand her."

Ingeborg and Haakan swapped looks of consternation. There had been no word from Sophie all day—not that one was expected, but there had been hope of a telegram. "Sometimes when a young woman thinks she is in love, she'll do crazy things."

"Hamre should have had better sense." Haakan beckoned Astrid to his side. "I hope you learn from her mistakes."

"Pa, I wouldn't ever do such a thing." She stared at him as if he'd accused her of stealing or some other awful thing.

"I don't think you would."

"Everyone was all upset at school. I found Grace crying behind the school during recess. Pastor Solberg moved Rebecca into Sophie's desk. Trygve is really mad at her. He said he'd go after them if they'd let him."

"Well, the best thing you can do is to pray for them all. Help me get supper on the table, please."

After grace Ingeborg paid little attention to the discussion between Haakan and Astrid, thinking instead about how to help Kaaren. Her sister-in-law's sorrow reminded her of the early years, after Kaaren's first husband, Carl, and their two small daughters died. *Lord, please comfort her. I know you will bring good out of this, but I don't know what to say.*

After supper, with Haakan reading the paper and Astrid studying, Ingeborg searched her basket of carded wool. She found a satisfactory hank and sat down at the spinning wheel. Pulling out a strand of wool, she picked up the end of the thread on the wheel, wrapped the new bit to the former, and started the wheel, continuing to pull the strands out as the wheel turned. Spinning wool always gave her comfort, the whir of the wheel a good accompaniment to her thoughts. If only they could be spun into order as easily as the wool formed into yarn.

When Astrid bent down to kiss her mother's cheek good-night, Ingeborg realized several hours had passed. "Good night, dear one. Sleep tight." Haakan sat in his chair, the paper in his lap, head back, sound asleep. "Wake your pa as you go by."

"Are you going to bed now?" Astrid asked.

"I'm going to spin awhile longer. I should be getting my basket ready for quilting tomorrow, but I'm out of yarn."

"You want me to dye some tomorrow when I come home?"

"That would be good. We have onion skins for yellow. I can gather oak bark for brown, and I think I have some blue dye left from last year. Maybe Grace would like to help you."

"I thought of asking her to come spend the night."

"Good idea, but she'll need to work with her signing students too." She watched her daughter head up the stairs. Life would be terribly quiet here if Astrid weren't around. And the day was coming far too quickly when that would be a probability.

⁂

"What do you mean you aren't going?" Ingeborg asked Kaaren the next morning.

"I have too much to do here." Kaaren's eyes were red and puffy.

"Come with me. You need to be out. Perhaps Hildegunn will be outrageous, and we can all get mad at her."

"Hildegunn." Kaaren shook her head. "I can't bear the thought of anyone looking at me and thinking awful thoughts about Sophie. You know she will."

"But not the others. We are all your friends and want to comfort you. Quilting is good for the soul. It seems someone we both know told me that more than once."

"I hate eating my own words."

"I know. Come on. Pick up your basket and get your shawl. It's chilly out."

"Should be. It nearly froze last night." Kaaren glanced around her kitchen. "I don't have anything to take for dinner."

"I brought plenty."

"You have an answer for everything."

"I try." Ingeborg took Kaaren's shawl off the peg and held it out.

"Bossy today, aren't you?"

The sun set the ice-sheathed grass blades to glittering, flashing fire winks as they passed by. Honking geese flew their formation south-ward, singing a song of fall.

Ingeborg stared up at the dark V. "I'd love to be out hunting."

"You gave that up years ago."

"I know, but when the geese honk, the urge comes over me.

Remember the goose down we saved so carefully for feather beds and pillows?"

"Not just goose down but feathers of all kinds." Kaaren pulled her shawl tighter to her shoulders. "Trygve brought in a couple of ducks last night, and I kept the breast feathers from them too. I'm thinking I should make some things to send along with Sophie's trunk when we hear from her. You think they got married?"

"Is that the hardest part?"

"I think so."

They pulled up at the hitching rail, and both climbed down using the spokes of the wheels for steps. While Ingeborg tied the horse, Kaaren retrieved their baskets from the wagon bed. She sucked in a deep breath and turned toward the church.

"It's not the firing squad."

"Ingeborg!"

Together they walked up the steps and entered, the opening door letting out laughter and the fragrance of soup cooking on the stove.

Penny dropped what she was doing and came to hug Kaaren, murmuring softly for her ears only. "We'll get through this too."

"I know. I wanted to stay home, but resisting Ingeborg is like keeping the snow from falling." Kaaren peeked around Penny's shoulder to see the others either staring at them or trying hard not to. Sucking in a deep breath of courage, she pasted a smile on her face and said, "Good morning. I guess it is a good thing we made one wedding ring quilt ahead, isn't it?"

"Ja, that is good." Mrs. Magron nodded, smiling brightly and glancing at Hildegunn at the same time.

"If they were married." Hildegunn spoke under her breath but just loud enough for most to hear.

Mrs. Magron ignored her and continued. "We will put it in the mail to them as soon as you have an address."

Ingeborg hid a smile. Good for Brynja. It looked like she'd finally crawled out from under Hildegunn's thumb and was thinking and speaking for herself. "All right, Kaaren. I'll iron if you'll cut."

"That leaves the sewing machine for me." Ellie looked down at her front. "If I can get close enough to the machine."

A chuckle danced around the room, lightening the mood and releasing the normal chatter.

"What did Dr. Elizabeth say when you saw her?" Ingeborg asked her daughter-in-law.

"She thinks the baby could come early." Ellie cradled the bulge under her apron.

"I better hurry on knitting those soakers I promised you." Kaaren leaned over and kissed Ellie's cheek. "Somehow I never seem to get the knitting done in the summer."

"So who is running the post office?" Penny asked the postmistress as she took a seat beside Hildegunn at the quilt stretcher.

"You think I am not doing my job?" Hildegunn bristled.

"No, not at all. I just know how hard it is to be gone when I have a business, and I figured you'd find the same."

"It is. But since the mail doesn't come in until the afternoon, I can close the doors for a few hours."

"True. I'm hoping we have some more people move into town who want work."

"I heard they hired a man for the flour mill." Mrs. Magron looked to Penny for an answer.

"Looks that way." Penny threaded her needle and took a couple of stitches in the same spot to anchor her thread. "Hjelmer says they might be open within two weeks."

"Mr. Valders said it will be longer before they have enough men to work there."

Ingeborg exchanged a glance with Kaaren. Mr. Valders. Why could the woman not use her husband's given name? If someone said black, Hildegunn would say white. "I think she's getting worse," she whispered to Kaaren.

A nod was her answer as Kaaren carefully cut the two-and-a-half-inch squares for a nine patch. They used different sized squares depending on how big the piece of fabric they had. Everyone brought whatever leftovers they had, and some pieced at home for their own quilts and brought the tops in to be quilted or tied. The one on the stretcher belonged to Hildegunn.

All the years they'd been meeting, all the heartbreaks they'd worked through in their discussions, praying and sharing, surely by now they knew each other well enough that there should no longer be dissension. *Oh, Lord, I wish it were so.* But no matter how much she had prayed, Ingeborg knew that Hildegunn still blamed her family for the fight between Toby and Andrew the summer before. She never could admit that Toby had done anything to create the tension that finally blew after the fire.

When they broke to eat, they spread the food out on the table and dished up the soup. After grace they fell to, and lively conversation picked up again. Discussion about the fall celebration took over—where they would have it and what would be served.

"With no houses to build or barns to raise, we might need a new excuse for gatherings," Penny said with a laugh.

Kaaren pushed her soup away. "I can't eat," she whispered. "I'm going to the outhouse. Ask what they want me to read when I come back."

"All right." After the door closed behind Kaaren, Ingeborg raised her voice. "What do you want Kaaren to read this afternoon?"

"First Corinthians thirteen."

"Philippians—all of it."

"Psalm one thirty-nine."

Ingeborg wrote down the requests as fast as they came.

"Do you think Kaaren would mind if we had a party to get things for Sophie's house?" Brynja asked. "I mean, I thought . . ."

"I think that's a very nice idea," Ingeborg said. "But let's wait a bit and see how things go." *Perhaps Sophie will come back.* The thought was appealing, but somehow she thought it more a dream than a real possibility.

When Kaaren returned, she opened her Bible and began reading with the psalm. Only a slight hoarseness betrayed that she might have been crying again. That and an occasional sniff.

Later, on the ride home, she sat silently.

"You did well."

"Thank you. You were right. This was better than staying home."

"Mrs. Magron wants to give a house party for Sophie."

"And Hildegunn said . . . ?"

"Nothing, and I didn't even look at her. I just suggested we wait a bit. But I'm glad they want to mail Sophie her wedding ring quilt."

"I think they will be living at the boardinghouse Hamre has been staying at."

"So no home of her own?"

"No. At least not right away. I keep trying to remember every little word to see if she dropped any hints."

"You don't think they'd been planning this all along?"

"No, I don't. Hamre told Lars he would wait a year, so I think Sophie convinced him. When she realized he was leaving so soon, she turned so sad. I didn't know what to do for her, but I never dreamed she would run off, and neither did Grace."

"Poor Grace. Astrid is inviting her to come dye wool after school and spend the night."

"Leave it to Astrid. Between her and Trygve, it's a good thing Sophie is nowhere close to Blessing. They'd have dragged her home again. And Lars would've been right along helping them."

The two shared a smile, albeit a heavy one.

"If only Seattle weren't so far away." Kaaren sighed.

"Ah, but you can take the train out there, you know. And there are letters."

"Ja, and if I don't get one soon, I might just get on that train and go find her."

"You ever think of taking the train and going to see other parts of the country?" Ingeborg asked.

"Sometimes. Once I dreamed you and I took our daughters and went to California."

"California?"

"I know. Crazy, isn't it?" Kaaren looked around at the men working the fields and said, "When this place is so dear and perfect, why would anyone want to leave?"

"I used to think our children would stay right here with us, but now I know they will leave. Hopefully they will come back. To visit, at least."

11

SNOW ALREADY WHITENED the Rocky Mountains.

Sophie rode with her nose pressed to the window to not miss a thing. Hamre teased her that she would get frostbite, but she persisted. "Have you ever seen anything like this?"

"Ja, in Norway. And there you have the fjords too."

She put her hand over her eyes. "It's too far to look down. What if . . . ?"

"Don't worry. The engineer takes the train this way all the time. He won't drive it off the tracks." He took her hand and squeezed it. "Why, they haven't had a train wreck in at least two weeks."

"Hamre!" She tried to glare at him, but even the nearness of him made her smile. *I am married to this handsome, fine man.* The notion made her smile wider. But the thought that followed dimmed her joy. If only she'd not had to run away. Knowing she'd hurt her family stabbed pain through her heart, but she couldn't have imagined Hamre going off without her. And here she'd been laughing at Ellie, who could hardly bear to let Andrew out of her sight, especially after his weeks in jail in Grafton. How lightly she'd taken the idea of falling in love, thinking herself immune, loving to flirt, including enjoying the brief kisses she'd experienced. Until Hamre looked into her eyes and she felt she was drowning.

Do not think of home. Think of Hamre and our adventure. Not just mine but ours. She traced the veins on the back of his hand with a trembling finger. Mrs. Hamre Bjorklund. She could feel his gaze upon her and glanced up from her tracing to smile into his eyes. "What?"

"You are beautiful."

Heat flared up her neck and across her face. Her breath caught in her throat so she couldn't swallow. Laying her hand against her throat kept her from touching his cheek with questing fingers. No one had said love meant wanting to be in the other's skin. Or did she just have a worse case than most? "Thank you." She cleared her throat and tried again. This time the words could be heard.

The outside flashed dark.

"What?"

"We're in a tunnel." Hamre leaned close to nuzzle her ear, and when she turned her face, he kissed her.

"Oh." Breathing against a man's lips was another new and heady experience. It was a good thing she was sitting down, for she was sure her legs would not hold her up.

A snowfield outside sent sparkles into the car as they cleared the end of the tunnel. "Oh." This time the beauty outside caught her attention again, but she left her hand securely in his on the seat between them.

Sleeping with her head on his shoulder was an experience she loved, but waking with her neck aching, soot coating her skin, and her hair tumbling about her face made her wish for a basin of warm water and her comb and brush. Forests, lakes, valleys, plains of sagebrush and grass all passed by the windows. Then more meals, more sleep, more mountains, and finally they were approaching Seattle.

"Mrs. Soderstrum, who runs the boardinghouse where I live, will be delighted to see you," Hamre said after breakfast.

"I hope so."

"She has been introducing me to young women. She said I needed a wife and a home of my own."

"Well, now you have part of that."

"We will find a place to rent soon."

But looking at his face, she wondered at his certainty. Something was bothering him, clouding that incredible blue of his Bjorklund eyes. "What is it?"

"What?"

"You . . . you . . ." She struggled to find the words. "Ah . . . are you worried?"

"No. What makes you say that?"

"Your eyes, they . . ." She nibbled at her lower lip.

He touched a finger to her bottom lip, making her gasp. "You are not to worry, wife. I was just thinking on things."

"But . . ." Her skin burned where he touched her.

His voice deepened. "Tonight we will be in our own room."

"Ja, tonight." Her eyes widened at the thought. "Our own . . . room."

❧

They stepped off the train into a drizzle that wilted the feather on her hat within five steps so that it dripped water onto her nose. She brushed it to the side and stared around her. This wasn't what she'd dreamed of at all. Everything looked gray, including, she was sure, herself.

Hamre nodded toward a horse-drawn buggy. "We'll take that to Mrs. Soderstrum's." He carried one bag under his arm, his hands full of the other two.

"I could carry a bag."

"No. I have them. Follow me."

Sophie did as he said, slightly miffed at his abruptness at her offer to help. After all, she did have two good arms and hands. But keeping up to his stride, even laden as he was, took some paying attention, especially to keep her skirt from dragging in the puddles.

Once they and their baggage were loaded into the buggy, he pointed out the sights as the horse clip-clopped along the cobblestone streets. Never had she seen such steep hills and such huge evergreen trees, and though he said a large body of water called Puget Sound was off to the west, she couldn't see it through the gloom. While he'd warned her that her new home would have foggy and rainy days, she'd still not been prepared. At home after it rained, the clouds blew away, clearing the skies again. *At home. You have to quit thinking that,* she ordered herself. *This is your home now, here in Seattle where your husband is delighted to live.*

Wind blew the rain into the buggy despite canvas coverings rolled down for protection. Sophie sniffed and shuddered. "What is that smell?"

Hamre inhaled once, then again. "What smell?"

"Stink, actually." She put her handkerchief to her nose. Whatever it was, it smelled worse than the outhouse on a hot summer's day.

"Oh." Hamre smiled. "The tide's out. That's all."

"Tide's out?" Was he trying to be funny? That's all? "You mean this happens regularly?" She'd read about the tides of the oceans, governed by the pull of the moon, which never had made any sense to her. No more than planting the garden by the phases of the moon. How could something so far away have a pull on things on the earth? Not like the sun that gave warmth and light.

She tried to breath without inhaling the stench but quickly learned the only help was a scented handkerchief.

Hamre sighed and spoke slowly, as if she weren't too bright. "When the tide goes out, it leaves the mudflats bare, like when the Red River dropped again after a flood. Things didn't smell too good there either."

"Oh. So when the water comes back in . . . ?"

"No more smell. The good thing is that when the tide is out, we can go dig clams and gooey ducks."

"Gooey ducks?"

"Huge clams." He drew the size in the air. "They can dig faster than a human with a shovel. But once ground up, they make the best clam chowder. I'm sure Mrs. Soderstrum will share her recipe with you." He paused for a moment. "We get oysters right out of the sound also. You could live off the land here real easy. The winters are far easier than Dakota winters. Snow comes but not a lot, and blizzards are unheard of. Truth to tell, it rains a lot, but you don't get lost in a white-out or have to shovel it. I'm hoping to build us a house after I get back from fishing season."

The thought of his being gone made her catch her breath. Some-how, on the train trip with him near and touching her, she'd forgotten

they would soon be separated. How long had he said he'd be gone?

"When do you leave?"

"We'll be fishing one or two day trips here in the sound or off the Washington coast until November, when we'll load the boats and head for Alaska for the cod."

And what will I do all the time you are gone? She wanted to ask the questions that tore at her but decided to wait. She shivered in the cold draft and edged closer to his side. Even her wool coat didn't keep her warm, and she'd almost not brought it along. The cold damp seeped right into her bones. She slid her gloved hand into the crook of her husband's arm. Heat poured from him like a freshly stoked furnace, warming her both inside and out.

"Seattle is a big place." The little bit she could see, but they'd been in the buggy for what seemed like quite a while.

"Bigger than Blessing, that's for sure. We'll go back to visit Seattle when the weather is nicer. It'll be suppertime by the time we get to Ballard."

She knew Ballard was the home of the fishing fleet and where many of the Norwegians had settled. Those who'd been fishermen in Norway found a ready market for their skills in this part of America. She'd read of the Marquis de Mores, from the western part of North Dakota, who had shipped salmon from the West Coast to the Midwest and parts east on railroad cars filled with ice. He'd shipped cattle butchered in Medora the same way. In their family discussions her pa had called de Mores a man of foresight, using the railroads to change the way people lived. The fact that he was from France had captured her imagination.

Right now all she wanted was a warm stove and a place to wash away the grime of the trip. A bath would be heavenly, but a basin and pitcher of hot water would do wonders for her morale.

◈

"It won't be long now." Hamre covered her hand with his.

Sophie jerked upright. Had she dozed off? Her cheek was warm from leaning against his shoulder. "Did I sleep long?"

"Not long enough, I'm sure. But we'll go to bed early tonight."

Go to bed. Share a bed with Hamre. A shiver ran from her drooping hat feather to the tips of her frozen toes. Tonight she would learn what came after kisses. *Mor, I didn't get to ask you what happens. You always said you would tell me when the time was right. Now you're not here, and I'm not there.* She gulped back the tears that threatened to blind her. Often she'd heard an old saying that for the first time struck her as meaningful. *"You made your bed. Now you'll have to lie in it."* Another followed on the heels of the first. *"Think before you leap."*

"See, that is the boardinghouse up there."

She followed along his straight arm, his hand, and a finger pointing to a two-story house set off the street and against a green-decked hill. A hill that disappeared into the low clouds hovering. Were all these so-called hills tall enough to disappear into the clouds? Wouldn't that make them mountains? A giggle escaped the boulder in her chest. *Don't start to laugh. This isn't funny, and before you know it, you'll be bawling your eyes out and making Hamre think he married some kind of nut. Mor, what am I to do?*

The house. Look at the house. Clenched fists helped her concentrate on the orders she was giving herself. *Pay attention. Yellow paint, white trim, lots of windows, the front porch inviting—if anything could be inviting in this rain. Rust and yellow flowers lined the walk to the front porch. A white picket fence with a gate. Mor had always wanted a white picket fence with a gate. Do not think of home. Pay attention.*

The driver stopped the buggy, and Hamre stepped out first to help her down while the driver brought their bags from the boot behind. She watched Hamre count out the requested amount of money and stuff the dwindling bills in his pocket. Traveling was indeed expensive. For the first time she wondered how he would pay for everything. Was fishing for cod that good of a business?

He picked up their cases and nodded for her to go ahead. "Don't worry. Mrs. Soderstrum will love you immediately."

Ordering her stubborn lips to smile, she blinked away what must have been raindrops and opened the gate. *Here we go, Sophie Knutson . . . no, Sophie Bjorklund.* She sucked in another breath and followed the brick path to the front porch. An oak door with an oval cutout stood as the next barrier. But before Hamre could put down the bags and open the door, it flew open and a rounded woman, who looked so much like her grandmother Bridget as to make Sophie catch her breath, threw wide her arms and enveloped Sophie in a hug that smelled of flour and vanilla.

"Ja, you come. Velkommen to my boardinghouse. Hamre, bring her in. This must be your Sophie, ja?"

"Mrs. Soderstrum, I want you to meet Mrs. Hamre Bjorklund, my Sophie."

The way he said "my Sophie" brought more of those threatening raindrops to her eyes. "I am pleased to meet you. You look so much like Bestemor Bridget in Blessing that I almost thought I was home."

"Ja, that is good." She stepped back. "Come in, come in. You want some help with those bags?"

"No, I've got them." Hamre picked up the one he'd set down. "Have there been any messages?"

"Ja, I put them in your room. You go on up, and I bring hot water."

"Mange takk." Sophie smiled at the woman and then followed Hamre up the dark oak staircase. *I must look like a bedraggled chicken*, she thought as she admired the striped wallpaper and the pot of ferns on the landing. Mrs. Soderstrum knew how to make a house look like a home.

Hamre already had their bags on the floor of the room that was first on their right.

A bed with a crazy quilt took up much of the room, with braided rugs on both sides to warm feet against the dark painted floor. A tall narrow window with white starched curtains invited Sophie to cross and see what she could see. Perhaps one day there would even be sun shining through the sparkling clean panes.

"Welcome home." Hamre's deep voice made her turn around. He stood at the end of the bed watching her.

"Ja, home." Sophie forced herself to look past the bed to the man standing there. The bed was huge. She traced one of the nine patch squares in blue and white with one finger. Quilted, not tied. She could feel Hamre's gaze on the top of her head. Funny how her dreams of being married had never included a bed until just a few minutes ago.

12

October

"YOU GOT THE JOB, didn't you?" Helga asked.

Garth nodded to his sister. "It will be a good thing. Perhaps you and Dan might like to move there too, if I can put him to work at the mill. Blessing is a nice little town and growing." Garth steeled himself for Helga's refusal. He knew that Dan was happy with his job at the Pillsbury "A" Mill, the same place Garth had worked until just an hour ago, when he had turned in his notice.

Rather than letting him work the two weeks he volunteered, they said he needn't come back. So much for trying to be honorable and polite. He stared at his sister. "You had your baby."

"Ja, the day you left. A boy. This morning Dan brought your daughter here."

"Are you sure you should be . . . ?" At the scowl she gave him, he changed gears. "How are the little ones?"

"All sleeping soundly for the moment. Nursing two babies uses up a lot of my day."

"What happened with the woman the midwife found? You didn't have to bring the baby here so soon."

"It seemed best this way."

She looked haggard. But why wouldn't she when she'd just had a baby? While her first son, Nathan, was two months older than his son,

Grant, Helga had volunteered to take his two in and nurse his baby along with hers. The baby. He had yet to even name her. *Why did you have to go and die, Maddie? How can I manage? How can I live without you?* Returning to Minneapolis had ripped off the scab he'd laid over his sorrow and brought it all back. When he closed his eyes, he could see the blood all over the bed, Maddie's gray face, her transparent skin, her cool body. Without his ever saying anything to her, not that she could have heard anyway. The midwife had waited too long to come for him. How would he ever forgive the woman for that?

"Garth." Helga laid her hand on her brother's arm.

"Ja." He knew he spoke too abruptly, but all he wanted to do was go out the door and keep on walking. Anywhere.

The hurt on Helga's face lanced the boil of his anger. He backed away, fearing to spew the poison he felt on her. "I-I have to leave. I'm sorry." He spun and was out the door before she could get over her shock to respond. He heard her call from the doorway and, shaking his head, flapped a hand at her. "Later."

Where to go? Not back to his own house next door. Not to the cemetery where they'd buried that box holding his life. Not to the local saloon; he might never come out. Instead, he pounded the street down to the river whose rapids powered the mighty wheels grinding the grain from across the Midwest into flour. The river walk had been one of Maddie's favorite places. She loved the cool spray from the falls, the roar of the water, the sunlight dancing on the swirls and deeper pools. Today would have been one of her "gifts from God," as she called the sunny fall days of October. With the leaves exploding in all shades of red, rust, and orange swirling down the river, she'd dreamed of following the water all the way to the Gulf of Mexico one day.

"No-o-o, it's not fair! Not Maddie!" After roaring at the falls, he glanced around, hoping no one heard him. But the shocked look on an elderly woman's face said she had. She nodded and turned away. At least she hadn't run screaming like he wanted to do. He turned back to the falls to hide the tears that now gushed like the water between the rocks.

When he finally had himself under control again, he walked the mile back to his house and stared up at the blank windows. How could a house look so desolate in such a short period of time? One month since Maddie died. Weeds greened her flower beds. She'd pulled them all out just before . . . He could see her if he narrowed his eyes. . . .

"What are you doing?" He'd hurried up the walk, ready to lift her bodily.

"I'm getting the flower beds ready for winter. What does it look like?" Instead of kneeling, which was impossible with her girth, she sat on a low stool and dug out weeds and the annuals finished with blooming. The full basket attested to her efforts. "Grant is sleeping, so I snuck out here." She lifted her face to the evening breeze. "Don't worry, I checked on him just a minute ago and left the windows and door open so I could hear him."

"It's you I'm worried about. Didn't the doctor say to take it easy?"

"I am taking it easy, just sitting here on the stool. I could be scrubbing the floors, I suppose."

He couldn't resist leaning down to kiss her laughing lips. Never had she looked so beautiful. He'd heard of women who blossomed when they were with child, and his Maddie was one of those. She admitted to loving being pregnant, over and over saying they would have six children, three of each.

"Your supper will be ready in three shakes of a lamb's tail." She held out her hands for him to pull her up. "But you better brace your feet before lifting this elephant."

He pulled her up and into his arms.

"Garth, what will the neighbors think?" But she laid her cheek against his chest for just a moment before straightening.

"They'll pretend to be horrified at our show of affection, and inside they'll be jealous." He tucked her hand through the crook of his arm, snagged the stool with the other, and handed it to her while he carried the full basket. "Let's go around back, and I'll dump this on the pile."

She told him all the day's happenings as they strolled through the side gate and into the backyard. "Oh, there is Grant. Hear him?"

Garth paused. Sure enough. A small voice was calling, "Ma?"

"Out here, son. We'll be right there."

"Now he'll probably not want to go to sleep when he should, but I just wanted to finish a few things around here before the baby is born."

That was before the baby was born. When the world stood still. And collapsed around him. When the baby was born—and she left.

He dashed the tears away again and mounted the three steps to the front porch. Her fern hung in dead sticks with dry brown leaves. No one had bothered to water it and bring it inside like she always did before the frost. He'd been gone to North Dakota less than a week, but he'd not been back to the house since Helga came to take the rest of Grant's things and he'd gone along to her house.

A faint coppery scent still hung on the still air. The smell of blood and agony refused to be banished no matter how much the cleaning woman had scrubbed both the room and the linens. With his eyes straight ahead, he mounted the stairs to the second floor, retrieved a small trunk from the closet, and emptied the drawers from the chest into it. He added work clothes from the closet, a suit and shoes, and slammed the trunk closed. Their wedding picture occupied a prominent place on the dresser, but instead of packing it, he laid it face down in the empty top drawer. He hauled the trunk up to his shoulder and made his way down the stairs and out the door, locking it behind him. Helga could come get whatever else she needed for the children, if she hadn't already.

"Surely you will stay the night?" Helga insisted when he walked back to her house to tell her he was leaving.

"If you'd like to move into the house—well, it might be a good idea. It is bigger than yours, and since you are renting, it would save you some money."

"Garth, please wait until Dan comes home so the two of you can discuss that."

He shook his head. "I cannot." *If I see the children* . . . He swallowed hard. "It is better this way."

"But Grant asks for his pa."

"Once I am settled there, I will come for them. And you too, if Dan agrees."

"We need a name for the baby, Garth. You have to give her a name," Helga implored.

"You name her. What are you calling her now?"

"Baby."

"Choose whatever you want."

"She should be baptized."

"Go ahead." *I cannot. If I get started on what I think of God right now, all those pious church people will go running for the doors.*

All the way to the station and through the long night as he dozed on the hard bench, he castigated himself for not visiting his mother, for not showing Helga his gratitude, for not being the man he thought he was. The next morning he bought a cup of coffee and a slice of bread before boarding the train.

With each clack of the train wheels, he left his life behind. Staring out the window into the early morning darkness, he promised himself, *I will no longer dwell on that part of my life. It is over. Someday I will have my children with me again, but now I must look forward.* It was a good thing he needn't say his vow out loud, for the rock in his throat prevented any sound.

When he stepped off the train, dry-eyed and dryer of soul, he made his way back to the boardinghouse. The proprietress greeted him as if he had come home.

"Thank you. I'm hoping you rent one of your rooms on a monthly or long-term basis."

"Ja, we do that. Meals are included." She named a price that seemed to him an undercharge, but he smiled gratefully rather than suggesting she raise her rates. He stared at the book as he signed where she pointed. Was he doing the right thing? Maybe he should just . . .

"Mr. Wiste?"

Her gentle voice with the heavy Norwegian accent brought him back to the present with a start.

"I-I'm sorry, what did you say?"

"I asked if you would like us to pack you the noon meal or if you would plan to return here to eat."

"I don't . . . I . . ." He scrubbed a hand across his face. "May I make those arrangements after I see how things will be going at the mill?"

"Of course." She named the hours when meals were served and handed him a key. "We change the beds and clean once a week. If you want it more often, there will be an extra charge."

"No, that will be fine. Do you do laundry for your guests also?"

"You are the only one staying here for an extended time, so we could do that for you."

"You have my eternal gratitude, Mrs. . . ." He paused. "I don't remember your name."

"Mrs. Aarsgard. Bundle your clothes to be washed on the day we clean your room. That will be Mondays, I believe."

"And my mail will be brought here?"

"You can make arrangements for a box at the post office. It is in the same building as the bank. The new one just up the street."

"I'll take my things on up, then." He nodded and failed at encouraging his lips to smile. Climbing the stairs with his trunk on one shoulder and his bag in the other hand, his feet weighed half a stone each. By the time he reached the second floor, his lungs pumped like bellows, forcing him to stop and inhale deeply, letting the air out on a whoosh. Was his trunk that heavy or was it life in general?

Once in his room, which overlooked the street in front of the boardinghouse, he set the trunk down and surveyed his new quarters. A quilt in shades of browns and yellows covered the bed; a rag rug in similar tones lay by the bed to protect his feet on a cold morning. A five-drawer dresser against one papered wall, a stand with pitcher and bowl, a line of hooks taking the place of a closet or chifforobe—all the comforts of home. The last put a cynical twist on his face and in his heart. Home. Would there ever be a home again? He threw himself across the bed and covered his eyes with the back of his arm. Loneliness with sorrow behind rode him with quirt and spurs.

By the next morning when he could think again, he figured that with his lodging and meals taken care of, he would have sufficient money to send home, or rather back to Helga for caring for his children. He'd even thought during the long sleepless night that he should ask her to take them permanently. She and Dan could become their real parents. But that thought had brought on the struggle to dam the tears. *Lord, what are you asking of me?* He cut off the prayer like he'd cut off the tears and snorted as a Bible verse he'd once memorized floated through his mind. *God will never give you more than you can endure.* What a pack of lies. If God was the loving God some claimed Him to be, why would He take a mother from her babies and a wife from a husband who adored her?

13

GRAY WEATHER WEIGHED like a stone chain around Sophie's neck. It had been days since she'd seen the sun, although it had appeared a couple of the days she'd been here. Hamre had told her that October was usually a good weather month in Washington State and apologized for the clouds.

"Breakfast is served," Mrs. Soderstrum called up the stairs.

Sophie rolled over and pulled the quilt up to cover her ears. Three days with no return of the fishing boat that bore Hamre out to the sea beyond what he so lightly called the Puget Sound. After all his descriptions, she felt safer when he was fishing the sound rather than the open ocean. It wouldn't be quite so bad if she could go walking, but like a cat, she hated to get wet.

The mournful hoot of the foghorn made her even more aware of the gray day. The foghorn didn't call out on a sunny day. But the seagulls cried all day every day. At first she had enjoyed the squabbles, but now all she heard was shrieking.

She threw back the covers and hastily dressed. Better to visit with those downstairs rather than to hide under the covers. *I just need something to look forward to each day.* She brushed out her night braid and bundled her hair into a snood. Never in her entire life had there been time to be bored. She could hear her mother as if she were standing right in the room. *"One who is bored is most likely boring."* Sophie Knutson had never been boring. Granted, she'd called some tasks boring, but right now anything looked better than doing nothing.

She'd had a good time the last three days shopping, though. Not that there were a lot of shops in Ballard, but she'd found a new bonnet. The feather on her other one never recovered from the drenching. Actually she'd gone looking for a new feather, but this hat was made of fur for the winter. And the umbrella was a necessity in this rainy country, as were a tablet, envelopes, pen, and ink. Surely Hamre wouldn't mind her purchases. She kept reminding herself of that as she made her way down the stairs, trying to ignore his remarks about saving every penny for his own boat.

"Oh, good to see you, dear." Mrs. Soderstrum greeted her with a smile. "I'll bring your plate right in."

"Mange takk." Sophie settled in what had become her chair and laid her napkin in her lap. She smiled across the table at the elderly man, Mr. Chambers, who clerked at a bank. He nodded and slurped his coffee from the saucer. A sniff from the pale and precisely plain young woman at the end of the table made Sophie want to roll her eyes. *Be polite*, she reminded herself, fighting to ignore the barbs of jealousy that she felt coming her way. Miss Benson, as Mrs. Soderstrum explained after their first meeting, had decided that she and Hamre would make a good match. Miss Benson was furious that he'd brought a wife back with him.

Sophie pasted a smile on her face and turned to smile sweetly. "Good morning, Miss Benson. I hope you slept well." She received a glare in return.

"Here you go, dear." Mrs. Soderstrum set a plate of bacon and eggs with biscuits in front of her.

"Mange takk." Sophie poured herself a cup of coffee from the pot sitting on the table. It felt so strange to be waited on like this, but when she'd offered to help, Mrs. Soderstrum shook her head.

"You are a guest here," she'd replied.

Sophie buttered her biscuit and soaked up the egg yolk with it. While several of the boarders were already gone for the day, those remaining were not overly talkative in the mornings. The quiet made Sophie think of the hubbub of home: the deaf students getting ready for school; Pa and the boys coming in from the milking; Ma and Grace, along with Ilse, getting the food on the table; Pa saying grace; the bustle to get those with sufficient signing skills out the door and into the wagon with their lunch pails and books. What a difference here.

She set her biscuit down and sipped at her coffee. First on her list for the day was to add to the letter she'd started to her family. Perhaps today would be the day she'd hear from them. Only one letter so far, and that so formal she'd wondered who wrote it. Was Grace missing her as much as she was missing her twin? She finished her breakfast and wiped her mouth with her napkin, tucking it back into the napkin ring to be used again for dinner and supper. Since the other diners were gone, she took her plate into the kitchen.

"You didn't need to do that." Mrs. Soderstrum took the plate from Sophie and set it on the counter by the sink.

"I know, but I wanted to. Do you have a minute?"

"Of course. You want to sit here at the table and I'll bring more coffee?"

"That would be nice." Sophie did as she'd suggested, glancing around the cheery room as she waited. Sunny yellow walls with white trim took away some of the gloom of the day. A pot of geraniums bloomed pink in the window; a purple violet bloomed in a pot on the table. The fragrance of baking bread took her home again. Was her mother baking bread today? Most likely. Did they have snow back there yet? So many questions and all with no answers.

Mrs. Soderstrum set the coffee cups on the table, followed by a plate of molasses cookies, and took her chair. "Black, right?"

"Ja, thank you."

"Now what is on your mind?"

How do I ask this without sounding ungrateful? "I know this might sound strange, but do you know of any jobs around here? I mean, I have all day with nothing to do."

"About the only place hiring is the fish cannery. At least that I know of."

"Do women work there?"

"Oh yes. Someone has to process all those fish men like your Hamre bring in. And while men do the heavy work, women work on the line, sorting, cleaning, and gutting. I worked there one season and took the money I made to buy this house."

"You made that much money?"

"Not really. I put a down payment on my house. The bank and I own it together."

"Maybe I could help Hamre with buying his boat."

"I don't think you would like working there. It . . . well, it smells pretty awful. And cold, oh my."

"It can't be any colder than North Dakota. The blizzards there do their best to drive the farmers out, or bury them."

"Well, you are young and strong. If Hamre wants you to do this, you just go down to the wharf and in the side door at the cannery. Ask to see Mr. Oscar Trondheim. He used to board with me before he worked his way up to manager. Tell him I sent you."

"Mange takk." Sophie picked up a cookie and bit into the rich flavor of ginger and molasses. "My mother baked such good molasses cookies too." She ignored the comment *If Hamre wants you to*. Of course, how could she know he didn't if she didn't ask? *I'll surprise him with the extra money so he can put it in his boat fund.* She smiled back at her hostess. "What happened to your husband?"

"The fishing boat he was on went down."

Fear made Sophie's mouth so dry she couldn't swallow. After a mouthful of coffee washed the crumbs down, she reached over and patted Mrs. Soderstrum's hand. "When did that happen?"

"Oh, long time ago—six, seven years." She squinted her eyes to think. "Seven. How the years pass so swiftly when in the beginning you think a day will last forever. Sorrow does that to you."

"I'm so sorry."

"Ja, life changes in a blink sometimes, and there's nothing you can do about it. Good thing God helps us go on in spite of what happens."

"And you never married again?"

"No, and no children. The babe I was carrying came too soon. Some say the shock of losing Arnet caused it. I don't know, but I'm grateful I have my boardinghouse. It's like having a bigger family."

"We have one in Blessing. Bridget Aarsgard—we all call her Bestemor—owns it. I've worked for her some."

"Well, if I didn't have my girl to help me, I'd hire you. But you can earn a lot more money at the cannery."

"You said his name was Mr. Trondheim?"

"That's right."

Sophie drained her coffee cup. "Mange takk." She pushed her chair back and rose. "You've been a great help."

Sophie danced up the stairs. She'd finish the letter home and then go call on Mr. Trondheim. After making up the bed and dusting the windowsills and the top of the dressers, she dusted the small table Mrs. Soderstrum had given her when she mentioned needing something to write on and sat down. After finishing the first letter, she took paper, pen, and ink from her purchases and wrote.

Dear Grace,

Why have you not written to me? I know you all got my letter, for Mor wrote back. I could tell that she is still angry, as is Far, but you are not, are you? You know how much I love Hamre, and since I didn't want to go to school anyway, I couldn't let him go back to Seattle without me. I'm sorry I couldn't tell you. Please forgive me.

She nibbled on the end of the pen for a bit. How to include everything without using all the pages she had.

This country is so different from Blessing, I cannot begin to describe it all. Hills that go straight up and so many kinds of trees. The fir trees are the biggest. Perhaps next summer you can come to visit, and I will show you Puget Sound and the mountains, snow-topped year-round they say, but so often hid-ing behind the rain clouds.

Hamre's boat has gone out to sea but not to Alaska yet. He should be back by Sunday. I miss him so. Mrs. Soderstrum, who owns the boardinghouse, was so kind to me this morning, and we talked over a second cup of coffee. I am going to seek work at the local cannery so I can keep busy when Hamre is gone to Alaska. He leaves around the middle of November. I hope to have enough earned to help him buy his own fishing boat. That is the dream of his life.

How are things there? Please write and tell me what all is happening.

I know things will be better when we have a place of our own. I'll have plenty to do then.

If Hamre isn't back on Sunday, I think I'll go to church with Mrs. Soderstrum. The woman had invited her, but Hamre said he wanted to take his Sundays off to show Sophie around. Strange how easy it was to get out of the habit of church on Sunday. Another one of those things she'd better not mention. Her mother would be fit to be tied.

I love you and miss you dreadfully.

Your loving sister,
Sophie Knutson Bjorklund

Sophie reread her letter. She'd had to be careful not to mention feeling so blue on these gray days or being tired of the rain already.

She addressed the envelope and put it in her reticule. She'd buy stamps today too. Glancing out the window, she was grateful that she'd bought that umbrella. Mist and more mist.

"Do you have anything you want me to mail, or pick up for you?" she asked Mrs. Soderstrum a few minutes later as she was about to leave the house.

"Would you be so kind as to take those things in the box on the hall table?"

"Of course. And I'll be walking right by the store if you need anything from there."

"I just ran out of vanilla." The older woman hurried back into the kitchen and returned with several coins. "That should be enough."

Sophie opened her umbrella before stepping off the porch. It was a good thing she had sturdy boots and had found the grease stowed in Hamre's dresser. She'd spent a couple of evenings greasing her boots and letting them set over the heat vent in the hall for the grease to soak in before adding another coat. No matter what she did, it brought up thoughts of home. From boot greasing to molasses cookies. *Please answer quickly, Grace. I need to hear of home.*

She strode the four blocks to the cannery and found the side door just as Mrs. Soderstrum had told her. The door opened into an office area, but even so, the smell of fish permeated the air. It was not fresh fish she smelled either. She felt like putting a perfumed handkerchief to her nose, but the man at the desk was already giving her a strange look.

"How can I help you?"

Ordering herself to be brave, she stepped forward. "I've come to see Mr. Trondheim."

"And your purpose?"

"Mrs. Soderstrum said to ask him about a job."

"*You* want to work here?" His inflection on the word *you* made her square her shoulders.

"Yes. May I talk with him?"

"It won't do any good. We're not hiring right now. Come back in two weeks."

"Oh. Shouldn't I leave my name or something?"

"Have you ever worked in a fish cannery before?"

"No, but I grew up on a farm in North Dakota, and I know how to work."

He cocked an eye at her, clearly doubting her words.

"Sorry, miss, but we don't have any cows to milk here." One of the men behind him chuckled.

Her eyes narrowed, but she kept a formal smile in place. "It is Mrs. and I would like to talk with Mr. Trondheim."

"Look, he's not here right now. And he would say the same thing. If you would like to write your name and address on this piece of paper, I will give it to him." He pushed a piece of paper forward.

She took the pencil and wrote down what he asked for. "I will come back in two weeks, then."

"Let me give you a hint, miss"—he looked at her signature and cleared his throat—"Mrs. Bjorklund. Women who work here dress in warm work clothes, not—" His glance caught her new fur hat, her fitted black wool coat, and the edge of her wool skirt that peeked from below.

"I see. Thank you." She turned and let herself out the door before collapsing against the wall under an overhang. Was that what looking for a job was like? Why, he'd been barely polite. She stared down at her clothing. Of course she had on a nice coat. It was her only coat. She'd left her chores coat at home in Blessing. And she'd worn her new fur hat. She touched the soft fur with a gentle finger.

Perhaps she'd better ask Mrs. Soderstrum what women wore to work at the cannery. She'd been hoping for a glimpse of the work line to give her an idea what the work would be like. Putting up her umbrella, she stepped back into what had progressed from mist to a heavy drizzle, with drops big enough to splash into the puddles. She could hear it plunking on her umbrella as she walked to the post office to buy stamps and mail her letter. She picked up vanilla at the grocery and went into the dry goods store with determination. Then, knitting needles and yarn in her bag, she headed back to the boardinghouse to begin knitting a scarf for Hamre to take with him on the fishing boat. She didn't have time to do socks and gloves, but a scarf would both keep him warmer and remind him how much his wife loved him.

The thought of being alone for those months stabbed like one of her needles might. What if she were to go home for four months and come back just before the boat returned? She mulled that over on the walk back, ignoring the moisture that was weighing down her skirt hem.

What would Hamre say if she suggested that?

What would he say about her getting a job at the cannery?

What if she just waited until he left and didn't bother to tell him? The thought made her shake her head. One rule her mother and father always lived by was to talk over everything. Secrets were the weasel that dug into the hen house and killed the chickens when you were sleeping.

When Hamre walked in the door two days later, he found her knitting in the parlor of the boardinghouse. She threw down her needles and flew across the room to greet him.

"What a picture to come home to." He tucked her underneath his arm, and together they climbed the stairs to their room.

"Oh, Hamre, I have missed you so." She took his wool coat and hung it on a chair back near the furnace vent in the hall to dry. "How was the trip?"

"Very good. We already unloaded at the dock, and I had more fish to my name than any of the others."

"That's because you are the best."

"Every time I think of going in early, I remind myself that each fish brings me closer to getting my boat."

Should I mention getting a job?

He turned his boots over and set them on the register to dry inside, then padded back into their room, closing the door behind him. "Thoughts of you here waiting for me made me work all the harder so I wouldn't be tempted to try and swim home to you."

"Hamre, you couldn't swim that far." She caught the teasing glint in his eye and smiled in return.

"I know, but that boat went so slow." He put his arm around her waist and pulled her onto his lap as he sat down and nibbled on her neck and earlobe. "My wife."

"My husband." She melted closer against his chest, her head tipping back of its own volition. She'd never dreamed hugging and kissing could be so intoxicating.

He kissed along her jawline, and his lips finally found hers. Their sighs mingled as they fell back onto the bed.

Sometime later, snuggled against his solid chest, she reminded herself that she needed to talk about her job idea, just before she drifted off to sleep.

She was sure everyone knew what they'd been doing when they joined the others for supper. Her cheeks flamed at her own thoughts. If they had their own house, she would have made a good meal for him and they could have had the evening all to themselves. She let herself drift into daydreams while the conversation flowed around her. Once she caught a wink from Mrs. Soderstrum that had her burying her face in her napkin.

"Are you all right?" Hamre leaned close to whisper, his hand on her knee under the table.

She nodded. No wonder married women didn't talk about things like this in front of the unmarried. This thought made her sit bolt upright, wishing for a fan, needing it as if this were mid-July in Blessing rather than October in Seattle.

Later, back in their room, Hamre cupped his hands along her jaw. "Now, are you going to tell me what was going through that pretty head of yours during supper?"

She shook her head, wanting to laugh, wanting to tell him, but oh, how could she even say such things?

"Come on. I'm your husband. You can tell me anything." He kissed her cheek. "You are blushing."

"Am not."

"Oh yes, you are. Those must have been some thoughts."

She glanced at the bed and then looked back into his eyes, those Bjorklund blue eyes she could drown in.

"Me too. I thought we'd never get away from the table." His kiss deepened.

❧

The next morning after breakfast, Hamre helped Sophie into her coat to go walking.

"You have a new hat?"

"Ja, do you like it?"

"How much was it?"

That surely was not the reaction she was looking for. She told him, taking a step back at the darkening of his eyes.

"I thought we were agreed. We are buying only the necessities so we can save for my boat." He spoke slowly and carefully, as if she were not only hard of hearing but hard of understanding.

Your boat. Never our boat. Am I not part of this? "I didn't rob the bank or anything." She glanced at the blanket on the chair.

"You bought that too?" The tone of his voice kicked at her shins.

She nodded. "I've been so cold here. The damp bites my bones." Where had that loving, gentle man, the one she'd delighted in, gone? "I-I'm sorry. I . . ."

He towered over her. "Did you take the money from my pouch?"

Sophie backed up. "J-ja. You said that was our money."

"Our money to save, not to spend. I paid for our room and board. The rest is for the boat."

"So I am to have nothing?" If only she could quit stammering. She tried to damp down the flare of anger singeing her middle. Why was he acting so . . . so . . . ? She couldn't think of a good word.

"No." He paused, obviously thinking, his forehead ridging from the effort. "But you must ask."

She thought to the tin in the cupboard at home where her mother always stored her egg and butter money when they'd had any to sell. While she'd doled the pennies and nickels out with great care, she'd had money of her own. "And if I ask?" Sophie narrowed her eyes. "How can I ask when you are never here?" She kept her foot from stamping and her hand from picking up something to throw. At home when she was angry, her mother always found something for her to do. Or Grace teased her out of a snit, as Mor called it. *Mor, how do I make him see?* She stared at his face, her fists rammed onto her hips.

He crossed his arms over his chest and leaned slightly backward. She could see a line in his jaw. *Stubborn man. Not that I'm not stubborn too. I know I am. I've been told so often enough. How can I do what he says when . . . What do I say?* "So then, if I need money I must go out and earn my own?" Where had that tone come from? Surely the rest of the boarders could hear them.

"No, that is not what I said. You sound like a child. This isn't Blessing, where you can always have your own way."

"I'm not a child!" Sophie felt the tears burning the backs of her eyelids and nose. "My own way! You have no idea . . ." *I will not cry. No matter how hardheaded you are.* "I'm your wife, and I'm trying to talk some sense into that hard head of yours."

Hamre turned away and grabbed his coat from the peg. He slapped his hat on his head and jerked the door open.

"Where are you going?"

"Out." The door snicked softly behind him.

14

HOW WONDERFUL that they were finally having a party for the whole town of Blessing. From what Ingeborg could tell over the last weeks, they needed one.

"Mor, where do you want us to set this?" Astrid held the punch bowl and Grace the pitchers, ready to fill the bowl.

"There on the end of the table. We'll put the coffee at the other end." *And if anyone messes with the punch, I am personally going to rip them limb from limb.* That had happened at the party at the barn raising for the Geddicks. Who would do such a thing when the children drank the punch too? That had been a real discussion at the last quilting bee. When someone had mentioned Toby, Hildegunn had flown into a rage that ended with her storming out the door. Ingeborg could still hear Hildegunn shouting that everyone blamed Toby for everything that went wrong. And she was right. Toby was being unjustly accused, all for his attitude and actions that as far as Ingeborg could tell had changed dramatically since The Big Fight, as people referred to the fight between Andrew and Toby.

Lord, why can't people forgive and forget, as the Scripture says? A thought flitted through her mind. *Have I forgiven Hildegunn for her attacks on Andrew?* Ingeborg sighed. She thought she had, but . . . *Lord, if there is some residual left, please weed it out. I don't want any strangling*

111

vines and roots of bitterness growing in me. Nor in those I love.

"Mor."

She could tell from the tone that she'd been off woolgathering again. "Yes, Astrid, what is it?"

"Tante Penny is calling for you."

"Oh, sorry." Ingeborg headed out the barn door and back to the house. She glanced up at the sky as she walked. They might be forced to move the whole dance back into the barn if the gathering clouds decided to dump their load of moisture sooner rather than later. "Lord, please hold it off. I wish the Geddicks had offered their barn. The schoolhouse has gotten too small for a dance with all the people we have here now. If we hadn't had such a nice long Indian summer, we wouldn't have planned this for outside."

Her knee grabbed as she tried to take the first step up to the porch. She gritted her teeth and stopped to catch her breath. It seemed that since those bleeding episodes had started, she was getting aches and pains all over the place: knees, fingers, right hip. Surely that was only part of getting older, but she hated mentioning it to anyone. She'd been praying for God to heal her, and if she complained about the pain, then she wasn't praising God for the healing. After all, He'd said He would heal all our diseases and infirmities.

She moved her leg again. Ah, that was better.

"Are you all right?" Penny peered through the screen door.

"Ja. Just a bit of a grab." If Bridget could keep going as she had up into her seventies, surely she should be able to get past the fifties mark.

"A grab where?"

So much for distraction. "It was nothing. What did you need?"

"Just that we should have someone guarding the punch."

"I've asked Thorliff to do that."

"Good. I didn't want to say anything out in public."

"I know. Perhaps we need to ask Pastor Solberg to mention the evils of alcohol in one of his sermons."

"You'd do that?" Surprise rounded Penny's mouth.

Ingeborg shrugged and tipped her head slightly to the side. "I've thought of it more than once." The two exchanged smiles.

"Has Kaaren heard any more from Sophie in the last week or so? Now that the post office isn't in my store, I get to feeling like I don't know what's going on anymore."

"Just yesterday. They are still living in a boardinghouse. It looks like she will stay there when he goes out with the fishing boat."

"Won't he go out for months? Why doesn't she just come home while he is gone?"

"I think our Sophie might be just a tiny bit afraid of her welcome back home."

"Oh, my land. She knows we all love her. And Grace misses her terribly."

"So does Kaaren."

"So does Kaaren what?" Kaaren opened the door, carrying a basket on each arm.

"Let me take one of those." Penny stepped forward.

"No, I'll put them on the table. There is more in the wagon. What do I do?"

"Miss that daughter of yours."

Kaaren's smile dimmed. "Every moment of every day." She set the baskets down. "I swing between wanting to hug her and beat her. At least she writes."

"How's Lars doing with this?"

"He never says anything about her." Kaaren's sigh came from deep in her wounded mother's heart.

"And Grace?" Penny's tone shared her concern.

"She didn't want to come tonight, but Astrid refused to let her stay home. Thank God for Astrid. She can say things that would send Grace into tears or a rage if I said them."

"Grace in a rage?" Ingeborg's mouth dropped open. "I've not seen her angry since she was really little and frustrated in trying to communicate with the rest of us."

"It takes a lot to get to Grace, but Sophie did it." Kaaren started to head back outside, but Penny stopped her.

"I'll get the rest."

Ingeborg held wide her arms, and Kaaren walked into them, resting her head on Ingeborg's shoulder.

"Some days I don't know how I'm going to stand it. It's easier when I'm mad. And I can't even talk this over with Lars. I feel like I lost both of them when she left."

"You think Haakan could talk with him, or Pastor Solberg?" Ingeborg felt her shoulder grow wet. Knowing that words were never enough, she stroked Kaaren's back and let her cry.

Sometime later Kaaren lifted her head and stepped back. "I didn't know I still had that many tears left." She mopped her eyes with a handkerchief she drew from her dress sleeve. "I'm sorry. This is supposed to be a party."

"The others are out there and doing just fine without us. Shall we go sit in the parlor?"

"No. I'll just wash my face and we can go on out. I think I'm over the worst. About the time I think I'm all right, something triggers the tears. Tonight it was the girls all dressed up for the dance. How Sophie loved to dance."

"I'm sure she still does. There must be dancing in Seattle."

"Ballard actually. It is a fishing village north of Seattle proper. I just hope Hamre loves to dance too."

"He didn't used to."

"I know, but he has changed so much from that quiet boy who lived here."

Penny came back through the door, pitchers in hand. "We need more punch. Even cool as it is, everyone is thirsty from dancing."

"Out in the springhouse."

"We'll help you." Kaaren forced a smile. "If I stay in the shadows, no one will know I've been crying."

Elizabeth met them on the porch. "Can I put Inga down on one of the beds? She can't seem to sleep through the music and laughter."

"Of course. Put her on my bed and stack the pillows around her."

"I can stay here with her." Kaaren reached out and took the now sleeping child. She nodded to Ingeborg to go help Penny and headed for the bedroom.

"Is she all right?" Elizabeth asked as the three ambled to the well house.

"She will be. Sometimes a good cry is all one needs. She spends a lot of time keeping a smile in place for everyone else's sake."

"Something like someone else we both know and love?"

Ingeborg pulled the bent nail out of the hasp that formed the latch and swung open the door. "I put the jugs in the water to cool. This is one of those times I dream of having an icebox."

"I sure like mine, but buying ice off the railroad car is near to unreasonable."

"Soon the icehouse will be full again."

Elizabeth donned her doctor hat. "Tell me how you've been feeling."

"Truly?"

"Ingeborg."

"I take it that you mean really." Ingeborg sighed. "Sometimes I am so tired I could just lie down on the floor and cry myself to sleep, too tired to find a chair or a bed."

"You've never told me that." Penny stopped, a jug in each hand.

"Why would I? There's nothing you can do."

"I would have told Elizabeth."

"I know." The three women chuckled.

"Still bleeding?"

"Not hard or I would have said something, but it's been going a good three weeks now."

"That does it. I'm scheduling the surgery as soon as possible."

"We could wait until after Christmas." *Lord, I don't want to do this. You could just make this right. You did it for that woman who touched your garment.* Ingeborg looked to Elizabeth, a slight frown marring her forehead. "Will you do it?"

"No. That wouldn't be a good thing. I'm too close to you. I wish we could go to Chicago for it. Hmm . . ." She stopped to think. "I could take Inga with me. How Dr. Morganstein would love to see her."

"And you."

"Do you know any doctors in Grand Forks?" Penny asked Elizabeth.

"No, but I could ask for references. I'll do that tomorrow." Her look at Ingeborg was loving and stern at the same time. "But if I telegraphed Dr. Morganstein, she would say to get on that train and get there now."

"How long would we be gone?" At Elizabeth's shrug, Ingeborg sighed. Uff da. Why couldn't this be easy and God just heal her?

Ingeborg debated whether she should go back to stay with Kaaren but chose instead to follow the music to the barn.

"Swing your partners and do-si-do."

She was sure the caller could be heard clear to Bridget's boarding-house, the night was so clear and still. She saw Astrid laughing up at Knute Baard as he nearly swung her off her feet before twirling her on to the next partner. The swirl of skirts and the colors all catching the light spelled fun in the best way. When two hands sneaked around her middle she leaned back against Haakan's chest and clasped her hands over his.

"How did you know it was me?" he whispered in her ear.

"Who else would it be?"

"Well, maybe Thorliff or Andrew." Together they swayed in time to the music.

"Well, there's Thorliff with Grace right now and Andrew with Astrid."

"Always so practical, my Inge."

"Just observant. Besides, none of the other men would be so for-ward."

"They better not be." His voice deepened to a growl, making her laugh.

"Ah, Haakan, have you thought lately about how blessed we are?"

"Every day."

The music stopped and everyone applauded.

"This will be a waltz. Come dance with me."

"With pleasure, but I'm not so old that I can't square dance any longer." Ingeborg leaned against his chest.

"Nor I, but I got to admit to needing to catch my breath at times."

She reached a hand up and patted the side of his face. The music started again, and she turned in his arms, their steps matching, his hand firm on her back. Her heart picked up a beat or two at the look of love in his eyes. Imagine, after all these years, she thought, the man still sets my heart to fluttering.

At a tap on his shoulder, Haakan turned to glare at his oldest son. "You can dance with her another time. I got her now."

Thorliff half bowed. "I just thought perhaps we could exchange partners."

Haakan glanced from his wife to Elizabeth and back again. "Well." He stretched the word to three syllables.

"You go on and dance with him, Elizabeth. I plumb wore him out." Ingeborg stepped into her son's arms.

"So you're having the surgery after all?" Thorliff asked as he took his mother's hand.

"I thought you just wanted to dance with me." Ingeborg shook her head. "In answer to your question, yes. But I don't want to talk about it now. This is a party, and I . . ."

Shouting from the refreshment table caught her attention. "Now what?" A wave of laughter caught all the dancers as the music stopped and so did their feet.

"What is it?" Ingeborg stood on her tiptoes but couldn't see. Thorliff took her hand and led her between the milling and laughing folks just in time to see Samuel dive under the table.

Two weaner pigs darted out the other side and skidded around to head toward the musicians. The table bucked as Samuel bumped it coming out from under it.

Two of the other younger boys took off in hot pursuit. One dove for a pig's back legs. He grasped one just for a second before losing it and catching the other leg. But the second leg quickly slipped out of his grip as well. With four boys now in hot pursuit, the pigs tore through the people, who were laughing so hard they were holding each other up.

"Call Barney," Ingeborg said to Andrew, who'd come up to stand beside her.

"Why? And take away all the fun?"

At the look on his face, Ingeborg paused. "You didn't."

"Didn't what?" At the questioning look he shot her, she shook her head.

"Nothing. I just thought for a moment that maybe you let them out purely for entertainment's sake."

"Mor, the pigs might get hurt."

"Okay, boys, that's enough," Haakan said. "Let's just herd them back toward their pen." He was having a hard time talking, he was still laughing so hard.

"Shoulda greased them and offered prizes."

"Why? They couldn't even catch them without grease."

"Hey, Sammy, don't you go hurtin' those hogs." The bystanders made sure the boys heard their comments.

Andrew met Barney at the barn door. "Okay, boy, go get those pigs." He waved an arm toward the panting hogs. Folks lined up to protect the tables, and others stepped back toward the walls as Barney hunkered low to the ground and eased around behind his quarry. With a quick dart he got them moving toward the door, and when one tried to break away, he zipped toward him and herded him back.

"Thorliff, you and Pa go man the gate." Andrew took over, ignoring the laughter.

"That's some dog you got there," someone called.

Barney kept the two grunting pigs moving toward the pen, not rushing them but moving steadily. When they neared the pigpen, Haakan swung open the gate, and the two escapees squealed when they saw the rest of the weaner pigs and ran on into the pen.

"Any idea how they got out?" Haakan asked.

"Nope, none. Strange that only two got out. I'll get a lantern and check out the fence."

"Fine. I'll go get the party going again."

"Haakan, you sure do a good job providing entertainment." One of the men clapped him on the back.

"Thanks. How about a pols for a change?" He motioned to the musicians, who set down their punch cups and picked up their instruments to play the Norwegian dance.

"Someone going to teach the steps?"

"Nah. Some of you that know it, grab a partner that doesn't. They'll learn quick." Haakan watched as Astrid and Grace offered to teach the Geddick boys and showed them in the side-by-side position. The music started, and the couples moved around the circle, everyone laughing and having a good time. When Haakan felt a hand slide into his, he followed his wife into the moving pattern.

Ingeborg smiled up at her husband and turned under his arm. Blinking her eyes, she fought to focus. The dancers around her blurred and then grayed, and she could feel herself falling into blackness.

She woke lying on her bed with Elizabeth bending over her, a stethoscope applied to her chest. Haakan gripped her hand, and she could see his lips moving in prayer. "What happened?"

"You fainted."

Haakan covered her hand with his other. "I'm sorry, my Inge, I should have seen—"

"Haakan, you couldn't tell," Elizabeth told him. "You caught her before she hit the floor and injured herself." She straightened up. "Your heart is fine. It has to be from the bleeding. I think this gives you your answer."

⁊ᕝ

Later, after all the guests had helped clean up and gone home, Haakan returned to sit down on the bed next to his wife. "So you have agreed to have the operation?"

"I guess so. It looks like we have no choice." She turned her head to look at him when he didn't answer. "What is it?"

"What if something goes wrong?" He cleared his throat halfway through the thought.

"That is why Elizabeth would rather we go to Chicago to where she took her training."

"Would it be safer there?"

"She feels so."

"Is it necessary?"

"If we can't stop the bleeding."

"But women have been going through this since time began."

"True. Some with this have died; others kind of fade away."

"Then why do this operation?"

"So I can be healthier and not one of those others."

Haakan sighed again. "I don't want to lose you."

The pain in his eyes wrenched her heart and brought tears to her own.

"I trust Elizabeth to do her best, but I trust God even more. If He wants me to go home, it won't matter where I am."

He nodded and clenched her hand. "My head knows that, but my whole self is . . ."

Afraid. I know that fear too. "I don't think God would be leading us this way if He didn't want it to be."

The pressure on her hand increased. "Ja, I know. In my head, I know. But in my heart . . ."

15

SOPHIE WOKE TO HEAR the door opening. Her eyes ached from crying and her heart from fighting. "Hamre?"

"Ja."

She sat up, pushing her hair back out of her eyes. "I . . ."

At the same moment he said, "Sophie, I . . ." The pain on his face drew her from her cocoon. She flung herself at him, wrapping her arms around his neck as if she might never let go.

Their words mingled together. "Sorry." "I love you." "Forgive me." When they recovered, they huddled together on the bed, whispering their love and neither of them bringing up what they'd fought about. That night they fell asleep in each other's arms after enjoying a private dinner from the tray Mrs. Soderstrum brought up.

In the morning Sophie stroked her husband's scratchy cheek. "You think they heard the whole thing?" The thought made her shudder both inside and out.

"We weren't exactly quiet," he murmured back. He kissed her forehead. "I hate fighting."

"That's why you left?"

He nodded. "We better get dressed and go down for breakfast. We can't hide up here all day. I have to go to work."

"I know." She hurried behind the screen and washed her face in cold water. Usually Mrs. Soderstrum's helper brought up hot water, but she'd probably not wanted to bother them. Sophie peeked out from behind the screen and winked at her husband.

"Sophie, if you know what's good for you . . ." His fake growl made her giggle. Maybe this making up wasn't such a bad thing.

For days they pretended the fight had never happened, joining the others in the parlor in the evening or staying in their room, her knitting, him reading, sometimes her reading to him.

One night when they were talking in their room, Hamre went silent on her again, not looking at her, staring at his hands.

"Hamre, what is it?"

When he shook his head, Sophie started to withdraw too but instead of tightening her jaw, blurted, "Are you angry at me?"

He shook his head slowly.

"Then who—what? Please . . ." She went to him, kneeling in front of his chair so she could look into his eyes. Her voice softened. "What is it?"

He let out a sigh and stroked the backs of her hands. "I didn't live up to my word—with your pa." He shook his head. "I should have been stronger." He stared into her eyes. "It makes me sad but . . . I . . ."

Sophie fought off the urge to cry. She leaned closer. "I know . . . but I am glad we are together. Now and forever." The kiss they shared drove the worry from her mind—at least for the moment.

❧

Then, on the seventh of November, Hamre came home, face somber. "The *Sea Lily* is ready. We leave in the morning."

Sophie stared at her husband. Backlit by the lamp, his face shadowed, he might well have been a stranger. Perhaps he truly was. They'd had so much fun since making up. "I-I guess I hoped you might stay with me."

"How can you think that? For the past two months I've been telling you all the things we were doing."

"You could fish the sound. Other boats do." No matter how hard she'd tried to prepare herself for this moment, even to denying that he would leave, she couldn't keep the bite out of her voice.

"Sophie, we've been over this before."

"I don't want you to leave. What will I do here all alone?"

"Why, the same things you do now, I suppose." He shook his head and left off watching her, turning instead to drag his canvas bag out of the armoire. "Did you finish knitting that pair of socks?"

Sophie closed her eyes. What would she do now? Count the hours for Hamre to return? *I'm not ready for you to leave.* The unfinished stocking lay in the basket beside her chair. While she'd finished his scarf, she'd left the remainder of the second sock unfinished, always hoping he wasn't going anyway. "No." The word snapped across the room. She clamped her arms across her chest.

"Sophie, quit acting like a spoiled child."

"If I'm such a spoiled child . . ." She glared at his back, then bit back the other words she'd been about to fling at him.

"You could make friends with the other wives. They manage to keep busy."

"They have homes and children. That makes a difference."

"True, and perhaps when I get back, we will build a house."

"How can we do that when all your money goes into saving for a boat?" She knew she was being snide but couldn't seem to stop.

"Sophie, I . . ."

She could feel her face tightening at the now-familiar tone of his voice. If he thought she was being unreasonable now . . .

"You could go back to Blessing."

"I don't want to go back to Blessing. I want to stay here with my husband." *Who is being so unreasonable I could spit!*

"Then you could—"

"I could! What if I don't want to? You won't even be here for Thanksgiving, let alone Christmas." *And I don't have your present ready to send with you.* Guilt chewed at her heart. *Sophie, grow up.*

"We will have Christmas when I return. Perhaps I will bring you something from Alaska."

"I don't want something from Alaska." Her voice broke on the last word. "I want you here."

She watched as he returned to the chest and pulled out the last drawer, the one with his heavy sweaters, and carried both the gray and the navy ones back to the broadening bag. "I don't know why you brought me out here when you were going to be gone for four months or more."

He stopped with his hand in the canvas bag. "If I remember right, you were the one who insisted. I was willing to wait the year your father wanted, but you refused to wait." His voice grew tighter and quieter with each word. The ice in his eyes froze her to her chair.

One thing she'd learned in these last several weeks was that while other men might yell when they were angry, Hamre grew more quiet, and the words he did say were like steel. She peeled her hands free of the chair arms, rose, and stalked behind the screen so he wouldn't see her crying. He'd made it clear several days earlier, after their big fight, what he thought of her tears when she wanted something and he'd said no. How could she tell him she'd been planning to buy his Christmas present? *I have to have some money. I don't want him to leave.* She unclenched her hands and forced herself to dip the washcloth in the tepid water and hold the wet cloth to her eyes. *If he can do the silent treatment, so can I.*

She struggled with the buttons up the back of her dress, finally yanking the dress up so she could reach the back. Here she needed help to even undress. She yanked harder and heard a button ping against the washbasin. Fine. Now she'd have to sew a button back on, and it was all his fault. She ripped again and heard another clack. Two buttons. *All you have to do is ask for his help.* The little voice spoke softly from somewhere amidst the raging waves in her mind.

She thought of the times he'd helped her unbutton her gown and things had progressed from there. And now he would be gone. At least farmers were home most of the time. She thought of her mother those years when Lars went off with the threshing crew. *But then Mor had all of us. And family and friends all around. Here I am in a strange city with no family, no friends, and I'm supposed to be content within these four walls?*

Laughter, the hysterical kind, dueled with rage and fueled by sorrow, threatened to erupt. She stepped out of her dress and flipped it over the screen to be hung up later. She could hear him moving from the chest of drawers to the seaman's bag, his boot heels clicking across the wooden floor. The urge to run and throw herself into his arms made her even more furious. Traitorous body. She untied her woolen petticoat and flipped it over the screen, then her under petticoat and camisole. As the tears flowed harder in spite of her efforts, she sniffed them back, pulled her flannel nightdress over her head, and stepped out of her drawers. One of the hairpins caught in her hair as she tried to undo the roll she'd fashioned so elaborately just this morning. She jerked on it, and pain shot through her scalp.

I can't even undo my hair right. She shook her head, and one of the other pins flipped to the floor. When she finally got the rest of the pins out, along with several long strands of hair, she rubbed the tender spot and dropped the pins into the porcelain dish she'd bought just for that purpose. Another one of those things he'd scolded her for wasting money on. As she had learned his anger, she'd also learned the hard way that he resented any penny not saved for his stupid boat. He didn't care that she needed a few things. After all, everything she needed had not come in the trunk her mother sent. *Think back, Sophie. How long has it been since he told you that you are beautiful?*

Leaving her dressing area looking like a blizzard had blown through, she stomped across the floor and ripped back the covers, climbing into bed without giving Hamre a glance. The flannel sheets even felt cold, much like her feet and her shaking hands. The burning was inside. She buried her face in the pillow so he wouldn't hear her tears.

Stupid stubborn Norwegian.

She fell asleep with the salt of tears on her tongue.

And woke to a sunny morning—alone.

When she pushed her hair back from her face, she vaguely remembered him kissing her and whispering good-bye. *What have I done?*

Two days later the tears of regret and sorrow still hovered and brimmed over at the slightest nudge of memory and dreams. She'd had to leave the supper table when someone mentioned a fishing boat. Mrs. Soderstrum came up to check on her and brought back tea and toast when she said she was too sick to come down. Sick at heart for certain, but her entire body felt the ravages. Surely she would run out of tears soon. The pounding in her head that followed the tears forced her to lie without moving, eyes closed, because even the dim light of a rainy day coming in the window made the beat pick up like a zealous child beating a washtub with a wooden stick.

A gentle knock at the door made her groan.

Mrs. Soderstrum pushed open the door and poked her head in. "Ah, Sophie, dear, I have brought you a tray. You must eat, you know."

"No, thank you. I cannot." She covered her eyes with the palm of one hand.

Mrs. Soderstrum set the tray on the nightstand and laid a cool hand against Sophie's cheek. "You aren't running a fever."

"No. It's just this terrible pain in my head. If I move, the whole room goes into a spin." Even talking was more than she could manage without additional pain.

"Oh dear. Perhaps we should call the doctor."

"No. Surely it will go away." Even her voice sounded strange. Was she making sense?

"I brought you some peppermint tea. That is supposedly good for the headache. Here. Sniff this. Perhaps it will help."

Sophie inhaled the warm peppermint steam. She thought of trying to sit up to drink some, but the slight movement of her head convinced her that was not a good idea. She inhaled again without moving this time. "Nice."

"I know what I shall do. I will go down and make a compress of peppermint and bring it up for your forehead." As she bustled out, she called over her shoulder, "We'll get you back on your feet. Never fear."

The silence after the door click felt like a balm. If only the pounding would stop.

Sophie dozed, and dark shapes cavorting and dancing with the pain lanced her eyelids.

Another tap at the door and Mrs. Soderstrum entered with another tray. "I brought you some laudanum too. That's the only thing I know that can truly kill the pain, but you are going to have to swallow when I spoon it into your mouth." She laid a towel across Sophie's chest and up to her neck.

The clink of spoon to bottle sounded loud, but then every sound seemed magnified out of proportion.

"Open."

Slowly Sophie opened her mouth and swallowed obediently. Her eyebrows wrinkled at the vile taste, hardly covered by the sweetness of honey.

"I know. It is bad, but you should feel some effects quickly. In the meantime we'll go with the cloth on your forehead."

A warm, wet peppermint-infused cloth lay on her head, the fumes entering through both nose and pores.

"There now. Is that better?"

The voice seemed to come from a far distance. Sophie thought about an answer, her mind checking out the symptoms. Pounding still there, but slightly abated? Did her teeth hurt as much? "I-I think so." She pushed the words out without use of jaw or lips.

"Good. I'll come back in a bit. You just rest."

As if I had any other choice.

The door snicked again and she could hear only her own heart thundering in her ears. The vile taste of the medicine lingered on her tongue as she searched for any trace of the honey. A longing for the cool stroke of her mother's fingers brought the incessant tears back to trickle out her eyes and down into her hair and dampen the pillow slip. *Mor, I need you. Grace, oh, Grace, if only I could see your face and hear your voice. Lord God, help me, please. . . .*

❧

When Sophie awoke, she lay still, afraid to move but already realizing a sense of freedom. The thudding was gone. She blinked, and it didn't hurt. Slowly, carefully, she turned her head to see that the angle of the light had slanted the shadow toward the evening side. No pain, only a sense of feeling displaced inside, as though the strength had been drained from each muscle and bone, so tired she could do nothing but fall back into a sleep so deep she didn't hear or sense anything.

The tray on her table the next morning showed that Mrs. Soderstrum had been in, the blanket in the chair by the bed mute testimony to her landlady's nocturnal watch.

When Hamre gets home . . . She stopped the thought and bit down on her lip. Hamre would not be coming home for a long time. And his last conversation with his wife had been bitter. What a memory for him on those lonely nights at sea. Was his whispered "I love you" only a dream?

When her eyes burned, she sniffed and rolled her eyes toward the ceiling, catching sight of her fringe, the ends of which came past her eyebrows. She needed to trim them or comb the hair back. She eased herself up against the pillows and surveyed the room. Had Hamre left nothing behind? She picked up his pillow and held it against her face, his masculine scent faint but easily identified. Breathing in the scent with her eyes closed, she could picture him coming across the room, love lighting his eyes.

Four long months. And now she had to figure out what to do with her time. Basking in the lack of pain in her head, she laid the pillow on her lap and crossed her arms over it, her wrists sharing the warmth in the chilly room. First she needed to finish knitting that pair of socks she'd started. Grace was right; it was time she learned to finish the things she'd begun. After tipping her head from side to side to make sure the pain was gone and to stretch out her muscles, she huffed a sigh and threw back the covers. The time had come to get on with whatever she was going to do.

Her gaze fell on the Bible her mother had sent in the trunk not long after Sophie and Hamre arrived in Seattle. Vaguely she remembered praying during the headache—such an innocuous name for what she'd experienced—and after that she'd fallen asleep. Had God answered and had a hand in her recovery? She thought back, trying to clear away the cobwebs that veiled her recollections. Mrs. Soderstrum had brought peppermint and laudanum. Had God told her to do that? Tante Ingeborg would say so. She often said God sent her here or there and gave her wisdom in using her simples to help those suffering.

Sophie crossed to the dresser and brought the Bible back to her bed. Flipping open the cover, she found a letter from her mother. Why had she not opened the book before now to at least see the letter? "Ah, Mor, I am so sorry. So sorry for so many things." Shaking her head, she unfolded the paper and read through misty eyes.

My dearest Sophie,

I cannot tell you how brokenhearted your father and I are at your leaving like you did. I am so grateful for your letter so that we know Hamre is taking good care of you and that you were married before boarding the train. Your father did not ask you to wait because he wanted to punish you but because he felt you were too young.

Ah, Mor, if you only know. Even Hamre now knows how young I really am, although I think he figured it out some time ago. She could hear him. *"Sophie, don't act like a child." I have been such a foolish daughter. How can anyone forgive me?* She returned to the page, wiped her eyes with the edge of the sheet, and read on.

And he wanted you to become more mature to be able to handle the trials a marriage always has.

We miss you so and pray that you are well and happy and that you will turn to the Lord for wisdom and guidance. Grace will write to you herself. I believe she has suffered more than any of us, but I am sure that she will come around eventually. I know that she loves you no matter what, as do I. You might want to write to your father separately.

Sophie read the last lines again. Grace had not forgiven her, nor had their father. At least at that time. She had received one letter from Grace, but it had been more like from a distant cousin than from her twin sister. She returned to the letter.

Give Hamre our love, and I pray you make a fine wife and the two of you will become the people God plans for you to be.

Love always,
Your Mor

Sophie sniffed, dabbed her eyes, and read the missive again. *So what do I do now? Besides write a letter home, that is.* She felt her stomach grumbling. First thing better be to get something to eat.

A tap at the door caught her attention. "Come in."

Mrs. Soderstrum entered with a smile that showed the dimples in her cheeks. "You sound like yourself again."

"I am, but I woke too late for breakfast." She nodded toward the chair. "You stayed with me?"

"A bit." She set the tray down on the bed and turned to go.

"Thank you for taking care of me." Sophie picked up the cup and inhaled. "Peppermint. This is so nice of you." She sipped and inhaled again. "Please, can you take time to sit down?"

Mrs. Soderstrum folded the blanket over the back of the chair and sat. "You look a mite pale yet but much improved over yesterday."

Sophie spooned jam from the little jar onto her toast and took a bite. "Ah, this tastes so good."

"It must. You've not eaten for three days."

Sophie chewed and swallowed. "What I'd like is some . . . some advice."

"About what?"

"About my finding a place to work." There, she'd said it.

Mrs. Soderstrum rolled her lips together and nodded. "I know you had a bad experience at the cannery, but I heard that Oscar is hiring now. I'd say to try there again. They pay the best of anyone."

When Mrs. Soderstrum left, Sophie stared at the wall for a while and then threw back the covers. First the letters and then finish the socks.

Within three days she'd finished her list and had even gone to visit Mrs. Jorgeson, the woman whose husband owned and captained the boat Hamre worked on. Mrs. Jorgeson, gracious amid her beautiful large home above the harbor, had reassured her that she could write to Hamre in care of the *Sea Lily*, and when the boat docked in Ketchikan, mail would also be sent home. She'd also invited Sophie to join their church and get to know some of the other families.

Sophie had not confessed the guilt that gnawed at her for the way she'd behaved that last night that Hamre was home—not to Mrs. Jorgeson, nor her mother or sister. No one need ever know that secret.

The next day Sophie returned to the canning factory, hoping this time for a better reception.

"Can you begin tomorrow?" Mr. Trondheim, the manager, asked, his eyebrows raised in a question mark. "This is hard work, you know."

"I know, but it can't be any harder than farm work, and I grew up on a farm in North Dakota." Sophie repeated what she'd told the other man when she'd tried to get the job before.

"Your husband is off on Jorgeson's boat?"

"How did you know that?"

"I know all the boat owners and most of the men. Hamre Bjorklund worked here for a time before he got hired on a boat. He is a good worker. He'll soon have that boat he wants so badly."

Sophie nodded. "And I plan to help him get one." *That's the least I can do after the way I treated him.* Even now, the thought of that night made her neck warm.

"Be here at seven. We start at daylight. And wear warm clothes. You do have boots, do you not?"

"I do." What would she wear for a coat? If only she had brought her chores coat with her.

After the interview she climbed the hill to the boardinghouse and entered, hanging her coat on the hook by the door. "Mrs. Soderstrum?"

"Back here." The reply came from the sewing room.

Sophie tucked scarf and gloves into her coat pockets and, inhaling the good fragrance of fresh baked bread, made her way to the sewing room.

"Did you get the job?"

"I did, but I have a favor to ask. Do you have an old wool coat I could buy from you? Or borrow until Mor can send me my chores coat?"

"I do, but it is so raggedy that I am ashamed to offer it."

"I could patch it."

"Then, dear girl, you may have it and be blessed." Mrs. Soderstrum rose from her chair in front of the sewing machine and went to a trunk in the corner. "Good thing I didn't throw it away. Thought I could use the good parts for patches myself." She dug in the trunk and pulled out a black wool coat that had indeed seen better days. Giving it a shake, she handed it to Sophie. "Try it on. Good thing you aren't a slip of a girl, or it would fall right off you."

Sophie donned the coat, and while she could pull the two front pieces halfway around her, a belt would take care of that. "Do you have any scraps I can use for patches?" At home her mor always had leftover pieces from garments she'd make or good pieces left from a garment that had been so worn that what was left could only be patches.

"Look in that basket over there. I throw all the odds and ends in that." Mrs. Soderstrum tsked and shook her head. "Won't be fashionable, but it should help keep you warm."

After spending the afternoon and evening sewing torn seams and patching both elbows, along with sewing a new belt and mending the pockets, Sophie fell into bed and closed her weary eyes. "Ah, Hamre, maybe I should just stay here and take in sewing or something." But she'd said she'd be at the cannery to work tomorrow. And she would keep her word.

But you told Hamre you'd stay here. The little voice made her roll her lower lip over her teeth. Too bad. When she showed him her full pouch of money for his boat, he'd not bother to yell at her. And if he did, well, she'd deal with that when the time came.

16

"I DON'T WANT TO LOSE YOU," Haakan said, his voice breaking.

Ingeborg left off washing the dishes and came to stand behind him, resting her hands on his shoulders. "Would it help if you came with us?"

"I don't know. How can I leave all the work here?"

"Andrew and Lars can handle it. You could visit machinery lots while you were there." Perhaps that extra enticement would sway him. His shoulders felt as tight as hers. The thought of having him along painted her picture of the ordeal in lighter hues. Besides, Elizabeth would have baby Inga, and that baby loved her grandpa. The feeling was mutual. "And perhaps you could help with Inga."

A smile tickled the edges of his eyes along with his mouth. "How long?"

"Two weeks if all goes well."

"There is the rest of the plowing, and we were hoping to get some pasture fenced over to Andrew's."

"Ja, and Astrid could stay with either of her brothers or with Kaaren." She could tell from the way his eyes narrowed that he was seriously contemplating the trip. She leaned forward, resting her cheek on the top of his head. "I would like you to come." Her words fell softly in the evening stillness.

Two days later the four of them boarded the train for Chicago.

"You let us know how it all goes," Thorliff made his wife promise.

Ingeborg hugged Astrid one last time, both of them sniffing and mopping tears. "Don't you go worrying now."

"I won't." Astrid stepped back to Thorliff's side, her smile wobbling but still there.

Ingeborg smiled at her son, who held his little daughter as if they were trying to snatch her away. She reached over and took the baby. "Now you two can say good-bye, and we'll get us all settled." Haakan helped her up the steps and followed with their two valises. Thorliff set two cases up on the top of the steps and turned back to his wife.

Ingeborg watched through the window as Thorliff held Elizabeth close and said something to make her smile before handing her up the stairs. Ingeborg waved again to Astrid and blew her a kiss. The conductor's call echoed, and the train wheels screeched and groaned as the engine drove them forward.

Please, God, take care of all of them while we are gone, and you know how much I want to come back home here. Ingeborg sniffed and wiped her eyes, grateful that she was not leaving Haakan behind but had him right beside her. She heard him clear his throat. This was no easier on him than on her.

Every time a worry tried to weasel its way into her mind, she repeated *Fear not, for I am with thee,* and *Whatsoever things are true . . . whatsoever things are lovely . . . think on these things.* The verses flowed through her mind and heart, calming both mind and spirit. If only her stomach were as agreeable. At least the bleeding had stopped again. One more thing to be thankful for.

The train ride passed without fanfare. Inga's happy grin enchanted a pigtailed little girl, along with a snow-crested dowager and the conductor, who made many more trips past them than seemed necessary. Caring for the baby helped take Ingeborg's mind off the upcoming surgery, and her laughter poured joy into all of them.

But the closer to Chicago the train drew, the more Ingeborg repeated her Bible verses—and strangled Haakan's hand. *Trust me.* The voice in her heart kept time with the clacking wheels. *Trust me. Will you trust me?*

Of course I trust you. And, Lord, you know I'm ready for heaven any time, but no offense, I would like a lot more time with my family here on earth.

The views outside the window failed to hold her attention—or Haakan's.

She nearly gagged on the smells that assailed them when they dismounted from the train. Smoke and fuel, garbage and unwashed humanity. The noises made her want to clap her hands over her ears, setting her longing for the sigh of the breeze and the birdsongs of home. She stared at Elizabeth, who was waving at a man striding through the crowd, his top hat riding high above the shifting mass of humanity.

⧫⧫

Two days later Ingeborg floated up from the sea she'd been drifting in to find Haakan sleeping beside her bed, his chin on his chest, his right hand clasping hers even in slumber. *So I am still alive on earth, not in heaven.* The thought made her smile, at least inside. She squeezed his hand, her eyelids already fluttering closed.

"Inge?" His voice brought her back.

She nodded, or she hoped she did.

"Oh, thank God. Thank you, Father."

She could hear the tears in his voice. Had there been worry that she would go on to her heavenly home rather than return to this one? The thought slipped away before she could respond to it, and she drifted back down.

"Ingeborg."

She heard the voice. Ah yes, Elizabeth. "Ja." Had she responded or not? She tried again, putting all her energy into it. "Ja."

"Good. Haakan said you had been awake, but he didn't want to wake me."

"Ja."

"You are doing well, very well. The surgery went so smoothly we can rejoice."

Ingeborg nodded.

"How do you feel?"

"Thirsty. . . . Tired. . . . Hurt." The spaces between the words gave her time to think of the next.

"That's normal. You need to drink, but you'll have to rise up so you don't choke. It will hurt."

Ingeborg braced herself as Elizabeth slid an arm behind her shoulders. But even she wasn't prepared for the pain that sliced across her abdomen. She quit breathing and her eyes clamped shut, her fists strangling the sheets.

"I know. It will get better," Elizabeth promised, holding the cup to her mother-in-law's lips. "Just sip for now. Good. Good." She lowered Ingeborg down to the pillow and held her hand until she was breathing normally again. "When Haakan wakes up, I'll tell him how well you are doing. He's concerned that you've been sleeping so much."

"How long?"

"Since the surgery?"

"Ja."

"Thirty-six hours. I've kept you sedated so the pain would not be so severe."

Dr. Morganstein joined Elizabeth at the bedside. She checked Ingeborg's pulse with two fingers across the inside of her wrist. "You, my dear, are one strong woman."

Ingeborg shook her head. "Not right now." There. Her voice worked better.

Both doctors chuckled, exchanging knowing looks.

"We'll have you sitting up by evening." Dr. Morganstein smiled again and patted Ingeborg's hand. "Most hospitals would have you lying flat for a week, but we have realized that the sooner one gets on her feet, the stronger she will be. There will be pain yet, but we will ease that as much as possible. If you have any questions, please don't be afraid to ask."

Ingeborg glanced at Elizabeth. "Does she realize what she is offering?"

Elizabeth laughed. "Remember, she taught me. And I have told her all about the wonderful things you have done with such limited resources."

"I want to know more about the herbs and things that you have used so remarkably," Dr. Morganstein said.

Really? Ingeborg looked from one to the other and started to say something, but a wave of such exhaustion swamped her that she blinked and drifted off.

∞

"You look beautiful," Haakan said the next day, his smile deepening the creases around his eyes.

"What day is it?" Ingeborg yawned and blinked herself fully awake. She shook her head at her husband. "Haakan, are you so tired you are not seeing straight?"

"Day four. And you have roses back on your cheeks. They've been gone for a long time."

"Ah." She tried to wet her lips, but her mouth failed to produce the needed moisture. "Could you help me sit up so I can drink?"

"Ja, that I could, but should you do that?"

"Ja, I should. I am to drink plenty. The doctor said so. Besides, I was sitting up yesterday for a short while."

"Which doctor?"

"Both doctors." She lifted her head and started to push with her arms, grateful when he slid his arm behind her and used the other to stuff a pillow against her back.

"Another?"

"No, this is fine." She hoped he'd not noticed her intake of breath at the shot of pain when she moved her hips. Besides, it had already abated. He held the cup for her, and she drank, more than a sip this time, the cool water soothing her throat and puddling in her belly. She could feel it all the way down.

"You will have broth today and all the water you can drink so that you do not get any more dehydrated," Elizabeth said as she joined Haakan at the bedside. "Let's get you sitting even straighter, and after a while, you can dangle your feet over the edge of the bed."

Ingeborg drank some more water and pushed against the mattress to sit up straighter. Easy words for those who didn't have to do it.

Dr. Morganstein and Elizabeth walked in together the next morning and stood on either side of Ingeborg, who was sitting on the edge of her bed with her feet hanging down. "All right, Ingeborg, the time has come."

"Take our arms and we'll put the other around you just in case you need more assistance."

Ingeborg swallowed once and then again. Here she'd been thinking it was time to lie down again. Haakan was supposed to be bringing her knitting, but she might not get a lot done. "All right." She locked her hand over Elizabeth's forearm and then did the same with Dr. Morganstein. As they lifted, she slid forward, slightly hampered by the bandages around her lower abdomen. The pain accelerated no matter how carefully she moved. When her feet finally met with the floor, she closed her eyes to stop the walls from swirling.

"Lightheaded?"

She nodded, but that wasn't an especially good idea either. Clamping her jaw, she sucked in a deep breath, held it, and let it out slowly. She could feel the sweat trickling down her back under the bandages. Oh, for a bath, or at least a good wash.

"Better or worse?"

"Not good."

"You want to sit down again?"

"No. Then I'd have to get up."

Elizabeth made a slight snort of agreement. "We can do this later."

"No. Let's get it over with."

"Then put that right foot out and walk forward. We're not doing any races here. Just to the chair for today. Then you can rest while the nurse changes your bed."

Four steps and they helped her turn and sit down.

"Mange takk. I feel like I walked to Blessing and back home five times, carrying a full wheel of my cheese."

"So what did you do with my wife?" Haakan asked from the doorway.

"I'm here." Ingeborg peered around Elizabeth.

Two nurses entered the room, greeted the doctors, and smiled at the others.

"Beginning to feel like a convention in here," one said.

"Dr. Morganstein, there is a woman waiting for you in your office," said the other.

"Excuse me. You did well, Mrs. Bjorklund." Dr. Morganstein squeezed Ingeborg's hand and turned to leave.

After the doctor left, Ingeborg leaned into Haakan's hand that now clasped her shoulder. *I want to go home. Surely I would get well more quickly there.* When the nurses finished making up her bed, Haakan helped her stand and half carried her back to it. Once she was lying down again, she let out a sigh of relief. Tomorrow she would go twice as far.

"See, all your worrying was for naught." She laid her cheek on the back of Haakan's hand.

"No, it wasn't. It made me pray all the more." He dragged the chair over to her bedside and sat down, immediately picking up her hand again.

Such wisdom this man had.

"I have something for you," he said, laying a package in her hands.

"What?"

"Open it."

Ingeborg untied the string and opened the box, often glancing at Haakan trying to decipher him.

"Oh Haakan, how lovely." She lifted a clear glass cream pitcher, along with a matching sugar bowl, from a paper nest. A line of etched leaves circled the throat of each. She grasped his hand pulled him close for a kiss. "Thank you."

৵৽

Two days later Dr. Morganstein brought a pad of paper and pen along. "Do you feel like talking about some of the herbal compounds you have made and how they were used?"

"I will gladly do that, but do you really want to know of my simples?" Ingeborg laid her knitting in her lap. "I mean, you know all this." She made an encompassing gesture with her hand.

"They didn't teach herbal remedies in medical school, and many of them are quite effective. Elizabeth has been bragging on you, you know."

An hour later Dr. Morganstein was still writing and Ingeborg was describing the tinctures she made from sage, cinnamon, and willow bark that seemed to help both a cough and shortness of breath.

"But that helps when the shortness of breath comes from the lungs, not from a weak heart."

"Did you try adding cayenne to that?"

"No. What does that do?"

Elizabeth stopped in the doorway. "See? What did I tell you?"

"I see those notes you sent me were only the tip of this woman's knowledge." Dr. Morganstein turned back to Ingeborg. "When you get home, if you remember other things, would you write them all down and send them to me?"

"Of course, but I-I hesitate."

"Why?"

"Where will you find some of the ingredients? Not here in the city."

"No. I might have to have you pick them and send them to me."

৵৽

Five days later the good doctor released Ingeborg from the hospital, telling her to take it easy and follow Dr. Elizabeth's orders, and when she was well enough, to continue her lists and explanations. "We are all going to miss little Inga," she said with a smile. "She's been entertaining everyone."

Ingeborg smiled back. "She does us too. Thank you for all your help." She watched Dr. Morganstein leave the room and turned to her husband. "We're going home, Haakan, just think. I can't wait to see Astrid and home."

"I know. Get out of this city smell. Lars will be pleased with the parts I found."

She'd been glad when Haakan finally felt she was doing well enough that he dared to go looking for machinery. *Lord, let me never take the sight of his dear face for granted again.*

17

December

"THANK YOU FOR THE INVITATION. I will follow you home, then."
Garth Wiste nodded as he spoke.

Ingeborg and Kaaren both smiled back at him.

"It's not hard to find." Kaaren turned and pointed across the field.
"See that huge house? We added on to our home to make my school
for the deaf. Sunday dinners are pretty hectic, but one more just adds
to the general hubbub. Usually we have Sunday dinner at Ingeborg's,
the white house to the right, but she is still recuperating."

"I heard of your trip to Chicago." How these two women managed
to make him feel like he was a long-lost member of their family just
come home, he would never understand. Both of their husbands had
been inviting him to church since he arrived in October, and finally he
had acquiesced. The first day of December wind bit through his heavy
wool coat and into his shoulder blades.

"Do you have a horse or buggy?" Kaaren asked.

"No. It is not far to walk."

"True, but you can ride with us." Ingeborg waved her arm toward
the buggy.

"Thank you, again." Garth touched the brim of his hat.

"Come, let's get out of this wind. The horse is ready to head home
without us if we don't hurry." Haakan took his wife's arm and helped

her up to the seat and nodded to Garth. "Glad you are coming."

With everyone loaded, the laughter and teasing caught Garth with a slug to the midsection. No matter how busy he kept, the loneliness gnawed like a rat at the grain bin. Sometimes he felt as if he could hear the teeth gnashing at night when he lay in an empty bed. No matter that he would be going home to see his children at Christmas. He tightened his jaw and looked out across the prairie so no one would see the tears blurring his vision. It would have been easier going back to work rather than coming to church with all these fine people.

But he knew folks were beginning to think him surly when he kept turning down invitations for supper or Sunday dinners. He'd not shown up at a party over at the Baards', even though he'd said he would. Before, it would not have been like him to be rude.

"So how do you like living in Blessing?" Ingeborg asked.

"This is a good town," Garth said over his shoulder. *Perhaps it is time to talk.* He'd ignored the prompting earlier, but everyone had been so welcoming and nice to him. Taking in a deep breath, he continued. "Coming here after my wife died was a good thing."

"Sometimes a change of scenery makes the grieving easier."

"I hoped it would. Keeping busy helps."

"I found that to be true when my first husband died. Nearly worked myself into an early grave, but God and His grace brought me through."

Her smile to her husband gave Garth more courage. Here was someone who understood.

"That was why I left Minneapolis and my two children with my sister. I hope to build a house and bring them here soon." Until he said that, he'd not realized he'd been thinking on it.

"You'll be needing a housekeeper then?"

"He needs a house first," Haakan said dryly. "You might talk to Andrew, our younger son; he'll be at the house too. He bought a package house from Sears and Roebuck out of their catalog. We put it up in no time."

"It came in on the train." Astrid spoke up too.

"Really? I think I read something about that but never paid much attention. Is there land available?"

"I'm sure we could find you a lot in town, or were you thinking on farming?" Haakan asked.

"No, I'm a mill worker, not a farmer." Garth watched as a mottled brown and gray dog shot off the porch and tore down the lane to greet them. "Town would be best."

"Then you'll want to talk to Hjelmer Bjorklund. He is selling off some of his land in town."

"He was at the interview. He's in government. Right?"

"Ja and has the blacksmith shop and machinery sales." Haakan stopped the team in front of the white gate of the picket fence that fronted the huge Knutson house.

Garth stepped out of the buggy to assist the two ladies behind him. Astrid gave him her hand and a saucy smile as she stepped out.

"Thank you."

He nodded and took her mother's hand. Mrs. Bjorklund's smile dashed any thoughts that she might still be ill from her surgery.

"Thank you." She settled her skirts and slid her hand through the bend in his arm. "We are delighted you could come today." She walked with him up the stairs. "We want you to feel welcome and at home here."

He opened the door for her, and she preceded him inside.

"Oh, it smells wonderful." Garth inhaled the aroma of roasting chicken overlaid with a hint of cinnamon.

"Dinner will be ready in just a few minutes." Ingeborg hung her shawl on the coatrack by the door. "Make yourself at home. The others are right behind us. I'm going into the kitchen to help Kaaren."

He could hear the laughter and exchanges outside as two other wagons arrived. Did all of Blessing come here for Sunday dinner? He remained in the parlor as the various families streamed through, the men remaining, the women carrying food to the kitchen, and the children heading back outside to play off some of their bottled-up energy from church.

He remembered days like this, freed from church and making sure no adults were nearby to remind the children that Sunday was to be a time of quiet and reflection. Perhaps things were different on farms where cows had to be milked and animals fed no matter what day of the week it was.

Pastor Solberg came up and shook his hand. "I'm glad to see you, Mr. Wiste. I've been meaning to visit you at the boardinghouse, but somehow after school starts, time gets away from me."

"You teach at the school also?"

"Yes. We are in desperate need of another teacher, our school has grown so much. I keep hoping one of our young people will come back to teach here, but we'll most likely have to petition the state for another teacher for next fall. We hope to add on to the schoolhouse next summer. Blessing is growing."

"I heard that a man wants to open a saloon here."

"Really?"

"Ja. You hear all kinds of discussions at the boardinghouse."

"He won't be the first with that idea and most likely not the last. But our women are rather adamant that there will be no liquor served publicly around here."

"You mean no one is making moonshine?"

"Not that I know of, and somehow I seem to get all the news one way or another." He turned to greet the young man who'd come up. "Hello, Andrew. Have you met Mr. Wiste yet?"

"Now I have." Andrew extended his hand. "Ah, Mr. Wiste, Pa said you wanted to talk to me about my Sears and Roebuck house?"

The man could have been an ad for young Norwegian manhood with his blond hair and intense blue eyes. Garth felt old and dried out next to him, even though probably not many years separated them.

"Yes. Yes, I would."

"I'll leave you two, then." Pastor Solberg turned to answer a question from someone else.

After all his solitary days since he'd arrived, Garth was beginning to feel boxed in by all the people swirling around him.

"Come, let's go out on the porch." Settling in the two rocking chairs on the porch with the pale winter sun burnishing the floor and posts, they both sat back with a sigh. The shrieks of the young children came from far away; the laughter from those in the house had closed to a murmur until someone opened the door to let more air in.

"What did you want to know?" Andrew asked.

"Why did you buy a package house is my first question."

"Look around. Do you see a lot of trees?"

"Well, no."

"That's the first reason. We have to have all our lumber hauled in anyway, so when I read about the Sears and Roebuck houses, my curiosity got the better of me. I looked them up in the catalog at Tante Penny's store. They said the houses went up fast, and everything needed came in the package."

"And was it so?"

Andrew nodded. "Our only complaint was that the package didn't come when they first said it would. They had fallen behind with too many people ordering the houses. But when it did come, we had most of it up in one weekend. We had dug out the cellar earlier and poured concrete walls so we were all ready. If you order one, we'll help you put it up."

"You would do that?" He didn't add *for a stranger?* but thought it.

"Of course. We work together in Blessing. It's one of the blessings of this place, according to Pastor Solberg."

"Haakan said there might be a lot for me to buy?"

"Talk with Tante Penny. Hjelmer won't be back for another week or two. I know there is a plot out by the church, and I think she is willing to sell some behind her store. If you want to be out of town—"

"No. I see no need of that. The closer to my work the better." The thought of possibly having his children here in time for Christmas set his mind to whirling. He'd not realized how much he missed Grant until he thought of having him with him. And his daughter—it was past time to be getting to know her.

"Wait a minute. I think Tante Kaaren has one of the more recent catalogs." Andrew rose and went back into the house.

Garth stared across the fields, the flat land broken only by buildings and haystacks and the trees along the river flowing in from the west, none of which looked big enough to become lumber. Perhaps one of Blessing's older women would agree to be a housekeeper and care for his children. Or was it better to leave them with his sister? *Lord, is it selfish of me to want to see them, to be with them?*

Andrew returned. "Here, you can take this with you. But Pa said you might want to wait until spring. We've already had snow, and all signs say we are going to have a hard winter."

Garth took the offered catalog. "Thank you."

"Dinner is ready," Astrid announced from the doorway. "Andrew, will you go call the children?"

After Pastor Solberg prayed, the men lined up first, and then the children, followed by the young people. Each person dished a plateful and then found a place to sit. The men gathered in the parlor, the young people in the schoolroom, and the children on the stairs, as if all knew their places. Garth joined the men, sitting off to the side, not taking part in the conversation unless asked a question. One learned a lot by listening, something he had discovered long years earlier. Maddie used to tease him about his quietness, but he'd always responded with the old saying, "God gave us two ears and one mouth for a reason." He'd learned that one from his grandfather.

Haakan was most likely right. Starting a house now would be folly. But he could start the process. First he would have to sell his house in Minneapolis, and that meant going back there perhaps more than just for Christmas. Back to all the memories. Maybe it was good Helga and Dan decided not to take over his house. How would he find either the heart or the time to get it ready to sell?

18

Dear Sophie,

I meant to write to you earlier, but when the baby came, I learned an important lesson—several in fact. One, my worries and fears were for naught. While having a baby is not an easy task, Dr. Elizabeth got here just in time, and all went as it should. She and Ingeborg had gone to Chicago for Ingeborg to have an operation. I was in labor when they got off the train on November 28, and Carl was born in the early hours of the next morning. I am happy to say that both mother and baby are doing well, although Grandma Ingeborg was sorry to have to miss this birthing.

The second lesson? A baby takes up every hour of every day and most of the night too. Even when he is sleeping, I am washing diapers or trying to get the meals made for Andrew or—come to think of it, I'm not sure where all the time goes. Mor came to stay with me for a while, and she reminded me that all babies are like this. I guess I'd forgotten, or else it is different when it is your own. I love rocking him to sleep. When he has the colic, Andrew helps walk him in the night hours, as the rocking chair is not enough. My dear far made me the best rocker. I told him he should go into making only rocking chairs, but he didn't think there was enough market for that to keep him and his workers busy.

Remember how we used to dream of our lives? I wonder how your dream is coming and when I will see your dear face again and hear you laugh. Sophie, I miss you, as does everyone. I pray all is well with you, though I can't even imagine what it would be like to have my husband gone to sea. Grace let me read your letter. I hope that was all right.

Love from your friend,
Ellie Bjorklund

P.S. Have you thought of coming home to Blessing for the months that Hamre is gone? Love again. E.

Sophie read the letter a second time before laying it in her lap and letting the tears run. There was no way she could go home. Grace rarely wrote; Pa never had. What country did Ellie live in to think all was forgiven? Besides, there was no way she could make enough money in Blessing to help pay for the boat Hamre wanted. Three weeks now she'd been working at the cannery, and never had she been so tired in her life. Surely by now she should have gotten used to standing on her feet at the gutting line all day. It wasn't that different from milking and canning and gardening and all the things she did all summer long at home. She and Grace had always worked hard. That's what everyone did, and no one thought anything of it.

She closed her eyes and leaned her head against the chairback. She could hear the bell ringing for supper, and she hadn't washed yet. Her stomach rumbled as if set off by the bell. Heaving a sigh, she rose, poured the now cooled water into the basin, and scrubbed her hands and up her arms. Her clothes she'd hung on a peg by the door, as far from her as possible. She'd thought to ask Mrs. Soderstrum if she could undress in the washroom near the back door and leave her work clothes there. She'd never get the fish smell out of them anyway.

After dressing again she made her way downstairs, dreading the thought that she'd have to go back up again. She could just sleep at the table with her head on her hands. She'd done that at work on her noon break one day.

"Are you sure you feel all right?" Mrs. Soderstrum asked after supper was cleared away.

"Just tired."

"That is a hard job working the gutting line. I did it one year before I married my Arnet and then again after he died." She set a cup of tea in front of Sophie. "You sure that's all it is?"

Sophie shrugged. She wasn't coughing or running a fever. Just incredibly bone tired.

The next night when she came home, Mrs. Soderstrum met her at the door. "Perhaps this will help." She waved a letter and then, with a wide smile that showed her missing lower front tooth, handed Sophie the envelope. "From your Hamre."

"Really?" Sophie threw her arms around her landlady, hugging her in spite of the fish smell she wore. After removing coat, muffler, and boots, she headed up the stairs.

"I will bring you some hot water."

"Thank you, yes." Sophie stopped at the large grate from the furnace and let the warm air flow up under the skirts and around her legs. No matter how many layers of clothes she wore, she always came home frozen clear to the bone. Cold in Seattle was so different from cold in North Dakota. Here it slipped past the skin and seeped into the bones and muscles, where it took up lodging in spite of the warmth of the house. She opened the envelope with shaking fingers.

My dearest Sophie,

We are here in Alaskan waters, and the fishing is some of the best ever. I row my dory out and many times have filled it three times in a day. The seas are relatively calm, so that is easier on all of us. You should see me. I stick that pew in and unload fish in record time. Knowing that you are waiting for me makes me work all the harder. Captain Jorgeson says I must have the fish all corralled, or I've got something in the boat that makes them come to me because I fill my dory up so fast. My shares from this season are adding up quickly. They are saying we might have a record season.

I am writing by lamplight, as all of our daylight is used for fishing. Were I not writing to you, I would be sound asleep like most of the others. Every night before I fall asleep, I think of my beautiful Sophie and thank God that you are my wife.

Love,
Your Hamre

P.S. You can write to me here at the cannery. They will hold our letters until we dock again. H.

Sophie wiped the tears away. Not one hint of resenting the way she had sent him off. Or rather, didn't send him off. Before he left he'd taken her on board the fishing boat to show her what his life would be like. She'd seen his narrow bunk, the galley and where they ate, the dories and the pew that resembled a wooden pitchfork but with only two points and used for scooping fish instead of pitching hay or manure. Now she could picture him there, writing at the wooden table with a kerosene lamp swinging overhead, the entire room so low he had to stoop to come through the door. He'd be wearing his oilskins, a jacket that came to his hips, with the turtleneck sweater underneath and wool long johns and pants.

"Ah, Hamre, I don't know if I can bear this all winter long." Of course, he thought she was warm and snug here in the boardinghouse. He had no idea she was standing on the fish line with a slender knife in one hand, slicing from the tail up the belly to the gills, pulling out the guts, and sliding the fish on to the next in line, where it would be washed, fins and head removed, and sent on to the next. The assembly line of silver fish started at dawn and ended just before dark.

She eyed the small packet of letters she had written to him. Not telling him about the job left her with little to say, other than the news from Blessing and the gossip she heard in the dining room at the boardinghouse. She'd tried hard not to whine about the unending gray days but knew some had leaked through her pen.

Reading his letter again, she had to smile. Hamre had not wasted a word—so typical for him.

She thought of addressing the letters but decided to put them all in one envelope and send them that way instead of individually. Sitting down on the bed to reread the letters she had written had been a mistake. She knew it as soon as her head felt the pillow, but moving took more energy than she had to give.

A knock at the door woke her. "What? Ah, I'm coming. I'll be right down."

"No, I brought you some supper. Are you all right?" Mrs. Soderstrum pushed open the door as she spoke.

"You didn't need to do that."

"You slept through supper, and I knew you needed the rest, so here you go. Bring the tray down with you when you come in the morning." She set the tray on the low table by the chair. "I brought you tea because I thought it might sit better. Would you rather have coffee?"

"No thank you, dear Mrs. Soderstrum. You are so good to me." Sophie rubbed the sleep from her eyes with the knuckles of her fingers, making a face at the fish smell she'd not washed off. Would she ever be free of the odor again? The smell made her stomach roil.

The next morning she woke more sluggish than ever. Turning over set her stomach to sloshing, so she lay flat for a few moments, massaging her middle. Whatever was the matter with her? She sat up, then stood and drew the chamber pot out of the stand. The smell made the gorge rise in her throat, and the next thing she knew, she was heaving into the basin. When finished, she wiped her face with the washcloth still damp from the night before. *How can I possibly get dressed and . . . You will do this, Sophie Bjorklund. You said you would work, and you will.* She dressed and clung to the rail down the stairs. But when they passed the platter with sausage patties, usually her favorite, she handed them on. Perhaps toast and tea was her best option this morning, although now she was feeling a whole lot better.

"Are you all right, dear?" Mrs. Soderstrum whispered in her ear as she went around refilling coffee cups.

"Why?"

"You're just a mite pale. I worry about you."

"No, I'm better." She had dumped her chamber pot in the slop pail on her way down to breakfast so no one would know. "No need to worry."

But when the same thing happened three days in a row and once on the way home from work, she'd begun to worry herself. Should she tell someone? What if something was seriously wrong? If only she could talk with her mother.

ॐ

Two days later the smell of the cannery line made her gag. She fought the feeling all morning until suddenly the world around her tilted, and the next thing she knew she was lying on the floor, her head pillowed in a woman's lap, a voice saying, "No, she's coming out of it. Sophie, can you hear me?"

Sophie nodded. "What happened?"

"You fainted."

"F-fainted?" *I have never fainted in my life. Oh, Lord, what is wrong with me?*

"Okay, ladies, back to work. Smith, you move into her place. Mrs. Bjorklund, you go sit in the lunchroom until you get your strength back." The supervisor gave the orders, and everyone went back to work.

Sophie tried to stand, but the world went around again, and she clutched a wooden post.

Her neighbor left the line, shot the supervisor a look of contempt, and put an arm around Sophie's waist. "Here, dearie, let me help you. Don't worry none, I'll be right back. Them fish ain't going anywhere without us." Together they made it to the relative quiet of the eating room, and Sophie sat on a bench.

"Put your head between your knees now, and it'll pass."

Sophie did as instructed and in a few moments did indeed feel far better. She raised her head to find the woman watching her, one hand holding up the other elbow.

"You been missing any of your monthlies?"

Sophie shrugged. "I don't know. I hadn't thought about it. Why?"

"Just look suspicious to me. You been feeling like heaving your guts every morning?"

"How did you know?"

"Hmm." She nodded as she studied Sophie. "Breasts tender?"

"Only when I roll over."

More nodding. "I'd be willing to bet you are in the family way."

"Family way?"

"Pregnant . . . with child . . . carrying."

"But . . ." Sophie could feel her eyes widen and her mouth fall open. Of course. She had all the symptoms, but no one to point them out to her. "Does every woman feel like I've been feeling lately?"

"Not every woman. Didn't your mother tell you about these things?"

"No. I ran off before she had a chance. I'm sure she'd have told me more otherwise, but you know no one talks of such things to innocent young girls."

"I know."

"How long? I mean, will I be sick like this for long?"

"Couple of months possibly. Perhaps not."

"Lady, get back out here. We'll have no lollygagging on my shift."

She made a face. "You come out when you can, or they'll dock your pay."

Sophie worked the rest of the day, wanting to rub her middle as if to reassure herself. She was carrying Hamre's baby. A shiver of excitement tickled her backbone. And he wasn't there to get the news. She plummeted into sadness. Cupping her hands over her lower belly brought back the thrill. What a surprise. No wonder she'd been so tired.

Hugging the secret to herself, she made her way home and up to her room, where she washed and lay down for a nap. She would not miss the supper bell this time. She had to eat to keep up her strength, both to work and to feed the baby floating inside of her. Tonight she would write again to Hamre, and tomorrow send the letter. If only she could be there to see the delight in his eyes. Hamre was going to be a father.

But I thought you didn't want to have children so soon? The thought caught her by surprise. *That's right. How can I go with Hamre on his fishing boat when I have a baby to take care of?*

In spite of her excitement, the next morning she felt worse than ever. She lay in bed with her eyes closed, trying to breathe around the nausea. But no matter, she was heaving into the basin within minutes, only this time when she lay down for a few moments more, it didn't go away. How could she get up and get to the cannery when the room kept spinning? Instead, she fell back asleep.

"Sophie, you're going to be late for work." Mrs. Soderstrum shook her gently.

Sophie drew in a deep breath, and this time when she opened her eyes, she felt weak but not sick. "I know. I couldn't go earlier."

"You're carrying, aren't you?"

"If you mean I am going to have a baby, I think you are right. One of the women figured it out yesterday when I fainted on the line."

"Oh, my dear, how wonderful."

Sophie threw back her covers. "And now I'm going to be late. I just pray he doesn't fire me."

"Do you think you should go?"

"I don't remember my mother ever taking a day off because she didn't feel well. Of course she would not have told me what the matter was. I don't know how she disguised such things. She had two more children after Grace and I were born." All the while they were talking, Sophie had gone behind the screen to get dressed, putting on layer after layer to keep warm.

"I'll warm you up some breakfast."

"Please fix something that I can eat as I walk."

"I will, and your lunch is waiting for you." Mrs. Soderstrum bustled out, and Sophie sat down to brush her hair and braid it to stay out of her way. When she stepped out the door, she blinked against the shining sun. She'd begun to believe it would never shine again, so at the corner she lifted her face to the warmth as a heavy wagon with four up drove by.

"A good day to ye, miss."

"And to you." She waved to the driver and continued on to the cannery.

"You are late." The superintendent turned on her when she donned her apron and made her way to the line.

"I know. I was sick."

"But now you aren't?"

"I'm here."

"That'll cost you the morning's pay."

"I understand." She kept her shoulders straight and looked him in the eye.

"Get to work, then. But remember, one more mark and you're out of here. Go on down there and relieve Miz Hanson."

Sophie did as told and stepped back into the sea of scales and slime that flowed by on the moving belt.

In the lunchroom she sat next to Alice Hanson and opened her lard pail, just what she'd had all those years in school. For a moment she wished she were back there, laughing with Grace and Astrid, groaning about the homework assigned by Pastor Solberg.

"How you feeling?"

"Better now. This morning was terrible. I thought to close my eyes for a moment, and Mrs. Soderstrum woke me an hour later."

"You might try waking earlier and eating stale bread, just a bit, then lay back. My sister said that worked for her."

"I'll try that." Sophie took a bite of her beef and cheese sandwich, wishing she had a cup of hot tea to go along with it.

"This isn't a good place for you to work, Sophie. All the cold and standing all day."

"So where else can I work? I can't sit in my room and twiddle my thumbs all day."

"Perhaps someone needs house help."

"Perhaps. But they pay a lot more here. I'll stay as long as I can get up to the table."

That evening after work, she took her packet of letters to the captain's wife, who promised to get them on the next supply boat going north.

"Good to hear they are having such a good run, wasn't it?" Mrs. Jorgeson said with a smile.

"Yes. Perhaps next year Hamre will have a boat of his own."

Mrs. Jorgeson leaned a little closer. "Don't tell anyone, but I think the captain has a proposition to offer Hamre. To make him a partner and let him pay off his boat over time. That way they could work together."

"Does Hamre know this?"

"No, so don't write it to him. But Captain Jorgeson mentioned again how pleased he is with Hamre's work, and they've been talking about ways to work this out that will make both of them happy."

"Ah, thank you for telling me."

"He's looking for a boat. I'm sure he will mention it to Hamre soon if he hasn't already." She thought a moment. "In fact, I know he has, because he said he would soon, and you know how long it took to get the letters down here."

Sophie's feet didn't touch the ground as she hurried back to the boardinghouse. Hamre was going to have his dream—two dreams. A family and a boat. The more money she could earn, the sooner they would pay it off.

"My, you look like you swallowed a candle." Mrs. Soderstrum handed her a pitcher of warm water to wash with.

"I know. I just took my letters over to Mrs. Jorgeson, and she told me that the captain is planning on going into partnership with Hamre and buying another boat. We will be paying it off as soon as we can."

"Why, that is wonderful. Captain Jorgeson has such a fine reputation. Such good news all around." She held a bite of stew on a spoon. "Taste this and see if it needs more salt."

Sophie chewed and thought before shaking her head. "Tastes fine to me."

"All right. Supper in a few minutes. I'll be ringing the bell. Oh, and Sophie, I forgot. There's a letter for you on the table."

"Thank you."

Sophie picked up her letter and nearly kissed the envelope. Grace had finally written again. She hurried up the stairs and poured the water into her washbowl. Mrs. Soderstrum had even come up and made her bed. No wonder Hamre always kept a room here. They had the nicest landlady around.

As soon as she washed and slipped into clean clothes, she sat on the bed and ripped open the envelope. One sheet. She swallowed her disappointment and read.

Dear Sophie,

I hope you are well. School is fine. Astrid and I, well, all of us had a good time at the fall party.

Ellie's baby is so tiny and sweet.

We all miss you.

Your sister,
Grace

Sophie ignored the tear meandering down her face. Grace had not forgiven her.

ॐ

The next morning Sophie ate a little bread as soon as she awoke and lay back down. Within a few minutes she got up and felt almost like she used to. Breakfast tasted good. The sun was lighting the east. Surely this would be a wonderful day. She inhaled and smiled at the crisp air. The frost that rimmed the pine and fir needles and whitened the rooftops lent a sparkle to the day and a skip to her steps. *Oh, Hamre, I hope you are having a glorious day and the fish are jumping right into your dory.*

She donned her apron and, after checking the edge on her knife, wielded a couple of swipes on the whetstone before heading for the line.

"Miss Merry Sunshine you are," Alice greeted her.

"I know. How can I resist? The sun is shining. I was beginning to think it would never return."

"There is no lovelier place than Seattle when the sun shines."

"Quiet! There'll be no more jabbering."

The women rolled their eyes and, as the fish line started up, went to work. As if they couldn't talk and gut fish at the same time. Perhaps men couldn't, but they could. If only they could convince the Grouch, as they'd all come to call him in secret.

The sickness caught Sophie by surprise after the break, and before she could ask to be excused to go to the necessary, her world went black again.

"Easy now. You cracked your head on the way down." Alice held a folded apron against Sophie's forehead.

"I didn't faint again?"

"I'm afraid so. Can you stand so we can go to the other room and put a bandage on it?"

"In a moment."

The superintendent was right behind her. "Bjorklund, stop by the paymaster on your way out. You're fired."

"But I—" From the look on his face, she knew he meant it.

19

"HE FIRED ME BECAUSE I fainted again." Sophie's jaw ached from clenching it so hard.

"Oh, my poor dear." Mrs. Soderstrum gathered her close, patting her back and checking the bandage on her forehead. "You hit your head. That's where all the blood is from." She turned Sophie's chin to look for more blood. "You're not hurt anywhere else?"

"N-no. I wanted the money to help pay off Hamre's boat, and the man fired me, just like that."

"I know. I know." Mrs. Soderstrum set her charge down on a chair and took off her coat and scarf. "Let me fix a cup of tea, and that will make both of us feel better. Can you get your boots off?"

"Y-yes." Sophie bent over and started to unlace her boots, then groaned. "Oh, my head."

"Keep your head down and relax." She laid a hand on Sophie's back. "Perhaps this is for the best. That was not a good job for a young woman who is carrying a baby. Not clean enough and smelly. No, I'm sure this is for the best. There will be another job. I know it might not pay as well, but you know that God will always light a way." Talking all the while, she bustled around, setting out cookies and fixing the teapot for when the water boiled.

Sophie kept her eyes closed as she slowly straightened again. She couldn't even take her boots off. She ignored the throbbing in her head. At least she could tell the difference between pain and wooziness.

"Just leave the boots, and let's get something hot in you. That will help more than anything."

"Did you get sick like this?"

"Somewhat. But my sister was puking for months. She swore she'd never have more children."

"Did she?"

"Nine and was sick with every other one." Mrs. Soderstrum knelt to remove Sophie's boots.

"You're teasing me."

"No, I tell the truth on a stack of Bibles. My older sister had nary a trouble. Sometimes we hated her for it. Well, not really. But then two of her little ones died of the diphtheria. Babies have a hard time of it in the winters—all the dampness, you know."

Sophie stared down at the part in Mrs. Soderstrum's hair. Babies did die. What if her baby died? Mor had buried two children, and Ingeborg's baby was born too soon to even bury. She laid a hand over her belly. Not Hamre's baby. And it would be born while Hamre was at home from the Alaskan fishing waters. *I wish I could see the look on his face when he reads my letter. I promise you, Hamre, I'll be different when you come home. I will be a good mother and a good wife. You wait and see.* She wrapped both arms around her middle, fighting weariness so intense she let her head fall forward.

❧

Sunlight woke her the next morning. "Oh, I'm late." She threw back the covers before remembering the defeat of the day before and then sank back down on the bed. She had no job to go to. After using the necessary she climbed back in bed, sat a moment, and slid back out again. So far so good; no morning sickness. After dressing, she made her way downstairs and into the kitchen.

"Well, you are looking so much better, dear. A good sleep is one of the best restoratives. Breakfast is in the warming oven. You sit down and I'll bring it."

"No bacon or sausage."

"No. Oatmeal and toast for you. I figured that might be the best. The coffee is hot if you want to start with that."

Sophie shook her head. Just the thought of coffee made her grimace. After breakfast and straightening her room, including hanging up her clothes from the day before, she sat down to write a letter to her family, telling them the good news. At least she hoped they'd think it good news. When her eyes refused to stay open any longer, she climbed back in bed and fell into a deep slumber.

"Dear Sophie," Mrs. Soderstrum whispered.

She woke to her landlady shaking her gently. "What? Is it dinnertime already?" She rubbed her eyes and stretched, catching a yawn on the way.

"No. You slept through dinner. But dear, you have a visitor."

"Oh, I must look a sight. Who is it?" She threw back the covers and sat up with her feet over the edge. Already that too-familiar feeling was overriding her pleasure. "Oh no. I thought this was supposed to be morning sickness!" Instead of fighting it, she leaned over the basin and heaved until she had no more to give up.

Mrs. Soderstrum handed her a damp cloth. "You lie down again, and I will bring her up here."

"I . . ." Sophie swallowed and closed her eyes. Surely this too would pass. She heard the two women talking as they mounted the stairs. How rude of her to not go downstairs to meet her visitor, but the lassitude made even sitting up difficult. At least she had combed her hair that morning.

"I'm sorry to bother you, Mrs. Bjorklund, but—"

"No, I am sorry not to come down to greet you. My first visitor and here I am lying in bed." She smiled at Mrs. Jorgeson, the captain's wife, but the smile died at the sight of reddened eyes and nose. Fear wrapped icy fingers around her throat. "Something is wrong. Tell me."

"A boat returned from Alaska. The *Sea Lily* went down in a terrible storm." Her voice broke and she blinked back the tears that brimmed over. "There were no survivors. I'm so sorry to bring such terrible news."

Sophie stared at her. No survivors. Surely not. The *Sea Lily* was a strong boat. Hamre always said Captain Jorgeson was the best captain around. "It cannot be. Surely there is some mistake."

"If only it could be so, but . . ."

"No. I won't believe it."

Mrs. Jorgeson turned to Mrs. Soderstrum, who took Sophie in her arms and let her cry against her shoulder. "I'll let myself out. I have another call to make. I am so sorry for your loss."

"Wait. How can you know for sure?" Sophie wiped her eyes with her fingertips.

"They would never bring us news like this unless it was true. They would wait." She turned and headed for the door, her shoulders curved as the weight of her burden wore her down.

Sophie cried herself to sleep, woke in the night, and cried again, trying to stifle the sound so she wouldn't wake the other boarders. The next time she woke, she found Mrs. Soderstrum asleep in the chair by her bed. The rustling of the covers as she got up to use the pot woke the older woman.

"I'm sorry to wake you."

"No, I need to go back to my bed. I heard you crying in your sleep."

Sophie's eyes brimmed again. "I can't believe he is really gone."

"I know. It doesn't seem possible. But in the fishing trade, these things happen. Must have been a terrible storm."

"I never said good-bye." Sophie could hardly speak the words.

"I know, I know. None do."

Sophie shook her head, the burden of her sorrow slowing the motion. "The night before he left—" she sniffed and wiped her nose— "I wanted him to stay home. I thought he wouldn't leave me. . . ." A hiccup caught her. "I was so mad, I just went to bed and fell asleep before he came to bed. I was hateful and . . ." Her voice dropped to a whisper, strangled by sobs. "Hamre, you can't leave me. You have to come back." *So I can tell you how sorry I am. God, why would you do such a thing? You didn't have to let this happen.*

"Shh. Hush. He knew that you loved him. All married people have fights at times, but that doesn't mean we love any the less."

"But he wasn't fighting. He just looked at me like I was the greatest disappointment of his life. He didn't want me to come west with him, but

I talked him into it. He wanted to wait like my father said." Hope had tucked tail and run, leaving her voice thready. She sank back against the pillow and turned her face away, letting the persistent tears wet her pillow.

When she slept, nightmares of towering waves threatened to swamp her, jerking her awake to cough and choke as if she'd inhaled the seas. She fell asleep again and slept round the clock.

Only in sleep was there surcease from the pain. Often, she woke crying for her mother and Grace.

This time she awoke to Mrs. Soderstrum shaking her shoulder again. "Come, Sophie, you must get some nourishment in you, or you'll be sick. You could even lose the babe."

Sophie stared around the room, as if searching for something she couldn't see. "Hamre?"

"Ah, poor child, he—"

"He's gone." She covered her eyes with her hands, letting the tears leak between her fingers. "I-I'm not hungry."

"Yes you are. And thirsty. Here, drink this." She handed her a cup. "It is only warm water. Drink it down."

Sophie took a sip and gagged. "I can't."

"You can or I will call a doctor."

"No!" She shook her head. "Just let me be."

"Do you want to let that baby die?"

"No, of course not. I—"

"Then drink." Mrs. Soderstrum held the cup to Sophie's lips. "And then you will eat this toast, and if that stays down, I will bring up a poached egg. I have a chicken stewing so you can have chicken broth. You have to have liquid and nourishment to keep your baby growing."

Sophie drank a couple of swallows and started to push the cup away, but drank again instead.

"There's a girl." The older woman took the cup back and set the plate with toast and honey on the bed. "If you scoot up, I'll stack the pillows behind you. Will be more comfortable."

Sophie did as told, as anything else took far more effort than she could find. *Hamre, oh, Hamre.* She gagged on the first bite of toast but chewed anyway, taking small bites and chewing them to a mush that slid down easily. When she'd finished half a slice, her head fell back against the pillows. "I can't eat any more."

"That was good for now. Can I get you anything else?"

"No thank you." *Unless you could work a miracle and bring my mor here.* Her eyes drifted closed before Mrs. Soderstrum made it to the door.

Go away! She kept from screaming the words, or even whispering them, with the greatest effort.

Later, opening her eyes, she saw afternoon sun on the floor.

"They say I make the best chicken soup, so I brought more than just the broth. You got to feed that baby. Remember?" Mrs. Soderstrum set her tray down. "You sit up and I'll put this across your lap. I'll take out the pot and bring you back some warm water. Washing will help you feel a hundred percent better, and then I'll brush your hair. My sisters and I used to brush each other's hair, and it always felt so nice. There's nothing like having someone else do it for you."

Gritting her teeth against the onslaught of words, Sophie did as she was told and realized her landlady was right. She did make good chicken soup. Sophie had cleaned the bowl before Mrs. Soderstrum returned with a clean pot and a pitcher of hot water.

"There you go." Mrs. Soderstrum stuck the chamber pot in the cabinet and poured the water into the bowl on top of the stand. "Will you wash? Or I can help you."

"I'll do it."

"Good. Then I'll be back to brush your hair. If you feel faint, sit down quick."

"I will." Sophie sighed. While her stomach felt better, the thought of getting out of bed made her sigh again. She watched as Mrs. Soderstrum picked up the tray and left the room. She didn't deserve anyone being so good to her. When she stood and looked in the mirror, she almost didn't recognize herself. Her hair was knotted and flying every which way, her face gaunt with black half-moons under listless eyes. Her skin looked nearly as white as the sheets she'd climbed from, except for the bruise around the bandage on her forehead. But what did it matter? Hamre would never come up behind her, never slide his hands around her waist and draw her back into the safe haven of his solid chest. Tears streaked down her cheeks as she dipped the washcloth in the cooling water and buried her face in the wet warmth. *Oh, God, I cannot bear this.*

I will never leave thee nor forsake thee. She turned around, searching for the voice that spoke those words. No one else was in the room. That's all her baby needed—a crazy mother. Already it had no father. It. Her baby was not an it. He or she. She needed to choose two names, one of each kind. Now that was something that bore thinking on.

She finished washing and drew clean underclothes from her drawer. Was she planning on getting dressed? No. But a clean nightdress would feel wonderful. She slid the flannel gown over her head and settled the bands around her wrists. Her hair, now that was another matter.

Mrs. Soderstrum bustled back in. "I brought clean sheets. I thought we might as well remake your bed while you are out of it. My, don't you look better. Even a bit of color back in your cheeks."

"I'm sorry to be such trouble."

"No trouble. You'd do the same, I'm sure." She pulled the blanket and quilt off the bed, then the sheets. Together they tucked the clean sheets under the mattress and finished making the bed, Mrs. Soderstrum plumping the pillows after donning clean cases and stepping back with her hands on her ample hips. "Now you sit down on that bench, and while I brush your hair, you tell me about what life was like growing up a twin."

The more she told, the more she wanted to go home. "Sometimes I miss Grace so much. . . ." The thought of missing Grace brought on the tears of missing Hamre. Ignoring the tugs as Mrs. Soderstrum worked the tangles out of her hair, she closed her eyes and pictured Grace doing the job instead, tsking at the rats' nests, as she called them, scolding Sophie for not taking better care of herself. She saw Grace signing to the deaf students, her hands patiently forming the symbols so they could learn to talk. Grace was already a fine teacher, so full of love for her pupils that they strove hard to please her.

"There you go. Do you have a ribbon to tie off the end of this braid?"

Sophie dug in the carved wooden box that had been in the trunk her mother sent. Onkel Olaf had made it, and Ellie gave it to her for Christmas one year. "Here." She handed over a white ribbon.

Mrs. Soderstrum hummed a tune as she finished the loose braid, weaving the ribbon in with the sections of hair. "You have such lovely hair. Does Grace look just like you?"

"No, her hair is as fair as mine is dark. She's more slender, like a reed that bends in the wind. Our faces are similar, but her eyes are gray and more dreamy. Grace was born deaf, yet she learned sign language, which we all learned, and she also learned to speak. She worked so hard to be like everyone else. My sister is the bravest and kindest person I know."

Mrs. Soderstrum stepped back. "There now. Why, I do see a trace of that spunky Sophie I met a few months ago."

Sophie nodded and sighed again. Exhaustion settled on her like a Seattle fog, so thick she almost felt she was breathing in the dense mist.

"I think I need to go back to bed." Her stomach was picking up the morning nasties again. As she settled in, she thought, *I wonder if Tante Ingeborg has something to help me feel better? Or Dr. Elizabeth?*

❧

What would happen if I went home? The thought jarred her awake for the second time the next morning. The first she'd spent with her head over the basin again in spite of the dried bread Mrs. Soderstrum had left for her on the nightstand.

Mor had already written and said she could come home for the winter until Hamre came back from fishing. Surely Grace would want her home; she had written at least, even though the letter was so stilted. But Far? He had not written her a line nor sent a message by either of the other two. Somehow she knew that was where the trouble lay. But they didn't know that Hamre had died. First things first. She took out paper and pen and wrote the briefest of notes, her tears splashing blots on the ink.

"I'm going to the store. Do you need anything?" Mrs. Soderstrom asked from the doorway.

"Just mail this for me, please." She handed off the envelope. "Thank you."

When she heard the front door close, she went back to contemplating what to do. "So I won't go home, er . . . back to Blessing.

My room here is paid until Hamre returns or would have been return-ing." Her voice caught. Spring would come, but Hamre would not return. She stared at the ceiling. If I stay here, I need to find work of some kind for as long as I am able. I can sew, though I'm not the best at it, or teach or clean houses. The last I can do just fine but don't much like it. I could care for someone's children, but how would I explain that I was getting fatter because of the babe I carry? I enjoyed working in Tante Penny's store. I can read well and do sums. Surely there must be a store that needs a good worker.

After two days of visiting every store of every ilk, even a ship's chandler, where they sold shipping goods, all she had was aching feet and a runny nose. No one required a young woman who, while she claimed to have worked in a cheese house, a general store, and a board-inghouse, had no proof and who, in one case, had to run to vomit before she could talk again. She forced herself to hike up the hill to the boardinghouse, stopping to lean against light posts and trees ever more frequently. After three stops on the stairs to her room, she flung herself across the bed and slept until the supper bell.

༄

The next day she packed all of her belongings into a trunk, drew the pouch of money from the back of the chifforobe, and announced she was going back to Blessing on the morning train.

"Much as I'm going to miss you, I do believe you are making a good choice." Mrs. Soderstrum dabbed at a tear. "Having you here has been such a blessing for me. You are almost the daughter I never had." She hugged Sophie close. "Will you telegraph your folks?"

"No. Someone there will take me in."

"I'll pack a basket of food for you."

༄

But the rocking of the train forbade her to eat any of the things packed, and Sophie made visit after visit to the necessary, where the stench made her even sicker. The wheels clacked off the minutes, and the piston drove past the hours as the train headed east, each turn taking her closer to Blessing and home . . . if Far would let her come home.

As she drifted in and out of consciousness, she vaguely remembered a woman with a black hat and feather encouraging her to drink water and a woman wearing purple who fed her crackers and held her head when she lost them—at least she thought the two women were real. Perhaps not.

"I've telegraphed ahead to the doctor in Blessing, miss."

Had the conductor said that, or did her mind make it up? She had made herself a nuisance to everyone on the train. It seemed something she was good at. She'd been a nuisance to Hamre the night before he left. . . .

"Can you stand, miss?" A man in uniform, but not the same man as before.

"I-I don't know." Sophie opened her eyes enough to realize the train was no longer rocking. "Where . . . ?"

"We are at the Blessing station. Let me help you off."

"Ja, help me off." But when he helped pull her to her feet, she swayed, and he caught her before she fell. "Sorry."

"That's all right. We get you the help you need."

Sophie clung to his neck as he picked her up and descended the steps to the platform. Had he said Blessing? How would she make it home from the train station?

She felt strong arms reach for her, saw the Bjorklund blue eyes above her. Hamre? Hamre with such beautiful blue eyes. Everything would be all right now. "Hamre."

20

"MOR, YOU CAME FOR ME." Sophie tried to sit up. Relief made her dizzy. *Mor is here. All will be well.*

"No, dear child, you came home on the train. Don't you remember?" Kaaren smoothed her daughter's hair back. "You've been here at Elizabeth's for two days."

"Hamre—he carried me here." Sophie's heart leaped. "Tell him I'm here. I must see him . . . tell him I didn't mean . . ." She clutched her mother's hand.

"No, Sophie, Thorliff carried you here. The conductor carried you off the train." Kaaren held a cup to her mouth. "Drink this."

Sophie did as her mother ordered. *Hamre won't be here. He's gone.* Reality stabbed her with deadly accuracy. She had no strength to fight the tears. When she could speak again, she asked, "Where's Grace?"

"She has been here off and on. She's at school now."

Sophie lay back in the bed. "I was really sick on the train. Some women took care of me, I think. It is all so confusing."

"We got the letter two days ago, Sophie. I am so sorry. Hamre was a fine man." Kaaren took her daughter in her arms as the tears flowed again. "You wrote the date in the letter. Grace knew. That day she wanted to get on the train and go to you. She said something terrible had happened."

Sophie mopped her eyes. "The captain's wife came to tell me. There

170

were no survivors." The bleak words lay where they fell. "I thought my world had ended. Hamre gone. Fired from my job. Pregnant."

"Pregnant? You are with child?" Kaaren's face bloomed with joy.

"You did not get my letter? I wrote and told you, before the letter about Hamre."

"No, that one did not come. Oh, Sophie, no wonder you were so sick on the train. Did you have much morning sickness?"

"Morning sickness? I get sick any time of day or night." Sophie lay back against the pillows, her eyes closing, too weary to keep awake. "I don't remember you being so sick with either of the boys."

"I wasn't, for which I have always been grateful. The two of you were another matter."

"Oh."

"This will pass."

"I hope so. The thought of months of this makes me want to run screaming." *Or throw myself under the wheels of the train.* Down in her middle, it started again, the roiling that worked its way up to her throat. She swallowed, hoping she could calm down before erupting again. Sometimes she succeeded but not this time. "Excuse me." She pushed to the side of the bed and reached for the basin Elizabeth had placed there for her.

Kaaren held the pan with one hand and smoothed her daughter's hair back with the other. When the spasms passed, she handed Sophie a warm, wrung-out cloth to wipe her face. "Have you kept anything down since you got here?"

"I don't know. But there was nothing in my stomach to heave out."

"I'll bring some tea and toast. That sits better than most anything else."

"Thank you." Ah, the pleasure of her mother's voice, the cool hand, the warm hug. Sophie slipped back into the gray land that she wasn't sure was sleep or imagination. Either way, her body felt better when her mother returned with a tray holding two cups of tea and a plate of toast.

"Tante Ingeborg sent this?" She had already swallowed three bites and some tea before talking.

"How did you know?"

"Her bread tastes different, that's all."

"I think you are imagining things. We use the same receipt."

"I can tell." Sophie choked on the words, then inhaled and breathed out a sigh. "Mor, this isn't the way life is supposed to happen." She wiped her tears, knowing that fighting them was futile.

"I know."

"What am I going to do?"

"You could go back to school."

"With child?" She stared at her mother, shaking her head all the while.

"No, I suppose not." It was Kaaren's turn to sigh. "I will bring the sleigh back this afternoon so you can come home. Or perhaps I'll have Grace bring it, and she'll bring you home."

Sophie studied her fingertips. The silence stretched like a spider's web caught on the breeze. Finally she voiced the words that were screaming in her head. "What about Pa?"

"What about him?"

"He . . . he never wrote. Does he hate me?" The words tumbled over each other, fleeing those coming behind. "Has he come to see me?"

Kaaren shook her head. "No, he doesn't hate you."

"But?"

"But your running away like that after he gave what he thought was a wise answer hurt him. Though he doesn't say much, he feels deeply. Kind of like the river. It seems placid on the surface, but there can be deep holes and whirlpools."

"I told him I was sorry in my letter."

"I know. Sometimes sorry isn't enough, though."

"All I could think of was Hamre. I thought surely I would die if Hamre left me behind." Her tears flowed through her fingers. *And I wanted an adventure. Now Hamre has left me forever.*

"I know. Young love can be so impetuous, but sometimes there are pieces to pick up later."

"Like now? Here I am, seventeen, a widow with a baby on the way. I could only think of coming home. Maybe I can't do that either."

"Have you prayed about it?"

Sophie returned to studying her fingers. How to answer that? She'd prayed all right, prayed that she would get here before she died on the train. Before that, she'd prayed about what to do, and home seemed the only answer. If you could call *God, help me* a real prayer. Had she been down on her knees praying? No. Had she been desperate? Yes. And who else was there?

"I've prayed, but not about what to do once I got here. I guess I figured everything would go back to the way it has always been." *At least that's what I suppose I was thinking.* "Actually, I didn't think beyond seeing you again."

Kaaren blinked a couple of times quickly and sniffed. "I am so sorry for all you have lost."

"D-don't say things like that. It just makes me cry again. I wake in the night and think it was all a nightmare, and then when day comes, I know it is true. Hamre is gone." She shook her head. "And he will never know his baby. I don't even know if he got my letter. I doubt it. They didn't go ashore very often. Mor, how am I going to raise a baby?"

"I don't know right now, but there will be a way."

A pain pounded her heart at the words. If her mother didn't know what to do . . . *All I want to do is go home and forget all this that has happened. But what do I say to Far?*

"Grace will come for you. Do you need help getting dressed?"

"Just with the back buttons. Most of my things are in the trunk. I hope it got off the train when I did." Sophie sighed. "Everything is so complicated." *And I don't really want to be back here. I don't want to be pregnant. I don't want to be a widow. I want Hamre and the life we were just starting.* She finally forced herself to look at her mother. "How did you get here?"

"Trygve dropped me off and then took the others on to school in the sleigh. Thorliff said he would take me home."

"Can't I go with you?"

"If you want. I just thought you and Grace . . ."

"We'll talk tonight." Sophie swung her feet out from under the covers and started to stand.

"So you think you're well enough to leave and follow the doctor's orders?" Elizabeth stopped in the doorway. "I think you'd better eat before you try to get dressed."

Sophie stood and immediately sat down again, blinking away the dizziness. "How did you know?"

"Remember, I've had a baby too, even though I didn't get as sick as you have. But then I'd not been hit with all the tragedy you have either. I'll have Thelma bring you some soup. You kept down the toast and tea?"

"Yes."

"Then soup it is." Elizabeth crossed to the bed and took Sophie's wrist to count her pulse. "No fever?" She looked to Kaaren.

"Not that I can tell."

"How many monthlies have you missed?"

"One for sure, perhaps two. I wasn't paying attention." Sophie battled back the thoughts of Hamre and their evenings together. Never again would he hold her close or whisper in her ear, tickling the hair around it with his breath. She closed her eyes and fought the battle inside.

"Sophie, listen to me." Elizabeth tipped up her chin with a loving finger. "Crying it out is far easier on you than battling back the tears. Tears are healing. Fighting them just makes you hard and bitter. And hard and bitter is not good for your baby. That baby needs to grow in love, surrounded by all the love you have to give."

"Amen to that." Kaaren laid her daughter's clothes on the bed. "You knew you needed home, and that was wise. I'll go get the soup myself."

What if Pa doesn't want me? If only she could keep her thoughts at bay.

"Bring a bowl for yourself too." Elizabeth cocked her head. "Oh-oh. I hear Inga. I'll bring her in here and feed her while you two eat. That way we can visit longer."

"You have other patients waiting?"

"Yes, but Inga comes first, or the entire town will think I've been beating her."

Sophie smiled back. Her stomach rumbled, making them all smile more widely. "It is so hard to believe that I really have a baby growing inside me." The tears simmered again. *Hamre will never know his son or daughter.*

"You'll believe it as soon as your clothes are too tight. Once this morning sickness is past, you'll feel really good, I hope. Most women do. God designed us to carry babies, and we do it well. Then once you are close to term, you'll feel like a tub with feet." She rolled her eyes as a wail came from the nursery. "Be right back."

Later, as the sleigh with Sophie and Kaaren bundled under the warm robes stopped at the Knutson house, Sophie closed her eyes, holding her mother's hand tightly. She was home, yet not home. Her father held the key to the future in his hands.

"Easy now." Thorliff helped her from the sleigh and kept her arm tucked in his on the way up the steps.

"Thank you," she whispered when he stepped back at the door.

"You take care," he whispered back. "It's going to come out all right." He squeezed her hand as he looked into her eyes. "Many are praying for you."

She nodded, tears clogging her throat again.

He headed back to the sleigh with a wave.

"Bye, Thorliff," Kaaren called. "And thank you."

Sophie shut the door behind her and stared around the kitchen. Nothing had changed. The big cookstove, shiny as ever, took up one wall. Braided rugs on the dark brown-painted wooden floor, yellow-and-white gingham curtains in the windows, a pot of red geraniums on the windowsill. But the smell was what she had remembered in her dreams of home. It had to be apple pies that lined a shelf, ready for supper. The nutmeg and cinnamon mingled with smoke from the kerosene lamps, a tang of woodsmoke, and surely there must be molasses-ginger cookies in the jar. They'd had bacon for breakfast, and bread had been baked either this morning or yesterday. Home—she breathed it in, allowing the fragrances to soothe her soul.

"Are you all right?" Kaaren had removed her coat and hat and was donning her apron.

"Ja, I am. Where's Ilse?"

"In the schoolroom. We have three new students who are still learning to sign so they can go to school with the others."

A wave of weariness washed over Sophie as she hung her coat on the peg and crossed the room to sit down in the rocker. "Where's Pa?"

"Most likely down at the machine shed. He and George are doing something to the tractor."

"Does he know I am home?"

Kaaren shook her head. "I didn't know if you'd be able to come."

At least he didn't say I couldn't. Sophie knew she was searching for comfort anywhere she could find it. Surely her pa wasn't the kind who would throw his pregnant daughter out. She heard the jingle of the harness and boys laughing as the schoolchildren arrived. Samuel and Trygve did manage to make a lot of noise considering the others were silent.

When the students filed in, they smiled at her and went to their rooms to put their things away. Samuel burst through the door. "Mor?" He slid to a halt, staring at Sophie. "You're home."

Sophie nodded. What do you say to your little brother after all that had gone on? Samuel looked an awful lot like Hamre. She'd never noticed that before.

"You talked to Pa?"

"Not yet. We just got here." *Please, Samuel, look happy to see me.*

"I wouldn't want to be in your shoes. Where's Ma?"

"She was here a minute ago. I don't know."

He headed to the counter for the crock with the fitted wooden lid and took out four ginger cookies. "You want one?" He almost smiled.

"Yes, please."

He handed her one, and they took bites at the same time.

"My favorite."

"I know. You haven't been gone that long." He handed her another cookie and headed for the stairs to change clothes. "You helping us milk tonight?" he called over his shoulder.

Sophie sighed. One down. But where was Grace?

Trygve came through the door, saw her, and looking the other way, headed for the stairs, his shoulders rigid, his boots heavy on the stairs.

Sophie left the haven of her chair and crossed the kitchen to put wood in the cookstove. She wasn't a guest, and she'd better pitch in to help—or go upstairs and not come down again. "Where's Grace?" she asked Samuel when he came back down in his barn overalls.

"She went home with Astrid. They were going to Dr. Elizabeth's to visit you."

"Why didn't you tell me?"

"You didn't ask." He grabbed another handful of cookies and headed out the door.

When Grace finally came through the door, Sophie was sitting on a chair by the stove peeling potatoes. She looked up with a smile that died as Grace stared back at her. Sophie could feel the tears forming, burning the back of her eyes. She rolled her lips together, blinked, and sniffed. Laying the knife down, she rose slowly to her feet. She tried to speak, but no words would come. Clearing her throat, she tried again. "I-I'm sorry, Grace. I . . ."

Grace's tears were welling to match Sophie's. The two took three steps each and met in each other's arms, needing no more words. Kaaren came and wrapped her arms around both of them with mother murmurings as familiar and soothing as the heat of a fire on a cold night.

"Are you all right?" Grace spoke carefully, around her tears.

Sophie nodded. "For right now."

"Good." She tapped Sophie's wrist three times, their signal for talk later.

When Sophie carried the bread and butter into the dining room, she checked to make sure everything was the same as when she'd left—the schoolroom on the other side, sofas and chairs around the stove, lamps on the small tables where everyone gathered in the evening, Mor's spinning wheels, the shelves and baskets of wool to be carded, wool to be spun, and yarn for knitting. All of the girls who came to the school were required to learn the steps of wool preparation and knitting, plus how to use the sewing machines in the sewing room. After supper the long table would change into a desk for doing homework. One of the boys was starting a fire in the fireplace. He looked up and smiled at her. She turned at the sound of someone coming down the stairway against the wall that led to the bedrooms upstairs.

Later, when they were gathered for supper around the oversized table, Sophie took her old place next to Grace. This year they only had ten students in the school and only three of them new. The smallest of the girls sat between Ilse and her husband, George, who'd been one of the first students at the school for the deaf.

Please, Pa, at least look at me. I don't care if you say anything or not, but look at me. Afraid to be the first to say something, knowing that if he didn't respond, she would run from the table and hide in the bed, Sophie did her best to fit in. She smiled at Trygve, who had been copying his father's actions. Samuel had patted her shoulder as he walked past and given her a smile that made her heart glad.

Far looked older, the lines carved deeper in his cheeks, the furrows in his forehead more pronounced. And did he not stand quite as straight either? *Pa, look at me.* She wanted to say it, but the saucy nerve that used to make him laugh had died, along with her heart, in Seattle. After supper she helped Grace clear the table, and two of the students did the dishes.

That evening by the time she and Grace climbed the stairs to their room, her far still had not even looked at her. Once they were in their nightdresses, they sat cross-legged on the bed facing each other.

"I never meant to hurt you," Sophie said, clutching her sister's hands. "Not Ma and Pa either. I am so sorry. Can you forgive me?"

"I already have." Grace held Sophie's hand to her cheek. "I knew something terrible happened."

"Mor told me."

"And I knew you were happy. When you got sad, I knew it."

Sophie nodded. "Did you know I'm pregnant?"

Grace shook her head. "Oh Sophie, that's why my stomach was upset."

"Really?"

Grace nodded. "Really."

The two stared at each other, until Sophie grinned. "I hope you've not been puking like me."

"Ah, Grace . . ." Sophie shook her head and caught a yawn. "I am so tired."

"Go to sleep. We can talk tomorrow." Grace leaned forward and hugged her sister, then pulled back the covers and blew out the lamp while Sophie crawled into bed with a deep sigh.

Grace had forgiven her. They fell asleep with their arms around each other, just as they had when infants.

⬿⬿

Sophie woke to a quiet house and an empty bed. How had they all gotten off to school and she had never heard a peep? She turned over cautiously and waited. Amazingly, she felt well, so she sat up and wrapped the quilt around her. The grate in the hall brought up warm air from the furnace that roared in the cellar. Far and Haakan had put coal-burning furnaces in each of the houses the year before, so they no longer dressed by the stove in the kitchen. Even so, there was frost on the inside of the window. The sun set the ice fronds to glittering. Sun when she woke up in the morning. Now having it back, she realized how much she had missed that in Seattle. When the sun shone there, it had to be the most beautiful place on all the earth, but the gray days far outnumbered the sunny ones, and rarely had she awoken to sun pouring in her window.

She chose a looser fitting dress that she could button the back by herself and, after brushing her hair, made her way downstairs. Her mother and Ilse would be in the classroom teaching the new students to sign, along with reading and writing. Few had had any schooling before coming to the deaf school, and the first year here was mostly catch-up classes for them so they could soon attend the regular school, where all the students and teachers signed right along with regular speech.

She cut herself a couple slices of bread and toasted them on the rack over the open flame of the kitchen stove. A pleasant aroma came from some kind of stew cooking in the oven for the noon meal. For a change, the smell didn't make her feel sick, a regular occurrence in Seattle. Why did she feel so much better today? The toast, along with cheese cut off the small round under the clear glass dome, and a dish of applesauce made a fine breakfast. And the sun shining on her shoulder as she sat in her mother's rocker made it all complete. Contentment. What a good feeling.

If only Hamre . . . The thought slapped contentment like a cat on a mouse. Tears trickled down her cheeks. So many *what if*s and *might* *have been*s. If only she had kissed him good-bye. Instead, she had acted like a small child, stamping her foot for not getting her own way. *How . . . how could I have acted so? I knew he had to leave. He'd told me over and over. He was a fisherman at heart and never as happy as he was on a boat on the sea. I knew that.*

The tears poured harder. She leaned her head against the back of the rocker and let the sobs take over.

"Ah, dear heart." Her mother's voice came softly, as gentle as the hand on her head.

"Oh, Mor, I cannot tell you how terrible I acted. You would be so ashamed of me." She took the handkerchief offered and, after blowing her nose, wiped her eyes.

Kaaren pulled up another chair and took her daughter's hands. "Just tell me and get it over with. They say confession is good for the soul."

Sophie stumbled over the first part of the story, and then it gained strength in spite of the tears she had to keep wiping. "You see, I failed him so terribly. And there is nothing I can do about it now."

Kaaren continued stroking Sophie's hands, except when she had to dab at her own tears. "Losing someone you love is always terribly hard, but when you add guilt to that, the burden becomes unbearable. Remember God's Word: 'If we confess our sins, he is faithful and just to forgive us our sins, and to cleanse us from all unrighteousness.' You memorized that years ago, and God never changes."

"But I let Hamre down. He would have waited the year that Far asked, but I pushed him into taking me."

"We guessed that."

"And then I blamed him for leaving me." She stared into her mother's eyes. "And I can't ever ask him to forgive me."

"I know, but you can ask God. And He will. And since Hamre believed in Jesus, he is standing now with all the heavenly hosts, and there is no lack of love or forgiveness there."

"Oh, Mor, are you sure?"

"As sure as I see you sitting here." Kaaren used the corner of her apron to wipe Sophie's face again. "You know to read your Bible and spend time praying."

Sophie sniffed and stared at her hands clasped in her mother's. "Not like you do."

"No, because you lived on our faith. You haven't all the years of experience. I could not make it through a normal day, let alone all the hard places like this, without the comfort and the instruction I find in His Word and trusting that it is true."

Sophie shook her head slowly from side to side. "You say God forgives me and that Hamre has, but what about Far?"

"I can't answer for him. You will have to go to him and ask. Tell him the truth and ask for his forgiveness."

"I'm afraid. What if he doesn't love me anymore?"

Kaaren looked up at the sound of sleigh bells. "We have company." She rose and went to look out the window. "Why, what a surprise! It's Bridget and Henry in Thorliff's sleigh."

"I must look a sight." But finding the energy to rise and wash her face took more than Sophie had to give. When she tried to stand, her knees felt like unset jelly, and she sat back down. All she wanted to do was go back to bed, crawl under the covers, and sleep, for in sleep there were no memories and harsh realities. Instead, she smoothed her hair back and used her apron to dry her face.

"Come in, come in. What a wonderful surprise. Just leave the horse there for now. He might like a bit of the sun too."

"We can't stay long. Dinnertime will be here before you know it." Bridget, her cheeks bright red in the cold and her eyes sparkling like the sun on the snow, let Henry help her out of the sleigh. "Bring in the bricks too. I'm sure Kaaren will warm them in the oven."

"Of course." Kaaren went down the steps to help the older woman up.

"I have come to see Sophie."

"She's right in the kitchen." At the top of the step Kaaren turned to the gray-haired man. "Hello, Henry. Welcome." As they stepped inside, she held out her arms. "Here, let me take your coats."

They both hustled over to the stove and rubbed their hands in the rising heat.

"That sun sure is deceptive. Looks so warm, but the wind has a bite. Feels like another blizzard coming on." Henry was known for his accurate weather predictions.

"So we enjoy the sun while we can. You have to admit this has been a rather easy winter so far." Kaaren hung up their coats, scarves, and hats. "Sit down here, and Bridget, you talk with Sophie while I fix something to go with the coffee."

"Welcome home, my dear." Bridget took the chair with a sigh. "I've come to ask for your help."

"Mine?" Sophie laid a hand against her throat.

"Ja, yours. I need more help with the boardinghouse, and I think you need a job." She turned to Kaaren. "Unless she is going back to school?"

"Ask her." Kaaren looked up from cutting squares of eggekake, a yellow cake with creamy frosting.

"I don't think Pastor would want a woman with child back in the schoolroom."

"Ah, I see. And from the pale look I see about your eyes, you are still feeling poorly?"

Sophie nodded. "Although today I feel better."

"Because you are home where your Mor can take care of you." Henry smiled at Sophie. "We are so sorry to hear about Hamre. He grew up to be a fine young man."

"Ja." Bridget shook her head with a sigh. "He looked so much like his grandfather Hamre, Gustaf's brother, I nearly choked when I saw him return from Seattle. He got his love of the sea from generations back."

"She's a hard mistress, that sea." Henry smiled when Kaaren handed him a cup of coffee on a saucer. "Mange takk."

"So, to go back to why we are here. Would you come work with me? I need help with the front desk—you know, making folks to feel to home—and with the bookwork especially. I just can't get up and down those stairs like I used to."

"You're an old woman, and I'm an older man. Saints be praised we hung on this long."

"Speak for yourself." She pushed at Henry's knee.

"Careful, you'll make me spill my coffee." He poured some in the saucer and blew on it before slurping it down.

Kaaren set a slice of cake in front of everyone and then took a seat herself.

"But what will you do when I start to show?"

"Why, we'll make you bigger dresses. You and the baby will have a room of your own, and you'll carry him or her in a sling like your mor did with you and Grace."

She has it all figured out. Sophie stared at the woman she'd known as Bestemor all her life, even though the relationship technically wasn't so. But since Kaaren had once been Bridget's daughter-in-law, that made her the honorary matriarch over all the families.

"Just say you will, Sophie, and we will go back and fix up a room just for you. I will love to have you close to hand."

Sophie sighed and nodded. "I will come. When?"

"Is tomorrow too soon?"

"She'd take you back with us today if you let her." Henry leaned forward and patted Sophie's hand. "A pretty face like yours is just what the boardinghouse needs. Always a sight for old eyes."

"But . . . but what about when I am sick in the morning?"

"We will work around that. Soon you will feel much better."

Henry laid his fork back on his plate. "Now we got that settled, we best be on our way."

"You could stay for dinner." Kaaren held up the coffeepot, the universal signal for refills.

"Nei, I'm needed to be home."

"She's just afraid Mrs. Sam might realize she can get along without her," Henry confided as he helped his wife to her feet. "You sure you don't want to come along with us now?"

Sophie thought a moment. *Uff da. How am I supposed to know what to do?*

21

"I WILL INTRODUCE YOU to all of our guests at supper."

Sophie felt like she was on an out-of-control buggy ride. Choosing to come in with Bridget and Henry rather than waiting until school was out to have Grace bring her to the boardinghouse had seemed the best decision at the time. The easiest for everyone. There hadn't been many guests for dinner, but that was the usual, Bridget had told her. Shortly after they had arrived, Henry had gone to their room for a nap, causing Bridget to check on him frequently in between fixing up Sophie's new room.

"You've made some changes since I left."

"That we have. Haakan and Lars, they took out a wall to make bigger the dining room. Since the flour mill got going, we have needed more room. We are talking about adding on another section. With more people living here in Blessing and around the area, we have more drummers passing through too."

Sophie knew drummers meant salesmen, not musicians. "You have a good reputation. They even knew the Bjorklund name in Seattle."

"Bjorklund cheese?"

"Ja, and people on the train knew of this boardinghouse. They said if you want a good meal, stay here."

"That is good." Bridget beamed. "I will show you how to register people."

"Like a hotel more than a boardinghouse."

"Ja, if you say so. They must write their name and home address and business, if they are on business. Some of the rooms are different prices; those are listed here in the front. We have three rooms that men can share if they want to go cheaper. This is the list of guests."

Sophie glanced down the list, seeing no names that she recognized. But then when she thought of it, she'd not paid a lot of attention to the boardinghouse last summer. "What do all these people do?"

"Mr. Vell, he is the barber. Mr. Wiste runs the flour mill, and these two work at the flour mill also. Miss Maisie Christopherson owns the Dress-Making Shop. She sews mostly ladies' dresses, but she makes some hats too. This one works for the railroad, and this man runs the grain elevator. Blessing is really growing, you know."

"Looks like it. In Ballard, at Mrs. Soderstrum's, she had one long table where everyone had their own place, not small tables like those in your dining room."

"Did you like that better?"

"I don't know about better, but you can pass the serving dishes from one person to another more easily."

"Ja. We are more restaurant style, but mostly we have too many for one long table. And everyone does not eat at the same time. We serve Mr. Wiste after eight every night, so we keep food warm for him. I think he has had some tragedy in his life. He never smiles."

"And the barber?"

"He closes his shop at six, so he can eat on time. He likes his meals nice and hot, that one."

"And Miss Christopherson?" While she asked the question, Sophie wondered what this woman looked like. She must be brave to come to a strange town and start her own business.

"The same. When Penny started closing her doors at six, the others followed suit. The Garrisons, who own the new grocery store, they got their house built, so they moved out a week or two ago. Andrew started something with his Sears and Roebuck house. There are three of them in town now."

Sophie tried to get all this information in her head, but all she could think on was that one man's tragedy. What could have happened to him? Tragedy she understood. *Ah, Hamre, if only . . .* She swallowed the thoughts and the tears. Right now she wanted a nap, something she could have had at home. Had she made another hasty decision she might come to regret?

They could hear the whistle of the westbound train, and the entire building shook as the train squealed to a stop just past the boardinghouse. Not long afterward two men came laughing through the doorway.

"Ah, Mrs. Aarsgard, it's hoping I am to have a room and a bath."

"Ja, Mr. O'Rourke, did you want a single or shared?"

"Single if you have one."

"This is my granddaughter, Mrs. Bjorklund. She will be helping you." She turned to Sophie. "Mr. O'Rourke is a regular."

"Welcome to Blessing Boarding House. I am pleased to meet you." Sophie could feel her knees trembling, along with her stomach. *Please don't start now.* She concentrated on what the man was saying.

"Ah, and a lovely lass like this would make any man feel welcome. Haven't I seen you before?"

"Most likely. My sister and I helped out here sometimes in the summers."

"Summer is good. That wind today nearly blew the train off the tracks, let alone us poor working men as we stepped off it. Dillingsworth here, I had to grab him by the ankles to keep him from flying away."

Sophie handed him a pen. "You need to sign here."

"You already have my address."

"Perhaps so, but if you will fill it in again, that will make it easier." *Please don't give me an argument.* If her face was turning as pale as she feared and her stomach kept churning, she might have to leave in a hurry.

"Easier for who?"

"Now don't you go giving her a bad time. Just because she is young and pretty, don't make her up to your jokes." Bridget scolded him like he was one of her own kin.

Now Sophie did almost smile as the man took a step back and sketched a bow.

"I beg pardon, miss."

"Mrs."

"Aye. I thought perhaps I misheard, Mrs. Bjorklund." His right eyebrow cocked in a way that said surely she must be joking. "I thought both of the Bjorklund boys were already married."

"Sophie married my great-nephew," Bridget informed him.

"Ah, now I remember. You are one of the Knutson twins." He smiled at Bridget. "She has grown into a lovely young woman, hasn't she?"

"Uff da, the way you go on." Bridget rolled her eyes at him, and he smiled in response.

Sophie might have laughed had she felt able. She flipped to the front of the book to check the room rates. "You will be staying how long?"

"Only overnight this time. Just needed to get me a fill of good fare. You have no idea how bad some of the food is when you're a traveling man." He leaned an elbow on the desktop. "That's why I tell all my friends about the Blessing Boarding House. Dillingsworth came because I recommended it. Right, my friend?"

"Ja, if his blarney can be believed."

"Blarney?" Sophie asked, pushing the registration book toward him.

"It's Irish for blather."

"Blather?"

"You know, friendly talking like we been doing."

Sophie rolled her eyes. "That'll be one dollar and fifty cents."

"I'll take a shared room," the shorter man said, smoothing his mouse brown hair back with one hand.

"And what do you sell, Mr. Dillingsworth?"

"Washing machines."

"Washing machines?" Sophie stared at him.

"Would you like to see a picture? I'm hoping Mrs. Bjorklund over at the store will decide to carry them. My mighty machines will save the backs and hands of all the women of Blessing, leaving them far more time to cook and care for the children. Cleaner clothes in half the time. No more hand wringing and rubbing knuckles raw on a scrub board."

"I see." Sophie glanced at the picture he laid on the counter. "What a contraption."

"Just wait until you see a demonstration. Why, Mrs. Aarsgard, you need two of these right here in the boardinghouse. Launder all those sheets and wring them dry enough to freeze real quick. Why, in the summer a nice breeze will dry them before you can bring another load out."

Sophie and Bridget exchanged amused looks. Get that young man going and he didn't know when to stop.

"Complete satisfaction or your money back."

"I saw his demonstration," O'Rourke added. "What a miracle machine he has. You ought to look at it. Can't hurt none." He tipped his hat. "First room on the right at the top of the stairs, right?"

Bridget nodded. "That is so. And you, Mr. Dillingsworth, follow him and four doors down, also on the right. Take your pick of the beds. No one else is in there yet."

As the men started up the stairs, talking and laughing, Bridget turned to Sophie. "You did just fine, but I warn you, watch out for such as O'Rourke. He's got a silver tongue and a way with the women." She lowered her voice. "And he always has a flask along—or two."

"How do you know that?"

"He leaves them on the chest of drawers or beside the bed. You just need to be careful, is all."

Sophie took in a deep breath, but nothing helped. "Excuse me." She headed for the basin in her room. Afterwards, she lay down on the bed, hoping she would feel better soon. She thought back to the boardinghouse in Ballard. If there had been flasks in the rooms, she'd sure never heard of it. But then there were saloons aplenty out there—not like here, where the women had made sure such a business never came to town.

She drifted off and awoke when Bridget brought a tray with tea and flatbread.

"I thought this might help."

"I'm feeling better now, thank you. I'm sorry for leaving like that."

"I wondered. You were getting whiter by the minute." Bridget set the tray on a small table by the rocking chair. "Come drink this and see if it helps. I've found that flatbread is good medicine. You keep some here in your room for the mornings."

After drinking the tea, Sophie straightened her clothing, smoothed her hair, and made her way back to the kitchen, where supper preparations were well under way. She donned an apron and asked what she could do to help.

When Trygve arrived with her trunk on his shoulder, she led the way to her new room on the first floor, right next to Bridget and Henry's. While they had a sitting room, her bedroom was large enough to have space for a bed for the baby too. She also had a chest of drawers and a dressing table.

He set the trunk in the corner. "You could stay at home with us and come in here every day."

"I know, but Bridget wants someone to be here in the late evenings, so this will be better." She couldn't look at him or say what she was thinking: *Besides, I don't think Far wants me there anymore.*

"Grace was disappointed that you had gone already." He parked his fists on his hips and looked around. "Well, at least it's closer than Seattle."

"True."

"Did you like it out there? Hamre sure did."

"It rained a lot."

"Instead of snow."

"It snowed in the mountains. You've never seen anything like Mount Rainier. And there were mountains on both sides of Puget Sound. The Cascades to the east and the Olympics across the water."

"You could see across the water?"

"Oh yes. Islands too, all covered with fir trees. Trees so big you couldn't believe it and some even with red bark that sheds like birch trees. We went for walks up among the trees. There is a lot of brush that grows. We picked huckleberries, smaller than our blueberries, so blue as to be almost black. Hamre says . . . said," she corrected herself, a pang slicing into her chest. "He said that bears love the huckleberries. People can live off the land there. And the fishing—oh, you would love it, Trygve, all the different kinds of fish—and huge. My word, at the cannery some came through big as a pig."

Trygve gave her one of his "Oh sure" looks.

"I'm not exaggerating. Someday we'll go there, and I'll show you."

"You would go back?"

"If I could. There are so many places I want to see. I've even thought of someday going to Norway and taking Mor and Tante Ingeborg along too."

"Nothing wrong with staying right here."

"No, not for those who want to. But some of us want to see other things."

"You went to see other places, yet you came home again."

"I know." *But not because I wanted to—I had no other choice.*

Trygve shook his head. "I got to go milk the cows." He surprised her with a quick hug, and off he went.

Sophie swallowed the lump in her throat and returned to the kitchen.

That night after meeting more of the guests, Sophie studied the list of room rates and wandered the halls, seeing what rooms were different, remembering cleaning and changing beds when she had previously helped Bridget. Not that much had changed, but she'd never paid attention to why Bridget charged the way she did. She put some of her things away, hanging her dresses in her chifforobe. Feeling a chill, she wrapped a shawl around her shoulders. The bell over the door brought her out to the desk to check in another guest. When it rang again, she looked up to see a man dusted in white walking through the door.

"May I help you?"

"No thank you. I'll be down for supper as soon as I clean up." He paused. "I'm Garth Wiste. I run the flour mill."

"I'm glad to meet you. Bestemor said you'd be coming in late. I'll go heat up your supper."

"Thank you, Miss . . . ah . . ."

"Mrs. Bjorklund. I am Lars Knutson's elder daughter."

"Ah, the one who went to Seattle. I'm sorry to hear about your loss." After looking like he would say more but didn't, he touched the brim of his hat, sending bits of powder floating down. "I'll go shake my coat and hat out the back door. Sometimes the wind blows me clean, but it is calm out there tonight."

So everyone in town knows about me, even strangers. The thought made her uncomfortable. What all had happened in Blessing since she'd left only three months ago? Perhaps more than she'd thought. She walked under the arch to the dining room and through the swinging doors to the kitchen. Mrs. Sam had left soup to heat, and in the icebox, a plate full of the short ribs, potatoes, and string beans with bacon that had been served for supper. Sophie set the plate in the oven, added wood to the firebox, and set the small kettle of soup on the front burner, pulling the coffeepot to the hotter part of the stove also. Half an apple pie sat on the counter. She sliced bread and carried a tray with the bread, butter, jam, and some beet pickles out to a table near the kitchen door.

"I usually eat in the kitchen," Mr. Wiste said as he entered the dining room.

"Oh. Well, if you would rather."

"I would. The kitchen is cozier than this big room when I am alone. I do hope you'll join me for a cup of coffee. Bridget . . . er, Mrs. Aarsgard usually does."

"I see." Sophie picked up the tray again, but before she could turn, he took the tray from her.

"Let me."

"But you're a guest." She let him take the tray and followed him into the kitchen. "If my grandmother sees this, she might fire me."

"Oh, I doubt that. She was so hoping you would come and help."

Does Bestemor talk everything over with this man? Since when? I've just been home a few days.

"She's gotten older while I was gone." Sophie fetched the kettle of soup and dished up a bowl for him.

"You just notice it more. Thank you."

"Would you like coffee now or later?"

"Now would be fine."

She filled his cup and set the pot back on the stove.

"Aren't you going to have any?"

"Oh, I guess." Sophie got another cup and saucer and poured some for herself. "Do you take cream or sugar?"

"No thanks. Black is fine."

While he ate his soup, she checked on the plate in the oven and cut him a large piece of pie. Sitting down, a wave of weariness rolled over her, threatening to drag her under. She trapped a yawn before it stretched her jaw. Perhaps working in the boardinghouse wouldn't be as easy as she remembered. Or was it the baby? Hadn't Elizabeth mentioned she would be feeling tired? As if being unable to keep much food down wasn't bad enough.

Later in bed, she thought about the day. *So many changes in one day. No wonder I'm tired.*

22

January 1902

"I HAVEN'T THROWN UP IN four days."

Sophie stared at the face in the mirror. Gone were the black shadows under her eyes, the gray cast around her mouth. She sucked in a deep breath and let it out. Although the waistband of her skirt was too tight to take a deep breath, she almost smiled. She felt good, really good, for the first time in . . . she couldn't think how long.

Here I am, a grieving pregnant widow in the middle of the winter in North Dakota, and I'm only seventeen years old. She straightened her arms, hands on the dressing-table surface, and let her head fall forward. What was there to rejoice about in all that?

At least I am not losing my breakfast over the chamber pot. That is something to be thankful for. And the sun is shining on new snow. She crossed to the window and scraped enough frost off the pane to be able to see across the flat land dotted by chimneys with smoke trailing straight up. No wind. Something else to be thankful for.

She thought back to Christmas, the worst one of her entire life. She'd chosen to stay at the boardinghouse so that Bridget and Henry could enjoy Christmas with the entire Bjorklund family. And because she was tired of everyone seeing her crying. No Hamre, not that he'd have been home anyway, but all she could think was that he was never coming home, that there would never be a home of their own for them.

Sophie had given the socks she'd knitted for Hamre to Trygve and the hat to Samuel. Had Hamre worn the scarf?

Everyone else went to church, to the program at the school, to family gatherings. Sophie had been invited to everything but turned the invitations down. Especially anything her father would go to. He'd still not spoken to her—not that he'd had many chances.

She heard footsteps and then a knock at her door.

"Sophie, we need a hand in the dining room," Lemuel said as she opened the door. "Lily Mae just slipped and dropped a tray. It's a mess." Lemuel and his sister, Lily Mae, both worked at the boardinghouse, along with their mother, the cook who everyone called Mrs. Sam. Lemuel had come back to work there after all the fieldwork was finished for the year and hoped to get hired at the flour mill.

"Coming." She stuck one more hairpin in her upsweep and headed out the door. Another thing to be thankful for—life was never dull at the boardinghouse.

She'd just closed the door behind her when she heard what sounded like a sob from the next room.

Henry staggered out the door, tears streaming down his face. "H-help. It's Bridget."

"What?" Her heart in her throat, she strode past him.

Bridget lay in the bed, a smile on her face. But when Sophie touched her, she knew. Bridget had gone home.

"Oh, Henry, I'm so sorry." She tried to say more but couldn't speak around the sobs of her own. She turned and stepped into his arms, and the two cried together.

"I woke up and she was gone. I didn't even get to say good-bye." Henry pulled a white handkerchief from his pants pocket and mopped his face, then sank down on the bed and took Bridget's hand in his.

Lily Mae skidded to a stop in the doorway.

"Go get Pastor Solberg please," Sophie said, "but don't tell everyone here yet. Let people finish their breakfast and go on their way. No, wait." She wiped her eyes and sniffed. "Go get Dr. Elizabeth first."

"No need of that." Henry looked up at her. "Nothing Elizabeth can do."

"I know." Sophie rolled her lips together, trying to stem the tears. Like Henry, she didn't get to say good-bye to Hamre and now not to Bridget either. "Pastor Solberg first and then Thorliff, all right?"

Henry nodded, curved over as if the whole world had just landed on his shoulders. "She wasn't even sick. Tired some but not sick."

"She looks so peaceful. You think that smile means she saw Jesus?" Sophie whispered the words. "Mor always says we'll see Jesus coming to meet us." She wrapped an arm around Henry's shoulders as if he were one of the children. "Can I do anything for you? Coffee?"

He shook his head. "You done all you can. Thank you for coming to help us here. That made her so pleased."

"I-I better go check on things. I'll be right back." Sophie pressed her handkerchief to her eyes again and blew her nose. *I must look a sight.* She straightened her shoulders and, blinking again, headed for the dining room. Empty for all but Lily Mae clearing the tables amid her tears. Mrs. Sam looked up from kneading bread dough, rivulets of tears on her cheeks.

"That de best way to pass—go to sleep in your bed and wake up in heaven." She sniffed and used her apron to dry her eyes. "But, Lawd above, I'm goin' to miss that woman."

"Me too. Henry's heart is broken."

"I do believe that. He loved his Bridget something fierce. Such a shock." She flipped the bread over and gave it a couple of good thumps before forming it back into a round, settling it in the huge crockery bowl, and then placing it on the wide shelf behind the stove to rise. "I knows de angels are rejoicin'. Bridget done gone home."

Sophie sighed again, the tears trickling down her cheeks. "I'm glad I got to be with her for these weeks."

"She was gladder I think. Right hard on her when you left las' fall without saying good-bye."

Sophie nodded. So many *sorry*s and *if only*s, and yet if she hadn't gone, she'd never have known what loving Hamre could be like. Or being loved by him. Or having his baby. Today she could rejoice for that. Funny how much easier it was to rejoice when she wasn't throwing up. She poured a cup of coffee and carried it back to the room where Henry sat, still holding Bridget's hand. She paused, not wanting to intrude, for she could hear him talking to her softly.

He looked up as if sensing her presence.

"I brought you a cup of coffee."

"Thank you." He waved his hand toward the bedside table. "Just set it there."

Sophie heard someone behind her and turned. "Pastor Solberg, thank you for coming so quickly." She started to say something else and stopped. An apology didn't seem appropriate at the moment, and when he squeezed her hand, she nodded.

"I left Astrid in charge at the school." He passed Sophie and strode to Henry. "Ah, dear friend, she's gone home."

"And left me behind." Tears flowed again. "I always thought it would be me to go first."

"Just went in her sleep, did she?" Pastor Solberg laid a hand on Henry's shoulder. "She looks so happy."

"I know. I know she is. It just seems I should have sensed her going or something. I didn't know it until I woke up this morning surprised to find her still in bed. She always got up so early, even when Mrs. Sam kept telling her she didn't have to."

"I sent Trygve to tell Ingeborg and Kaaren. They'll all be here soon."

Thorliff arrived at the doorway, then crossed to Henry's side. "I'm sorry, Henry."

Sophie set the cup down and returned to the kitchen to find Mrs. Sam refilling the coffeepot.

"They all be coming, so I fixing cake to serve. I set up in the dining room."

"Thank you. I don't know what to do or say or anything. All I can do is cry." Sophie heard someone behind her and turned to step into her mother's arms, her father right behind her.

"Mor." Together they cried, Lars patting shoulders and sniffing himself.

"She lived a long and good life, blessing so many people." Kaaren leaned back against her husband. "Including us." She kept hold of Sophie's hand.

"Ja, she did." Lars stepped back. "I'm going to Henry. Haakan and I will build the box this afternoon."

"You go on, Mor. I'll be fine." Sophie dabbed at her eyes again and thought to what needed doing. Most likely Mor and Tante Ingeborg would take care of the body and dress Bridget in her Sunday dress. They wouldn't be able to bury her until spring came and the ground thawed enough to dig the grave. *At least they have a body to bury.*

Her father had patted her shoulder. Had he forgiven her? *You haven't talked to him like your mother told you to do.* She headed back to the kitchen. Keeping busy was always the best remedy.

By the end of the day all the people of Blessing and the surrounding area had come to pay their respects. The engineer and train crew even left the westbound train and stopped by to tell Henry how sorry they were. The women had lined the box with a quilt, and Bridget did indeed look like she was sleeping.

That evening the family gathered in the dining room after the guests had been served. They shared stories of Bridget's coming to America and starting the boardinghouse, all the while wondering if it could be kept operating.

"When all is said and done," Henry said, "this place can go on as it is. Mrs. Sam and her family do the heavy work, and Sophie is doing a fine job at the front desk. What it really comes down to is that Bridget and me, well, we've not been as helpful as we used to be. We been talking, and Bridget wanted to train Sophie to run this place so she could own it after we are gone. Bridget didn't sign a will or anything, but that is what she wanted. I do too."

Sophie nearly choked on her breathing. Own the boardinghouse? At her age? What had Bridget been thinking? Surely this was a joke. She could hear the others murmuring. They were as shocked as she was.

"What would you like to do, Henry?" Haakan asked.

"Stay right here if it is all right with the rest of you. This been my home since Bridget and me ..." He heaved a sigh and dried his eyes again. "I'll help Sophie as much as I can."

"Of course it is all right." Haakan turned to Sophie, staring into her eyes as if searching her soul. "And you are agreeable with this?"

Sophie nodded. "Yes. If you want me to stay, I mean. I have a lot to learn." *Surely that wasn't her own voice she heard. No, I don't want— yes, I do—* She clamped her hands together in her lap to keep them from shaking.

"So true, but Mrs. Sam will gladly teach you. And if you need more help, we'll find it."

After they all left, Sophie stopped by the coffin. "I'll try to make you proud of me," she whispered. "I never told you how much I loved you and admired you." *Why do I always think of such things too late?* She blew her nose again, being careful of how tender it had become. *Bridget, you don't go giving away a boardinghouse like you would a tablecloth and napkins.* Sensing someone behind her, she turned to find Mr. Wiste standing in the doorway.

"I didn't mean to intrude."

"No, it's all right. Come in."

"She was a mighty fine woman. She made everyone feel welcome here. That's a real gift."

"And most likely why the boardinghouse is so popular." Sophie looked back down at Bridget. "I remember coming by here with Grace when we were little, and she always took time for us. We'd sit out on the back porch and snap beans, and she'd tell us stories of life in Norway before she emigrated. Her stories always made me want to go to Norway and see for myself." She dabbed at her nose this time. "Pardon me. Here I am running on, when you—"

"No, please. I like hearing about her. She'd become my friend."

"Mor and Tante Ingeborg have told me about New York City when they came off the ship. I want to go there too." Sophie leaned over the side of the box and straightened the front of Bridget's dress. "What a day this has been."

"Thank you for remembering to save supper for me."

"You are welcome, but thank Mrs. Sam. She remembers everything." She gave Bridget one last look and turned to leave, weariness dragging her footsteps.

"How is Henry?"

"He's so terribly sad. I think he's already gone to bed."

"I won't bother him tonight, then."

"Do you need anything?"

"No thanks. Good night, Mrs. Bjorklund."

"'Night." She watched him walk up the stairs. Surely there would be no one else coming by tonight. She turned down the lamp they kept burning on the counter just in case someone came in. A bell lay on a paper that said *If you need a room, knock on door number 3.* The number 1 had been crossed out and the 3 inserted. Number 3 was Sophie's room. She peeked into Henry's room to see him in bed, lying on his side, slight snores saying for sure he was asleep.

In the morning when she came out, the casket was gone. The men had come in early and taken it to the icehouse, where it would wait until spring.

Sophie fixed a tray and knocked on Henry's door. When he didn't answer, she nudged the door open and carried the tray to the bedside. Henry lay flat on his back, eyes closed, and a slight smile on his face.

"Henry?"

He didn't answer, didn't move, and she knew once again. She touched his cheek, and her eyes filled. "God bless, Henry. At least you didn't suffer either." She made her way into the kitchen, returning the tray.

"He not hungry?" Mrs. Sam asked.

"No, he's gone."

"I din't hear him go out."

"No. I mean, he died—in his sleep." Sophie wiped the tears from her cheeks.

The black woman didn't look surprised. "Ah, his heart broke yesterday, and God took pity on him and took him home to be with Bridget. Blessed be de name of de Lord."

"That's what I thought." Sophie sniffed. "But it still makes me sad."

"Yes, we always be sad but glad too. Sad for us and glad for them.

Till one day we all be there, praisin' Jesus in the heavenly throne room. What a day that will be."

"Would you have Lemuel go tell everyone again?"

"He go in a minute. He fillin' de woodbox now."

"I'll make sure things are all right in the dining room." Since most of the guests had already left, she helped stack the dishes and poured one man another cup of coffee. As usual, Mr. Wiste had been one of the first to leave. She thought back to the night before. He was such a nice man.

Grace blew through the door.

"Why aren't you in school?" Sophie asked.

"Something is wrong. I had to come to you."

Sophie held out her arms. "Ah, Grace, Henry died during the night, and I'm so sad." The two sisters hugged and cried on each other's shoulders. Finally Sophie stepped back so Grace could read her lips. "Thank you. That helped more than anything."

"Should I go tell Pastor Solberg?"

"Lemuel has already left. Mrs. Sam says Henry died of a broken heart. I always thought that was just a saying."

"Mor said he would probably get sick with something. She said that often happens. How old was he?"

"Seventy-seven. He mentioned that yesterday. Said Bridget had married an older man, and that this older man had a hard time keeping up with her."

"They're together again." Grace smiled through her tears. "That's good. I better get to school." She hugged Sophie again. "I miss you."

"Grace."

"Ja."

"I'm scared."

"Why?"

"Who's going to run the boardinghouse now?"

"Why you, I guess, and Mrs. Sam."

"But I . . ." She shook her head and raised her hands, letting them fall to her sides. "But I'm not ready to be in charge of the whole thing. I mean, I . . ." She shook her head again. *Too fast. This is going too fast. No, not this.*

23

THANK YOU, GOD, *for Mrs. Sam.*

In the week since Bridget and Henry passed away, Sophie caught herself praying more than once. When an order for the kitchen came in on the train, Mrs. Sam showed her how to check the supplies against the invoice and against the order to make sure she got all that Bridget had ordered. Nothing matched. They'd shipped an extra bag of flour, which was not a problem in the long run, but they hadn't shipped sugar. She would have to buy sugar at Garrisons' Groceries. No lard caused more troubles. By the time she got it all straightened out and the letter written to the supply company, she had a headache of mountainous proportions. When it didn't hang on like the one had in Seattle, she found something to be grateful for.

The mice in the pantry and storage room had to go. She asked around and finally found a half-grown cat that Mrs. Solberg was willing to give away. It having never been in a house before, they had to be careful to keep it inside until it decided it was happy at the boarding-house. Bits of leftover chicken, a dish of milk, and crumbles of cheese convinced it to leave off playing shadow and come when the food appeared. Sophie hoped the mouse problem would soon abate.

When Mrs. Sam came down with chills and a fever, Sophie wanted nothing more than to go home to her mother and cry her eyes dry in her mother's aproned lap.

"You go home and get well," she told Mrs. Sam, forcing her lips to smile and her hands to not tremble.

"But what will you do?" The few words sent Mrs. Sam into a coughing spell.

"We'll manage. I'm sending Dr. Elizabeth out to see you."

"No. I'll be all right."

Lily Mae, Mrs. Sam's daughter, looked up from mixing pancakes. "I'll cook; you serve. Tables need setting." She turned to her brother, Lemuel. "You set the tables."

"I'll start the coffee, then." Sophie dug out the coffee grinder. They had run out of ground coffee the night before, and Mrs. Sam had said she'd grind it in the morning. Something had awakened Sophie early, for which she was thankful. "Oh, the oatmeal." She pulled out the deep kettle and half filled it with hot water from the reservoir, then measured in the salt and rolled oats. It should have been cooking already.

Since Lily Mae was cooking, Sophie took over the dining room, with Lemuel bringing the heavy trays of food out so she could serve their guests, Lily Mae's usual job.

"Is Lily Mae sick?"

If she heard the question once, she heard it twenty times.

"No. Her mother is, so Lily Mae took over the kitchen."

"Mrs. Sam is sick? It must be really bad." Mr. Vell, the barber, shook his head. "First time I know of she wasn't cooking."

Sophie made sure all the coffee cups were refilled and that the men who took dinner boxes had them before they headed out the door.

Miss Christopherson, who owned the Dress-Making Shop, stopped on her way out. "If you need more help, things are slow in the shop right now, and I could hang a *Closed* sign on the door. From the looks of the weather, no one will be by today anyway."

Sophie started to turn down the offer, but at the look on the young woman's face, she changed her mind.

"Are you sure? I mean, you have nothing to do over there?" *What a thing to say. You better think before you let your tongue get away from you.*

"Oh, I have plenty to do, but most of it can wait. If you need help, that is."

Sophie swallowed a lump in her throat, not realizing until that moment how close to tears she was. "I do, and I really appreciate your offer. I was about to run over to the school and drag my sister out of there for the day."

"Good, then. I'll be right back."

Sophie returned to clearing the tables, stacking the dirty dishes on the trays for Lemuel to carry back to the kitchen.

"You eat now." Lily Mae pointed at the table where Lemuel was pouring syrup on his pancakes.

"I better—"

"Eat. That's what I said."

Sophie's stomach took that instance to complain loudly at the lack of sustenance, and at Lily Mae's giggle, she gave up. "You sound just like your ma."

"Bossy and demanding?"

"You said it. I didn't." Sophie dished up a bowl of oatmeal and sat down at the table, where Lily Mae passed her the cream and brown sugar.

"Pancakes and eggs?"

"No thanks. This is plenty. Have you eaten?"

"Going to right now."

As the three of them finished their meal, Sophie thought about all that needed doing. Today was wash day. That could wait, at least until the afternoon. The main thing was to get the meals ready. Unless they had a large group arrive from the train, they should have only five or six for dinner, and supper could be up to fifteen, depending on the train. The more she pondered, the more she realized how much the boardinghouse depended on Mrs. Sam now that Bridget and Henry were gone.

"What had Mrs. Sam planned for the meals today?"

"I sliced the last of that roast for sandwiches so we can make soup on the bone," Lily Mae said. "That with fresh bread and apple cake for dessert should be enough."

"Those men come in really hungry. Do we have any ham to slice?"

"Hangin' in the storage room. Might be half froze."

"Then let's bake that for supper. We can slice off enough to serve with fried potatoes for dinner if we need to. That's something to fix quickly." Sophie rubbed her temple, where a headache had been hinting toward an arrival for some time. Her stomach felt woozy again too. *Go away*, she mentally ordered the nausea. *I have no time for you.*

"If'n I bakes a pie or two, that always make de men happy."

"Good idea. One apple and one from the canned Juneberries." She rubbed her stomach and stopped as if listening for a faraway voice. The movement continued, like the faintest of fluttering wings. "The baby is moving." She spoke in a whisper, as if a loud voice might scare it away.

"Ma says that the most heavenly feeling in the world."

Ah, Hamre, look what you are missing. Not that he would have been able to feel it yet. Her hand didn't but her insides did, especially her heart, which seemed to be expanding and breaking out into a smile. Her whole body was laughing. If only she had time to go talk to her mor, Ingeborg, or Dr. Elizabeth. Even the snow blowing outside could not dim the feeling. Her baby was real. He or she was moving, alive and growing.

The sound of the bell over the front door brought her out of her reverie. Miss Christopherson slipped through the door before Sophie could even get to her feet.

"All right. Tell me what to do." She unpinned her hat and set it on one of the tables. "I'll take that to my room after we get dinner going."

The morning passed in a whirl, with Lemuel hauling wood in to the rapidly emptying woodbox, then bringing carrots, turnips, and potatoes up from the cellar, and Miss Maisie, as she insisted they call her, taking over the pies so Lily Mae could chop vegetables for the soup. That left Sophie to change the bed in a vacated room, dust, and make sure everything was ready in all the empty rooms for new guests. Half of the twenty rooms had permanent guests like Mr. Wiste. She paused as she walked by the closed door to his room. Today his room should have been cleaned and the bed changed. Should she leave him a note of apology? *I'll explain things to him tonight*, she thought and continued down the hall. The baseboards needed dusting and the wall sconces needed polishing. Bridget would never have allowed such slack. A two-pronged attack of guilt and sorrow made her catch her breath. Guilt for letting things slip and sorrow that Bridget wasn't there to order more cleaning.

The windows rattled as the westbound train steamed into the station. She bundled the sheets tighter as she made her way down the stairs, keeping one hand on the railing. Good thing Bridget bought the washing machine from that drummer. Lemuel turned the crank just fine, and the paddles inside the belly of the contraption beat the clothes clean. But today even he didn't have time. Amazing how one never realized how much work another did until they weren't there. The porch along the back of the house was a good thing. They hung up sheets and other linens there until they freeze dried, then brought them into the storage room to finish drying and be ironed.

She dropped the linens into a box kept for such in the storage room and headed back to the counter in the lobby, arriving just as the wind blew two men through the front door.

"Brrr. You forget how cold North Dakota can be until you come back in a storm like this," the taller one said, unwrapping a muffler from around his neck.

"You get used to it." The shorter, rounder man pulled off his gloves and stuffed them into the square patch pocket on his coat.

"Don't think I'll ever get used to it. Next winter I'm putting in for a southern route. If I never see snow like this again, it will be too soon." He stamped his feet and brushed the snow off the shoulders of his black wool coat. Then he looked up to see Sophie behind the counter, and a grin split beard from mustache. "Well, look who we have here."

"Good morning, gentlemen. Welcome to Blessing."

"A good morning it is, after all." He nudged his carpetbag forward as he removed his coat. "I sure do hope you have room for two hard-working men."

"I'm sure I can find something. Have you been here before?"

"Oh, many times." He looked around. "Where is Bridget?"

"Bridget and Henry both died a week ago." Sophie fought to keep her voice steady and a welcoming smile in place.

The grin left his face. "I'm sorry to hear that. Must have been sudden like." He shook his head. "I thought she'd go on forever, not that her replacement isn't a sight for near frozen eyes. I'm Larry Borden, purveyor of the latest in household goods." He turned to his companion. "And this here is Ernest Frieburg. He's in machinery."

"I'm glad to meet you both. If you would sign the register here, I will give you your keys. Do you want single or dormitory style?"

"Oh, I always take a single." Borden sniffed. "Dinner smells mighty inviting."

"Thank you." If they only knew. But the fragrance of fresh bread and beef soup always made one's mouth water.

"And who might you be, miss?" Borden looked up from signing his name.

"I'm Mrs. Bjorklund." Sophie caught herself. She'd almost said Sophie Knutson. What was the matter with her? But then, how often had she answered that question since she'd come back to Blessing?

"One of the Bjorklund girls, eh?"

Ignoring his forwardness, Sophie smiled at the other man who finished signing his name. "Dinner will be served in about half an hour. Do you need someone to show you to your room?"

"No thanks, miss, er, missus. We know the way."

"Then here you are. The rooms are down at the end of the hall on the second floor."

"I'm sorry to hear about their passing. Mrs. Aarsgard made everyone feel at home here," Ernest Frieburg said as he turned toward the stairs.

"I hope you continue to feel that way. Thank you." Sophie smiled at him again.

"So, who will be running the boardinghouse now that they're gone?" Borden asked.

"I will."

At his guffaw Sophie started to say something but then stopped and stared at him, one eyebrow slightly raised. "Interesting that you find that amusing." Where had that all come from? Sometimes she surprised even herself.

"A chit like you? Barely out of the schoolroom? You won't last a year."

"Really?" Her eyes narrowed a tiny bit, and she smiled in spite of gritted teeth. "As I said, dinner will be served shortly."

"Something you might think on . . ."

I have several somethings to think on, like there will be no single rooms available next time you come. "Oh, and what is that?"

He leaned forward and dropped his voice. "If'n I were you, I'd turn a couple of these downstairs rooms into a saloon. It'd make you more money than all the rooms combined." He picked up his bag. "Good advice, that. And I won't charge you a dime."

Sophie shook her head slightly. "I guess you don't understand the folks of Blessing. They've turned down several people who wanted to open a saloon. They'd run me out on a rail if I did that."

"Not one of their own. Don't you know the Bjorklunds can do anything?"

"No, I didn't know that." *And if one of my uncles walked in now, you'd be right sorry for this conversation.* "Excuse me, but I'm needed in the dining room." She spun so quickly her skirt swirled. The nerve of the man. Barely out of the schoolroom. The audacity. And a saloon? She could just hear the women if she proposed such an idea. Why, Mrs. Valders would faint.

"Are you all right?" Miss Maisie asked as Sophie entered the kitchen.

"Yes, of course. Why?"

"You look ready to do battle."

"Oh no." Sophie wished she had a mirror. She sighed and shook her head. "One of the guests who just arrived made me want to invite him to leave."

"Was he unseemly?" Heat suffused her face.

"If I'm going to run this boardinghouse, I have to learn how to deal with men like that. Do you know a Mr. Borden?"

"A drummer who sells household things?"

"That's the one."

"I don't know how he makes a living, crude as he is," Miss Maisie said.

"Probably does all right dealing with men." Sophie gave herself a shake. *I wish Bridget were here. She'd know what I should do. And Henry would want to escort the man out the door, rather forcibly, I should think.*

Maisie leaned closer. "He thinks he's God's gift to womankind."

Sophie rolled her lips together to keep from giggling. "He called me a chit. Barely out of the schoolroom." *Of course, that last is true. Had I not gone with Hamre, I'd still be in school. And not working here. My boardinghouse. I'm too young to own a boardinghouse.*

She turned away from her thoughts. "What still needs doing?"

"Slice the bread. I put dumplings in the soup. Hope that is all right."

"Good idea. What do we have for dessert?"

"I made the pies like you said."

"Maisie, you're a lifesaver." She heard the scrape of chairs being pulled back from the table and the sound of male voices along with the jangling of the bell. "Sounds like we have guests. Lemuel, you bring the coffeepot. They're all going to want hot coffee to warm them."

I should have set up only the tables closest to the kitchen, Sophie thought later as she and Lily Mae cleared off the last of the dishes. They could have saved a lot of steps that way. And maybe she should have moved a couple of the tables closer together to make one long one and served family style like Mrs. Soderstrum used to in Seattle. *I have a lot to learn. I do hope Mrs. Sam is back tomorrow.* She had a sick feeling that that wouldn't be the case. What if someone else caught it? What would they do?

24

I DIDN'T THINK IT WOULD *be colder here than in Minneapolis.* Garth stamped his booted feet on the swept stair tread, grateful he didn't live farther from the flour mill. The wind, on top of the dropping temperature, was enough to freeze one's bones. Stepping into the warmth of the boardinghouse, he paused to catch his breath. Even though he was later than usual, he could still smell coffee, beef something, and cinnamon. Had they baked apple pies again?

No matter how much he'd thought lately on missing Grant and having his children with him, he knew how fortunate he was to have a place like this to live. He unwrapped the muffler and shook off the snow before draping the scarf around his neck and removing his hat— the hat he'd nearly lost to a blast of wind intent on denuding him of as much apparel as possible. Sophie—no, he reminded himself, *it's Mrs. Bjorklund. You have to call her Mrs. Bjorklund, no matter how clearly she has already become Sophie in your mind.* Their evening chats while he ate his late supper had become something to look forward to.

She wasn't working at her books behind the counter, as she often did in the evenings. He peeked into the dining room. Not there either. Surely she hadn't taken ill like Mrs. Sam? The thought made his stomach lurch. He made his way up the stairs to his room and divested himself of coat, hat, and boots, sliding his feet into the moccasins he'd purchased at Penny's store, warm sheepskin that covered his ankles. Seeing a letter lying on his nightstand, he sat down on the bed and slit it open with his penknife. News from his sister had gained even more importance since his visit home at Christmas.

Dear Garth,

Thank you again for coming home when you did. Grant asks every day when his pa is coming back. He goes to the window and looks for you, and yesterday I heard him telling Linnie about going to live in Kota with his pa.

"Linnie." Garth closed his eyes. His anger at Helga for naming his daughter Madelynn after his beloved was volcanic when he first heard the news, but now he was grateful that she'd had the foresight to give him one more link to Maddie. His lips curled upward as he continued to read.

One of these days he'll get all his words correct, but for now I enjoy his attempts to talk right.

Linnie is growing right before my eyes. I am grateful I have enough milk for our two babies. You'd almost think Micah and Linnie are twins, both with their dark hair, although I would wish his curls for her. They lie on the quilt on the floor and gurgle and coo at each other. Grant was telling them something yesterday, and they both watched him as if they understood every word. Perhaps they did, for I didn't.

I believe this was our nicest Christmas ever, even though I know your heart grieves so for Maddie, as does mine. I've been writing down the clever and funny things Grant says so that one day you can show him how much we loved him. He's quit asking for his ma. But our mother is inclined to spoil him.

Well, I hear Linnie waking from her nap, and I better get her quickly so Micah can sleep a bit longer.

Dan is seriously thinking about a move to North Dakota. I was so surprised when he showed interest. I thought he was happy at the mill here. When I mentioned it to Mother, she nearly cried. On that cheery note, I'll close, wishing you a happy new year and may this year be far better than the last.

Love from your sister Helga and your two sweet children.

Garth folded the paper and put it back into the envelope, thinking back to his visit while he did so. His first meeting with his daughter had not been pleasant. When he tried to hold her, she arched her back and nearly threw herself out of his arms, screaming all the while. But as Helga reminded him, to her he was a stranger. How tragic that he was a stranger to his own child, yet he knew it was his own fault. Somehow he would try to make up for this time apart.

By the time he was ready to leave, he could hold Linnie in one arm and Grant on his knee and thought perhaps they would make a family after all. He was glad he'd not given them to Helga and Dan permanently, as he'd contemplated. Grief can make people do strange things. He tucked the letter into the drawer next to the others he'd received from his mor and from Helga and brushed his hair before making his way downstairs. He was about due to visit Mr. Vell at the barbershop, but the hours he worked made it difficult for him to get there. Maddie used to cut his hair. So easy it was to find reminders of her even when he wasn't living in their house.

His stomach rumbled and he headed for the kitchen.

"Ah, there you are. I thought I heard someone come in." Sophie turned from stirring something on the stove when she heard him come through the door.

"Good evening, Mrs. Bjorklund. You are all right?"

"Of course." Her smile banished any worries he'd had. "Why do you ask?"

"Well, you weren't at your desk." *And I'm getting used to seeing your smiling face when I come through that door.* He sniffed appreciatively. "What is it that smells so good?"

"I baked apple pies for tomorrow," Lily Mae said as she lifted one out of the oven.

The aroma made him think of home. How Maddie had loved to

bake. She'd always said she was one of his best customers, the amount of flour she went through. For a change a memory made him smile, inside and out. Far different than the crushing blows they had brought for so long.

"I'll cut you a piece soon as you finish your supper."

"Thank you." He studied Sophie as unobtrusively as possible. Her apron no longer hid the babe she was carrying. While they'd not discussed the baby, he had recognized the signs long before the mound pushed out her aprons. Now he realized what was different. She had a softness about her, a glow of . . . could it be happiness? Maddie had worn the same look. She'd said being with child made her happy beyond measure. And so it had done the same for him.

Sophie drew a plate from the warming oven and dipped gravy from a kettle keeping warm on the back of the stove to pour over the potatoes and meat. "Do you want both string beans and pickled beets?"

"Yes, please." His stomach added a rumble for emphasis.

"Shame you can't get off in time to be here when supper is at its best." She started toward the dining room and stopped, turning back to set the extras on the kitchen table. "Sorry."

"I like eating in here. It's warmer and easier for everyone. Then you can both sit down and have your coffee, and we can visit." He glanced around. "Did anyone get the paper?"

"Of course. You can read it while you eat or take a copy to your room." Sophie brought his plate to the table, and Lily Mae brought a napkin and silverware.

"Thank you. Did you notice the headlines?"

Sophie shook her head. "I've not taken time to look yet."

"Ah, then I have a favor to ask." At her nod, he continued, "Perhaps you would read to all of us while I eat." His smile included Lemuel, who came in just then and dumped another load of wood in the woodbox.

"I-I guess I can do that." Sophie paused. "My mother used to read to us in the winter evenings. I didn't realize how much I missed that until now. She has the loveliest reading voice. All the women ask her to read when they are quilting. She says it keeps the bickering down."

Garth smiled when she clapped a hand to her mouth, as if to grab the words back. "Surely, Mrs. Bjorklund, there is no bickering in Blessing."

"I really wouldn't know. I've never been to the quilting meetings."

She sat so prim and proper that it made him smile again. "I suspect that wherever people are gathered, there is some bickering and dissension. People just seem to be that way."

"I'm sure you aren't referring to only women with that remark."

"No, of course not, although I wouldn't say that men bicker. They argue, true, but . . ." He nearly laughed as Sophie's eyebrows disappeared under her fringe but realized a slight smile might be the better part of valor. *My word, surely there isn't a women's suffrage advocate right here in front of me.*

"Let me get this straight." Sophie put a fingertip to her chin. "Women bicker, and that is a bad thing, but men argue, and that is a good thing?" She tipped her head slightly to the side. "Do I have that right?"

"I . . . ah . . . perhaps you would be so kind as to read—the headlines at least?"

"Are you insinuating that I cannot read beyond the headlines?" Sophie unfolded the newspaper.

Lily Mae never raised her gaze from the rim of her coffee cup, but Garth could tell she knew exactly what was going on.

"No, not at all. Ah, could I please have my coffee heated up?" He raised the cup and smiled at Lily Mae. How strange it was to have more than Sophie with him in the kitchen. Usually the others had gone home long before now. They must be missing Mrs. Sam.

"Yes, sir. Would you care for more meat or anything?"

"No thank you. There is pie for dessert?"

"Yes, sir."

"We were going to save that for tomorrow, but . . ." Sophie looked at him over the top of the *Blessing Gazette*. "Would you like to hear about President Roosevelt's latest speech or about the current outrage against the increased railroad rates?"

He ignored the barb about the content of the newspapers. "I plead for the pie. The fragrance greeted me at the door. Coming in from that awful cold, I smelled the apples and cinnamon, and I knew I was home."

"Sweet words will get you nowhere."

He could tell she was fighting to keep a straight face. "Thank you." He smiled up at Lily Mae as she refilled his coffee cup and then turned his attention back to Sophie. "Must I get on my knees and plead for a piece of pie?"

Sophie slapped the paper down. "Do you want me to read or not?"

She has a dimple in her right cheek. He'd not seen that before. "Can't you read while she brings me the pie?" He tried to look forlorn, but he was enjoying himself too much.

"Do you know that you have flour in your eyebrows?" Sophie ducked her head and peered at the paper. "There's also a story on the weather."

Lily Mae set the plate of pie on the table. "Can I get you anything else?"

"Aren't you having any?"

Lily Mae glanced at Sophie, who nodded.

"Of course we are. Cut one for Lemuel too." Sophie motioned toward the young black man, who was now carving a new rung for one of the chairs.

Sophie studied the paper. "I wish Thorliff would write another story and run it in the paper in installments like he did last year."

"I read the one he wrote several years ago. The *Minneapolis Tribune* carried it. Of course, I didn't know Thorliff at the time, but we all enjoyed his stories."

"I didn't know other papers beside the Northfield paper carried it." Sophie looked over the top of the paper again. "Dr. Elizabeth's father owns that paper. Did you know that?"

"No, I didn't."

She began reading about Roosevelt's speech as Lemuel joined them at the table. Garth took a bite of the pie and let it melt on his tongue, savoring every crumb. He enjoyed listening to her read, mostly because then he could watch the expressions flit across her face. Though he was tired enough to fall asleep in his chair, he hated to leave the warmth of the kitchen and the time he spent with her. He needed a friend so badly and was still surprised to find her as one. Her eyebrows drew together when she wasn't sure of a word or disagreed with something written. She had a mind of her own, that was for certain. One of these days when he was feeling mighty brave, he'd like to ask her about living in Seattle and the man she'd been married to so briefly. Talking with Bridget one night he'd learned a little about her. He scraped the last of the apple filling from his plate.

Here he was teasing a young woman and truly enjoying himself and not giving a thought to Maddie. *Forgive me, dear one, but perhaps it is time to look forward instead of back. As soon as I can bring the children here, we could be a real family again.* Was that possible without their mother? Perhaps they were better off left in Minneapolis with his mother and sister caring for them. He'd had this discussion with himself many times before. Until he could buy the lot and build the house, it would have to remain a dream.

"Mr. Wiste, am I boring you?"

Garth saw Lemuel wink at his sister.

"Why, no. Whatever makes you think that?"

She rattled the paper again. "I-I asked you a question, and you didn't answer. I thought perhaps—"

"No, I . . ." He shook his head. "Forgive me, but sometimes my mind just takes off on its own and leaves me behind." He pushed his chair back. "Thank you for a delicious and enjoyable meal." He stood as he spoke and nodded to the group.

"Would you like to take the paper?"

"No thanks. I'd be asleep before I read two words. Thank you for keeping me up on the news." *And on my toes.* "See you all in the morning."

That night he dreamed of his wife, for the first time in quite some time. When he woke, all he remembered was her going away from him and blowing kisses, her smile dimming as she drew farther away. Happiness and joy seemed to flow from her, washing over him, curling around his heart, and lapping against his cheek. He lay in bed, hesitating to brave the cold. His dream had felt like spring. Somehow the wind whining at his window made spring seem like it would never come. *Lord, this may be the longest winter of my life, but I know that you are here, and I thank you for the dream.* It had seemed so real. Was there a message in it? He thought a moment more. *When had he started praying again?*

25

Dear Mr. and Mrs. Bjorklund,

It is with great delight and yet trepidation that I am writing to ask a monumental favor. I nearly boarded the train to come and ask this of you in person, but I decided it might be easier for you to say no in a letter or telegram, if that is your decision.

Ingeborg paused in the reading. Considering how long it had been since she'd heard from her New York friend, this was certainly a strange beginning to a letter. She returned to the letter.

My son Jonathan will be graduating from preparatory school and has been accepted at Harvard in the fall. I would like him to spend the summer working on a farm so that he gains an understanding of a way of life different from that in which he was raised. I want him to work with his hands and his back and not just his brains, for I am afraid we have spoiled him somewhat with all the privileges he has had of wealth. Could he possibly work on your farm? I would request that you give him the same jobs you give your children and without any pay. I am the one who will pay you for his room and board and the training I hope you will give him. If you do not have room for him to live with you, then he can live at the boardinghouse, but I do hope you can find room for him with you.

I know this is a burden on both you and our friendship, but I beg of you to consider it. How dearly I would enjoy having you all come here to visit. My city has changed greatly since you were here. I know of wholesalers who would like to stock your cheese and will write about that later. You have an excellent reputation here and everywhere.

We are all well here, and I hope the same is true for you.

Your friend and servant,
David Jonathan Gould

Ingeborg laid the letter in her lap and stared out the window. Gould's son coming here? To live with them? What a preposterous idea. Why, he was used to servants and a huge house and every advantage imaginable. She glanced through the letter again. Nowhere did he say his son was in agreement. Would he feel he was being banished to the prairie for three months? They did have room. He could use Andrew's room, and they always needed more hands in the summer. But this young man knew nothing about milking cows or running machinery. He probably knew how to ride and drive horses—well, ride anyway. They had a coachman to drive the horses. And they most likely had one of those new automobiles by now.

What would Haakan say about this? But after all that Mr. Gould had done for them, how could they say no?

Haakan reiterated her thoughts after he read the letter. They finished dinner before she gave it to him. He looked up, then returned to read it again. "We can always use more hands. Of course the ones we usually use are well callused and already know what to do. What do you suppose 'somewhat spoiled' means?"

"I don't know."

"Hmm. I wonder. Does the son want to do this?"

"He doesn't say."

"Well, if he wants to work, this is the right place to come."

Ingeborg nodded. "He must be close to the same age as Astrid. Such different lives they have led."

"But how can we not?"

"I know. Shall we talk it over with Thorliff and Andrew?"

"And Astrid. She'll be around him the most. We better pray about this and not make a hurried decision." Haakan folded the paper along its creases and tapped the fold on his other forefinger. "I wonder what ever gave Mr. Gould an idea like this."

❧

That first Sunday in February when the family all gathered for dinner at Ingeborg's, she passed the letter around. While Kaaren and Andrew had already read it, the others laughed and joked at the possibilities.

"So what are you going to do?" Thorliff asked while his wife finished reading.

"We're all going to talk about it. We want to hear what you think." Haakan tipped his chair back on two legs, caught Ingeborg's glare, and eased it back to four-point contact with the floor.

"What if he doesn't want to come?" Astrid asked.

"Or comes and doesn't want to stay?" Andrew started to copy his father in leaning his chair back, caught his wife's throat clearing, and changed his mind.

"Guess that's between him and his pa." Haakan picked up his coffee cup and propped his elbows on the table. Taking a sip, he wrinkled his nose.

"Need a warm up?" Ingeborg brought the coffeepot and, after filling Haakan's, motioned to the other family members gathered around the table. As she went around filling cups, she rested her hand on the shoulder of the cup holder. When one of them passed the cream pitcher, she thought back to Chicago and Haakan's bringing her the lovely clear glass pitcher and sugar bowl as a gift. He who never went shopping but for machinery. She smiled to herself. Ah, the joy of all those present. No longer did she take having everyone home around the table for granted. Both of her sons lived in their own houses, and the death of Hamre still lay heavy on her heart. So unexpected.

When Ellie's baby kicked up a fuss, Ingeborg held out her arms. "Here, let me hold him. You finish your coffee."

Taking the baby, she strolled around the kitchen, baby Carl against her shoulder with Bestemor patting the tiny back. How good it felt to hold a baby again, to have babies in their house. She hummed and brought herself back into the discussion.

"What could it hurt?" Andrew raised and dropped his hands. "We get a free hand for the summer; he gets a taste of farm life. He goes back to New York, we go on as we always have. Shame he can't be here to go with the crew on harvest. Now, that would be a real education for him."

"His name is Jonathan."

"Okay, so getting his hands dirty for a change might be real good for Jonathan."

Ingeborg raised an eyebrow at the tone of her son's voice, especially the inflection he put on the young man's name. "I doubt he'll be afraid to get his hands dirty."

Andrew had the grace to flush at the censure in his mother's voice. He cocked an eyebrow and grinned at her. "We all know that city boys have a hard time of it in the country." His sally made the others laugh.

"And country boys wouldn't have a hard time in the city?" It was Haakan's turn to raise his eyebrows.

"Nah," Andrew said. "Country boys are more adaptable."

"Andrew Bjorklund." Ellie smacked her husband on the shoulder. "What a thing to say."

"We should all go to Minneapolis to see the wonder horse, Beautiful Jim Key. That'd give you a taste of the city," Thorliff told his younger brother. "See how you like it."

"Oh, wouldn't that be marvelous." Astrid clapped both arms around her middle. "You think he can really do all those things they say, or is it all a fake?"

"I think he's really that smart. Remember how we taught old Jack to shake hands and bow?" he asked his sister over his shoulder. "And he was a mule, a stubborn old mule."

"I've heard it said that mules are smarter than horses." Haakan sipped his coffee and caught his wife's eye with a smile.

"I don't know if mules are smarter, but they sure are sneakier," Astrid said with a grin. She'd been pushed into the stall wall more than once by Jack.

"Well, think how fast Paws took to herding cattle. He'd watch for hand motions—didn't even need us to shout at him." Thorliff smiled at his wife rocking Inga, who was almost asleep.

"Wouldn't it be fun to go?" Astrid leaned on her father's shoulder.

Haakan turned to look at her. "Who would milk the cows?"

"Don't you want to go?" She stared at him, surprise widening her eyes.

Haakan shook his head. "Not really. I like it right here. That Chicago trip about made me sick, all the stink and noise and dirt. Big cities aren't for me."

"Minneapolis isn't as bad as Chicago." Elizabeth added to the conversation. "Having been both places, I'd say there's a world of difference. If we went, we could go to Northfield and visit my parents. I know they'd love to keep Inga with them while we went to the show."

"You could write it all up for the *Blessing Gazette* and then sell the article to other papers." Astrid smiled at her brother.

"Now there's a thought," Thorliff said. "I never would have come up with it myself."

"Go ahead and be sarcastic," Astrid countered. "I think it would be the most wonderful thing in the world to do. He's almost as famous as Black Beauty."

"Black Beauty wasn't real. Beautiful Jim Key is." Andrew turned to his wife. "You think he could spell Thorliff or Trygve?"

"Would you like to go?" Haakan looked to Ingeborg, now swaying from side to side with a sleeping baby in her arms.

"Yes and no."

"Now, there's a definitive answer for you." Thorliff grinned at his pa.

"Yes, if we could all go. No, if you decided not to."

Haakan nodded. "We shall see."

They all stopped talking at the jingle of sleigh bells. Ingeborg handed the baby back to Ellie and went to the door. "Pastor Solberg, come on in."

"No. I just came to get you all," he said from atop his horse. "There's something you have to come and see."

"Right now?"

"You wouldn't want to miss out."

"Where?"

"At Hjelmer's."

"I thought he was in Bismarck."

"He was. You have to come see." Solberg backed his horse. "I'm going over to Lars's. See you in a bit."

"It must be something really important if he wants us all to come." Haakan shoved his chair back.

"Are we all going?" Astrid asked.

"Why not? It's Sunday afternoon and awhile before chores need to be done," he said. "I'll get the sleigh."

"We'll take our sleigh and go home from Hjelmer's." Thorliff stood too and patted his wife's shoulder. "Figured it was someone needing a doctor. Come on, Andrew. You can help harness up."

The women bundled themselves and the children and were ready when the teams drove up to the house. Once they were all snuggled under the buffalo robe that was kept for winter travel, Ingeborg said, "And here we were all having such a serious discussion and never decided anything about Mr. Gould's son, Jonathan. We just took off about that horse and now this. Uff da. You just never know."

"But going to see Beautiful Jim Key would really be fun, don't you think?" Astrid tucked her mittened hand through her mother's arm and laid her head on her shoulder. "Ride the train to Minneapolis and see the sights. Go to Northfield. Maybe Thorliff would give me a tour of St. Olaf. I wonder if they have a nursing school there now."

"Would you want to go there?"

"I don't know. I'd like to see the place."

"But Elizabeth really wants you to go to Chicago."

"I know, but there is the nursing school at the college in Grand Forks, and that is closer to home. I could come home sometimes on the train for even a couple of days."

Ingeborg heard a note of wistfulness in her daughter's voice. "You know, you don't have to go away at all if you don't want to."

"I know. I read about some doctors getting all their training from another doctor. So I suppose nurses can do that too. But if we build a hospital here and I want to work there, then I want to make sure I know all I need to know."

"I don't ever want to leave Blessing again except to go visit ma and pa," Ellie said, snuggling her baby close. "I have all I want right here."

Ingeborg put her arm around Ellie and hugged her. "I love having you so close."

"Actually, what she means is, if you go visiting, you can leave the baby with her." Astrid leaned forward enough to see Ellie's face. "She's as happy as a pig in the mud with babies to hold."

"That's a fine picture," Ingeborg said. "Thank you so much."

"Would you look at that?" Haakan turned over his shoulder so they could all hear.

Astrid scrambled out from under the robe in the wagon bed. "What? What do you see?"

26

"MRS. BJORKLUND, CAN YOU BE GONE for a bit?"

Sophie glanced up from her ledger. "Why, whatever is wrong, Mr. Wiste? You look all flustered."

"Not flustered, but you must come see this." He stayed on the mat by the front door so as not to track snow all over the entry.

The man was nothing if not polite. "And what is it that I must come see?" She glanced down at the columns in the ledger as if they were the most important thing in her entire world. She really didn't feel like getting all bundled up to go outdoors. While the February sun was shining, although heading toward the horizon, winter had yet to lose its lock on the land.

"I think everyone in town is there."

"Really?" She couldn't help but get her interest piqued. "I need to be helping Mrs. Sam with supper soon." She thanked God daily that Mrs. Sam had finally gotten well enough to return to work. Otherwise she and Lily Mae would be hard at it themselves. Finally she'd been able to take some time with her bookwork. Besides, no matter what was going on, stepping outside with Mr. Wiste would be pleasant. *He makes anything pleasant.* Now, where had that thought come from? "I'm sorry to hear that. It would be a shame to miss out."

At the saddening look on his face, Sophie pushed back her chair.

"All right, but I can't be gone very long." Feeling like giggling at the pleasure lighting his face, she fetched her wool coat out of her room, stopping in front of the mirror to nestle a black felt hat into her upswept hair and pin it in place. To keep her ears from freezing she added a long scarf under the collar of her coat so she could cover neck, ears, and even face if need be. At least she had warm boots on already, along with wool socks and a quilted woolen petticoat. There was always a draft coming down the lower hall and into the vestibule where her small desk hid right behind the higher counter for checking in guests.

"Sorry it took so long." She smiled at the waiting man as she joined him.

His appreciative glance made her neck warm. "It was worth the wait." He held the door for her and took her elbow as he let it close. "Be careful. It's icy."

"That's because we're in North Dakota. You didn't have ice in the winter in Minnesota?"

"Not to the degree as here."

Sophie heard laughter and people calling to each other from the other side of Penny's store. She glanced up at Mr. Wiste.

"You have to see it to believe it."

"Hjelmer brought back another contraption."

"What gives you that idea?"

A bang that sounded like three rifles firing at the same time made her want to duck. "Who's shooting?" Surely there would be no hunting today, although anyone would be grateful to bag a deer. In fact, if someone shot one, she'd gladly pay for half of it. They'd not had venison on the menu for some time.

"I don't think anyone is."

"Crank her again!" That was Hjelmer's voice.

"Horses don't need no cranking," someone shouted.

They stopped at the end of the porch that fronted Penny's store so they could see over the crowd. As Mr. Wiste mentioned, most everyone in Blessing was there—all in a big circle around a contraption, as she'd guessed.

"It's a horseless carriage." Sophie had heard of them and had seen pictures of them in Thorliff's newspaper. Riding in one would surely be an adventure. *Interesting that there might be adventures even here in Blessing.* Now where had that thought come from?

"They're calling them automobiles now."

"How long do I have to crank?" Andrew straightened from his efforts.

"Until milking," someone shouted.

"It'll fire any time now." Hjelmer fiddled with some knobs and levers. "There now, try it again."

Another explosion that puffed smoke out of the rear of the conveyance sounded even louder this close up. But this time the monster coughed and stood shaking with the engine rumbling.

"Who's going to ride with me?" Hjelmer asked, looking around the crowd.

"You take it out on the roads here and you'll get stuck for certain." Haakan shook his head.

"Well, I drove it off the train and right to here, so I imagine we can go to the boardinghouse and back. Come on, get in."

Haakan climbed in and settled into the seat. "Can't be any worse than the steam engine." He waved to Ingeborg. "Hang onto the horses, all of you. Over in Grafton they had two teams run away when the first of these came to town." He turned to Hjelmer. "All right, what are you waiting for?"

Hjelmer shifted into reverse and gunned the engine. The wheels spun on the snow, throwing ice in every direction, but the automobile gave a little jerk and started backing up. The *putt-putt* of the engine made Sophie want to cover her ears.

"Do they have to be so loud?"

"They're getting better. I rode in one in Minneapolis before I came here. This must be the first one to come to Blessing."

"As far as I know. I've seen pictures but never one moving. Look how fast they are going."

"Won't be long before they take over the horse."

"Pa said the horseless carriage is just a fad."

"I hate to argue with such a lovely young lady, but mark my words, they are here to stay and will only improve as time goes on. The combustion engine is just in its infancy."

"How do you know so much about it?"

"Thought of buying one, but there aren't enough roads for them yet."

"Sophie!" Astrid and Grace pushed their way through the crowd and stepped up beside Sophie.

"Good afternoon, Mr. Wiste," Astrid said politely and then turned to Sophie. "I want to go riding in it. What about you?"

Sophie shook her head but nibbled on her bottom lip at the same time, the shaking turning to nodding. She leaned out to watch Hjelmer turn the car in the middle of the street and pick up speed again on the return. They were going almost as fast as the train. But when Hjelmer tried to slow the thing down, it swerved and headed for the people gathered along the road to watch.

"Look out! He's in a skid," Mr. Wiste yelled and began pulling people back. "Move fast. Get out of the way."

"Hjelmer Bjorklund, what in the world are you doing now?" Penny leaped out of the way as the front end of the monster connected with one of the posts on the steps to the porch of her store. It shook and shuddered and the post and rail splintered, the crash of it filling the air. With a snort, the beast shivered to a quiet that sounded loud after the racket.

"I'm sorry. I pressed on the brake pedal, and the thing took off all on its own." Hjelmer stepped out of the carriage and lifted his hat to smooth his hair back. "Now, look what you went and did." He shook his head at the car and the destruction it had caused.

"You could have killed someone."

"Or at least injured one of us."

Hjelmer raised his hands, asking for silence.

"I'm sorry for the scare. Guess I have more to learn about driving."

"At least horses stop when you *whoa* them."

Astrid leaned close to Sophie's ear. "They all jumped around and ran like rabbits."

Sophie tried to keep a straight face, but a snicker caught her by surprise. She clamped her mittened hands over her face to keep from laughing out loud, although her heart had nearly leaped out of her throat when that thing was heading straight for Penny. When she heard a *harrumph* behind her, she turned just enough to see Mrs. Valders glaring at her.

Oh, now what? Sophie tried to close her ears, but it didn't work.

"Not even six months since her husband died, and here she is with another man."

I hope Mr. Wiste can't hear her. All I did was walk over with him to see what all the ruckus was about. No wonder even Mor complains about that woman at times.

"No regard for others."

Sophie's ears burned. She clamped her teeth and sucked in a deep breath. The cold burned her nose all the way to her lungs. *Say something or just ignore? What would Mor do?* She heard her mother's voice as clearly as if she were standing next to her. *"A soft answer turneth away wrath."*

What kind of soft answer? The old bat didn't speak directly to me. *What do I do?*

"Sophie?"

She could tell by the nudge that Astrid had most likely called her name before. "Sorry. What?"

"We're going to have a popcorn-ball party when we get home. Can you come?"

"Please do." Grace added, speaking carefully, since she couldn't sign with her hands in mittens. She smiled at Mr. Wiste. "You are invited too."

Sophie closed her eyes for a moment. *I want to go, to have fun for a change, to laugh and forget about the boardinghouse.* She faced Grace so she could read her lips. "I'm sorry, I can't. Mrs. Sam still wears out easily. I need to be there to help with supper."

"Come for a little while."

"I could bring you back as soon as you need to." Mr. Wiste's smile made her want to go even more.

"All right, I'll go, but I can't stay too long." There, she'd followed what her heart wanted to do for the first time in months.

"Oh, wonderful." Grace threw her arms around Sophie's shoulders.

Sophie hugged her back. "I'll go tell them I'm going." She started out and turned to find Mr. Wiste beside her. What would Mrs. Valders be saying now? Ignoring the thought, Sophie hurried so as not to keep the others waiting. She was going to a party, a time for fun and laughter, with people her own age. The thought made her want to jump in the snowbank.

Garth held the door for her, and she breezed through, stamped her feet to get rid of snow, and started for the kitchen to tell Mrs. Sam. She met Lily Mae flying across the dining room.

"What's wrong?" The wide-eyed look told her it wasn't good.

"Ma fainted."

All the pleasure left Sophie with a whoosh to be replaced by fear. "Is she all right?"

"She awake, sort of. I sent Lemuel for Dr. Elizabeth."

Sophie turned to Mr. Wiste. "You go on out with the others and have fun. Tell them why I couldn't come. You'll get a chance to meet more of the folks of Blessing."

"But I could help you here."

"Thank you, Mr. Wiste, but that is not necessary." She nodded in dismissal and turned to head for the kitchen. "Where is she?"

"In the storeroom. I fixed a pallet for Ma there." Lily Mae's voice cracked, her dark eyes wide with fear.

"Why didn't you put her on my bed?"

"That wouldn't be proper."

"Oh, for—don't be silly. The storeroom floor is cold." Sophie flew across the room as she spoke and pushed the half-open door so it banged against the wall, Lily Mae right on her heels. Dropping to her knees beside the pallet, Sophie smoothed her hand over Mrs. Sam's forehead. "Do you hurt anywhere?"

"Not so's I know. I jes' found myself on the floor."

"As soon as Lemuel comes back, we'll carry you into the other room, where you'll be more comfortable."

"Where he go?"

"To get the doctor. You shouldn't have come back to work yet."

"Thought I was good enough. 'Sides, you need help here. Lily Mae, you get dat roast out and let it set before slicin' it. Better be no lumps in dat gravy, girl."

"Yes, Ma." Lily Mae scurried back into the kitchen.

Sophie laid a hand on Mrs. Sam's forehead, as she'd seen her mother do when anyone was sick. "Do you have a fever?"

"Jus' a headache. Nothin' to go worryin' yerself over."

"We'll each take a corner of the quilt and carry you to my bed."

"You do no such thing. Don't you go liftin' me. I can get up and sit on de chair by the stove. Be fine."

"Why? So you can faint again?"

Mrs. Sam snorted, but Sophie didn't see her pushing to get up right at the moment. What to do? Mrs. Sam was right. The two of them couldn't carry the old woman into the other room, but she couldn't lie there either.

She looked up to see Mr. Wiste coming through the door, a quilt over his arm.

"I sent the others on. Perhaps I'll go later."

"I say bring me dat chair." Mrs. Sam rolled onto her side and propped herself up on one elbow. When she saw Mr. Wiste, she made a disgusted sound and hid her face behind one hand but smiled when he spread the quilt over her.

Sophie heard the bell tinkle over the front door and boots pounding through the dining room.

"They back here," Lily Mae called.

Sophie rose.

"Hep me up."

"I don't think so." She turned to see Elizabeth following closely behind Lemuel. "Thank you for coming."

"How is she?"

"I's jest fine."

"Then why did you end up on the floor?" Elizabeth knelt and took the patient's wrist to check her pulse, checking for fever with the back of her other hand. "Any pain in your head?"

"No. Well, not enough to fuss over."

"Anywhere else?"

"No. I jest want to get up."

"Mr. Wiste, you take her one arm and, Lemuel, you the other. Let's help her up to sit on the chair. Sophie, you go get the chair." Elizabeth smiled at Mrs. Sam. "You tell me if you get dizzy now."

With only a couple of grunts, they had the older woman sitting in the chair with her eyes closed.

"Dizzy?"

"A mite."

"Put your head between your knees." Elizabeth gently pressed down on the back of Mrs. Sam's neck. "We should have gotten you up in stages." With gentle fingers she explored the old woman's head. "No bumps, so you must have fallen easy like."

"You were lucky," Sophie said.

"We won't be so lucky if we don't get de supper on de tables," she muttered from her knees.

"We take care of that." Lemuel flashed a smile at the doctor. "Thank you."

"I didn't do anything yet."

"Nothin' to do. I be fine now. Sorry to bother you." Mrs. Sam sat straighter and glared at her son. "Never seen an old woman faint before?" She mumbled some more under her breath. "Weren't de first time I fainted. Most likely not de last."

"I'd say you should go on home and take it easy for a day or so, then come see me." Elizabeth turned to Sophie. "You want me to send Thelma over to help for a day or two?"

"No, we can manage." Sophie laid a hand on Mrs. Sam's shoulder. "You can go home or go lie down in Bridget's room. Might be better to not go out in that cold."

"I sit right in de kitchen and make sure—"

"I will make sure all goes well. Which will it be? The bed here or go on home?"

"I could go get Pa," Lemuel offered.

"Good idea. As soon as we get the food served."

Sophie turned to see that Mr. Wiste was still there, standing back out of the way and watching the proceedings. "Thank you for your help."

"You are welcome."

"You could go on out to the party now."

"I'll stay here." He smiled at her. "I'll keep out of the way."

For some reason his smile made her feel comforted. He had chosen to stay just because he saw a need. "Would a cup of coffee help?" she asked.

"That it would. Dr. Bjorklund, would you like one too?"

Sophie turned back to see Dr. Elizabeth checking Mrs. Sam's pulse again. "Coffee?"

"That would be marvelous, but here in the kitchen where I can keep an eye on my patient." She studied Mrs. Sam. "I think she needs a cup too."

"My land, this ain't de way—"

"You can have coffee or tea, in here or in the bedroom." Elizabeth spoke in her doctor's orders voice that even Mrs. Sam obeyed.

"Coffee . . . in here."

That night after crawling into bed, Sophie sighed. What would they do without Mrs. Sam again? And what if something was truly wrong? She thought back to when Mr. Wiste told her thank-you and good-night, as if she'd done something special for him. He was the one to be thanked. She smiled to herself. He was always so proper to call her Mrs. Bjorklund. She tried to remember what being a missus felt like but could hardly even remember what Hamre looked like. His face seemed to be fading like a figure going off in the fog. Three months since he'd been gone, and she'd thought she'd never laugh again. Yet today she'd laughed and almost went to a party.

She rolled over onto her side. Would she ever get to attend popcorn parties again?

27

March

"YOU HAVE A LETTER," Sophie told Garth as he stood before the desk in the boardinghouse lobby.

He took the letter she handed him and smiled. Not a wide smile, because he could scarcely hold his head up, but his lips moved in spite of the fatigue. "Thank you."

"Are you all right?"

Her concern made him straighten—barely. "Just tired." He paused and then for some strange reason, added, "I've not been sleeping well."

"Too much coffee with your supper?"

"Perhaps."

"Your supper is waiting."

"Thank you. Let me wash some of the flour off, and I'll be right back." And no, it wasn't the coffee. He half folded the letter in his hand. He knew by the handwriting who it was from. His mother. And he most likely knew what was in it. She was urging him to return to Minneapolis and resume the care of his children. But he didn't have to go there to do that. All he had to do was build a house here in Blessing and have his sister bring the children out, and they would be a happy family again. All the better if Dan decided to come work for him at the flour mill.

Strange how lately the face he thought he would never forget, that he would mourn forever, seemed to be fading away. That was one of the reasons he'd not been sleeping well. While he fought to remember the shape of her eyes, the memories of their earlier years together always brought joy to his heart. The first time he met her, the way she laughed, their wedding, the birth of their first child—a boy who was, as the old saying went, the apple of his eye.

Some days he missed little Grant so much his heart tried to quit beating, but mostly he concentrated on his job to the point of thinking of nothing else. Going home at Christmas had made matters worse, not better, as he'd hoped.

His mother pleading for him to come home, to return to a house that was home no more, didn't help either.

He washed his face and hands, brushed the flour from his hair, eyebrows, and mustache, shook out his suit coat, and left the letter lying on his chest of drawers. He headed for the kitchen, a place that had come to be the symbol of home to him.

Sophie—he couldn't keep calling her Mrs. Bjorklund—turned from drawing a plate from the warming oven and smiled at him. Her smile could drive away demons.

"Will you sit with me, Mrs. Bjorklund?" He asked her the same thing every evening.

"I will." She set the filled plate at his place.

He sat and tucked the napkin into the collar of his shirt.

Sophie brought the coffeepot to fill his cup. "Are you sure you wouldn't rather have tea?"

"No. This is fine, thank you." He waited for her to sit, started to cut his meat, paused, put the knife down, and bowed his head. Why all of a sudden he felt the need of saying grace, he wasn't sure, but for some reason it seemed important.

Perhaps it had to do with Pastor Solberg's sermon on Sunday. He'd spoken of finding joy in Jesus, of talking with the Father about everything.

Heaven knew he needed a friend. When he opened his eyes again, he found Sophie staring at him. Was a man saying grace such a shock?

Go ahead and ask her, he ordered himself while he buttered his bread. Instead, he cut his meat and took a bite. Even warmed up, the food tasted better than any other he'd had in his life. Maddie had not been a particularly good cook. His mother was adequate. What her meals lacked in flavor, she made up for in quantity. He could feel Sophie watching him.

He stopped to take a drink of coffee. "So how has your day gone?" Her smile made his heart kick up.

"Busy. We have two new boarders, and they each paid for a month."

"I'm glad to hear that. Who are they?"

"A Mr. John Snyder. He is looking for work here. He came from Indiana and is thinking of heading on west if he finds nothing here. I wondered if you might be needing another man."

"I'll talk with him. And the other?"

"A woman, Miss Bergstrom, from Minneapolis like you." Sophie leaned forward and lowered her voice. "She says she is a nurse and is looking to build a hospital."

"A hospital?" He stopped chewing.

"I know. She said she was planning to talk with Elizabeth. She heard of her through that doctor in Chicago. It takes a lot of money to start a hospital."

"I'm sure it does. Perhaps she has a lot of money."

Sophie shrugged. "She is dressed very well." She steepled her fingers and rested her chin on them. "She's been to Europe and New York and lots of places. Why would she come here to start a hospital? You'd think a doctor would be more interested in starting a hospital than a nurse."

"Why don't you ask her?"

"I plan to the next time I see her."

Garth laid down his fork and picked up his cup to cradle in both hands, his elbows, like hers propped on the table. He took in a deep breath of courage. "I have a favor to ask."

"Of course. What is it?"

"I am getting tired of calling you Mrs. Bjorklund when in my mind I always think of you as Sophie. Might I call you Sophie and you call me Garth?"

Sophie stared at him, surprise lifting her eyebrows, then the corners of her mouth. "I think that would be very nice, but please don't let Mrs. Valders hear of it. I've been castigated by her enough."

"She seems to do that well." He sipped his coffee. Sophie's eyes sparkled in the lamplight. While her middle expanded, her face grew only more lovely. Like many women he'd heard tell, pregnancy became them, as it had Maddie. If only he dared to continue down that lane of thought. But society would condemn them both as being in too big of a hurry, and she had already tasted the censure. He'd heard the woman hiss at Sophie during the runaway automobile fiasco. What a nosy busybody. Running the post office must yield plenty of fodder for her nosiness.

"Good. That's settled, then." He buttered another piece of bread and continued eating.

"Would you like more? I could reheat some."

"No thanks. Why don't you tell me more about Seattle?"

"I always talk. I think it's time I got to ask the questions."

Sophie's chin tilted slightly, a sign he'd learned to recognize as her determined look. *Please don't ask about my wife.* He looked down at his plate so she couldn't read his eyes.

"What was life like in Minneapolis?"

He breathed a sigh of relief. "Well, I worked at a flour mill."

"Not much different than here?"

"One major difference. Here I run it; there I had several bosses."

"That would make a difference." Her grin turned saucy. "Being boss is better."

"Except you have all the responsibilities, like you here in the boardinghouse."

"True."

"And if people don't show up to work, you have to do it."

"Or find someone else."

He guessed by the shadow that flitted across her face she was thinking of Mrs. Sam. "How is she?"

"She says she's all right, but I see her stop to catch her breath at times. I don't know how we would manage without her." She paused, then tossed her head. "There you go, getting back to me. We decided that it was your turn. Remember?"

"We?" His eyebrows rose on the question.

"Well, I did, but you didn't disagree. So tell me about your family. You've met most of mine." Her eyes took on a sheen.

She still misses her husband. What kind of fool am I, forgetting that?

"I mean, if you want to. If you'd rather not, I understand."

"No." He swallowed hard. "I would be happy—" *Not happy at all, but I will tell you because it is necessary.* He prolonged the pause with another sip of coffee. When he made a slight face, she jumped up.

"I'll warm that up for you."

Wiste, when will you get yourself in order? It is only fair that you tell her.

She returned with the coffeepot and a sober face. "I'm sorry. It is not proper for me to intrude on . . . on your grief." After filling his cup, she poured her cup half full and set the pot on the table. When she sat down, she filled the cup with cream and took a swallow.

You are so young for all you've been through. The thought made him want to reach out and take her hand. "Thanks for the refill. I never could abide lukewarm coffee." He hoped his smile would reassure her, but she didn't look at him.

"I own a house in Minneapolis not far from my mother's house. My sister lives next door. Ma is helping to take care of my two children. My son, Grant, is two and a half, and my daughter is now six months old. My wife, Madelynn—she went by Maddie—died giving birth to our baby girl. I—we found a wet nurse for the baby, and I . . . not long after that I heard of the opening here in Blessing, and the rest you know. My sister Helga took the baby to her house as soon as she had her own baby."

"I'm sure your little boy misses you."

"Yes, and I miss him. But I like my job here. I like Blessing, so when spring comes, I will build a house, and my sister will bring the children. I'm hoping her husband, Dan, would like to work here for me. We would build them a house too, or they could live with me." *There, he'd said it aloud, stating his plans. Now to write and let his mother know for sure. She would not be happy.*

"Is your father still alive?"

Garth shook his head. "He was killed in a flour-mill explosion."

"Oh." Sophie's eyes grew wide. "Does that happen often?"

"Not often, but the fine flour dust is extremely flammable. If there is an open flame or a spark—well, it can happen."

"How long ago? I mean, your father's death?"

"Four years. My older brother still works in Minneapolis at the Pillsbury "A" Mill. My mother would rather none of us worked in one."

"I don't blame her. Would she come here too?"

"No. She is near her other grandchildren there."

"How many brothers and sisters do you have?"

"Three of each. I'm the youngest."

"You've met all of mine. Two girls and two boys."

"You don't see them often."

"Oh—I forgot to get your dessert." She pushed herself to her feet. "We have chocolate pudding with cookies."

He watched her walk away. While her twin was finishing school, she'd already been married and widowed and carrying a baby. Along with managing a boardinghouse.

And dreaming of adventures. She'd told him about that during one of their kitchen visits.

She has no idea what having a baby is going to do to her life. The thought made his forehead wrinkle. He could feel it, along with the certainty that she was not thinking of a man with two children and a house in Minneapolis. Although that might be a bit of an inducement. There were many adventures to be had in Minneapolis. *But I don't want to return to Minneapolis. I want to remain here in Blessing.*

She set down a plate holding a bowl of pudding and four cookies. "Maybe I should have brought more."

"You usually eat your dessert with me."

"I know, but"—she rubbed the rise under her apron—"some things just don't sit well."

"According to Maddie, that is not unusual. She said that some babies like some foods and some others. She quit eating bacon with Grant, and it was chocolate with the girl."

"What is her name?"

He stared at her, caught with the spoon halfway to his mouth.

"I just thought . . . you never say her name. I'm sorry. Ignore what I said. My mother always said, 'Fools rush in where angels fear to tread.' Often she meant me."

Garth swallowed, took a breath, ordered himself to say it, and swallowed again. "Her name is Madelynn. They—we—call her Linnie. My mother and sister chose to name the baby after my wife." He could feel his throat clogging. Now was not the time to cry. And here he'd been doing so well. He pushed back from the table and stood. "Good evening, Mrs. Bjorklund." He only kept from running from the room with the kind of resolve that he'd groomed much of his life.

You didn't need to be rude like that! His inner voice sounded amazingly like that of his paternal grandfather, the one who'd terrified a little boy with his dictums.

Garth pushed open the door to his room and, after closing it, leaned his forehead against the cool wood. Why did he react like this now? He thought he was beyond this. For the first months the only safe place was at the mill, where he was able to concentrate on work to the exclusion of all else.

"Dear Lord, what do I do?" He sank down on the edge of the bed, his heart bleeding tears that his eyes refused to shed. Perhaps there were no more tears. He'd cried the well dry those days afterward when he wore a trail in the rugs pacing the house, upstairs and down. Filled with rage at times, broken at others.

"Lord God, what do I do now?" *I'm praying again.* The thought or the prayer brought a sense of peace, something else he'd not felt in a long time. If talking to Sophie about his family brought him to running again, was that good or bad? Would it always be like this? He noticed the letter and opened it, quickly perusing the news. With nothing surprising he tucked it into the drawer. She *really* didn't want them moving to Blessing.

28

March 17, 1902

Dear Mr. Gould,

Thank you for the honor of choosing us to host your son. If you believe his coming here for the summer would be advantageous, we are pleased to provide a home for him for the time he is here. While Blessing has changed a great deal since you were here, you must remember we are still a small town, a farming community without all the luxuries found in the cities. We look forward to hearing from you as to the date he will arrive.

Spring is finally taking over winter; the sound of dripping icicles is music to my winter weary ears. Although it has not been a terribly hard winter, the sight and sounds of spring always give me a lift.

Graduation here will be on Sunday, May 25. We have been discussing the program and thought of asking you to be the speaker here this year if you are considering coming west with your son. We can change the date to accommodate your schedule. You have been so generous with your gifts to our graduat-

ing students all these years, and I know they would be thrilled
to thank you in person.

I look forward to hearing from you.

Your friend,

Ingeborg Bjorklund

Ingeborg read her letter again and laid it aside to dry while she
addressed the envelope. Did she want a rich man's son living in her
home for the summer? Her gaze traveled around the kitchen from
where she sat at the table. They were in need of new curtains, the rug
on the floor was getting ragged, the cabinets needed painting—she
shook her head. No. No matter what they did, their house would not
begin to compare to the home this young man had grown up in. His
father had said the boy was a bit spoiled. Shame the soddy had melted
away in that terrible flood of '97. Living there would have really made
his life different. She chuckled to herself as she folded the letter. What
would be would be. He would come and either enjoy himself and work
hard, or he would hate it. Although how anyone could hate living in
this bowl of God's plenty, she could not understand.

She dripped a dab of candle wax on the envelope, thus sealing it
shut, and propped it against the clear glass sugar bowl in the center of
the table. She paused for just a moment, thanking God for Haakan.
Keeping his gift on the table prompted these prayers for him more
often. Perhaps she'd go into town and visit with little Inga and mail
this letter and some bills she'd prepared to send for cheese orders. Her
account books for the cheese house needed to be brought up to date,
but these first days of spring tugged on her and drew her outside. A
sneaky thought reminded her that winter probably wasn't all done with
them, but she tried to ignore it.

Just for a minute, she promised herself and followed the call of the
dripping icicles and the wind that blew so gently over the drifts and
hollows of snow sculpture. Standing on the back porch, she raised her
face to the sunrays that for the first time in months promised warmth
and the new life of spring. She, who at times still struggled through the
dark days of winter, inhaled the sun and the breeze, the odors of cow,

hay, and manure from the barn, the slight taste of woodsmoke from someone's cooking fire.

Barney came bounding across the snow, yipping his delight at seeing her.

"You need a bone. Every good dog needs a bone. Be right back." She returned with a bone she'd removed earlier from the stew and presented it to him, his wagging tail her reward. She took in one more deep breath that tingled all the way to her toes and returned to open the oven door. After thumping the bread to make sure it was baked enough, she pulled the pans from the oven and tipped them over one by one onto the wooden cooling rack. Then dipping her fingers in the butter bowl, she smeared the crusts with butter and flipped a clean towel over the loaves.

With the bread cooling, she gave the stew a good stir to keep the meat from sticking to the bottom. After beating two eggs in a bowl, she got out flour and a bit of cream, stirring in some herbs dried from her garden, and dropped the dumpling dough into the stew, one spoonful at a time. Covering the kettle, she pushed it to the back again so it wouldn't burn, added wood to the firebox, and finished setting the table.

With all ready, she stepped back outside and gave the triangle three good licks with the bar, enjoying the echo as the call bounced off the barn. She could hear the men clanging about down in the machine shed, getting the machinery in shape for spring work. Both Haakan and Lars were sticklers about watching for wear and fixing things before they broke, when at all possible. Andrew had learned from the best.

The three men followed the dug-out path back to the house. Even as lovely as it was today, she knew it would fall below freezing again at night, and perhaps there would be even more snowstorms. One never trusted spring in the Dakotas until the ground was bare, and even then they could get another freak storm.

"Sure smells good in here," Haakan said as he hung his hat on the coatrack by the door.

"Fresh bread and stew with dumplings ought to smell good." Ingeborg set the kettle next to her place so she could dish up the plates.

"Ellie said to tell you thank-you that she didn't have to make dinner. With Carl teething, she didn't get a lot of sleep last night." Andrew washed his hands at the sink, following his pa.

"That poor baby. Teething is harder for some than others. Did you rub his gums with your finger to help those first teeth come through?"

Andrew held up one finger. "He nearly gnawed it off." The look on his face made the others laugh. "Did we have trouble with teething when we were babies?"

"I don't remember much about you. Tante Kaaren and Thorliff took care of you while I worked to save the homesteads after your pa died. But Astrid sailed through without much trouble."

As soon as Haakan said grace, she dished up the stew while the men passed the plate of sliced bread around. Andrew picked up a piece and sniffed it, closing his eyes and smiling at the fragrance.

"No one makes bread as good as you do." He stopped. "Ellie's is real good too."

Ingeborg smiled to herself. *Leave it to her Andrew to always stick up for Ellie*. He'd done so ever since they were little. "You are most fortunate that your wife is so good at so many things."

"I know."

The discussion meandered from machinery repairs to which cow was due soon and whether the river might flood again this year. If they had a nice slow melt without a lot of heavy rain, they might get by without the river rising over its banks.

"I'm going to town this afternoon," Ingeborg mentioned as she refilled coffee cups again.

"You want I should hitch up the sleigh?" Haakan put his hand over his cup. "Thanks. I've had enough."

"That would be good. I thought of walking, but I need some things at the store."

"I could use some tobacco."

"Anything else?"

Haakan's eyes furrowed in thought. "Not unless that box of bolts I ordered arrived."

"I'll check. I'm mailing the letter back to Mr. Gould."

"Good." Haakan pushed back his chair. "Better get back out there." The three men thanked her for the meal, took their hats off the rack, shrugged into coats, and trooped on out the door.

Ingeborg put things away and washed up, humming all the while. Though she hesitated at donning her wool coat, she did so, pinning her black felt hat in place and looping a scarf around her neck. Winter could turn on them at any second, thundering down out of the north like a buffalo herd on the run. After placing her mail and a shopping list in her reticule, she followed the path, lined nearly waist high with shoveled-off snow, to the barn, where horse and sleigh stood waiting. How wonderful it would be to see the green grass again instead of piled high snowbanks, although she had to admit that the wind-sculpted snow waves, as she called them, were indeed beautiful. In the summer the wind created waves in the grass and wheat; in the winter, snow waves with crowns like surf, all gifts of the wind.

She stopped first at Penny's store.

"Well, look who's here." Penny, her smile as wide as her face, came around the counter, hands outstretched. "What did you think of all the excitement the other day?"

"You mean about the horseless carriage? Haakan couldn't quit talking about his ride. Uff da. Such goings-on."

"Ja, men and their toys. I'm sure we'll be selling automobiles out there with the machinery before long. What can I get you today?"

"I sometimes wish you carried everything here like you used to. That was far more convenient, not that I don't like the Garrisons, mind you." Ingeborg looked at her list. "Haakan wants to know if his bolts came in yet."

Penny shook her head. "Sorry."

"Then I need sewing-machine needles, white thread, red and blue dye if you have it—"

"I do and some nice green." Penny led the way between aisles as they talked. "What are you dying?"

"The yarn left from my last spinning. I still have some fleece to card and spin, and here it is nearly time to shear again. You should come out. We have the sweetest crop of lambs." She tapped her chin with one finger. "I think I'll spin some really fine and dye it pink for a sweater for Inga. I finished more soakers for Carl. Oh, and do you have any flannel for diapers? They never seem to have enough diapers, so I'll hem some for them and for Sophie's baby too. Ellie is already sewing shifts for the summer."

"It's hard to believe the girls will be graduating." Penny pulled out a bolt of blue dimity with a touch of green. "I thought of this for Astrid's dress. Her eyes would really sparkle against this."

"Just so they don't sparkle too much and catch the eyes of the young men around here."

"That's part of life, and if you've not noticed, she's been catching the eyes of several young men already."

"I know, but she has her eye on nursing school, just like Thorliff did with going to St. Olaf. He'd like her to go there, but she might go clear to Chicago."

"To Dr. Morganstein?"

"Ja. I don't know how I'll bear it. All three gone from our house."

"I'll send you one of mine."

"Which one today?"

"Take your pick." The two women laughed together and then turned at the dinging of the bell over the door.

"Good day, Mrs. Magron," Penny called. "I'll be right with you."

"No rush."

Penny turned back to Ingeborg. "Is there anything else you need?"

"Let's measure out enough for that dress you mentioned, and I'll take this lace too. I wish I could surprise her, but trying to get away with anything secret around her is nigh to impossible. She's like her pa in that."

"Oh, I nearly forgot. I have a new washing machine in. I'll show it to you both at the same time." Penny tucked the bolts of goods under one arm. "Come on. You won't believe it."

"Have you already tried it?"

"Of course. Would I sell something I hadn't tried? Every woman in

Blessing needs one before spring cleaning starts. Why all those curtains and bedding would be done in a jiffy."

"And how long, pray tell, is a jiffy?"

"I'll just set these things up here on the counter. Come on, I have this washing machine all set up. No more boiling clothes or using a scrub board. Scrub boards are going the way of the walking plow—out, out, out."

Ingeborg stared at what looked like a washtub on legs but with a cover, a crank on one side, and a strange thing on top composed of two tubes in a frame.

Penny removed the lid. "See these paddles? You pour in hot water, add soap and the dirty clothes, then turn this crank, and it beats the dirt out. No more scraped fingers. Then, and this is the greatest part, no more wringing. You feed an end of the towel or pants into these rollers and turn this crank. It squeezes the water out as it pulls the shirt through. When you hang them on the line, they are dry in no time."

Ingeborg stared at the machine. "Somehow this reminds me of when we first ordered our sewing machines."

"That it does, only men are finally inventing machines for the house too. And I saw a picture of a new flatiron. You put hot coals right in it, and there is another one that uses kerosene. I'm going to order them the next time the salesman comes by."

"My land, what is our world coming to?" Mrs. Magron walked around the machine. "Have you sold very many?"

"This just came in two days ago. I tried it yesterday. Outside will be better, since it tends to slosh some. And just think, children will be able to turn the crank, leaving your hands free to feed clothes into the wringer. This one is even better than the one at the boardinghouse."

Ingeborg thought a moment. "I'll have to talk this over with Haakan. How much is it?"

Penny named a price that made Ingeborg swallow. "But think how much men spend for their machinery. This is nothing like that."

"But it won't bring in money like their machinery does," Mrs. Magron said.

"True, but if you didn't have to spend so much time doing the wash, you could bake bread for the store and thus bring in more money."

Ingeborg shook her head. Penny had been asking her to bring in fresh baked bread for years, but she never had the time. "You don't sell food anymore, remember?"

"Ah, but Mrs. Garrison would be singing like a meadowlark if you would take that on."

"Will you put it on our bill?" Mrs. Magron's voice took on a firmness that made Ingeborg blink.

Penny turned to the little woman who so rarely did or said anything without Mrs. Valders' approval. "Of course."

"Then I want Mr. Magron to pick it up tonight—or tomorrow."

Ingeborg and Penny exchanged glances, both of them obviously thinking the same thing. What was going on here?

"Are you sure?"

"You will still take returns if something is not satisfactory?"

"Of course."

"Then I shall use my egg and cream money for my new washing machine. And I'm going to try that new soap that you have also."

"Let me finish Ingeborg's order, and then we'll write that up. Since you'll be the first in town to have this new machine, would you mind if I ask you questions after you've used it?"

"I would be delighted."

"Oh, there is an instruction book with it, and since Thorliff wrote about Hamre's automobile for the paper, perhaps he'll write a story about your new washing machine."

"Whatever you decide. I need to go to the grocery store, and I'll come back. Good seeing you, Ingeborg." And out the door she marched, leaving both Bjorklund women staring after her.

"Well, can you beat that?" Ingeborg said softly.

"And now I don't have one to sell to you."

"But you will order another and let me know as soon as it arrives. Since I don't have Astrid around to help me wring sheets and men's pants, this will be wonderful."

"You can always hire help."

"I know, but we already hire so many people between the harvesting and the cheese house. I wish Goodie were still here. She and I worked together like sisters. I'd put her in charge of the cheese house."

"I will let you know when the next one arrives. I wish we could go to the big fair in St. Louis. They show all the new things that are coming from all over the world. One of these days we are all going to have telephones and electric lights, be able to see moving picture shows on big screens, and . . . and—"

"You've been reading too many magazines."

"We will. The next ten years will bring enormous changes."

"How do you know that?"

"Hjelmer said so, and you ask Thorliff. He's seen and learned lots more than he is telling us." All the while she was talking, Penny was measuring yardage and trims, wrapping the packages, and adding the bill.

Ingeborg paid what she owed and headed for the door. "Tusen takk."

"Ja, anytime."

Leaving horse and sleigh in front of the store, Ingeborg walked the block to drop her letters in the slot at the post office and finished up at the grocery store. Since she needed only vanilla and brown sugar, she took her package and returned to the sleigh.

She'd just settled into the sleigh and was backing the horse when an explosion set her horse to rearing. He took the sleigh with him as he tore out of town. Ingeborg hung on to the reins and braced her feet against the sleigh front. But no matter how hard she pulled, he had the bit in his teeth, heading for home. *Dear Lord, keep us on the road and upright.* "Whoa," she yelled, sawing on the reins. What could have caused such an explosion?

29

THE EXPLOSION IN THE FLOUR MILL threw Garth up and into a hard object, then dropped him on the floor. Debris beat down on him, and then something heavy crushed him into the floor. It all happened so fast, he could do nothing but fight to breathe, not sure if he was really injured or just had the wind knocked out of him.

"Fire! Fire!" Men shouting, someone screaming. "Get out! Call the fire wagon!"

"Mr. Wiste? Garth? Where are you?"

"Here." But he knew his words went not farther than his breath. He forced himself to move hands and feet, checking to see what was working. Every movement brought pain, but he could move. A deep breath made him gasp. Ribs, most likely. "My men. Got to get the men out." He tried to roll over, but something heavy pinned him down. The smell of burning flour seared his nose. Smoke, heat. The flour floating in the air would burn hot and fast.

Where in the mill had the blast occurred? While questions sifted through his befuddled mind, he forced himself to think where the workers would be. His assistant had gone to the necessary. The millmen could be anywhere. Ten men. He had to find them. But he couldn't move. He ran his hands over whatever was pinning him down. A beam? Something big. But it wasn't actually resting on him or he'd have been crushed for sure. He braced against it and tried to pull himself out.

"Garth? Wiste, where are you?"

"Here." This time he was sure he'd spoken aloud. "Over here. I'm trapped under something."

"Keep talking."

"Here. I'm here." Any words brought on coughing. The pain nearly knocked him out.

He heard someone near him say, "Under something." The beam shifted as two men heaved it off him and dragged him to his feet.

"Thank God we found you. Can you walk?"

"I-I hope so. Where are the rest of the men?"

"Don't know." They half dragged him across and around shattered walls and pieces of the roof.

Staggering down the corridor, smoke burgeoning, they tripped over part of a damaged wall, and Garth went to his knees.

"Mr. Wiste, come on Garth, we gotta get out of here."

"What about the others?" With their help, he managed to get to his feet again.

"Don't know."

"Who was screaming?"

"Don't know." One of the men took his arm and pulled him down a hallway, heading for the back door. Hearing moaning, they stopped, followed the sound, and found another man on the floor. Between them, they picked him up and dragged him with them. A crash behind them said something had caved in.

Hearts pumping, lungs screaming, they stumbled outside and collapsed into a melting snowbank.

How bad is it? Where are the rest of my men?

Thorliff ran up. "We have two men on the other side of the building. Do you know about the others? How many?"

"Ten . . . working today." Garth doubled over coughing. He kept from passing out from the pain by sheer will. "Besides me."

The clanging of the fire wagon caught their attention.

"How bad is it?" Garth asked.

"Still don't know. Get out in front so we can make a count. I'm going on around."

Garth put a hand to the back of his head and felt the warm wet of blood. He checked the man now unconscious at their feet. "Let's get him over to Dr. Bjorklund's." Together, coughing every other step, they dragged him around the burning building and out to the street.

"Here, take him." Garth turned and headed toward the front of the building. With only five out, there were another five still inside.

"You can't go in there!"

He ignored the shout and picked up his pace, pulling off what was left of his coat as he moved forward. A force caught him in the back of his knees, and he hit the snow-packed ground. Rage smote him as the tackle grounded him.

"I need to get my men out." He tried kicking at the attacker, but he couldn't move with a body lying on him.

"You can't go in there. It's too late." The voice in his ear softened. "I can't let you kill yourself like that."

"But my men—"

"I'm sorry. Maybe more got out the other side." The man relaxed his hold, rolling to the side so Garth could breathe more easily.

Garth tried to sit, but a fit of coughing forced him back to the ground.

"You need to see the doctor. You've a cut on the back of your head and now blood on your chin. Sorry, but I think you got that when I tackled you."

Garth turned to see who was talking. "Toby?"

"Yah, I had gone to the grain elevator. Hopefully the snow on the roof is going to save that building. The fire wagon is concentrating there. Nothing will save the flour mill. If this were summer, there'd be sparks everywhere and half the town would be burning." He stood and extended a hand to Garth. "Come, you can lean on me."

Garth let the younger man help him up. Right now one step in front of the other was about all he could manage.

Toby dug a handkerchief out of his pocket. "Here, let's stop that bleeding if we can." He pressed the folded compress against the wound on the back of Garth's head. "Though you don't look too good from the front neither."

Garth tried raising his hand to hold the cloth in place, but the pain refused to let him even lift his arm. The burning in his throat and chest brought on another coughing spasm. He leaned against Toby, knowing he'd be on hands and knees again without his support.

When he finished, Toby pulled him forward.

As they staggered out of the smoke, Thorliff came running back to help. "How bad?"

"Ribs, I think."

"And a few cuts?"

"Come over and sit on the rear gate of the wagon before you collapse."

"My men . . . how many . . . ?" Coughing stopped his words.

"We've taken five over to the surgery. The two that dragged you out over there are okay, and then there's you two. That leaves two missing."

"Who?"

Thorliff gave their names. "I'm sorry."

Garth closed his eyes. *Lord, have mercy.* He listened to the shouting as more men arrived to help, but there was nothing anyone could do except watch the mill burn. He couldn't bear to do that. One of the men had a family—the other was single, one of the Geddick boys. Fine men. Was there anything he could have done? They'd followed all the safety rules that he knew of, but it could have been a spark from the grinding stones.

The thoughts flitted between the wheezes.

Thorliff returned. "Let's get you over there."

Every turn of the wheels sent spears through Garth's chest. At least it felt that way.

The wagon stopped.

Thorliff and Toby helped him out of the wagon, but when they tried to wrap their arms around his waist to hold him up, he shook his head. "Easier if I walk myself. Hurts less."

"We won't let you fall."

One step in front of the other, just like in the smoke, although now at least he could see. Up the three steps, bring one foot up, follow with the other, set it on the same step and lift the right again.

A scream came from within the house. The stench of burned flesh hit them when they opened the door. Someone groaned; another whimpered.

"Let's set you in here. I'll go see what is needed." Thorliff left them.

Garth leaned back against the chair, and once settled, the pain lessened some until he had to cough.

"Here." Thelma, the woman who assisted Elizabeth, stopped in front of him with a cup on a tray. "Drink this. It will soothe your throat and lungs. It's warm honey water."

Garth took the cup in both hands, only to realize he was shaking. Strange, he didn't feel that cold. But he could hardly hold the cup to his mouth. Some sloshed down his front.

"Let me." She took the cup and held it for him to drink. "Easy now. I'll get some blankets. If you'd like, we can make a pallet on the floor."

"No. Sitting up is better." Each word came through a fire.

While the drink helped ease his throat, the shaking made his chest hurt worse. *But this is nothing compared to what those other men are going through.* His thoughts faded in and out. He felt the blankets wrapped around him from his head to his feet. Clenching the blankets closed, he tipped his head back and let the darkness come over him.

"There's not enough room at the surgery. Bring the less injured over to the boardinghouse."

Sophie's voice. He would get to see her again. And his children. Relief poured over him like warm water.

Through a haze he felt someone messing with the back of his head, the prick of something sharp several times, but when he tried to ask what was happening, he coughed. He drank something warm and sweet again, and when he woke he was in his own bed at the boardinghouse.

Were it not for the pain in chest, throat, head, and hand, he'd have thought he dreamed it all . . . a horrible nightmare. How could he ever thank the men who had dragged him out?

30

"GOOD MORNING." Sophie leaned over him and smiled. "I thought perhaps you'd sleep all day too."

He stared at her, sure he'd never seen anyone more beautiful in his entire life. "Morning?"

"Ja, you slept through the evening and night. When you started to cough, we gave you the syrup Dr. Elizabeth sent over, and it helped."

He laid a hand on his chest and felt a tight wrapping. "My ribs?"

"She is sure a couple are broken, and others may be cracked. The explosion must have thrown you against something."

"A desk maybe. I woke up on the floor under a pile of debris." He kept his voice to a whisper, hoping to keep from coughing. It didn't help much. Coughing cut him in half.

When he could he let his mind rove. "You said *we?*"

"Mrs. Sam, Lemuel, and I took turns."

He nodded, just enough to realize that wasn't a good idea either. Actually, not moving at all seemed the best plan.

"Are you hungry?"

"No."

"Doctor said you had to drink."

"Later." He paused. "How many died?"

"Two in the fire, one is failing, and Dr. Elizabeth said if she can beat the pneumonia—that mostly follows smoke inhalation—the others will live. We're all praying."

His eyes closed whether he wanted them to or not, and he slept again.

∽

"Is it night?" he asked Sophie the next time he woke.

"No, but we had to board up your window. Most of the windows on this side of the building were blown out in the blast."

"Have you been here all the time?"

"No, we take turns."

While a deep breath hurt like sabers slashing, shallow breaths weren't so bad. His throat felt gravelly but not on fire. "I'm hungry."

"Good. We have soup hot. I'll get it."

He watched her leave the room. How long had he been out? "What day is it?" he asked when she returned.

"Wednesday. The explosion happened on Monday."

"And the men?"

"One more died."

"And the other two, or was it three?"

"It looks like they'll make it, at least if Dr. Elizabeth has anything to say about it." She spooned rich beef soup into his mouth.

He swallowed carefully. "I think I need another pillow."

"I'll get one." Returning in a moment, she gently lifted his head and pushed the pillow in place. "The doctor said you were lucky you didn't have more cuts with all the glass flying." She dipped another spoonful.

At least I am alive. Thank you, God, I am alive.

"Knock, knock. I'm here to check on my patient." Dr. Elizabeth smiled as she entered the room. "Now this is what I like to see, a man taking sustenance. How are you feeling?"

"Some better, I'm sure. Not coughing all the time anyway." While he spoke slowly and carefully, he could at least talk.

"You need to take deep breaths." She demonstrated a slow deep breath. "I know, I know. You think I'm a sadist, but you don't need a bout with pneumonia. So far so good. No fever. So in spite of how much it hurts, breathe as deeply as you can." She turned to Sophie. "Give him plenty of pillows. The more upright he is, the easier on the lungs."

"Anything else?"

"No, but no heavy lifting for you, Sophie." She turned to Garth. "When you need to get up, you call Lemuel and let him help you."

"I will."

"And for those ribs—it just takes time. The sooner you are on your feet the better, but no races or lifting for you either. The pain will let you know what you can do. I've left more syrup here for you. Take it as needed."

"Thank you."

"You are indeed welcome."

"And my men?"

"The two in my surgery, barring any changes, will make it. I'm sorry for the others. They found one body and . . ." Her voice softened. "And most of the other."

"I see."

"Pastor Solberg wants to come see you."

"Later please. I can hardly keep my eyes open."

"You eat and sleep again. I'll tell him." She patted Sophie's shoulder as she passed by. "And you make sure you get enough sleep too, young lady. That baby needs a mother who's gotten plenty of rest."

"Yes, ma'am." Sophie felt like saluting. Dr. Elizabeth was good at giving orders.

"More soup?"

He took a few bites. "Enough. Thank you." He was asleep before she reached the doorway.

The next day he sat in the chair, and the next he walked into the dining room for dinner. While there weren't a lot of guests eating, those who were gave him hearty applause.

He collapsed into a chair and shook his head. Dr. Elizabeth was right to a point. She said no racing, but he should walk. Why did he feel like he'd run a mile and gotten beat upon with a club the whole way?

❧

Sadness sat upon Blessing like a cloud.

Sophie caught herself staring at the wall—again. Three men dead. One minute they were working, doing the things needed to be done in the mill, and the next they were gone. No, that isn't quite right, she reminded herself. One man took another day to die, and she could still hear his screams. How terrible must the pain have been to make a big man scream like that?

Even though Pastor Solberg had gone around talking with the families and the others in town, she couldn't get her mind around it. That, along with the miasma that seeped into every corner of the buildings. If someone laughed, they quit because laughter seemed out of place. Instead of making the load lighter, it cut like slivers from the piece of obsidian her father had on the shelf at home, cuts so fine one didn't realize until the blood dripped from a finger. The fog was black too, but surely light could sneak through. Or did it only bounce off and go another way?

No matter that spring had come to the prairie.

Hamre had died. She understood that, but she'd not been right next to it like she was here. She mopped the tears she didn't realize were falling—again. The screams, the horrible agony, it had taken forever for the last man to die.

A knock at her door caught her attention. "Come in." If only no one would come in, if she could hide out here, cover the window, seal off the door so the fog would have to go away.

"Sophie?"

"Oh, Mor." Sophie pushed herself up out of her chair and ran to throw herself into her mother's arms. "How did you know I needed you so badly?"

"You could have come home."

"I can't leave the boardinghouse."

"What do you mean, you can't—"

"The fog. I'd get lost. I can't see, I . . ." Her words slipped into incoherent sobs. "And Hamre." She burrowed closer. "The men."

Kaaren eased her daughter to the bed and sat the two of them on the edge, murmuring mother comfort and stroking her daughter's back. "Go ahead and cry it all out." When the tears finally subsided, Kaaren fetched a cloth from behind the screen, dipped it in the basin, and after wringing it out, wiped her daughter's face. "Now you lie back here"— she fluffed up the pillows and stacked them—"and tell me all that's been going through your mind." After getting Sophie comfortable, she sat beside her and held her hand.

"Hamre's gone."

"I know."

"And the men at the mill."

"Um-hmm."

"Mother, it's not fair."

"No, it's not. We all think we'll live to get old like Bridget and Henry, but that's not always true."

Silence except for sniffs held for a time.

"Did God do this?"

"Some would say He did, and some would say Satan did it."

"But which is right?"

"Do you believe God is who He says He is?"

"Of course. Since I was little you taught us that."

"The Bible teaches us that. We read of His promises over and over. He said, 'I will never leave thee, nor forsake thee.'"

"Then why did they die?"

"He also said that He will walk with us, will carry us when we walk through the valley of the shadow of death. Death came into the world when sin did."

"But God could have stopped it."

"Yes, He could have. But one thing He cannot do is stop loving us. He promised."

"Funny kind of love."

"Seems that way at times. These are the hard questions of life, and we don't know why things happen the way they do. But we can trust Him to take care of us."

"I know Hamre is in heaven."

"Good. Would you want him back here when heaven is our real home?"

Sophie shook her head slowly but with tears seeping again. "I used to miss him terribly and now sometimes I can't even see his face."

"That's part of the healing God is giving you. You won't forget him. The good memories stay around forever, but now you go on with your life, asking God every day to show you the way."

"I don't do that very well." Sophie stared up into the love in her mother's face.

"You can learn to."

"You do it."

"I know. I've been learning a long time. When Carl and our two little girls died that winter, all I wanted was to die too. But God and Ingeborg wouldn't let me. And if I had died, I would never have had you and Grace. Look what we would have missed." Again the silence, only this time it felt lighter, like sun beginning to burn the fog away and peeping through the gray shreds.

"What if my baby dies?"

"We'll do everything we can to see that that doesn't happen. You are good and strong, and we will all be praying for the baby to be born easily and healthy."

"I think God listens to you more than to me."

"Maybe you need to learn to listen to Him."

Sophie thought about what her mother said. Her eyes felt as if sand had been thrown in them. She sighed, one of many. "Life is hard, huh?"

"Yes, at times."

"Mr. Wiste is getting better." She almost called him Garth but restrained herself.

"As are the other men."

"I should get up and go help with dinner."

"In a while. You lie here and rest, and I'll go make us some tea."

Sophie heard the door click behind her mother. "Lord, thank you for my mor."

She must have fallen asleep, because the next thing she knew, she heard the clink of cups and saucers on the tea tray and smelled tea and cinnamon. When she opened her eyes, her mother handed her a warm washcloth.

"This will help your eyes; the tea will help your throat."

"Mor?"

"Yes."

"I'm sorry."

Kaaren smiled and waited.

"For all the sadness I caused you."

"You are forgiven." She hugged her daughter again, the two clinging together. "Remember, that is over and done with now. Did you ask Jesus to forgive you?"

"A long time ago."

"Then He did, and I do."

"And Pa?"

"You need to ask him."

"I will."

Sophie pushed herself up against the pillows and took the cup her mother poured for her. "You are so good to me, Mor. How I love you."

"And I love you always, no matter what."

"Like God?"

"As close as I possibly can."

⥻

"Are you sure you should go help yet?" Sophie asked as she set Garth's breakfast in front of him three days later.

"I have to." While still hoarse and prone to coughing, Garth could at least talk in a normal tone. "I've been lying around long enough."

"Would you like more of the honey syrup Dr. Elizabeth brought over?"

"I'll take the bottle with me. Thank you." He looked up and studied her face. "You look lovely, Sophie." His voice softened on her name.

Sophie met him smile for smile yet thought, *How can he say that when I'm getting broader by the day and I have circles under my eyes so I look like a raccoon?* "I think your eyes must have been affected by the fire." But his words warmed a band around her heart that seemed to be widening by the day.

"Have you eaten yet?"

"No, but I need to finish caring for the guests. I'll bring my coffee over later if I can."

"Tonight I'll see you at supper."

"If I can." Why did the thought that she might be too busy to have their usual visit bring the fog back? *Don't be silly*, she admonished herself. *Sitting with him is not that important in the overall scheme of things.* Even after telling herself the same thing three times, she turned to another table without her usual smile. What was happening to her? A thought flitted through her mind. Perhaps it was the baby. She'd heard that women who were in the family way often had the vapors. Whatever that was.

When Garth didn't show up for dinner the next day, she thought of going to look for him but convinced herself that would not be a good idea. He would come when he was ready. But when he didn't have an office anymore, where could he be? Did he go somewhere else to eat? Should she save food or put things away?

That afternoon she walked into the kitchen to find Mrs. Sam sitting on a chair, her head resting back against the wood.

"Are you all right?" Mrs. Sam only sat down to peel potatoes or snap beans, neither of which would be what she'd been doing.

"Jes needed to catch my breath."

Sophie studied the woman before her. "Where is Lily Mae?"

"She gone to the store."

"And Lemuel?"

"He helpin' his pa for an hour or two."

Lemuel often helped Mr. Sam at the blacksmith/machinery shop in the afternoon if not needed at the boardinghouse.

"I think you should go see Dr. Elizabeth."

"Now why for would I do dat?"

"You don't look good."

"I be better in jes a minute."

The tinkle of the doorbell caught Sophie's attention. "I'll be right back." While she hurried to see if she was needed at the front desk, she wondered how to get Mrs. Sam to do as she was asked.

A man stood at the counter surveying the room as if measuring or appraising it.

"May I help you?" If he were to be measured by his well-fitted suit of black herringbone and the white of his shirt, the man had plenty of money. Tall like the Bjorklunds but with a more slender build, an inside man from the look of him. A dark mustache was clipped in a fine line above a rather narrow upper lip. His long-fingered hands had never shoveled manure and probably not even snow.

"Why, yes, Mrs. Aarsgard?" His clipped voice said he was from the East.

"No, she passed away several weeks ago."

"I'm sorry to hear that. Could I speak to the owner please?" He looked right through her as if she were invisible.

"Yes." She stepped behind the desk and studied him while he in turn studied the staircase. Proper was a word for him but not friendly.

When he turned back, a frown dug lines between his caterpillar eyebrows.

"Would you fetch her please?" He was used to speaking to servants.

"Fetch who?"

"The owner. I would like to speak with the owner of this establishment." He spoke slowly, as if she might not understand him. "As I asked before."

Sophie picked up the letter opener and squeezed it. Hard. Of all the—She cut that thought off, remembering Bridget's *You always catch more flies with honey than with vinegar.* As if she wanted any flies. But her mother's training in manners came through.

"Could I have your name please?"

"Walter Cumberland."

"Mr. Cumberland, I am Mrs. Bjorklund, and I own this establishment. Now what can I do for you?"

While he stifled the look of surprise before it covered his entire face, she read it in his eyes first. It was worth the good manners.

"I beg your pardon. From all I've heard, I assumed that . . . I mean, I was sure the owner was an older woman."

"It used to be, until she died." Sophie let him chew on that, not having any spare sympathy to offer him at the moment. "She was my grandmother." That wasn't really an exaggeration. After all Bridget believed she was grandmother to all the people of Blessing, both by blood and by adoption.

"I-I'm sorry, er, pardon me."

Sophie let him stutter a moment before she smiled. "That's all right." Sophie knew how to clip words too. "Let's start again. How may I help you?" Having the upper hand felt exhilaratingly wonderful. "Would you like a room?" *For a week or a month?*

"No, not today, thank you. I . . . ah, could we sit somewhere and discuss a business proposition?"

Sophie's eyebrow arched.

"No, no. Excuse me. I am . . . I . . ."

"Please come into the dining room and have a seat. I'll bring in some coffee, and we can talk." She showed him the way through the arched doorway.

"Thank you." He removed his coat and scarf and hung them over the back of another chair. As nice as it was outside, his coat must have felt too heavy, but that was none of her concern. What did he want? Walter Cumberland. She knew she'd never seen his name on any of the papers she'd looked through. Who was he and what possible business could he have with her if he didn't want a room?

"I'll bring in de coffee." Mrs. Sam already had a tray set with two cups and a plate of raisin cookies.

"Cream and sugar too, please." Sophie stepped closer to Mrs. Sam, knowing full well she'd had a view of the man. "Have you ever seen him before?"

"No."

"I wonder what he wants."

"Ask him."

"Thank you. I plan to." Why did she feel as though she were preparing for a battle? What a strange thought.

He stood when she arrived at the table.

At least he has good manners. Perhaps his manner at first was— Another thought interrupted. *His attitude changed when he found out I am the owner, not just someone who works here.* All the while her mind was whirling, she was allowing him to seat her and then take a chair himself.

Mrs. Sam poured the coffee and offered cream and sugar, which he declined with barely a shake of the head.

Sophie let him take a swallow of his coffee before asking, "Now, how may I help you?" While she smiled, she knew there was not a lot of warmth to it—deliberately.

He set his cup down, glanced at the cookies, and turned to look her fully in the face, his smile precise. His gaze dropped to her lips, then raised again to her eyes.

Please, she thought, *I learned that little trick in school. I could make any boy blush with it. Tsk, tsk.* If they were playing cat and mouse, he thought he was the cat, but she knew she was.

He wanted something.

"Mrs. Bjorklund, let me be frank with you. I work for a company that is contemplating moving west and we heard about the boarding-house here—"

"Pardon me, but what is the name of your company?"

"We either build or purchase properties as hotels in smaller towns along the railroad, towns that appear to be growing and in need of our services." He sat back in his chair and brought the coffee cup to his mouth, watching her over the rim.

Sophie copied his actions, only leaning forward instead. "What did you say the name of your company was?"

"Cumberland and Associates."

"I see." So was he the Cumberland or was it his father? "What exactly do you mean?"

"I mean that we might possibly be interested in purchasing this property."

"Oh really?" She kept the leap of interest locked inside and off her face. The few times she'd played poker with the boys, unbeknownst to her mother, she'd won. Someone said she took after Hjelmer, who'd been quite a successful gambler when he was younger, or so the stories went.

Dear Lord, give me wisdom please, and I need it right now. She started to say something, and then stopped.

He glanced around the dining room. "Of course, we would have a lot of work to do on this place."

Sophie felt herself bristling. He'd have to go far to find a place more inviting and with a better reputation. At the moment she was grateful she'd lived in the boardinghouse in Ballard, for she had something to compare it to.

"How many rooms do you have?"

"Twenty-four."

"Could you possibly give me a tour of your premises?"

Sophie thought a moment. "I can show you around, but since many of the rooms are occupied, I can only show you one or two."

"You mean that all your rooms are occupied?"

"Usually." *Easy, Sophie, don't go stretching things or giving him more information than he needs.* But what if he, or rather they, bought the boardinghouse, and she could use some of the money to take a trip somewhere, anywhere? Perhaps she could move to Minneapolis or Chicago or visit St. Louis and the world's fair there. Possibilities chased each other through her mind while all the while she kept a pleasant expression in place and passed him the plate of cookies.

"Would you care for more coffee?"

"No thank you. I would appreciate it if you would show me around, and then if I could stay for dinner?"

"Of course. The charge is fifty cents for a single meal." *Sophie,* her inner voice chided, *be polite and invite him to eat here without charge.* But then she quickly answered herself, *Not on your tintype. He wants to buy; he can pay.*

"You know, if you would prefer, I could see myself around, in light of . . . of . . ." He glanced to her waistline.

Of all the nerve! Sophie clamped her teeth. Proper gentlemen did not refer to one's state like that. Not that proper women allowed their approaching motherhood to show as she did. But she had a business to run, and withdrawing to her parlor was not possible. Her mother had run her school right up until Samuel was born. Her full white aprons had helped disguise her state. Perhaps she needed to don more protective clothing.

"Thank you for your concern, but I manage quite well. After all, having a baby is a normal event for women, is it not?"

"Ah, well, ah . . ."

She had him there, but she took little joy in the barb. His narrowed eyes gave away his ire. Taking him upstairs first, she showed him a single room and then a bunk room before continuing down the back stairs, where the linen closets were and on down the hall to return to the lobby.

"May I see the kitchen?"

"Of course, but remember we are getting ready for dinner."

"But of course. May I ask how many staff you run here?"

"There are four of us."

"You do all this with four people?"

"Yes."

She showed him the kitchen, the pantry, and the back porch before returning to the dining room, where she invited him to sit until the meal would be served in fifteen minutes.

Leaving him, she headed for her room and sank down into the rocking chair in her sitting area. Her back ached, her stomach felt like it was doing flip-flops, and the baby had taken to dancing a polka on her rib cage.

Had she done what was best? What if he—they—wanted to buy

the boardinghouse? What if they didn't? Could her dream of adventures be starting?

Reality hit like slipping on an ice patch. How could she go on adventures when she had a baby coming?

31

"SO HOW DID YOU GET HOME?" Elizabeth asked, a week and a half after the explosion.

Ingeborg turned with a plate of cookies to go with the coffee she had pulled to the front of the stove. "Getting home wasn't the problem; getting that horse stopped was. He took that turn into our lane with the sleigh on one runner. I thought sure I was going to tip over. But when he slipped, it was like all the fight went out of him. I jerked the reins hard enough to get the bit out of his teeth, and he trotted into the yard as if nothing had happened. Other than he was flecked with foam, as was I, and his lungs were pumping like bellows."

"Thank God we didn't have another casualty due to the explosion." Elizabeth picked up her daughter, who immediately reached for her grandmother.

"Here. Let me take her." Ingeborg settled the little one in her lap and blew on her neck, making her giggle.

"Mo, Gama."

"I thank God every day there weren't more injured, including me." She blew again. It wasn't like Elizabeth to just sit like this. They'd had coffee and cheese toast, discussed the progress of the injured men, and shared community news.

"Oh, Penny said to tell you that your washing machine should be here in the next day or two. I'm buying one for the surgery, but I'm sure Thelma will appreciate using it for the household too."

"Good. Haakan just rolled his eyes when I said I was buying one."

"What can these machine-conscious men say? Thorliff brought up the automobile again. He says it will help me on my rounds. I can just see trying to start that engine after birthing a baby all night."

"Many was the time I'd sleep all the way home, knowing my horse knew the way."

"Me too."

"Speaking of which, what's happening with the hospital idea?"

"I don't know. The woman left, and I've not heard from her. I was thinking of approaching the co-op, but by the time they rebuild the flour mill there won't be any extra money for building a hospital. No matter how much we need it."

Ingeborg wrapped her arms around Inga and rested her chin in the little girl's near white hair, humming a little tune. Inga nestled her ear against Ingeborg's chest.

"She loves listening," Elizabeth commented.

"I know. Must be like before she was born when she could hear your heart beating."

"You think babies can hear when they are in utero?"

"I've wondered that myself. I believe they can sense things, like how much they are loved or aren't."

"Has Thorliff told you our news?"

"You're pregnant again?"

"He did, then."

"No, but I've known for some time. Just waiting for you to tell me."

"How did you know?"

"You have the look."

"The look? I don't recognize that in women."

"You will after you've been at this as many years as I have."

"Thorliff asked me to start writing a column for the paper with simple suggestions on health issues for families."

"What a good idea."

"Speaking of machines, he wants to buy a new printer. That one my father gave him is too slow for all the editions he is putting out now."

"That's a big expense all right. If you need more money to do that, I can contribute some."

"He wouldn't ask you."

"I didn't wait to be asked. I'd rather invest in my children than in the bank."

"But if Astrid goes away to school, that will be a big expense."

"The cheese house has done very well these last years. We'll be all right." She kept how well to herself. Even with all the expenses, the growing total in her bank account was a constant source for her gratitude. "God has blessed us far beyond any of our hopes or dreams." She kissed the top of Inga's head as the little girl wriggled and then slid to the floor. Inga would tolerate being held only so long before she needed to be moving again. She reminded her grandmother of a happy bee that zipped from flower to flower, never staying long at any.

"So Mr. Gould's son is indeed coming here to work all summer?" Elizabeth asked.

"Jonathan, yes. The girls are all atwitter."

"Astrid said he would have to prove himself."

"I know. Instead of being awed by his family's wealth, she figures he is most likely spoiled rotten and will be nothing but trouble."

"Leave it to Astrid." Elizabeth reached forward and snagged her daughter as she danced by. "Come, little one, we need to be heading on home. I'm sure the waiting room is full up by now. I'm looking forward to having Astrid help again this summer. She learns so quickly. Thelma's good with the housekeeping, but she never has gotten over her squeamishness at the sight of blood. She fainted when we were treating the burn victims."

"I could help you out when things get too busy, you know."

"Are you sure you're feeling up to it?"

"Thanks to your insistence on the surgery, I feel better than I have for years."

"I'd be happy to have you help me. Especially as we get nearer to this one being born." Elizabeth stood and arched her back, rotating her shoulders. "Come, bring your coat, Inga. We need to go home."

Ingeborg held the child's coat as she slid her arms into the sleeves. The sky had clouded over and a breeze kicked up, dropping the temperature quickly.

"You hurry on home. From the looks of things we could get more snow."

"But spring is here."

"We've had snow as late as June. You can't trust Dakota winters to stay gone even after spring has arrived."

Elizabeth shivered. "True. It froze pretty hard last night. Give Grandma a kiss, Inga."

Ingeborg cupped her granddaughter's cheeks in her hands and kissed nose and forehead, bringing forth a giggle, along with a smacking kiss. "Bye, little one. Come again soon."

"Soon." A vigorous nod accompanied the parroted word.

After they left, Ingeborg returned to her bookwork for the cheese house. What used to take a couple of hours a month now took a good part of a day every week. Never would she have dreamed that she'd be writing invoices and bills of lading, ordering such large amounts of supplies, and keeping track of the amount of milk and cream purchased from so many farmers. Along with paying them and those who worked in the building itself. If they kept growing, she would need to add on to her building again.

She leaned back in her chair in front of the rolltop desk Onkel Olaf had built for her so she would have spaces to store all the paperwork. This year she had added a second file cabinet to the first.

She pulled out the payroll file and returned to her chair. This was not her favorite part of the business, but Haakan had slowly but surely handed his bookkeeping for the farm over to her too.

Someone had to go to the bank to get cash to pay all the employees. She totaled up the hours worked and figured how much she needed. Taking out a packet of envelopes, she wrote each name on the front and the amount due in a lower corner. Mr. Valders had suggested she pay everyone with a check, but she knew they wouldn't all have time to go to the bank and cash them.

Mr. Valders had trained her in the bookkeeping systems she

needed, including the leather-bound ledgers that now lined bookshelves Haakan had made. The office was taking up more and more of the parlor, hardly leaving room for her spinning wheel. The loom had been moved to their bedroom long ago. Not that she had much time for weaving anymore. Besides, now she could buy many of the things she'd been forced to make those earlier years.

The accounts didn't balance. She stared at the two numbers and rubbed her forehead. Now she'd have to add them up again.

Instead, she strode into the kitchen and pulled the coffeepot to the front of the stove. Of course the fire had nearly gone out, so she rattled the grate to let the ashes fall into the ashpan and laid slivers of pitch wood on top of the coals. She opened the vent to get a draft on the coals and added several sticks from the kindling box. She knew better than to let it die down like this.

"Uff da," she muttered, at the same time turning to check the time. The children would be home from school soon, and she'd hoped to have all this done before they came.

Astrid barreled through the door a few minutes later, Grace right behind her.

"Mor, Sophie is selling the boardinghouse," Astrid blurted out.

"N-no. S-Sophie . . ." Grace stuttered, her agitation so great she fell back on signing. "Sophie wouldn't do that."

Ingeborg held up both hands, palms out. "Wait a minute. Let's calm down here."

"But, Mor—"

"Let Grace talk."

Astrid started to humph, looked at her cousin's face, and flinched. "I'm sorry, Grace, but this is such terrible news."

Dear Lord, let this not be so. Ingeborg reached out with both arms, one for each girl. "Grace, you go first. There's no hurry."

Grace took a deep breath. Speaking slowly and carefully, she spoke and signed together. "Sophie would not do that without talking with Far or someone."

"She ran away without telling anyone."

Ingeborg shook her head and made a tsking noise. "Astrid."

Astrid flounced again, then turned to Grace. "I'm sorry, Grace. That wasn't fair."

Grace's eyes did not smile with her mouth. "That's all right." Even her fingers looked sad.

"Here, let's sit down and think this through." Ingeborg brought the plate of cookies she'd fixed for herself and Elizabeth. "Do you want something to drink too?"

"Is there buttermilk in the house?" Astrid asked.

"Yes, in the pantry."

Astrid slid back her chair and headed for the pantry. Bringing back the jug, she motioned with it to Grace, who shook her head. With cookies in hand, both girls looked at Ingeborg.

"Now tell me exactly what all you heard and from whom. Grace, you go first."

"At noon recess I saw the girls talking. They forget sometimes that I can read lips. I don't know who started it, but I saw it was something about Sophie, so I just watched. But then they drew closer together, and I couldn't see any longer. I saw them mention the boardinghouse too."

"Rebecca asked me if I had heard that Sophie was selling the boardinghouse." Astrid shrugged. "That's all I know."

"So it is gossip." Ingeborg chewed on the inside of her lower lip, something she usually did when thinking hard. *Lord, you know how much I hate gossip, and I know you do so even more.* "So what do you think we should do about this?"

"Go and ask Sophie if this is true?"

Ingeborg nodded. "What else?"

Astrid swapped glances with Grace, both of them not sure how to answer. Then Grace's face lit up. "Pray first."

"Ja, that is my mor." Astrid smiled at her mother. "She always says to pray first."

"And mine." Suddenly Grace made an O with her mouth. "Trygve will have told Mor." She pushed back her chair. "I need to go to her."

Ah, poor Kaaren. Please, Lord, not another heartbreak for her.

Grace fluttered a good-bye wave, and out the door she went.

"You think Tante Kaaren will be mad?"

"Sad more likely."

"But she'll be praying too."

Ingeborg nodded.

"Pray first, yell later?"

Ingeborg blinked at her daughter. "What?"

"Well, you and Tante Kaaren always say pray first."

"Ja."

"That's hard to remember."

"I know. It takes lots of practice. Years of practice."

"But sometimes you just have to yell."

"Ja, sometimes." Ingeborg picked up the now empty cookie plate. "But then I am often sorry afterward for the yelling. I am never sorry for the praying. I need to go to the bank. Would you like to come with me?"

"To see Sophie?"

"Possibly."

"I'm coming."

As they were leaving the bank, Kaaren and Grace drove up.

"You want to come with us?" Kaaren asked.

"Will she think we are descending on her like the wrath of God?"

"I brought the soakers and blanket I knitted. And Grace sewed several buntings."

"I should have thought of that. Ah well, yes we'll come."

When they arrived at the boardinghouse, Sophie showed them to her quarters and, after asking Mrs. Sam to bring in a tea tray, joined them, closing the door behind her. "All right! Who started such a stupid rumor?"

"That's what we came to find out." Kaaren patted the bed beside her. "Let's talk this out and see if we can come to some conclusions. What have you heard?"

"That I am selling the boardinghouse. Can you believe such rot? I could just . . . just . . ." She stuttered to a stop, eyes narrowed, jaw set. "The nerve of that man."

"What man?" Kaaren leaned forward.

They all turned when they heard a tap at the door and Mrs. Sam poked her head around the door.

"Tea's ready. And Sophie, Thorliff is here. He say he want to talk wit you."

"Tell him to come on in. Might as well get the truth in the newspaper too."

Mrs. Sam set the tray down and returned to the hall.

"Ah, so we are having a family meeting?" Thorliff set his hat on the table by the door. "Where are the men?"

"Home working like they should be. It's hard to hear gossip when you are sharpening plowshares and repairing machinery." Ingeborg leaned forward. "You want me to pour, Sophie?"

"Please do. This whole thing started when Mr. Cumberland asked if he could speak to the owner. He was a bit put off when I said I own the boardinghouse. I talked with him and showed him around, including the kitchen. He asked if he could stay for dinner. I'm sure it was to see how well we do. He asked if he could talk with me a bit more, but when he made an offer to buy the place, I nearly laughed in his face. I'm sure he thinks that because I am young I am stupid or would think the amount he offered would be a lot of money."

While Sophie paced, Ingeborg made sure everyone had what they wanted, all the time hiding her smile at Sophie's dilemma. She might be young all right, but Sophie had come a long way.

"So what happened after that?" Thorliff asked.

"He thanked me and left. And I think he went around town telling everyone he is buying the boardinghouse."

"Why would he do that?"

"I don't know. What I do know is that I would not sell him the boardinghouse no matter how much he agreed to pay."

"But do you want to sell this place?" Ingeborg asked as she refilled the teacups.

"I never thought about it before. You know how I wanted to go places and see things. I've always wanted that, but between a baby and a boardinghouse, it looks like I'm stuck right here."

"I am glad you came back." Grace stared hard at her twin.

Sophie reached for her hand. "Oh, Grace, I am glad too."

"You are?"

"Could have fooled me," Astrid muttered.

"Why do you say that?"

"Well, we never see you, and—"

"If you haven't noticed, every time I leave this place, something happens. No wonder Bridget never got out much. I went out to see Hjelmer's car, and Mrs. Valders told everyone I was not honoring Hamre's memory, running around like that with another man." She paused to take a breath. "And none of you ever come to visit me." She glanced at her mother. "Well, rarely."

"You never invite us."

"Why do you have to be invited? You're my sister and my cousin and my aunt. Do you invite each other over?"

"Sometimes!" Astrid started to say more but hushed at a look from her mother.

Grace had turned pale, like she'd been struck. "I'm sorry." Her bottom lip quivered. "I-I thought . . . I mean, I didn't think you wanted me to come here."

"Why would you think that?"

"You . . . you seem different, not like my Sophie, and I thought . . ."

"Well, I thought you were all still mad at me." The words hit the surface of the silence with a splash. Sophie locked her arms across her chest, then loosed them and leaned forward. "I know I hurt you all when I left, and when I came back I was so miserable it seemed I cried all the time. When Bridget invited me to work here, I was so tired all the time, and since she died, I've been up to my eyebrows in learning how to run this place, and then Mrs. Sam got sick, and—"

Grace took Sophie's flying hands in her own. "I am sorry." She spoke slowly and distinctly, looking directly into Sophie's eyes. "We are sisters, and nothing should ever come between us."

"Not just sisters, twins, and I've been missing you every day. Please, can you forgive me?"

"I did, long ago."

A tap at the door broke the intensity.

"Yes?" Sophie sniffed and mopped her eyes as she spoke.

Mrs. Sam peered around the door. "Dat man, he be back and wantin' to talk with you."

Sophie's eyes narrowed. Astrid and Grace stared at each other, wide eyed and suppressing giggles.

"Let him have it, Sophie." Astrid nodded at her.

Ingeborg and Kaaren stood.

"Don't leave." She looked to Thorliff. "You either. This will only take a minute." Sophie rose and straightened her shoulders. "Mrs. Sam, please bring more tea. I'll be right back."

Late April

LIFE IS TOO SHORT *for waiting.*

Garth stared at what he'd written. If this was now what he truly believed, what would he do about it? Or rather, what *could* he do about it?

Pondering. That was an interesting word, and it seemed to apply to his way of thinking since the explosion. B.E. had come to mean Before the Explosion. A journal seemed a good way to ponder, so he'd purchased one at Penny's general store and had just written the first line. *Life is too short for waiting.*

Looking back, he realized that B.E. he'd been marking time and doing his work competently, but in all other areas, just letting life happen. Like with his house in Minneapolis, his children growing up without him, recognizing his growing feelings for Sophie . . . He paused at that last one.

"So," he muttered to himself, "when did she . . . or rather, when did I start thinking about her so much?" Dreaming about her even. He thought back to their conversation the night before. While he could make it to supper on time now, he had asked if they could still have supper later.

"If you want." The look she had given him was woven with question marks. "But why? Supper is better when it is hot the first time."

"That may be true, but you are so busy during the regular supper hour."

"You do not get good service? Is something wrong?"

He shook his head. "No, nothing is wrong." He paused and stared at the floor for a moment, waiting for inspiration. When he looked up, he searched her face. So young. Was she too young? No, she'd already been married and lost her husband. She'd been forced to grow up quickly. "I just like being with you." Not that he was an old man by any means, but some days twenty-seven seemed very old next to seventeen.

Her cheeks turned a charming shade of pink. "Why, ah, thank you."

And I don't want to share those precious minutes of my day with all the others in the dining room at the regular suppertime.

So after the others were finished and the dining room set to rights again, they had their supper.

"What did you say to him?" he asked after Sophie told him about the man who'd assumed he would be buying the boardinghouse.

"I told him that spreading rumors showed he is not the sort of man I would want to deal with and that the boardinghouse was not for sale."

"Then what?"

"He offered me more money." She sat straighter. "I guess he thinks I am young and stupid."

"What if he offered a great deal more?" The question brought her gaze back to his.

"Before I sold this place, I would talk it over with Far and Haakan and the others." She shuffled her silverware around, then polished the knife blade with her napkin.

He waited, buttering a slice of bread while she fidgeted.

"I thought about using the money to travel, to go live somewhere else."

"Where would you go?"

"I don't know, but . . ." She realigned the knife and fork. Giving a sigh, she looked up with a half smile. "Can I get you anything else? We have apple cake with lemon sauce for dessert."

"I'd love some, thank you." *But what were you going to say?* He watched as she pushed her chair back and rose with a grace only barely impeded by her expanding waistline. He knew the baby was due in July, and now it was nearly May. Would she have answered the man differently had she not a baby to consider?

A baby. He had a baby who was seven months old. And he'd not seen her since Christmas. He closed his eyes against the pain that welled up, choking off his air. Working long and hard hours had been a good antidote for the pain of grief, and now it didn't come as hard or as frequently. Even when he concentrated as hard as he could, he could no longer see Maddie's face clearly.

He and Sophie had talked of that one night, both of them wondering at the same thing. They had so much in common, grief at losing a mate a big part of their discussions. He'd been surprised how easy it was to talk with Sophie.

He studied what he'd written again. Life is indeed too short to spend it waiting. Waiting to bring his children north to live with him. Waiting until spring to start building a house. Waiting to tell Sophie that he would like to court her. One wait was done. The co-op of Blessing had decided to rebuild the flour mill, and they wanted him to continue on as manager. The vote was unanimous to both. He and the remaining men who worked there, along with others who could spare the time, had been cleaning up the mill site, salvaging what could still be used, hauling away and burning the refuse. It was dirty black work, but they talked of possibilities. The grinding stones were proof that fire couldn't destroy everything.

He left off staring at his writing and paced the room instead. *What do I want to do most of all?* The questions continued.

Back to his paper and pencil. Write both the questions and the answers.

But instead of writing, Garth let his mind wander. Sophie. Sophie backing down that buyer, Sophie pouring his coffee with her hand on his shoulder. The place where her hand lay stayed warm for hours. Sophie laughing at the horseless carriage. He didn't see her laughing very often, now that he thought about it. Sophie taking care of Mrs. Sam. . . .

He rubbed his fingers over his scalp. Even with all the clearing out of the flour mill, he had too much time on his hands.

"Sophie," he said on the way out of the dining room the next morning, "I have something I want you to look at. Would you be available later this morning, at . . . say eleven?"

"Why, I believe so. What is it?"

He smiled back. "I'll see you then." As he headed out the door whistling, he could feel her gaze drilling into his back.

First stop: the flour mill. With all the wreckage cleaned out of the site, they were ready to rebuild. All they needed were the supplies. He had a partial list in his pocket. The grinding stones had been rolled out of the structure and now rested between the grain elevator and the two remaining concrete walls. The blast had taken out much of the other two, and the remaining rubble had been carted off. Sand and gravel to mix with the concrete had to be hauled in from a gravel pit west of Grafton via the railroad. The cement and timbers for the roof would come from Minneapolis, along with the rest of the interior construction. All the milling machinery would come from parts east, as it had before. Some of the metal pieces could be restored. The people of Blessing had great faith to be willing to start over.

His whistling continued as he walked the block to Penny's store, where he picked up pages that showed house plans from the Sears and Roebuck catalog.

"Is Hjelmer around?"

"He's at the bank, I think," Penny answered.

"Good. I'll catch him there. Thanks for these plans."

"You're going to build a house here, then?"

He nodded. "Soon as I can. You know some men who might help me?"

"I'm sure all of them will. Last house we put up was Andrew's. We're in need of a house-raising again. It puts everyone in a good mood."

"I meant to hire someone."

"Here in Blessing we work together. You're a member of our town now, and we'll all be glad to help. Last house that came in came two months late. I hope they've gotten caught up by now."

Garth groaned. "I hope so too." More waiting?

"Where are you going to build?"

"That's one of the things I want to talk to Hjelmer about. Thanks for the information."

"You're welcome."

Garth tipped his hat and headed out the door, pausing a moment to let the sun warm his face before he strode down the boardwalk to the bank.

"Good morning, Mr. Valders. Have you seen Hjelmer?"

"He was here a few minutes ago. I think he went to the barbershop." Mr. Valders pushed his green visor up with his remaining hand. He'd lost the other hand and arm in a threshing accident years earlier.

"I see."

"Can I help you with anything?"

"Perhaps soon. I'm planning on building a house here."

"Good for you. Can't live in a boardinghouse all your life."

I could if I didn't have children. And if Sophie ran the boardinghouse. "Thanks." Garth turned and went back the way he came. Male laughter came from the section of the building on the other side of the post office. How wonderful to be able to have doors open again. The North Dakota spring wasted no time once it got around to arriving.

He stopped in the doorway. Hjelmer reigned from the barber chair, telling a story that made the barber and the man waiting laugh.

"Garth, good to see you." Hjelmer extended his hand from under the white cloth drape.

The two men shook hands. "Hank, you know Mr. Wiste here, and Herman, you too?" Hjelmer asked.

"Of course. We both live at the boardinghouse, and I been cutting his hair ever since he moved here." Hank Vell's German accent lent ponderance to his words. He held a scissor in one hand and a comb in the other, snipping as he talked. "You need a haircut again?"

"No thanks. Just came to talk with Hjelmer."

"Good. You ready to buy that lot, then?" Hjelmer tipped his head forward at the barber's nudge.

"I believe I am. I picked up house plans. Once I decide which one, I'll turn in the order. Then I need to return to Minneapolis and tie up some loose ends there."

"Will you be back to start construction on the mill?"

"I'm not sure. I'm planning on it, but—"

"Are you going to look for new equipment while you are there?"

"Finished." Hank removed the drape and used a large fluffy brush to remove the stray hairs from the back of Hjelmer's neck.

Hjelmer stood and dug in his pocket for change to pay the bill. "Thanks." He tipped Hank with a nickel.

"Next."

Hjelmer clapped a hand on Garth's shoulder. "Come on over to the house and we'll discuss this over a cup of coffee. I think I smelled cookies baking before I left." The two men left the barbershop and strolled back toward the store.

"You hear that we are going to have a café opening in our little town?" Hjelmer asked.

"No, really?"

"At least the Geddicks are thinking on it. Might take a bite out of the revenues for the boardinghouse, though."

"Have you mentioned it to Sophie?"

"Not yet. We'll be having a meeting on it soon. Might make it easier on her in the long run if she no longer had to provide dinner or even breakfast. What with Mrs. Sam getting sick and all. Plenty to think on."

"I heard someone wanted to open a saloon here."

"That won't happen. The women would drive them right out of town. Someone tried a few years ago, and we learned really quick who holds the final word in Blessing." His laugh made Garth smile. Hjelmer was a great storyteller, as well as a good businessman. No wonder he kept getting voted back to the legislature.

"So which of the lots are you thinking on?"

"The one on the other side of the church. That's what—half an acre?"

"About that. I haven't paced it off myself. I heard that someone south of town might be selling his place."

"No. I want to be near enough to the mill that I don't have to keep a horse and buggy."

"Or a horseless carriage. I have another Oldsmobile on order. It should be here any day."

"You're going to be selling automobiles along with machinery?"

"I own the blacksmith shop too, but you mark my words, the blacksmith shop will turn into a machinery repair business in the next ten years as more farmers trade in their teams for tractors. Since most of the farmers around here already have their windmills, selling those won't be profitable much longer. You have to be willing to change with the times."

Garth smiled and nodded a response. However, sometimes change was not a choice but something forced upon one. Had his wife not died, he would not be here in Blessing. He'd still be in Minneapolis.

"Penny, is the coffee hot?" Hjelmer called as he pushed open the door to the family quarters.

"Will be in a minute," she called back.

Hjelmer peeked under the edge of a towel that covered something cooling on the table. "Molasses and ginger, one of my favorites. Have a chair." He indicated one on the other side of the table.

"Good to see you again, Mr. Wiste," Penny said as she pushed through the fabric hanging in the doorway between the store and the house. "I see you found Hjelmer."

"Garth says he wants to buy that lot on the other side of the church."

"Wonderful." She added several sticks to the firebox and pulled the coffeepot forward. "Have you decided which plan you will use?"

"Not yet. But whichever plan, I need to get a cellar dug before the house gets here. And since I need to return to Minneapolis to clear up some unfinished business, I want to find someone to dig it for me."

Hjelmer nodded slowly. "I'll talk to Thorliff. We've a crew that builds, digs—whatever needs doing. You lay it out, and they'll take care of it."

"I see. They pour concrete walls for the cellar too?" Garth glanced up at the clock over the kitchen sink. How could he hurry this conversation along? The hands were clicking toward eleven at an alarming rate. He knew Sophie didn't have a lot of time this close to the dinner hour.

"Of course."

"Will some of your men be working on the flour mill reconstruction?"

"Most likely. Seems lately we have more jobs here than men to do them. Blessing is growing."

"Ingeborg is looking for more help for the cheese house too." Penny set a plate of cookies on the table. "You take cream with your coffee?"

"No thanks. Black is best." Garth waited while she filled his cup. "How much do you want for that lot?"

"Well . . ." Hjelmer rubbed his chin and stared out the window. "I was asking two fifty, but for you I'd take two hundred."

Garth thought a moment. "How much for the other one?"

"That's about a third smaller, say one fifty."

"How about one seventy-five for the larger one?"

"You drive a hard bargain." Hjelmer looked up at Penny, then back to Garth. "Cash, or do you need time to pay it out?"

"Cash, as soon as I return from Minneapolis. I'll give you fifty now and the rest then."

"Deal." Hjelmer extended his hand. "You want a well dug, I can take care of that."

"How much?"

"Depends on how deep we have to go. Water table is pretty high here, but you need to go deeper for sweet water."

Garth glanced at the clock on the shelf between the windows. "Will fifty down get you started?"

"And possibly finished. I'll start as soon as you mark out your house. Do you want a windmill or just a pump?"

Before he left at five to eleven, Garth had a contract in his pocket and a decidedly different weight to his pocketbook. He wished he had time to pace out the house location, but he'd told Sophie eleven, and he refused to be late. Besides, someone else would be sure to tell her what he'd been doing if he didn't get there right away. News had a habit of getting around town faster than birds flew.

He took the boardinghouse steps in one bound and opened the door, still whistling. When he didn't see her behind her desk, he headed for the kitchen. "You know where Sophie is?" he asked Mrs. Sam.

"Miss Sophie in her room."

"Is she sick?" Sophie was usually right in here.

"Not dat I know."

"Lying down?"

Mrs. Sam shrugged and shook her turbaned head. "Just go knock on de door."

"Of course, thank you."

He crossed the dining room and went through the vestibule. Her door was closed. Taking a deep breath to throw off the feeling of apprehension, he tapped on the door.

"Come in."

Her voice sounded all right. He pushed open the door and stepped just inside so the door wouldn't close. "Sophie?"

"Over here." She rose from the wingback chair that faced the window overlooking the street. One hand clutched an envelope with a sheet of paper.

"What is it? Are you all right?"

"Yes, I think so." But her face looked pale, as if she'd received a shock. She held out the letter. "This is from Mrs. Jorgeson, widow of the captain of the *Sea Lily* in Ballard."

Garth waited.

A narrower piece of paper fluttered to the floor. He stepped forward and squatted down to pick it up for her. Handing it back, he stared into her eyes. He knew the paper was a check. *What could make her act so strange?*

THIS CAN'T BE REAL.

Sophie watched as Garth knelt to pick up the check. Thick dark hair, darker than her own, neither brown nor black but a blend. Although from this angle, she saw threads of silver in his. He wasn't that much older than she, or at least it seemed that way.

When he looked up at her, confusion carved lines in his broad fore-head, perhaps becoming wider as the hairline receded slightly.

"Here." He put the paper back in her hands. Hands that now had started to shake. "I think you should sit down. You look pale."

"Yes, I'm sure." She took back the check and tucked it into the folds of the letter as she sat on the edge of her chair.

"Sophie, what is it?" He glanced over to make sure the door was still open before sitting on the footstool in front of her.

Should I tell him? Who would I rather tell first? Mor and Grace? Her thoughts ran back in time again. *Ah, Hamre, so close you were to buying your boat. I don't know what a fishing boat costs, but this is a lot of money to have saved. No wonder you fussed at me. If you had only told me, perhaps I would have acted better.* All the while her thoughts were drifting, she inserted the letter back in the envelope, precisely, to make sure no edges were bent.

When Garth took her hands, she stared down at them. His broad with dark hairs on the back, hers slender, chapped, badly in need of lotion. When she and Grace were little, their mother had smoothed their chapped hands with goose fat because they had no money for lotions and nice soaps. These had become her one indulgence since she took over the boardinghouse. And still her hands were chapped. She brought her thoughts into focus. Why was he holding her hands like this? Were they such good friends?

"I can travel now." Her voice barely stirred the air in the room. *Go on all the adventures I want. Why am I not singing and dancing and announcing this to the world?*

"I see." But his face said that clearly he didn't.

She tapped the envelope. Since she'd already started telling him, she might as well finish. "With the fishing season over, Mrs. Jorgeson sent me the money Hamre had been saving for his boat, including his share from this year's catch. He'd invested his savings with Captain Jorgeson. No wonder Hamre loved fishing. He made a goodly amount of money." *But look at the price he paid, or I paid. According to Pastor Solberg, Hamre is in heaven worshiping at Jesus' feet.* Her nose stung and her eyes filled. *And I thought him stingy. Which he was.* "He got really angry at me one day because I took some money from the pouch and bought a new hat. I thought he'd think me pretty and be proud of me."

"I'm sure he thought you not only pretty but beautiful." Garth paused. "For you are."

"Thank you." She drew her hands free. They shouldn't be alone in her room, let alone him holding her hands like that. And yet it felt so good, so familiar. Ah, how she'd missed a man holding her hands. She peered into his face. A dear face still clouded with . . . with what? Confusion? Of course, so much information . . . and here he—*"Think of someone besides yourself, Sophie."* She could hear her mother's words ringing in her ears, words from long ago and inferences from not so long ago.

"Oh, you had something to tell me, to show me, you said." *Some friend I am, thinking only of myself like this.*

"I have a feeling your news is of more import than mine."

"Not at all." She leaned forward. "What is it?"

He pulled some papers out of the inside breast pocket of his jacket. "I want you to help me choose which house to buy. Like Andrew, I'm going to order a package from Sears and Roebuck. I picked these up at Penny's." He laid three pieces of paper in her lap. "On the front of each page is the exterior view and on the back are the floor plans." He held up the first of the front views, then the second and the third. "What do you think?"

Forcing herself to concentrate, Sophie looked at each one carefully. "I think they are all wonderful. Where will you build it?"

"I bought a half acre lot from Hjelmer. It's on the other side of the church. There will be room for children to play, to have a garden, and maybe a big shade tree or two."

"You have been busy."

"I decided life is too short to spend waiting."

Waiting. That's what I've been doing. She paused, feeling the baby moving. *After the baby is born, I can hire a nanny to travel with us.* She hesitated to think it, but ... she would be nearly rich. That would make things so much easier. Perhaps Grace would like to come along. This wasn't a new thought, but she'd never had the money to seriously think about anything. Unless, of course, she sold the boardinghouse.

"So which do you like best?"

His question brought her back to the moment. "Which do *you* like the best? That is the question."

"I narrowed it down to these three, and now I need a woman's opinion. Your opinion."

Then you better go ask my mother was her first thought, closely followed by a warm feeling that flowed around her heart. She returned her attention to the papers, turning them over to see the outlines of the walls and rooms.

"They are all big houses."

"I know. Remember, I already have two children. I like both the front and back porches on this one and the four bedrooms upstairs. I'm thinking of a coal furnace in the cellar. Like Thorliff has."

Who is going to care for your children? The question popped into her mind, and then she remembered another of their talks where he had said his sister might come and live there when he had a house.

"I need to sell my house in Minneapolis, but I'm going to order one of these first."

"So you are leaving?"

"For a while."

How long? "Who will build your house if you are gone?"

"I'll be back. You still didn't tell me which one you like best."

"What color will you paint it?"

"What color do you like?"

"White with green trim. And maybe some yellow or . . ." Her eyes narrowed in thought. "I saw a house in Seattle with dark green trim and some yellow as part of the trim. It was really pretty." She traced a line around a window on the picture he seemed to like the best. "Right in here. I vote for this one."

"We agree."

"We do?"

Staring into her eyes, he lifted one of her hands and brought the back of it to his lips. "We do." He leaned forward. "Sophie . . ."

A knock at the half-opened door shattered the moment. Feeling like something special had just started and now lay in shards on the floor, Sophie sat back. "Come in."

"There's a gentleman here to see you, Miss Sophie." Lily Mae peeked around the door.

"Who is it?"

"Man who was here the other day."

Sophie sat up straight, slammed her palms on the arms of the chair, and heaved herself to her feet. "I guess he just doesn't know how to take no for an answer." She whipped off her apron and threw it across the back of the chair.

"I'll speak to him if you want," Garth offered.

"No thank you. I'll do this myself." She marched across the room and out the door. Without bothering to paste a smile in place, she paused in the middle of the vestibule. The man was standing in the entrance to the dining room, watching something so intently he didn't hear her.

"Mr. Cumberland, to what do I owe the honor of this visit?" She could feel her mother at her own house wincing at the tone in her daughter's voice. Polite was not exactly a good description.

"Good morning, Mrs. Bjorklund. Such a fine day, don't you think?"

"It was." *State your business and get out of here. No matter how nice you act, I remember the furious look from the other day.*

"I talked with my associates. Could we sit down so I can show you what we decided?" He gestured toward the dining room.

"No, I think not. We are busy getting ready for dinner."

"Oh, I see."

She could tell he didn't see at all. Perhaps he wasn't used to not getting his own way. "Please, Mr. Cumberland, I have work to do. Just tell me what it is you decided." She put a twist on the word, like it left a bad taste in her mouth, which it did. He decided? He and his associates decided?

"Well, ah, I realized that I hadn't presented my best offer the other day, and I wanted to make amends."

"Make amends? I thought I explained to you quite clearly what my position was."

"But you haven't heard my offer."

She huffed a sigh. "What is your offer?"

He pulled a paper from his breast pocket. "I have the figures all written down here. Are you sure there isn't a man you'd like to have look at these? We've really put together a very good offer. Perhaps your uncle?"

"My uncle?"

"You know, Mr. Hjelmer Bjorklund? I think he would give you good advice. He understands the business world."

Sophie could feel Garth coming up behind her. She took a step forward and took the paper the man extended. Glancing down the column of figures, she reached the bottom line. Nearly double what he'd offered the time before.

"Is this the best you can do?"

His face tightened. "What are you asking?"

"First of all, I am not asking. I am telling you that I have no intention of selling the boardinghouse. Three times the amount you are offering would not be enough." She placed the paper back in his hands. "And furthermore, spreading rumors about town was not a way to make a good impression. Good day."

When she strode into the dining room, Mrs. Sam and her two children were lined up, clapping silently, smiles as wide as their faces. Fighting tears of fury, she blinked and started to grin. When she heard the front door slam, she hid a giggle behind her handkerchief.

"Well done." Garth strolled in behind her. "I wanted to make sure he left before I had to throw him out."

Sophie turned to see his expression of satisfaction.

"Remind me to never get on your bad side. You about flayed the skin from his bones."

"Dat she do." Mrs. Sam stepped forward. "I 'bout sent Lemuel here for reinforcements, but you done fine. Dat man don't deserve even staying for dinner, though I make the best chicken and dumplin's anywhere. He was sniffin' like a hound on a hunt."

The bell jangled over the front door, and Garth stepped back to see who had come in.

Miss Christopherson greeted him as she entered the dining room. "What a rude man. He nearly knocked me off the steps."

"Did he hurt you?" Sophie took a step toward her.

"No." She brushed off her upper arm. "But if I never see him again, it will be too soon. And to think he came into my shop the other day."

"He did?" Sophie frowned. "And did he tell you he was buying my boardinghouse?"

"No, he said he was looking for a gift."

"And did he buy something?"

"No. He fumbled around and then left, saying he'd come see me again when he returned."

Others were coming into the dining room, so Sophie signaled her help to begin serving. The next time she turned around, Garth was not sitting at his usual table. He wasn't in the dining room at all.

Later she found a note on the table in her quarters.

Congratulations on your skillful handling of that situation. Thank you for helping me choose a house. I've turned my order in and am catching the afternoon train to Minneapolis. Waiting even another day didn't make much sense. We have something more to discuss when I return.

Yours sincerely,
Garth Wiste

Sophie reread the note, especially the part, *Waiting another day didn't make much sense.* It didn't make sense for her either. She knew what she had to do. Taking her shawl off the coatrack and pinning her hat in place, she headed for the kitchen. While she figured she could drive the team, she knew her family would not approve. She would borrow Thorliff's team and buggy, and Lemuel would drive.

They had to go now before she lost her courage.

On the way she almost asked Lemuel to turn back three times, maybe more. She tried counting fence posts to override her fear, but they blurred with her tears. Where had the spunk she was known for gone? *Oh, God, let this work. Please give me the right words and Pa the ears to hear.* Would he be out in the fields? She searched the land as they neared her home. No one was out with either team or tractor. Was it too wet to be out there yet, or was something wrong?

"I wait here," Lemuel said as he handed her down from the buggy seat.

"No, you come inside for a cup of coffee."

He shook his head and looked out across the fields.

Sophie looked toward the machine shed to see if her father was there. She didn't see him, nor did she hear him working on the machinery. Not in the field, not in the machine shed—where was he?

Mor opened the door. "Sophie! How wonderful to see you. Come in, come in."

Better get this over with. "Where's Far?"

"Over at Haakan's. They are shearing sheep."

Now what should she do? "I have to talk to him."

"Then go on over. You want me to come with?"

"No, I want you to pray that . . . that all goes well." She turned back to the buggy. "Let's go." *Before I lose my courage entirely.* All she could think as the buggy wheels turned, carrying her back to Haakan's barn, was to keep on going and return to the boardinghouse. She could come on this errand later. But something wouldn't let her do that, so they turned up the lane she'd walked so many times through the years.

She could hear the sheep bleating before they neared the barn.

She waited for Lemuel to help her down. All she needed to do was slip on the step or something. Then he'd really think she was brainless, and careless too. She walked through the open door and followed the bleating through the barn to a corral behind where Lars was just letting a sheared sheep run back to the flock. Those waiting to be sheared milled around in a separate pen.

"Hey, look who's here." Andrew waved to her before grabbing another fluffy sheep.

Sophie smiled and returned his wave. She nodded at Haakan's greeting and looked at her father. "Far, can I talk with you, please?" The words had to be forced from her throat. She welded her shaking hands together.

"Now?" He motioned to the waiting sheep.

"It-it won't take but a minute." The look on his face did not bode well.

"Ja, I guess so." He set his clippers on a box and wiped the sweat off his face with his rolled-back sleeve. When he stopped at her side, he looked down with a frown. "Couldn't this wait until later?"

"I-I might never have the courage to try again." She peered into his eyes, gray like Grace's. "Please, Far."

He nodded and motioned to the shady side of the barn. The two walked the short distance in silence. When she stopped, he crossed his arms and waited.

Sophie shot another prayer heavenward and cleared her throat. "I know that I disobeyed you and caused great hurt to you all when I ran off with Hamre, and I have come to plead for your forgiveness." The words tumbled over each other once she started. "Please. I am so sorry, and I beg you to forgive me."

He stood motionless, his arms still clamped tight. "You've already asked for your mor's and Grace's?"

She nodded.

"Why did you wait so long to talk with me?"

Sophie rolled her lips together to try to keep from crying. "Because I was afraid."

"Afraid of what?"

"That you would say no. I couldn't bear that."

"Ah, Sophie, have I ever not forgiven you?"

"No, but I'd never done such a thing before."

"I was beginning to wonder if you'd ever come to me." He opened his arms and gathered her to his chest. "You, daughter, are forgiven." He held her while she cried into his sweaty shirt.

When she leaned back to dry her eyes, she pulled a piece of fleece from the side of her wet face. She sniffed through a wavering smile. "Guess I'm like the one the shepherd came to find. I've even got damp wool to prove it." She held up the bit between two fingers. "Thank you. I'm sorry I waited so long."

"Let this be a lesson to you, you know?" His hands clasped warm on her upper arms. "Waiting to ask for forgiveness just increases the fear and the pain." His face sobered. "I should have come to you like our Father does. I'm sorry too."

Sophie locked her arm through his. "I have so much to talk over with you. Could you and Mor come to supper at the boardinghouse so we can talk? I really need your advice."

"Ja, we will. How about tomorrow night? We'll be done shearing by then."

"I'll be waiting." She reached up and kissed his cheek. "Whew, you sure do smell like sheep."

Garth had been right. Waiting was not a pleasant situation. But now that Pa had forgiven her, she had one less wait to do. Why couldn't she have gone sooner to him?

She had nearly two months to wait until the baby came, and she needed some new clothes soon. Her others couldn't be let out any more. It seemed like she went to sleep one night, and the next day all of her skirts were six inches too small. Her aprons no longer could disguise her expansion either, so she took to wearing one of Mrs. Sam's.

"What da matter with you, child?" Mrs. Sam asked her several days later.

"Everything is too tight. I've let out all the seams, and I have no time to sew. Not that I'm very good at it anyway."

"Ask Grace. She help you."

"I don't think so. She's busy getting ready for graduation. Mor is too." *And besides clothes for me, I need things for the baby.* She thought of the check she had tucked away in her top drawer. She knew she should put that in the bank, but somehow if she did, it seemed she was severing her last tie with Hamre.

Silly, the baby will always be part of him, she chided herself. But if she spent some of the money, it would feel like stealing. Hamre had worked so hard for the money, and now his dreams were gone. And yet when she had told Far and Mor how she felt, they both said that the money truly was hers, and in honor of Hamre she should use it wisely. Far also reminded her that she could use money from the boardinghouse for her own needs. She'd told them that felt like stealing too, but they'd convinced her she'd earned her money at the boardinghouse. However, there was one more problem she hadn't mentioned. Well, two actually. Would that be dilemmas with an *s*? Or would it be two dilemma, like sheep? One sheep, two sheep. Somehow today she couldn't see the humor in playing with words.

She sniffed and made her way back to her room. Lying down on the bed, she allowed the tears to flow. Some days were just like that, and it didn't help that it was raining outside too.

And on top of everything she'd not heard a word from Garth since he'd gone to Minneapolis. She missed their nightly chats. That's all she could think about. What if he didn't come back? What if he met someone there?

She tried to roll over, but her belly got in the way. Maybe someone slender and lovely and wanting to be the mother to his two children? That thought sat her straight up. What difference did it make to her? Having a wife again would be a good thing for him. After all, he was just her friend. Someone she liked to talk with and share memories with, someone who understood what it was like to lose the one he loved.

She wiped her eyes and nose and made her way to her chair. But looking out at raindrops pelting the street made her feel like crying even more. Waiting. *I never have cared for waiting.*

34

MAY GREW HOTTER.

Sophie grew wider.

"All women don't get this big so soon, do they?" Sophie let Elizabeth help her sit upright again after an examination in the doctor's office. "I don't walk; I waddle."

"I see that. Let me listen again." She put her stethoscope to Sophie's mound, moving it around, listening carefully. "I can't be sure, but I have a feeling there might be two in there. If so, the hearts are beating so closely, I just can't be sure."

"Twins? Two babies?" Sophie laid both hands over her belly and stared down where one foot nudged against her hand.

"Well, it seems to run in the family."

"Do all twins have twins?"

"No, but the odds are higher, and you are getting pretty big. I'll check you again in a week or so. Maybe we'll know more then." She helped Sophie to step down from the table and stand upright.

"Two babies. I-I . . ." *How would I take care of two babies and run the boardinghouse? Maybe I should sell it after all.* "How am I going to manage?"

"I'd talk with your mother and ask her how they managed. And we'll have to find you some help, that's all. Often twins come early. You will need to rest more. Lie down every afternoon at a minimum. Grace and Astrid will both be out of school. I'm sure they will help you."

"Twins." Sophie kneaded her back with her fists. And Garth wasn't even here so she could tell him.

"If you notice your ankles swelling in the heat, get off your feet. You can lie on the bed and put your feet up on pillows."

Sophie stared at her. "You mean all this, don't you?"

Elizabeth assumed her most serious doctor face. "Yes, I do. If I need to, I will put you to bed here where we can help you." She rolled her lips in a fought-off smile. "I know what I'll do. I'll tell your mother, Ingeborg, and Mrs. Sam." At Sophie's moan, she turned serious again. "The choice is yours, Sophie. Do you want the babies to live or not?"

Sophie sucked in a deep breath. "You mean my baby or babies could die if I don't rest?"

Elizabeth nodded.

Sophie cupped her big belly with both hands. "Whoever you are in there, I will do everything I can to make sure you live." She shuddered. "Even go to bed if I have to."

When she dragged herself back into the boardinghouse, she headed to the kitchen.

"So what de doctor say?" Mrs. Sam asked.

Sophie sank down on a chair. How could walking those two blocks make her feel as if she'd run clear out to her mother's house and back? She and Grace used to run home from school, and while they'd be panting when they reached the house, in a minute and after a drink of water they would be fine.

"Could you please bring me a glass of water?"

"O' course. It weren't bad news?" Mrs. Sam's dark face wrinkled in concern.

Sophie drained the glass and fanned her face. "No, but interesting news." She sighed again. "I might be carrying twins."

"Yes."

Sophie stared up at her friend. "You mean you knew?"

"Well, not for sure, but you got de look. Stick out your foot, child."

Sophie lifted her skirt and held out her foot.

Mrs. Sam knelt down and pressed gentle fingers around the ankle-bones and up the leg. "Gotta watch dis."

"I don't understand. Watch what?"

"Swells up, it be poison in you. Hurt dem babies."

Lily Mae and Lemuel came in from working in the garden after washing up at the outside bench. "Carrots and peas is up, lettuce too."

"How are de potatoes?" Mrs. Sam pushed herself to her feet. "Any bugs?"

"A few. We doused 'em in the kerosene can," Lemuel said.

"And de corn?"

"We need a new rabbit fence," Lily Mae said. "They got some of it and some lettuce."

"Lemuel, bring some chicken fence tonight when you get back from the smithy. We fix dem rabbits."

"Put out snares," Sophie said as she pushed herself to her feet. "We can always serve fried fresh rabbit. I need to ask Samuel if he's running snares this year." She knew Trygve had given the job over to his younger brother, but now that Samuel was getting big, who did he have to pass the job on to?

That night Sophie collapsed on her bed rather than sitting down on the edge and brushing her hair the required hundred strokes. Her fringe had grown out, and she pinned it back—anything to let the cool air reach her skin.

❧

The next afternoon her mother came by. "Come, let's sit out on the back porch," Kaaren said. "That's where Bridget used to sit to catch a bit of breeze. You look done in."

Sophie sank into the rocking chair. "Thank you. This is nicer than lying down on my bed. Dr. Elizabeth said I have to lie down every afternoon." She told her mother that she might be carrying twins.

"I'm not surprised," she told her daughter.

Nobody is but me, it seems.

"I remember feeling as big as a house when I was carrying you and Grace. But at least you weren't born until the fall, so my summer wasn't as bad."

"Did we come early?"

"I'm not sure. We didn't know as much about due dates and things back then. Medicine has changed a lot in eighteen years. Not that having babies was considered part of medicine back then." She lifted a basket up to her lap. "We have some things sewn for you, but if you are indeed carrying twins, we need to crank up the sewing machines." She laid three little gowns in Sophie's lap, along with a knitted sweater and hat, and two soakers.

"Oh, Mother, they are so beautiful." Sophie fingered the narrow lace at the neck and the embroidered lamb on the chest.

"We made them light for summer. There are hemmed diapers in the basket too. We will need a lot of diapers for two."

Sophie gazed at her mother's face. She had used the word *we*. Such a good word, since she so often felt alone.

"Grace has some things made too, and I heard her and Astrid talking about a surprise."

"Which you won't tell me about." Sophie's smile lingered.

Kaaren looked up with a smile that matched her daughter's. "Why of course not. Then it would not be a surprise."

"Dr. Elizabeth said I might need to spend time in bed if my ankles swell. They were fine until it got so hot."

"It has been unseasonably hot for May. Grace will come help you as soon as graduation is over."

"Really?" Her heart immediately felt ten pounds lighter.

"You thought she wouldn't?"

"I hated to ask."

"Oh, Sophie, 'All will be well. All will be well. All manner of things will be well.' I read that in a book of devotions. A famous woman, Saint Juliana of Norwich, wrote it hundreds of years ago, and I think it such a reassurance."

"Say it again, please."

"'All will be well. All will be well. All manner of things will be well.'"

"Right now things don't feel so well."

"I know. But the 'all will be well' part depends on God's promises, not our feelings." Kaaren leaned her head back against the chair and set it to rocking. The gentle squeak and the soft breeze teasing the wisps of curls that framed her face lulled Sophie to sleep.

When she awoke some time later, her mother had left and Mrs. Sam kept the rocker singing, an old fan adding to the fitful breeze.

"De mail came."

"Good. Anything interesting?"

"Might be. A letter here from Minneapolis." She held the stamp closer to her eyes. "Yessum, that be where it come from."

"For me?"

"Looks to be." Mrs. Sam chuckled and handed the envelope across the small space. "How 'bout I bring you some lemonade?"

"You are so good to me."

"You easy to be good to. And it goes both ways." She headed back to the kitchen, humming as she went.

Sophie watched a pair of robins carrying grasses and twigs up into the cottonwood tree that Bridget had planted off the back porch, adding to the shade and breeze duets with the leaves.

She studied the envelope, prolonging the pleasure. Definitely from Garth. His block handwriting was distinctive. She slit the wax seal with a fingernail and removed two folded pages. Not just a note but a real letter.

Dear Sophie,

I've been writing this letter for a week and thought I'd better mail it before you think I fell through the cracks somewhere. Read the back page first if you want the news in chronological order.

She flipped to the second sheet, where the date showed two weeks earlier.

I am having to fix some things in my house, so I shall be here longer than I anticipated. But first I must tell you about my family. Linnie loves to laugh, and with her lower teeth sparkling, she makes us all laugh along with her. My son is a more serious child. He watches after his baby sister like she belongs to him. He has grown so much I hardly recognized him.

My mother is not happy that I will be taking her grandchildren away. While my brothers and sisters live in the area, they are not as close to her as these two are.

I realize now what a terrible mistake I made in leaving them behind. I lost precious time with them, but I still don't know how I could have done anything else, other than stay here, and that I couldn't bear.

I have a buyer who may be interested in my house, but first I need to finish repairing some water damage in the upstairs ceilings. Houses need to be lived in, that is for sure.

She flipped back to the front page.

So now you know all the news. My sister is still agreeing to come with me now that her husband, Dan, is willing to move to Blessing also. He doesn't want to work in the flour mill after all, but he is a good carpenter, so I will have him work on my house. As Andrew warned me, the house did not ship on time, but they promise it will arrive there before I do. I pray you are well and recovered from your shock.

What shock? She thought a moment. *Oh, he means the arrival of the check. He doesn't know the real shock that I may be carrying twins.* She smiled her thanks to Mrs. Sam for the glass of lemonade. "Where's yours?"

"I need to work on de supper."

"Not until after we drink our lemonade and perhaps have a cookie or two. I can't believe how I'm hungry all the time."

"That cuz you eatin' for three."

"Or how often I'm rushing to the necessary." She heaved herself from the chair and charged back into the building. She never ceased to be thankful that Bridget had installed indoor toilets. No more privy for her.

___

Two days later Sophie heard the whistle of the westbound train but went on making out her order for supplies. With strawberries coming on soon, she'd need extra sugar for making jam. She glanced over the inventory Mrs. Sam had completed just that morning and started another list. Talk to Samuel about supplying the snares to trap the rabbits so they could serve fried rabbit, and at the same time get rid of the destructive furry varmints. Even with the new fencing up, a rabbit had dug underneath one night and took out a good portion of a lettuce row—the new fresh lettuce, not the rows they'd already harvested a couple of times. Thanks to Mrs. Sam, who put in two new seeds for every plant she pulled, they had lettuce for sandwiches and salads, and for making the serving platters look pretty. She'd seen a picture of fried chicken served on a platter decorated with lettuce leaves and had trained her help in using the new look. Parsley was good for the same, so she'd had them plant extra parsley too.

"All dem folks care about is good food," she'd heard Mrs. Sam mutter, but when Miss Christopherson commented on how nice the meal looked, she knew she was on the right track. Just because they lived halfway to nowhere was no reason she couldn't make changes that might *attract more discerning customers*. She'd seen that line in an ad in a magazine. While Bridget had instigated high rules for cleanliness and Sophie kept that going, she knew she was adding class in another way. She never had forgotten eating in the dining car on the train going west with Hamre.

She looked up at the jangle of the bell. Garth Wiste stopped just inside, his smile bright enough to light a room. She felt her whole self respond in kind and, had her belly not gotten in the way, would have leaped to her feet and rushed across the vestibule to throw herself into his arms. Wherever had such thoughts and almost actions come from? One did not greet one's friends that way. Instead, she schooled her face into a more dignified manner. "Welcome home, stranger." Her voice cracked. Why did her eyes burn and nose heat up just because he walked back into her life? They were just friends, after all.

"Ah, and it is good to be home." He removed his hat and added it to others on the rack in the corner, glancing around the room as if to memorize it. When he allowed his gaze to lock on Sophie's, she immediately wished for her fan to cool off her neck and face. "And I hope I'm not really a stranger." His voice lowered, setting her heart to beat a singing cadence.

I was afraid you were never coming back. "You could have kept in better contact. I nearly rented out your room."

"Didn't I pay my bill?"

At the shocked look on his face, she leaned back and laughed, a light sound that had no relation to the pounding of her heart. *It's not fair to tease him, you know. Though it wasn't fair for him not to write sooner either. But you didn't answer his letter. It just came two days ago.* The thoughts zipped by like a honeybee carrying pollen back to the hive. *I missed you so. Don't tell him that; you have no right.*

Love gives me all the rights I need, so hush. Sophie nearly choked on that thought. *Love?* Who said she was in love with this man? He was just a friend. Wasn't he? *Since when has your heart danced like this when a friend walked in? Not since Hamre, that's for sure.*

"Sophie, you look so beautiful sitting there." Garth was staring at her, the corners of his mouth lifting slowly, the smile meandering up to his eyes and lighting his entire face. "I've missed you more than I can say."

"You have?" Fluster threw the deadbolt on all her rational responses.

"I have. I thought I'd be trapped there forever, when all I wanted was to be here in Blessing."

"To build your house. To take over the mill again?" The boulder that had moved into her throat forced her to swallow again and again.

"Those too, but remember I said I had something important to tell you?"

"You said a surprise."

He came around the end of the desk and leaned against it, extending one hand.

With no volition on her part, her right hand joined his. The shock that zinged up her arm and straight into her heart made her catch her breath. *Surely you must have something to say. Drowning in his eyes is not . . . is not . . .* She had no clue how to finish the thought.

"Welcome home, Mr. Wiste." Lily Mae tossed her comment and a knowing grin over her shoulder as she carried a stack of sheets fresh off the clothesline up the stairs to the upper linen closet.

Sophie snatched her hand back. If she thought she'd been warm before, now the heat was akin to standing in front of an open fire. A big fire. "Ah, supper won't be ready for a couple of hours. Would you like something cold to drink?"

"Later perhaps. Right now I'm heading over to see how far they've gotten on my house. Would you like to come along?"

"I'd love to, but I'm needed here." *And waddling across town is not appropriate, as Mrs. Valders reminded me the last time I went to the post office.* Why was it important for women to disguise or hide away something so natural as having a baby? That was another one of those questions that had no answer. Surely it wasn't scriptural.

Besides which, her feet were a bit swollen, and she knew that if she didn't lie down, Mrs. Sam would tell Dr. Elizabeth, who might make true her threat of bed rest. "I'll have some supper ready for you when you get back." *And we can talk after supper too. Oh, how I've missed our evening visits. I wonder what his surprise is.*

35

DO I ASK HER TONIGHT? *She was certainly happy to see me.*

No more than I was her. All I wanted to do was sweep her up in my arms and kiss those lips that smiled so brightly.

Surely this is love. Love! He wanted to shout it to the birds that winged overhead. Never had he understood dithering before, thinking it more a female thing. But one look at her face and he'd had a hard time breathing. A hard time keeping a sane thought in his head. Had he been like this when he was courting Maddie? The thought gave him pause. Probably, but it was long enough ago that he'd forgotten.

I love Sophie Bjorklund, and I'm going to ask her to marry me.

But will she say yes? What if she says no? This thought brought him back to rational thinking with a thump. He stumbled over a chunk of black soil, baked so hard it bore all the look and feel of a rock. But unless hauled in, there were no rocks in this portion of the Red River Valley, at least as far as he knew. Glancing around, he was glad to see no one smirking at his clumsiness. In fact he saw no one at all. But then, other than the farmers, most people were wise enough to find some shade or a breeze. He took out his handkerchief to wipe his face. No, not everyone. He could hear hammering from the direction of the church, from the direction of his house. It sounded like an echo of that going on at the flour mill.

It was all he could do to keep from running toward the sound.

"Welcome home," Pastor Solberg called from the door to the church. "I just took water over to the men working on your house. Would you like some too?" He came down the steps and reached out a hand. "Good to see you back."

"Good to be back. Being in Minneapolis sure made me aware of how much better I like it here."

"Did you get your house sold?"

"That I did. The day I finished the repairs, a man walked up and met my price."

"God's like that. Often right down to the last minute but never late. I'm glad it worked out that way for you. I know there were some prayers going up for you from here."

Garth glanced at the man walking beside him, a man who talked about prayer as if he'd just come from a visit with his best friend. "So what has gone on here while I've been gone?"

"Oh, graduation is this weekend. Mr. Gould will be arriving tomorrow. We've all been busy sprucing things up at the church and schoolhouse both. When they cut the grass around the two buildings, they went ahead and cut yours too. I hope you don't mind."

"Mind? Of course not. I'm very pleased." Garth stopped to shake his head at the two piles of sand and gravel waiting to be mixed with cement and water for the basement walls. "It looks like enough supplies here to build two houses." Stacks of lumber of various sizes took up a good portion of what would one day be his yard. He knew the crates held windows, but he'd not realized there would be so many. Would Sophie like this house? She helped pick it out, but still . . . Everything seemed to return to Sophie in his mind.

"It's some different looking at a picture, and then at the materials, isn't it?"

"You took the words right out of my mouth." They stopped at the edge of the hole in the ground, and he waved at the two men putting up forms.

"Hey, Garth, what do you think?" Toby Valders waved a hammer to indicate what they had done. "We'd have been farther along, but we were needed over at the mill a few days."

"Looks good to me." He studied the three wall frames already built. He'd never mixed or poured concrete. This would be a new experience. As far as that went, he'd never built a house either.

"We should be ready to pour these walls day after tomorrow. Then they can set over the weekend and we'll start on the floor joists on Monday."

"We've planned the house-raising for the next weekend, if that is all right with you," Pastor Solberg added.

"More than all right. It's wonderful." Garth turned to stare at the pastor. "You all planned this even when I was gone?"

"You said you were coming back, and we need you at the mill. Besides, you're a member of Blessing now, and we take care of our own."

"And anyone who happens to need something."

"If we can."

"My brother-in-law is coming out to work on the house too. He's tired of working in the mills."

"Is he a good carpenter?"

"Yes, a bricklayer too."

"I'm sure the Bjorklunds would be glad to have him on their construction company."

"My sister is coming with my children as soon as the house is finished."

"It sounds like you made some decisions."

"I did. This place is my home now." He turned back from watching the men nail up more boards and clapped the pastor on the arm. "Thanks isn't enough, but until I find a way to repay, it will have to do."

"Oh, I'm sure God will find a way to even it all out."

Garth flinched inside. "I haven't been on too good of terms with God since my wife died, but surviving the mill explosion brought this believer back to praying like never before. I don't take life for granted anymore."

"He's always waiting for us to come back. And looks to me like He's been providing too. Overwhelming grace, I call it."

Garth sucked in a deep breath. "For a while there I figured work was the only remedy."

"It helps. That and the folks He brings into your life. Spend time in the Scriptures and worship Him in spite of the pain. He understands when we blame Him for things we do not understand. Sometimes life makes no rhyme or reason, but He stays faithful, full of mercy and grace."

"I don't deserve—"

"None of us do."

The answer lay gentle on the breeze that tickled Garth's ear, much as if God were whispering to him himself. "Thank you."

"Anytime. Door's always open."

"Pa." A voice carried on the wind stopped them.

Pastor Solberg turned. "I'm being called. See you on Sunday."

"Yes." Garth watched the man stride off and let his own sigh join the breeze. Strange how much lighter he felt. He thanked the men in the cellar and headed back to the boardinghouse. Now if only he could find just the right time to talk with Sophie and see if she would do him the honor of becoming his wife and living in his new house.

✑

Sophie lay on her bed, thinking she should get up, but the breeze coming in the window teased the cream lawn nightdress that she'd donned after a cooling basin bath bade her rest a bit longer. Since there was no way she could see her ankles, even though two pillows held them up, without lifting her leg, she chose to not think about the swelling and just enjoy the comfort.

The babies didn't bother to rest at the same times she did, so sleeping had become somewhat hit and miss. "I wonder what you are going to be like," she whispered. "Are you two sisters, two brothers, or one of each?" She'd been thinking of names. Hamre if one was a boy—that was not even a question. But she needed another boy's name. Name a girl after her mother and sister? Kaaren Grace? Grace Kaaren? Her mind wandered off without asking permission. Thanks to the money Hamre had saved, she could now travel when and where she wanted. But every time she thought of places to go, guilt crept in and tainted the dream. Hamre had worked so hard for the money that at least part of it needed to be used for something lasting. A house? An addition to the boardinghouse? She'd thought of talking this over with her mor and far but hadn't done so.

While she knew the money was legally hers, it still didn't feel like it really was.

Besides, how could she travel with two small babies to nurse? Even with a nanny. She'd thought to take Grace along, but what if Grace didn't want to go? What did Grace want to do now that she was graduating? She'd talked of many things in the past.

A thought sneaked in on tiptoes. You could hire a wet nurse and be free to travel by yourself. What would it be like—to be free?

A tapping at her door sent the thoughts spinning off. "Yes?"

"You're awake?" Mrs. Sam opened the door and looked in.

"Yes, the babies decided to play a game of tag. Or kickball. Come on in."

"I brought you some cold milk. Thought that might taste good." Mrs. Sam shouldered open the bedroom door and set a small tray on a table. "Cookies too."

Using both of her arms, Sophie pushed herself up against the pillows and the headboard with a groan. "Standing works, lying flat works, but sitting? Not as good."

"Dr. Elizabeth come by. She say to let you sleep." Mrs. Sam handed Sophie a napkin to place on her belly and a glass of milk.

"Well, sometimes this shelf is good for something." She rested the glass on the napkin. "Thank you." Nibbling on a lemon cookie, she tried to keep from dropping crumbs.

"Storm coming up." Mrs. Sam pulled up the rocking chair and sat down.

"How do you know?"

"Smell it on de wind."

Sophie had given up trying to understand how Mrs. Sam knew so many things. She dampened a fingertip to pick up a cookie crumb. "So have you decided?" Sophie asked. "Is it boys or girls?"

"One girl, I think, not sure yet on de other."

"What does Dr. Elizabeth think?"

Mrs. Sam shrugged.

"Tante Ingeborg?"

Another shrug. "She say bring a potty chair in here for you."

"Speaking of which . . ." Sophie handed off the glass and swung her feet over the edge of the bed. She stuffed her arms into the sleeves of the dressing gown that Mrs. Sam held for her and headed for the necessary. The potty chair sounded like a wonderful idea.

When she returned to her room, she found a dress all laid out for her on the bed, the tray gone, and the curtains billowing at the windows. While the dress had been cut plenty big, already it was feeling snug around the middle. Whoever would've dreamed she'd be this big and six weeks more to go? She dressed, slid her feet into felt slippers since she could no longer button her shoes, and tied an apron in place with a very small bow. Even the ties were getting short.

Six weeks or so of lying around like this? It sounded like a lifetime.

After supper she and Garth took their coffee out onto the back porch. Lightning forked the sky like cracks in a celestial mirror. While thunder grumbled off in the distance, it came no closer. Sophie put her feet up on the stool they kept there for her and let her head rest against the back of the chair. The cool breeze kissed her skin while the crickets serenaded them. She could hear Mrs. Sam and her crew cleaning the kitchen, the clatter of dishes and pans a counterpoint to the night music.

"So what did you think of your house?" she asked.

"Farther along than I thought. Looking at that hole in the ground made the whole thing a reality." He then told her some about his conversation with Pastor Solberg. "He's a fine man and a good pastor."

"I guess. But then I don't really know any different. He's been the pastor here since about the time I was born, I think, and always my schoolteacher, other than my mother. I was angry at him for refusing to marry Hamre and me when we left here, but now I realize he was doing what he could in the hope we would stay here."

"Are you sorry you went with Hamre?"

"Never."

"Do you still love him?"

She thought a long while before answering. "In a way. But it is hard to remember at times. We were together such a short time. Almost like it was only a dream or a book I read. Until I move. Then reality is here." She laid her hand on her belly. "What about you?"

"I realized when I was in Minneapolis that Blessing is now home to me, and I want my life here to really begin. I thought I would wait until the house was finished, but like I told you, I'm tired of waiting." He paused for deep moment. "Sophie." He leaned forward, then rose and pulled his chair closer so he could take her hand. "I know that I have fallen in love with you, and I am asking if you feel the same about me."

Oh no. Please don't ask me. Before you came I was dreaming of adventures. "I-I'm not sure. I mean, I know that there is an attraction between us—just feel our hands to know that. But am I ready to really love again? I don't know. I care for you more than any man I know, and when you were gone, I was so afraid you weren't coming back that I cried. Is all that part of love?"

"I want to marry you, Sophie. I'm asking you to be my wife."

Sophie let his declaration lie between them. *Do I love this man enough to marry him? To be the mother of his two children and my two? Four children. How can I be a mother to four children? I want to travel. I'm still thinking on how I can. What does all this mean?* "I-I don't know."

"Well, that's certainly not the answer I had hoped for, but then I've had more time to think on this than you have." He lifted her hand to his lips and kissed her knuckles, his mustache tickling her skin, his lips searing it.

"Would you want me to give up the boardinghouse?"

"Not if you didn't want to."

"Is this why you wanted my opinion on the house?"

"You saw through me."

"Not until now." The rocker barely moved, as if it too were holding its breath. "Can I think about it?"

"I sure hope you will." He kissed her hand again.

She tried to draw it back but he didn't let her. "I can't think when you do that."

"Good. I've wanted to kiss you for a long time."

"Really?"

He stood and bent over the arm of her chair. "May I?" At her nod he lowered his head, brushing her mouth with his before settling his lips on hers.

Sophie kissed him back, her lips remembering how to fit against a man's, her hand seeking the hair that curled on the back of his neck. When he lifted his head, a lightning bolt outlined him with a shimmer.

That's just what she felt like inside, all shimmery and as if she might explode. She hadn't expected to feel this way, but oh, she'd missed being kissed. She blinked lazily and smiled up at him. "Mr. Wiste, you really pack a punch."

"And here I thought it was you. Let me help you up."

The first of the raindrops struck the porch roof and blew a breath of damp coolness over them. They stood watching the storm approach. The drumming increased, the sky got darker, thunder rumbled right next door. She laid her head against his shoulder and heard the steady drumming of his heart.

A shiver started about her knees and quivered its way up to run tingles around her scalp.

"I should get you inside."

"Only a moment more." Could she say yes? Was this love that flowed clear out to her fingers like rain drenched the leaves of the tree, washing away the dust of confusion?

"Sophie, I have something more to say. If you decide to travel, to go find the adventures that you've dreamed of, just know that I'll be waiting here for you to come home."

Thunder crashed so close she flinched, and he drew her even closer, sheltering her under his arm. Was it the rain on the roof or was her heart crying that she couldn't say yes?

36

"WHY COULDN'T I SAY YES?" Sophie asked the woman in the mirror.

Here it was, the day before graduation, and she had awakened with swollen ankles and enough puffy skin around her eyes to make her look like a stuffed cabbage. And if not for the potty chair, she'd have had an accident during the night. Why would any man even think of wanting to marry her looking like this? *If Dr. Elizabeth says I have to go to bed, I will miss the graduation altogether and the big party. I haven't been to a party for so long, and I was really looking forward to it.*

She turned at the tap on the door. "Come in."

Mrs. Sam pushed open the door, carrying a tray with coffee and toast. She took one look at Sophie's ankles and shook her head. "Oh, I was afraid of this." She set the tray down. "You get back in that bed, child. I'll bring in some comfrey tea."

"What does that do?"

"Take down de swelling some, we hope." She hustled out the door, throwing one more comment over her shoulder. "I'm sending Lemuel for Dr. Elizabeth."

Sophie moved the stool closer to the bed with her traitorous foot. Bending over was now an action of yore. How could things change so overnight? True, she'd not let anyone see the puffiness the day before, but this was beyond belief. She stepped up on the stool, turned, and sat on the bed, thinking it must have grown taller in the night.

Then lying on her side, resting before the act of rolling onto her back and pushing herself up against the headboard, she let the tears flow. They seemed to gush at any odd moment, whether finding a number in her account books that didn't match or seeing the daffodils in their spring glory. She should have paid much more attention to the legions of pregnant women she'd known in Blessing—the tears ran harder, making her gulp—back when she'd been so sure of herself in all things. That seemed another lifetime ago. Today, this moment, she knew nothing other than women had been going through this for gen-erations, which made the continual arrival of babies in Blessing that much more incredible.

Once she'd heaved herself into some sort of propped-up position, she mopped her cheeks with the edge of the sheet, wondering if the skin on her ankles would pop before her belly did.

Six more weeks of this. Her mother was a saint. Ingeborg was a saint. Any woman who went through this was a saint.

She'd dozed off when another tap came on the door and Dr. Eliz-abeth entered with her black leather bag. "Sorry it is coming to this. You've done well so far." She took out her stethoscope and checked Sophie's heart and lungs. "Are you having trouble breathing?"

"Only if I try to bend over, or when—"

"You stand up or sit down or . . . ?"

"Something like that. Even my skin hurts."

"I'll have Mrs. Sam rub some glycerin cream into it. Skin stretches, but you're pushing beyond an easy stretch." Moving down over the mound, she listened to the baby heartbeats. "Two for sure now." She smiled at Sophie, who did not smile back. What if . . . ? She had to ask.

"Elizabeth, they're . . . all right, aren't they?"

"Far as I can tell." She looked deep into Sophie's eyes. "You're thinking about Grace and her deafness, aren't you?"

Sophie nodded, ashamed she was so obvious. Her sister only gave joy to anyone who was around her. Why did it matter that she did it without hearing? Sophie wanted it not to matter for her babies, but deep inside, she knew it did.

"God only knows. Someday maybe we'll understand more, but right now, well, I'm grateful for every baby that is born whole and healthy." Taking a deep breath, Elizabeth straightened. "What I do know is that mothers taking better care of themselves have healthier babies. Not lacing their corsets also gives healthier babies. Imagine being pinched into smaller spaces while you are growing."

She pressed the skin around Sophie's feet and ankles and looked at her equally swollen hands. "Keep your feet up. The less walking the better." When Sophie started to say something, Elizabeth raised her hand. "I know. Graduation is tomorrow, and you want to go to the party, but even if you rode in a wagon or buggy, you'd be bumped around more than I want you to be. I'm sure it will be hot, and much as I hate to say it, you would be better off here."

Tears leaked out around Sophie's determination and rolled down her cheeks. "It's not fair." Hearing the familiar lament she'd uttered so many times since Hamre's death only increased her misery. Missing out on one more thing since she'd returned, like she'd missed out on the winter dances and dinners around the family table. This time Sophie would miss Grace's important day, a day they would have shared if Sophie had had sense enough to care back then.

Now she was bawling like a calf who'd strayed too far from its mama, and as she did, she accepted that she couldn't go to Grace's graduation. Her life was her babies now, and they needed her feet up.

Forcing the words out through the gulps, Sophie answered Elizabeth. "I-I know. I will stay here . . . for the babies."

The westbound train whistled and, even though slowing, shook the entire building. While Sophie hardly ever paid attention to it anymore, Elizabeth rolled her eyes. "You must have to straighten pictures every day."

"You've noticed we don't have a lot of pictures on the walls."

"Good thing. Do you have any questions?"

"I had one earlier, and now I can't remember it. I'm going to have to let out those two dresses. . . ." A sigh slid up from her puffy ankles and out her lips. "Maybe I should just wear a sheet."

An answering smile met her. "That's a thought," Elizabeth said. "We could sew two of them together at the shoulders and sides, hem them up, and away you go."

Sophie giggled and she could feel her arms and legs relaxing. "Now that would be a sight."

A bustle out in the vestibule caught their attention, then two male voices and Lily Mae answering.

"Oh, that must be Mr. Gould, and now I won't get to meet him either." She slitted her eyes in thought. "I sure hope those rooms are at their best. I reminded Mrs. Sam about that yesterday. I should have put them on the first floor; then I could have made sure."

"Sophie, Sophie, you know they took care of it all. And you'll get to meet him. I'll make sure of it."

"But not now. My hair's a mess. I'm a mess." She raised her hands and let them fall on her stomach. "Nothing is going right." Nothing had since Hamre. *That's enough. This muddling around in misery doesn't change anything.* Besides, it wasn't true anyway. Just not the way she wanted things. Well, then. Her thoughts had steamed up like the train that had just blown through, and the words fell faster and faster as she stared at the ceiling. "And on top of that Garth asked me to marry him—"

"Did you say what I thought you said?"

"And even after all this, I still want to travel—"

"Sophie!"

Finally another rib-rattling sigh. "And I don't know what to do."

"Garth asked you to marry him?" Elizabeth's eyes were wide.

Sophie nodded. "He said he loves me, but I couldn't say yes. I said yes too fast last time." Moisture joined the tears on her cheeks. "No. I made Hamre say yes too fast. I'm not the same girl. At least I don't want to be the same girl. What do I want now that I have a choice? A choice that includes two babies?" Blowing out a deep breath, she finished, her bottom lip in the pout she hadn't allowed herself for months. "All I know is I'm so huge the bed might break, and then I'll fall onto the floor."

Elizabeth rolled her lips together to keep from laughing. When the silence fell, they could hear someone walking in the room overhead. Sophie made a face and clapped a hand over her mouth.

"They couldn't hear me, could they?"

"I doubt it. But I have some advice for you. All you can do right now is take care of yourself and the babies. All the rest will work out in God's good time."

Sophie swallowed and mopped her eyes with a napkin. "Sorry."

"No problem. An outburst once in a while by a pregnant woman is not a bad thing. You've been through a lot, Sophie dear, and God isn't going to desert you now."

Sophie huffed a sigh that puffed out both cheeks. "Thanks. You won't tell anyone, will you?"

"Tell anyone what?" Elizabeth put her stethoscope back in her bag.

"About what I said."

"Doctors never tell anyone anything they've been told." She patted Sophie's hand. "You talk it all over with your mother. She's the best advisor around."

Sophie slept through much of Saturday, or rather napped, since sleeping for any length of time day or night was becoming more diffi-cult by the day.

Sunday morning she drowsed awake when she heard the church bells, shed some more tears at missing the graduation, and fell asleep again.

In the evening she heard laughter and recognized both Grace and Astrid's voices. Surely the other voice was her mother's, and when they trooped into her room, Ingeborg was along too.

"Since you couldn't come to the party, we brought the party to you," Astrid said, setting a handled basket on the hassock.

"Oh!" Sophie teared up again. It would be lovely to have a conver-sation without busting into waterworks. "I'm sorry I couldn't come. How did it go?"

"We are all graduated," Grace said. "That means we are women now, not just girls."

"Not in my mind," Ingeborg said. "You are all still my little girls."

She included Sophie in the warm glance.

"Little?" Sophie stared at her belly, making the others laugh.

"Well, in our minds you are all still little girls." Kaaren kissed Sophie's forehead. "Somehow I don't remember being this big."

"I don't remember that either, but maybe over time we've forgotten some things." Ingeborg walked around the bed and took Sophie's hand. "You and Grace were so little, I was terrified you wouldn't make it."

"I think these two are going to be born walking," Sophie said.

"We wanted to bring ice cream, but Mor said it would melt before we got it here." Astrid took a jar of canned raspberry juice from the basket. "I'll take this out to the kitchen and make swizzle to have with our cake."

"There's ice in the icebox. Just ask Mrs. Sam."

"We brought you some things to keep you busy," Ingeborg said, taking a roll of fabric from another basket. She unrolled it to show an open-front baby gown with two sets of ties. "I thought you could embroider on this, and I brought knitting needles and baby yarn too, along with the instructions. Plus you can finish the handwork on these little hats, so you will have one for each baby. Can you sit in the chair?"

"With my feet on the stool I can, for a while at least. I tried working on the books earlier this morning, but I didn't last long."

"Have you met Mr. Gould yet?" Ingeborg asked.

Sophie shook her head while fingering the little garments. "I wanted to, but . . ." She gestured to her hair. "I look a mess, and I can't do anything without huffing and puffing." Tears. She was going to shrink her face by the time these babies were born with all the water pouring down it.

"We'll take care of that." Grace brought the brush and comb from the top of the chest of drawers. "Can you sit up more?"

"With help."

Kaaren and Ingeborg helped her to sit on the edge of the bed with her feet on the stool.

"I don't have much bend in me. Almost slid off here during the night."

"Here, this will be easier." Kaaren brought a chair over and helped

Sophie put her feet on that. "Better?"

"Yes."

Grace knelt behind her and brushed through the long locks, using her fingers to work out some of the tangles.

"Oh, that feels so good." Sophie tipped her head back to make reaching the top of her head easier. "I just bundled it back in a snood earlier, but that's not comfortable to lie on."

"How about we braid it?" Kaaren drew up the rocking chair and sat down. "Elizabeth said those two dresses I sewed for you are getting too tight."

"I suggested we sew two sheets together. I'm bigger than one of the cows."

"I saw an elephant once," Astrid announced as she came through the door. "Mrs. Sam is making the swizzle. A cow maybe," she said, her grin impish. "But you're not as big as an elephant."

It felt so good to laugh.

"Sophie," Astrid said, lowering her voice. "Jonathan Gould has arrived." Her eyes sparkled like there was a story to be told.

Ingeborg and Kaaren both rolled their eyes. "Just because he is handsome . . ." Ingeborg began.

"Well mannered. . . ." added Kaaren.

"And has a charming New York accent . . ." Astrid piped in.

"Are those any reasons for all the girls to swoon over him?" Ingeborg finished.

"I didn't swoon." Astrid insisted, frowning at her mother.

"All right. We exaggerated a teensy bit. But it was fun to watch."

Grace finished braiding Sophie's hair and tied a ribbon on the end of the braid. She sat beside Sophie on the bed. "Jonathan says he is looking forward to his summer here in Blessing."

"Wait until he gets up to milk tomorrow morning." Astrid plumped up the pillows and set them back against the headboard. Then she climbed up to sit against them. "Can we bring you books or anything?"

Sophie shrugged. "If I can work on these baby things, that will take me plenty of time."

"Do you remember how to thread a needle?"

Ah, Astrid was quick. Sophie grabbed a pillow and thumped her cousin while Grace and the others chuckled. "I'll have you know I sat still long enough to read the paper here, and I read one in Seattle."

"One or once?" This time it was Grace, a slight smile sneaking over her lovely face.

Mrs. Sam carried in a tray holding a tall pitcher and glasses with ice. She set the tray down, poured the glasses full, and handed them around. "Congratulations to the both of you," she told the girls. "You all growed up now."

When Mrs. Sam left the others filled Sophie in on all the doings she'd missed hearing about, including the rebuilding of the flour mill and a letter Elizabeth had received from the woman who had been interested in building a hospital in Blessing.

"She is still pursuing the idea, she wrote, and is looking for investors." Ingeborg's fingers kept up her knitting.

"Blessing would be blessed with a hospital," Sophie said.

When Sophie began to yawn moments later, Ingeborg put her knitting away. "It is time for us to be on our way home. I've been thinking. Perhaps we should have the men build a place for you to lie down out on the back porch. That way you could enjoy the breeze and not feel so cooped in. Pad it with quilts, a feather bed. Make something easy for you to get on and off."

Later, reminiscing about the wonderful visit and rejoicing that she had people who cared about her, Sophie thought about Ingeborg's idea. "A bed to roll the cow off and on." She giggled, her words getting wispier. "But not as big as an elephant. So there." Sophie was almost asleep when the thought hit her. She'd not told Grace about Garth's proposal.

37

THE NEXT MORNING, thanks to Grace's help, Sophie was sitting on the back porch next to Grace with her hair combed, face washed, and wearing the blue calico dress with new inserts in the sides so it was comfortable when a knock came at the door. Her heart leaped. The knock sounded male. So Garth had not abandoned her. "Come on out."

"Pardon me, but I would like to meet the other Mrs. Bjorklund before I leave."

The deep voice was like none she knew. *Oh, do I look all right? How can I look all right?* She trapped her dithering and put a smile on her face. "Mr. Gould, come join us."

"Thank you." He stepped through the door and tipped his head. "I couldn't leave without meeting you, and now I've met all the family." He nodded to Grace, acknowledging her too.

Crossing the porch, he stopped at Sophie's side and held out a box wrapped in white with a yellow bow. "This is for you."

"Why, thank you." She smiled up at him, noticing that his silver hair was set off by dark eyes. "You look just like I imagined. Tante Ingeborg has told us the story of meeting you so often. Please, have a seat."

"I cannot stay long. I have a train to catch. I want to thank you for your hospitality and commend you for your fine establishment."

"This is all thanks to Grandma Bridget. I just run it now. Well, actually, Mrs. Sam runs it. We'd be lost without her."

"She is a fine cook. You are fortunate."

"I know."

"I hear that you dream of traveling."

"I always have."

"Well, if you travel to New York, we would be honored to have you stay with us. I tried to convince your mother and Ingeborg to come too. They might have new and better memories of the city if they came again."

"Thank you for the invitation."

"Well, I must be on my way. Thank you again." He held out his hand, and she laid hers in it. He bent over and kissed the back of her hand and then repeated the action with Grace. "Good-bye, Mrs. Bjorklund, Miss Knutson."

"Good-bye." They watched him leave, the door clicking behind him, then swapped astonished looks. "I think we should all go to New York," Sophie told Grace.

"Me too."

Sophie felt her mouth drop open as she stared at her sister. "Would you go to New York?"

"If I went with all of you, yes." Grace fetched the stool and put it in front of her sister. "Put your feet up."

Would wonders never cease? Sophie thought a bit more. Garth had said if she wanted to have adventures first before she made up her mind to marry him, it was all right with him. Perhaps a trip to New York would be a good way to start. Remembering how she'd felt when he didn't come back from Minneapolis as soon as he'd said made her wonder. And sigh. So many decisions to make.

৵৹

Two weeks later Sophie woke in the middle of the night frantically trying to decide whether to throw up or to scream for the pain knifing into her back. It rolled around to her front as she heaved into the wash-basin. When she finished, she wiped her face with a cloth dipped in the water pitcher and returned to the side of her bed, debating if she should ring her bell or just go back to sleep. Lily Mae had spent the night on a cot in the kitchen, hadn't she?

She wiped the back of her neck with the cooling cloth and drizzled some of the water down her front. Feeling restless she made her way to the window and let the breeze flow over her. Had one of the babies kicked her wrong, or what had happened? When she turned back to the bed, her stomach roiled again, and she staggered back to the basin. *But I've nothing left in my stomach*, she thought as nothing came up. She'd not felt like eating supper, so hadn't. Was that the problem? She was hungry? No, hunger wasn't it. The knife struck her in the back again. She stumbled to the bell and rang it, then opened the door and rang it again. Please, Lily Mae, hear this.

She leaned against the doorjamb, waiting for the pain to subside as it had before. When it did, she heard feet pounding down the stairs. Garth burst into the hallway.

"What is it? What's wrong?"

Never had she been happier to see someone. "I don't know, but I need Lily Mae or Mrs. Sam or Dr. Elizabeth."

"I'll get her. You sit down, lie down, however you can be most com-fortable." He charged across the vestibule and through the dining room. She could hear his shoes thumping on the floor all the way. Panting now, she leaned against the wall.

When the pain came for the third time, just as Garth got back to her, she knew she'd better see the doctor. Something was terribly wrong.

"Go for Dr. Elizabeth."

"I think we better get you over there."

"I can't walk that far."

Garth paused for a moment. "Can you sit in the chair?"

"I guess so."

"Fine. I'll get one of the men and we'll carry you."

"But I can't . . ." She might as well have saved her breath. He was now taking the stairs two at a time.

"What do I do?" Lily Mae asked, her eyes wide in the lamplight she'd brought with her.

"Go tell Dr. Elizabeth we are coming over there."

Nightdress flapping about her dark legs, Lily Mae ran out the door. The men Garth recruited—four instead of two—must have leaped into their clothes as they came flying down the stairs.

"All right, Sophie, skip the chair. You lie down on the bed, and we'll carry you by the corners of the sheets."

"I-I can't." She gripped the doorjamb and let the pain roll over and around her.

"Then sit on the edge of the bed and we'll do the rest." They entered the room, all of them trying to be mannerly and not look directly at her. They loosened the sheets and, as Sophie sat down, bunched them up around her. On the count of three, they lifted. She let her head fall back and tried to relax as they jostled their way through the bedroom door, the hall door, and finally out the front door and down the steps.

"All right, in step will make it easier on her. Right foot, left." Already beginning to puff, they marched up the street and down the block to the doctor's house, the full moon throwing their shadows ahead of them.

"Thank you," Sophie said to all of them as they mounted the ramp to the surgery.

Thorliff pushed open the door and held it.

"In here," Elizabeth called. She stood by a narrow birthing bed. "On the count of three now."

With great care they laid the sheets and their cargo in the center of the bed.

Sophie grabbed Garth's hand and dug in as another wave rolled over her. She gritted her teeth, fighting to not moan, and when it passed, she collapsed back against the bed.

"Sophie, if we can get you up and walking, this will be easier."

"Are . . . the . . . babies coming?"

"Looks like it." Elizabeth listened to the heartbeats and palpitated the abdomen. "Sorry, Mr. Wiste. I forgot you were here. You want to wait outside? Or you could return to your bed. I'm sure this will be long hours from now."

"Could I be of assistance in helping her walk?"

"We can get Thorliff—"

"Would it offend anyone if I stayed to help?"

"Not anyone here. Sophie?"

"Is it going to get worse?"

"Oh yes."

"Will it make Mrs. Valders shriek?"

"Oh yes."

"Good, then stay."

With all of them laughing, they got her back up and her feet moving. They staggered up and down the hall, into the kitchen and out onto the back porch, where they sat Sophie on a bench to let her rest for a bit. When the sun burned its way loose from the horizon, her water broke, leaking down her legs and onto the porch floor.

"Well, this was as good a location as any for that to take place. Now don't be embarrassed, Sophie. Things will really begin to happen now."

"You don't call all this happening?" Sophie leaned into Garth's side, her hand locked on his wrist.

"You are doing wonderfully for a first-time birthing."

"These two are in a hurry to come into the world." She could feel another contraction coming. "Here we go again."

"Okay, let's walk."

They paced, half carrying and half dragging Sophie for another hour until Elizabeth finally said, "Let's get her back to the bed. Now is when you can really be a help, or I'll ask Lily Mae to come back."

"You don't need to ask anyone. I'm here." Kaaren stopped in the hall. "Why didn't you send someone for me earlier?"

"For us," Ingeborg said from right behind her.

"I knew there was nothing you could do up until now," Sophie said.

"We could have been praying."

"You're right," Sophie said. "I'm sorry but glad Thorliff took it upon himself to do what was right. I am really glad you are here. Mr. Wiste, thank you for your help."

"If you can't call me Garth by now . . ." He squeezed Sophie's hand. "I'll be out on the porch. If you need me, let me know."

Sophie nodded and clamped her hands on the sides of the bed, her teeth gritted so hard her jaw was screaming too.

"I'll get behind her." Kaaren waited while Elizabeth and Ingeborg held Sophie up, then Kaaren took her place, braced against the headboard, and eased her daughter back. "Now, you push against me, for when you are half sitting, the baby comes more easily."

"Oh, Mor, I didn't know . . ."

"None of us know until we do this." Kaaren wiped her daughter's face with the cool cloth Ingeborg handed her.

"If you feel like screaming, Sophie, go ahead. Sometimes that helps."

"But . . . what . . . about . . . Inga?"

"Her pa took her out to spend the day with Astrid." Ingeborg wrung the cloth out and handed it back. "You and the babies are all we're concerned about now."

When it was time for the surgery to open, Dr. Elizabeth went to care for someone else while the two women worked with Sophie, rubbing her back when she could lie on her side for a time, singing softly, praying and praising in song and prayer. Thelma checked on the group occasionally to see if they needed additional help.

Sophie heard them at times, felt their gentle hands soothing her, but about the time she thought she might breathe easily, the pain came again.

The next time Elizabeth checked her, she patted Sophie's knee. "We're making progress. Looks like this one has dark hair like her mother." She raised her voice. "Sophie, can you hear me?"

Sophie nodded.

"On this next contraction, I want you to push for all you're worth and then relax. We're going to have a baby here pretty soon. All right, let's go. Push, Sophie, push."

Ingeborg clung to Sophie's hand, Kaaren to the other, and Sophie pushed with a cry torn from her. Two more big pushes, and she collapsed against her mother.

"A little dark-haired girl." Elizabeth laid the baby on her mother's reduced belly. "Little one, meet your mother."

Sophie stared at the round little face, eyes all scrunched shut, tiny fists waving in the air. "Oh, she is . . ." She looked to Elizabeth. "She's all here, I mean . . ."

"She looks perfect."

Sophie touched the tiny head and stroked down the cheek. The baby turned her head, seeking the touch, perfect lips moving. "It's coming again!"

"You take the baby, Ingeborg, and we'll get this job over with."

But after another stretch of pushing, no baby showed.

"All right, Sophie, you rest a moment here while your mother and I have a bit of a talk."

Ingeborg handed the newborn to Thelma, and the three women gathered in the hall. "Any ideas?"

"See if the baby is breech?" Ingeborg suggested.

"Yes. I thought the second would come right away. On the next contraction, I'll see what I can find out."

After the next contraction, Sophie whimpered, and Elizabeth looked up after her inspection. "We have an arm rather than a head."

"Can you turn it?"

"We can try."

"Wait. Let's roll her up on her hands and knees. I've done that in the past."

Between the four of them, with groaning and grunting and gasped instructions, Sophie knelt, braced on either side by her mother and aunt.

"I know this will hurt, dear, but bear with us." Elizabeth felt carefully and, with exquisite care shifted the baby inside.

"Coming." Sophie collapsed on her side, and they helped roll her over. With a loud scream, Sophie pushed again.

"Harder."

"I can't."

"Yes you can. Now on the next one, you push with every bit of strength you can find. And you two, pray like you've never prayed before. I don't want to do a cesarean."

Sophie panted. *God, please, I can't do this anymore. Please help me.* When the pain started again, all she wanted to do was quit. This was too much. She couldn't go any longer. But through the haze she heard a stern demanding voice.

"Push, Sophie, now push!"

Like choruses, she heard the same from both sides. "Push, Sophie. You can. Now p-u-s-h!"

She pushed and bore down with everything in her. The last thing she heard was "We have a boy." And darkness claimed her.

⟜⟛

Ingeborg shook Sophie's shoulder. "We have some hungry babies here. They want what only you can give."

Sophie blinked in the dim light. "It is babies? I mean they are both all right?"

"As I said, hungry little ones."

Kaaren laid one in Sophie's right arm, and Ingeborg did the same in the left. "Let's get you all set, and they will know what to do."

Sophie flinched as the first one latched onto a breast and began to suckle. "Ouch."

"It will take some getting used to. Come on, little boy baby. Your sister did it, now you." Ingeborg helped guide the tiny mouth to the nipple, where he latched on like a trouper.

While they nursed, Sophie looked from one to the other. Her dark-haired daughter, fair-haired son. "Hamre, you be like your pa, and you'll grow to be a fine man. But what am I going to name you, little girl? Sweet like Grace, full of love like your bestemor. What to name you?" She smiled up at her mother. "Have you ever seen anything so perfect?"

"They are beautiful." Kaaren leaned closer to her daughter and whispered, "And they both can hear."

"Thank you." Sophie kissed one downy head and then the other. When she straightened up, she stared down the length of her body. "Look, I can see my feet." She wiggled both feet, rubbing one with the other.

When the two finished nursing, Ingeborg took one baby and Kaaren the other. "Once these two are settled, I'll bring you something to eat."

"No, I brought her soup and bread." Thelma waited in the doorway. "You need to eat, to keep your strength up."

Sophie fought against the weariness that tugged her back to sleep. "Later. I'll eat later."

"No." Ingeborg handed Hamre to his grandmother and turned to Thelma. "You go help Kaaren, and I'll feed Sophie."

Ingeborg took the tray from Thelma and set it on the table by the bed. After putting a couple more pillows behind Sophie, she picked up the bowl of soup and held out a spoonful. "You need lots of nourishment to feed two hungry babies."

"They are so tiny." Sophie swallowed the soup. She didn't need to keep her eyes open for that.

"Actually they are big for twins. That's why you were so big." As she talked, Ingeborg kept the spoon moving, then offered the bread with butter and cheese on it. "You need to drink lots of milk too."

"Will I have enough milk to feed two babies?"

"We'll find someone else to help if we need to."

Sophie flinched as cramps tightened her belly. "It hurts."

"I know. But that's healthy. Keeps you from bleeding too much. One more bite of bread and I'll let you go to sleep."

"Thank you."

❧

"Has Garth been around?" Sophie asked the next afternoon when she woke up from a nap. For a change she didn't feel like she was being dragged up from a dark well.

"He is sitting on the back porch talking with Thorliff." Elizabeth sat down in the chair beside the bed. "You want to see him?"

"Has he seen the babies?"

"Yes, and he was in awe like any normal man." She leaned closer. "Don't you tell him I told you, but he had tears running down his face when he watched them sleep."

"Did you put them in the same bed?"

"Yes. Kaaren said that was the way you and Grace were most content."

"We always slept in the same bed."

"You want me to send him in?"

"Do I look terrible?"

Elizabeth rolled her eyes. "You look pretty as can be."

It was Sophie's turn to roll her eyes. "Even Mor couldn't work that miracle." She raised a hand to check her hair. Her mother had washed and brushed it in the morning but she'd fed the babies and slept again since then.

The sound of little feet improved her mood. "Inga's coming."

"I know, she's been in to check on you a couple of times. I can't believe how much time she spends watching the twins sleep."

"Ma?"

"Come in, Cupcake."

Sophie smiled at the nickname and watched Inga climb up into her mother's lap. She settled herself and reached a hand out to Sophie. "See babies?"

"Soon."

Elizabeth stood, holding her daughter on one hip. "We'll go see the babies and send Garth to see you. He's been the paragon of patience, sitting here watching you sleep."

"He was?"

"I'd hate to have tried to pry him out of here. Might have taken three men and a boy to do that. When he's not in here, he's often been in the nursery."

Sophie waved bye-bye to Inga and stared out the window. She

could hear his steps coming down the hall. Garth had figured out a way to get her here to Elizabeth's and had helped her walk the halls for those hours. He'd sat here watching out for her and the babies too. She glanced up to see him waiting in the doorway.

"Come in." She patted the side of the bed—not the narrow birthing bed but a regular, comfortable bed. "Sit down."

"Are you sure?"

"Of course. Elizabeth told me what you've been doing."

"Just wanted to be here if you needed me."

"I didn't know how much I needed you, depended on you." She studied his dear face. Whatever gave her the idea she would want to go off traveling and leave him behind? Or the babies? What kind of a ninny was she? She guessed it took a lot to make her see clearly.

"Remember when you said you loved me, and I—"

"How could I forget? That was one of the hardest moments of my life."

"I know my answer now." She watched his Adam's apple bobble as he swallowed. Laying her hand atop of his, she smiled into his eyes. He turned his hand over and clasped hers, leaning slightly forward. His gaze never left hers. "I love you, Garth Wiste, and if you want to marry a woman with two little babies . . ."

"I do. I most certainly do." He cupped her cheeks with both hands, gently, as if she were the most exquisite china and might break, and brushed her lips with his. His sigh warmed her lips even more. "I don't want to wait forever." He kissed her again, this time with all the love and longing that had been on hold. At last he breathed against her lips. "Two babies was a real surprise."

Sophie rested her forehead against his, the kiss leaving her gulping for air. "I forgot to tell you. I'm sorry. I meant to."

He chuckled softly. "Four children. I love you, Sophie, more each day. We could get married as soon as the house is finished."

Sophie straightened and looked into his eyes again. "Ah, Garth, one other thing."

"What?" His brow furrowed. "Is there a problem?"

"Well, I think you have to ask my father first. Isn't that proper?"

He blinked, then rolled his eyes. "I'll go do that right now."

"Could you kiss me again before you leave?"

"With pleasure." And he did.

Sophie lay back against the pillows. This time there was no rush. Garth would be right here with her all the way. And what was one month or two? Maybe she should bribe the men building the house to hurry up. Besides, if they married before her year of mourning was over, Mrs. Valders was going to have a tantrum. In spite of her giggle, she heard a baby whimpering. Was it Hamre or . . . *Lord, I need a name for my baby girl. Such joy you have given me.* Joy. Of course! Joy is a wonderful name. And Garth, you will be the first to know.

✑ ACKNOWLEDGMENTS ✑

THE MORE BOOKS I WRITE, the more people I get to know and the more stories and bits and pieces come my way. Thanks to Chelley, Kathleen, and Marcy for reading and commenting. New eyes are always helpful. RaeLynn contributes through her research of the period and the area. I have a cadre of pray-ers who help more than any of us know. Thank you.

I am always grateful for all the people at Bethany House Publishers who work so hard to bring books to life and get them out to readers. What a great family you are.

Thanks also to my personal team: Agent Deidre Knight of the Knight Agency, you are wonderful; Cecile, my assistant without whom I'd be lost; Round Robin friends who help keep me on track; husband, Wayne, who puts up with all the craziness of the writing life; Chewy, resident basset hound who makes me laugh; and Bidley, cockatiel of advanced years who announces visitors and Dad coming home, a watch-bird, if you will.

Thanks to all my readers who make it possible for me to continue to do what I love. You are the greatest. Most of all, thanks to my heavenly Father for all of life.